SURRENDER

Priscilla West

Table of Contents

Chapter One

"Leaving already?"

I'd tried my best not to wake my roommate as I collected the pile of client documents laying on the hotel room table. Riley Hewitt was a heavy sleeper, especially when she'd been out drinking the night before, her favorite vacation pastime. So I was surprised when she popped her strawberry-blonde head out from beneath the covers. Apparently, I hadn't been quiet enough.

"Sorry I woke you. I have to meet Richard downstairs in a few minutes so I'm just packing up." I'd been poring over the client strategy the previous night with my supervisor, Richard Hamm, in his hotel room, as if we hadn't already gone over it dozens of times this past week.

When I'd gotten back to my room, I went over the materials again, memorizing every detail, replaying in my mind the sequence of events that would lead to landing this client for our company. Closing this deal would mean a lot for my career: prestigious wealth management firms weren't in the habit of letting analysts with only three years of experience fly to Cape Town, South Africa to woo billion dollar clients. It was only through a series of fortunate events—a group of senior employees leaving to start their own firm, my recent promotion, and a chance encounter with one of the directors in the cafeteria—that I was in this position. To say this was big would be an understatement.

"No worries." She yawned and rubbed one sleepy eye while making a noise somewhere between a groan and a gurgle. "I wanted to get up anyway. Get some breakfast, catch some foreign television. It's not every day you get to see Big Bird speaking Afrikaans. You ready for your meeting?"

God, I hope so. I'd better be after all the practice and preparation. Thankfully the butterflies fluttering in my stomach did more to energize me than a cup of coffee ever could. "I think I'm ready. Besides, Richard's going to do most of the talking. He's got years of experience doing this. I'm just there for backup."

She flashed her winning smile. "And to be a pretty face. You'll do great, Miss Harvard grad."

I stuck out my tongue playfully. Riley was from Staten Island and went to NYU for college. Although we both ended up working in the finance world, Riley was a corporate tax accountant thanks to her parents' guidance, and often reminded me how her job was less exciting than mine. She generated plenty of her own excitement in her downtime, though. Her permanently revolving bedroom door guaranteed that she always had a juicy story to tell at our weekly mojito-and-Mexican "date nights." Watching her pore over a room service menu, I reflected for the millionth time that I was unbelievably lucky to have her in my life. We had met at a work-mandated, soul-deadening seminar on Expanding Corporate Productivity at the NYU Stern School of Business, where we learned absolutely nothing about expanding corporate productivity and almost everything about each other over the space of three hours.

Since then, she had been the yin to my yang, the weekend warrior to my librarian. We often joked about sending NYU a nice fruit basket to say thanks, though Riley always countered that "the two hundred thousand I dropped there for a Philosophy degree is thanks enough." Still, I couldn't suppress a surge of gladness every time I walked past the imposing steel-and-glass business school on my way to the gym; I knew that without Riley, my time in Manhattan would have been just as cold and lonely as my years at Harvard.

When I'd told her I was taking a business trip to Cape Town for a week, she insisted on using her vacation time to join me, much to my delight. Hanging out with her on the beach would be much more fun than tanning by myself or--god forbid--with Richard.

I packed the last of my files, zipped my shoulder bag, and smoothed my light blue blouse and black pencil skirt. The outfit had been painstakingly put together to blend professionalism and style. It was part of the strategy. "How do I look?"

"I'd trust you with my million dollars—if I had it."

"Hopefully bad boy billionaire Vincent Sorenson thinks the same way."

"I've seen you working nonstop for this meeting for a month now. You're more than ready, girl. Either way, we're going to have fun tonight. Don't forget about that."

Of course, a full afternoon and evening of adventure with Riley— a sweet reward for waking up at ass o'clock to woo a client who was, according to my research, notoriously difficult. With a wave, I left the hotel room and took the elevator down to the lobby to meet Richard. As I stepped onto the marble tile, heels clacking, I checked my watch. 7:30 a.m. on the dot. We'd agreed to meet an hour before the meeting, giving us plenty of time to walk the few blocks from the hotel to the client's office building and to go over any last minute details should they arise in our sleep. God knows I'd had dreams about this moment. Well, more like nightmares. And for some funny reason, all of them ended with me in my underwear.

I spotted Richard seated on the edge of a cozy lounge chair, eyes glued to his Blackberry. His slate-gray suit and cerulean tie knocked years off his age. Only a few strands of gray hair would betray that he was pushing forty.

"Morning," I greeted him.

"Have you eaten breakfast yet, Kristen?" he asked without looking up from his Blackberry. Though his dismissive manner had irritated me in the beginning, the last six months of working with him had taught me to hold entire conversations without once making eye contact. Unless, of course, the subject was money. Then Richard was all ears.

"I had an orange juice and a granola bar. I could go for some coffee though."

"Let's get going then. We can stop for a cup." He gathered his briefcase and I followed him as he left the hotel.

As we stepped out from beneath the overhang of the valet area, the view of the ocean in the distance helped calm my nerves. An early morning breeze ruffled my hair, and the mid-June sun streamed gold. As we continued strolling the busy Cape Town streets, I relished the sights, smells and sounds I had been too busy prepping to notice yesterday. Tall corporate buildings piercing the sky, honking cars, an eclectic mix of people commuting to work, a McDonald's on seemingly every corner—in a lot of ways, it reminded me of Manhattan. Still, the mix of bright colors, unfamiliar languages, and dreadlocked surfers streaming towards the beach to catch an early-morning wave gave this place its own charm.

Along the way, we paused for coffee and Richard took the opportunity to review our strategy.

"When we get inside the building, I want you to be all smiles, Kristen. I want to see your teeth at all times. I will be doing most of the talking, but you play an important role as well. Clients may have more money than some countries, but first and foremost, they're people. People are emotional. Men, in particular, are weak to feminine allure. You soften them up, and I mold them." He said shit like this on a regular basis, with absolutely no irony.

Sounds like my role could be replaced by a cardboard cut out with boobs. Great. Richard's back-handed compliment irritated me, but I wasn't in a position to rock the boat. Although there were plenty of women in the finance world, the upper echelons were men's clubs with their own rules. I said nothing when Richard made his sexist little comments, but that didn't mean I was going to compromise my personal integrity if he ever suggested I take things farther than a smile. After three years in this ruthless business, very little could shock me.

"Right. An emotion-driven approach." I used his own words to show I understood him.

He smiled. "I call it the Buddy System. In my experience, Vincent's a Type B. Hobbyist, passionate for recreational activities, doesn't really know how to run a company but got extremely lucky. A hands-off CEO who's unburdened by details but good at delegating responsibility to his VPs. The guy loves to jerk off and surf."

I had my doubts about his assessment, but I kept them to myself. Vincent had started off as an avid surfer and built a cheap waterproof camera that he affixed to his surfboard, allowing him to film his accomplishments. Soon, the YouTube generation of extreme athletes was clamoring for a similar camera to affix to a surfboard/bungee cord/skateboard/parachute, and Vincent's from-scratch company was generating billions in revenue. My research had painted Vincent Sorenson as a workaholic—his empire had expanded to include an extreme-sports TV show, a clothing line, and custom surfboards—but if Google Image had anything to say about it, he was a tattooed beach bum with a deep tan and heavy-lidded stoner eyes.

A bum with tattoos and chiseled abs.

Richard continued as we crossed the street. "These guys are fairly predictable. All the other wealth management firms vying for his money look exactly the same on paper. They're going to talk to him about alpha ratios, dividends, hedge funds, and it's all going to go over his head. We want our approach to stand out. Demonstrating your interest in what he's passionate about is going to win you half the battle. Watch, I bet he'll be in a t-shirt, shorts, and sandals when we meet him."

My sensitivity to incorrect initial assumptions kicked in but I wasn't going to argue with Richard. Our strategy was set. Fortunately, Richard's confidence helped quell the gnawing feeling that we were still unprepared. It was like the test anxiety I would get all throughout college except now failure meant losing millions of dollars instead of a few GPA points.

When we reached our destination, I faintly recognized the towering structure from our research. "Does Vincent own this building?"

"No. The company just rents out a few offices on the twenty-third floor for small operations in the area. He mainly comes here to surf."

I made sure to plaster my smile on before we passed through the revolving door entrance. After checking in, we took the elevator up to Vincent's floor where a receptionist ushered us to his office. "Just knock," she said before returning to her post.

"You ready?" Richard asked as he held his knuckle to the door.

This was it. I sucked in a deep breath and looked him in the eye. "Let's do this."

He knocked and I heard a distinctly male voice telling us to come in. Raising the corners of my lips to give my smile that extra perk, I followed as Richard led us in. My smile faded at the sight of the man seated behind the desk.

He was calmly poised with masculine refinement more befitting a Calvin Klein model than a Fortune 500 CEO. As I gazed at those rich brown eyes, sharply etched nose, and seductively carved mouth set in a bone structure undoubtedly designed by a master artisan I briefly thought we had stepped onto the set of a photoshoot. But there was no mistaking this was Vincent Sorenson, in the flesh. The hours I'd spent analyzing his images in the name of research did not—*could not*—prepare me for the real thing. In the most recent photo I could find, he was up to his waist in the sea and approaching the shore beaming a heart-stopping smile like some sort of mythical sex god eager to claim his offerings. It wasn't difficult to imagine virgins voluntarily sacrificing themselves to him.

But that picture was taken months ago and his dirty-blonde hair had been short then. Now it flowed, framing his features like a portrait fit for display in a museum. For an instant all I could think about was how it would feel to run my hands through those silky locks.

My footsteps slowed, matching my breaths as I watched him elegantly rise and circle his large oak desk, closing the space between us with economical finesse. After shaking Richard's hand, he stood in front of me. With brows furrowed in deep curiosity, his gorgeous eyes bored into my own, shrewdly assessing and evaluating. I felt strangely vulnerable and exposed under the weight of that stare, like I was undressed and naked before him.

I caught a whiff of something that made my mouth water and the area between my thighs ache. What was it? Cologne, after shave, his pheromones? Whatever it was, it smelled *good.*

Being so close, the raw magnetism he exuded jumbled my senses and made my pulse erratic. I felt compelled and pushed all at once; it was a potent male force that could never be bottled or captured on film, only experienced.

The sound of Richard's cough and subsequent nudge on my arm broke the spell.

My lips were dry so I licked them before speaking. "Hello Mr. Sorenson. Kristen Daley. It's a pleasure to meet you," I said evenly.

I held out my hand, feeling like the appendage didn't belong to me. I watched him take it with his own and squeeze firmly. The sensation alone was enough to summon pornographic images I neither approved of nor realized existed within me, ones where I was bent over his desk or splayed against a wall or on my knees. . .

"Vincent," he said, the velvety rasp of his voice flowing over me. The way he spoke his own name made it seem even more divine. "The pleasure's mine."

The heat radiating from his hand and up my arm seemed to reach my brain, and I forgot to squeeze back.

When he released his grip and shifted his gaze away from me, I was both relieved and disappointed to have the dirty mental images fade.

Pull yourself together. You're here for business.

"Great weather today," Richard remarked. "Perfect for surfing." He was already launching into the script.

It was then I noticed Vincent was wearing a t-shirt, shorts, and sandals—just as Richard predicted. The effect of the combination was more striking than I could have predicted and I figured he was the only man who could pull off sexy-casual well. Nevertheless, figuring the beach bum impression had been accurate, my fantasies subsided long enough to allow me to resume my feminine allure, smile included. It seemed to be working because I could feel Vincent's gaze slide over my profile as we moved to the meeting area of his office.

Vincent gestured and we took two accent chairs near the large glass wall facing the beach. It was a spacious office, bigger than any I had ever seen.

"I'd like to work on my cutback. I hear the Bali Bay is a great spot," Richard said. He had never surfed in his life.

Vincent sat across from us and I couldn't help studying him. Even in a position as benign as sitting, he exuded primal confidence. "It's one of my favorites." His deep voice resonated, inciting a restless energy in my legs. I shifted in my seat, trying to ignore the growing ache between my thighs. Fortunately, Richard was the one talking so Vincent's attention was trained on him.

Richard nodded enthusiastically. "From what I know, Kelly Slater got his chops riding those waves." This was part of the plan. Richard would open up with a softball about the weather then progressively use more surfing jargon, ultimately tying it back to investments through analogies. It was like a children's education program. I'd been skeptical—concerned the approach could be misconstrued as condescending—but when he spelled it out, the effective simplicity of the message was actually kind of brilliant.

Vincent's demeanor was impassive. "I see you've done your homework."

Receiving the anticipated signal, Richard continued, "The thing I admire most about him is his ability to read the water. They called him the Wave Whisperer."

We'd rehearsed the lines, me playing Vincent and Richard playing himself. It was standard best practice. Everything was going smoothly so far. Next, Vincent would say something along the lines of "I'm glad to hear you're a fan. Surfing's a big part of my company and you seem to understand that."

Vincent glanced at his expensive sea-diver watch. "I have another meeting soon, so if you don't mind, let's cut straight to the point. Why should I trust you with my money?"

Shit. This wasn't part of the plan. In a flash, I saw weeks of work flushed into oblivion. Panicking, I looked to Richard, hoping he'd pull something from a deep place of wisdom and experience.

Richard swallowed a hard lump, tiny beads of sweat dotting his brows. I'd never seen him so frazzled. "Of course, Mr. Sorenson. I'm going to let Kristen tell you more about our exciting investment strategies."

I reeled in horror when I realized where that deep place was.

My mouth opened to protest, but I quickly shut it to avoid ruining what remained of our facade of professionalism. I didn't dare look at Vincent, but I could feel his intense focus on me. Eyes wide, I fumbled through the documents in my dossier, trying my best to control my trembling fingers. If I screwed this up, Richard would blame me; he'd left me to drown.

"We've prepared materials illustrating the key benefits you'll receive from choosing Waterbridge-Howser," I somehow managed in a steady tone. I rose from my seat and walked over on shaky legs to hand Vincent the briefing materials we had planned to leave with him after we finished our pitch. What was I doing? Where was I taking this?

Stressed out by the situation as it was, I made an effort to avoid touching him in the exchange, but juggling the maneuver with everything else proved to be too complicated. I wobbled on my heels and fell, winding up with my chest and palms flat against his shirt, papers strewn across his lap.

I distantly registered strong hands catching my waist and my nipples instinctively tightened at the sensation. Something strange beneath my fingers caught my attention. Hard. Round. Circular. What was it?

He has nipple rings.

Curiosity overriding logic, my fingers pinched one of the rings through his shirt. I'd never met a guy who had nipple piercings before. His dark eyes locked with mine and I could swear for an instant I saw a spark turn into a smoldering fire.

When the silence passing between us became deafening, I collected my bearings and apologized emphatically.

"Are you okay?" he asked, his voice having the same effect on my body it had earlier.

No, your chest is too firm and I can't focus. "I'm fine, thank you. Sorry for the clumsiness. As I was saying, we have experts specializing in diverse strategies to fit your goals. Think of us as partners. Our firm helps your firm grow." He eyed me curiously and I felt my cheeks grow hot with embarrassment at the poor choice of words. "I mean wealth. Helps your wealth grow."

Awkwardly, I returned to my seat. It was the longest five steps I'd ever taken. Vincent was silent, his attention focused on the materials. I couldn't guess what he was thinking, only that the dark look in his expression couldn't be good. I tried to fill the void by verbalizing what he was already reading and in the middle of my meandering explanation about discretionary allocations, he cut me off. "Who made these charts?"

We were already bombing this presentation and this was going to be the nail in the coffin. Poor presentation, poor graphs. Could it get any worse?

"Kristen did," Richard said, surprising me. I made a mental note to strangle him when this was over.

Vincent looked at me with what I could only guess was a mixture of approval and fascination; it made him even more attractive, as if everything else wasn't enough. "They're good," he said, flipping the page and moving on to study the next document.

At the first sign of positivity, Richard attempted to salvage our chances. He cleared his throat and over the next fifteen minutes made an eloquent speech about value-added returns ending full circle with the surfing analogies we'd practiced. Apparently I'd bought him enough time to reformulate our strategy.

Still, only a few slight nods hinted Vincent had actually been listening. Mostly, he was just reading the materials I gave him.

"Any questions, Mr. Sorenson?" Richard asked.

"No. That's all I need to know." Vincent's rise from his seat indicated our meeting was over and we followed. "Thank you, Kristen." He shook my hand first, then Richard's. "Thank you, Dick." Richard paused then reciprocated the handshake, seemingly ignoring the misnomer.

When we left Vincent's office, my shoulders slumped and my body felt numb. Even the lively South African air couldn't reinvigorate me. On the walk back to the hotel, I was tempted to call Richard out on his behavior during the meeting, particularly the part where he threw the entire burden on my shoulders when things started going sour. I studied his features, expecting to find him dejected since he had more to lose than me, but he looked surprisingly calm.

"We blew it, didn't we?" I said, more as a statement than a question.

"Huh? I don't know why you think that."

"He wasn't responding to the emotion-driven strategy like we practiced. He barely said a thing."

Richard waved his hand as if dispelling an odor. "These brooding billionaire types, they just want you to think they're dark and mysterious. It gets the ladies but it's all an act. Did you see the guy? I was spot-on about his clothing. And I'm certain we aced that meeting. Don't worry."

I groaned. "Sure."

"Besides, I think he was into you. That move where you tripped and groped his pecs was perfect. We couldn't have planned something better." Richard chuckled.

"Don't tell anyone that happened," I snapped. It was bad enough Richard knew about that mishap, but it'd be even worse if more people at the firm found out—there was no telling how they would interpret it. The office gossip would be trouble.

"Your secret's safe with me." His finger to his lips completed the mockery.

"What are you doing the rest of the day?" I asked, wanting nothing more than to change the subject before my irritation with him made me speak out of line.

"Oh not much. Try the local cuisine, check out babes at the beach while I catch up on some emails."

"Which beach?"

"Clifton."

I smiled at him. Riley and I were definitely not going to that one.

Chapter Two

When I got back to my hotel room Riley was curled up on the bed watching television. Richard had gone to his own room to do who knows what.

"So how did it go?" Riley paused after I shot her a miserable look. "I'm so sorry, Kris. You don't have to talk about it."

I kicked off my heels and let my hair down, anxious to get out of professional mode. "Richard seems to think we did well. Sometimes I feel like he's in his own world though. Vincent was definitely not going for our pitch. You could totally read it in his body language."

Riley's expression was sympathetic. Remote in her hand, she switched off the TV. "I'm sure you did your best. Maybe luck just wasn't on your side today."

"That's the thing. I couldn't even do my best. I messed up multiple times." My mind replayed the awkward moments from the meeting and I shuddered. I didn't have anyone to blame but myself, but in my current mood I was eager for a scapegoat. "If Vincent wasn't so damn gorgeous, things might've been different."

"Oh, do tell." Her voice increased a pitch.

I told her all about my blunders, and when I was done she smiled. "Well at least you *looked* professional."

"Thanks for the sympathy." I gave her a wry grin.

"You know I'm always here for support. That's why we're going to have a blast today. You're going to forget all about that meeting and Mr. Abs Sorenson. Tonight we'll hit the bars and have guys buy us drinks. I know you haven't been dating much, all that sexual frustration must be eating you alive."

It was true. I'd only gone on a handful of unsuccessful dates since I'd met Riley. I told myself it was because I focusing on my career instead, but there were also personal reasons I didn't want to think about dating—reasons I never told Riley. Still, she was right about the sexual frustration. If my battery-operated boyfriend could talk, he'd probably say I was smothering him.

"I'm not really interested in the male species right now. Between Richard's chauvinism and Vincent shooting us down today, I think I'm a little burned out on testosterone."

"Fair enough. It'll just be us girls then. Get in that sexy bathing suit you brought." Riley untied her robe to reveal her bikini, its thin straps and enhanced bust leaving little to the imagination. "I'm all ready to go."

Having vented to Riley, I felt better about the situation this morning. I slipped into my bathing suit and left the hotel with her.

When we arrived at the aptly-named Bikini Beach just before noon, the shore was packed. There was a nice mix of tourists and locals, with lots of people both in and out of the clear blue waters. We laid our towels down on the heated sand and relaxed in cheap folding chairs we got from a nearby beach store. Once we were settled, Riley went to get us some drinks. I stared out at the waves and thought about how picturesque the scene looked. This kind of experience was rare when you lived in Manhattan and I took the opportunity to soak it in. As the afternoon wore on, the stress of the morning seemed to melt away like the ice cubes in our mojitos.

I spotted a few surfers in the distance zig-zagging along the water. I'd never been surfing before and didn't have much of a desire to change that. I understood the appeal, but I was afraid of the danger—I just didn't think the risks outweighed the benefits. A few thrilling moments versus the possibility of getting my arm bitten off by a shark or getting stung by a jellyfish . . . yeah, I'd be happy with just tanning—with sunscreen of course.

Vincent, on the other hand, loved risky activities. His whole business was based on extreme sports. I didn't really get it but it clearly made him very successful.

A few toned men with olive skin passed by and Riley directed my attention to them. I had to admit they were attractive from a purely physical perspective but that just didn't do it for me.

"Maybe your standards are too high," Riley said.

"Just because they have abs and a penis doesn't mean I want to sleep with them."

She laughed. "Keith had more than that. You never told me why you turned down my offer to set you up with him."

"He just wasn't my type."

"What *is* your type, Kris? I've hardly seen you date since I've known you, and don't say it's because you've been too busy with work." She nudged me with her elbow.

"I'm not sure I have one." I was only vaguely aware of rubbing my own pinky finger.

"Oh come on. Every girl has a type, some just aren't willing to be honest about it."

Now I was the curious one. "What's your type then?"

"Let's see . . . tall, strong, handsome, smart, dark, dangerous . . . oh and let's not forget rich."

"Sounds more like a fantasy than a real person." Actually that sounded a lot like someone I met this morning. "Why don't we just say I like the 'nice and caring' type."

"Basically boring then, huh?"

"Boring to you, satisfying to me. Why would you want someone dark and dangerous? And if he's so hot, wouldn't you be concerned he'd cheat on you?"

"I'd just have to blow his mind." Her mischievous wink made it clear what she meant. "But to each her own."

We spent the rest of the afternoon bathing our skin in UV rays and trying out the local food. Fortunately, there were enough tourists streaming through Cape Town that the restaurants provided menus in English. I thought chicken would taste the same no matter where you were but whatever special sauce they used made it exceptionally delicious. We explored the area, stopping periodically to point out unique architecture or unusual occurrences. Although I'd told Riley I wasn't interested in dating, I couldn't help but indulge in idle thoughts about Vincent. Maybe I'd spent way too much time memorizing his files.

It was evening by the time we were hungry again. Despite wearing comfy sneakers, our feet were killing us from all the walking. Riley suggested we rest at a local bar to relieve our weary legs and grab some grub. We were off the beaten path by this point and the bar she picked looked sketchy.

"It'll be fun. Don't you want to get an authentic experience? We didn't fly thousands of miles just to go to some bar we could go to back home."

"Yeah, but we're two American girls in a foreign country. There are horror movies based on this situation."

"What's the worst that can happen?" Her grin made me ill at ease.

"Don't say that."

"Look, I have some mace in my bag. If anybody tries to get frisky with us, I'm going to melt their eyeballs." I pictured Riley as the female version of Rambo.

"All right, fine. If we get abducted, it's your fault. I just don't want you saying I'm a party pooper."

She laughed. "I've never said that. You just like to be cautious, which I respect. Remember when you warned me about Danny? You were right, he did turn out to be a creep."

Riley had dated Danny a few months prior. When she brought him over to our apartment he kept giving me shifty-eyed stares. I expressed my concerns to her and it turned out he had done time in prison for theft. He wasn't even the worst of Riley's extensive dating history. I honestly didn't know how she found some of these guys.

Upon entering, we found the place was full of mostly locals. There were a few expats in the corner who sounded British and were probably out for some adventure. Somewhere there was a speaker putting out exotic tribal music. The hypnotic beats were catchy but it certainly was a far cry from American pop music—no Miley Cyrus here. When we found a seat at a table and ordered margaritas, I found myself easing into the atmosphere.

"Man, check this place out." Riley sounded excited. She pointed at the decorations around us. "Animal bones hanging on the walls, a shrunken head behind the bar, and a beat-up sign that says 'Ompad'. Isn't it cool?" She whipped out her phone to snap some pictures.

The distinct sound of a shot glass slamming against wood alerted us to a commotion brewing near the bar. A group of onlookers surrounded two men with tumblers in hand and a bottle half-full of amber liquid between them. The one on the left was a juggernaut of a man; a gruff beard and mean stare completed the intimidation factor. The gathering of curious spectators obscured my view of the man on the right.

"What's going on over there?" Riley asked.

I knew we shouldn't have gotten closer. The feeling in my gut that whatever was going on over there was trouble told me we should leave, but intense curiosity pulled us near the action like moths to a flame.

We settled at a table nearby, giving us front row seats. It was when I saw who the figure poised on the right was that I realized why my alarm bells had gone off.

Vincent.

What was he doing here? He was wearing a white button-down and khakis that showcased his lean muscular build. By now the crowd around the bar had grown considerably, tantamount with the noise level. Most huddled around Vincent's side. Some of the admirers included beautiful, curvaceous women that were all but rubbing their breasts against Vincent, and a pang of jealousy hit me from who knows where.

Riley shouted to me over the ruckus. "Is that who I think it is?"

"Yeah, it's Vincent," I said. "Looks like he's in the middle of some kind of drinking game."

I couldn't hear her response over the cheering. The only two words I managed to decipher were "fucking" and "hot."

I leaned in closer to her. "I can't hear you."

"I said you should go over there. This could be your second chance to win him over."

"What? I don't even know what he's doing. He might not even remember me."

"You pinched his goddamn nipple, of course he'll remember you. Go find out." She nudged my shoulder but I remained steadfast in my seat. As serendipitous as this encounter was, I wasn't comfortable with the idea of approaching Vincent in this strange social situation. If Richard had been right about the meeting going well, talking to Vincent could sabotage our efforts rather than help.

"Let's just watch them a little first."

We witnessed the burly guy down his shot, slam his glass against the counter, and grunt something in Afrikaans. I couldn't understand it, but if I had to guess by the tone, it meant "Is that the best you got?" He then reached into a nearby bag sitting on the counter and produced a large clear jar. I squinted my eyes to identify the contents. Thin strands, black dots scurrying.

Cobwebs and spiders.

The crowd didn't seem surprised, instead they clamored approval like they were at a sporting event. Why would he have such a thing? And here of all places. *I hate spiders.*

My disgust and surprise must have been palpable because Vincent turned his head in my direction as if attuned to my specific frequency. For the second time today, we locked eyes. A part of me wanted to hide from the embarrassment of this morning, another part of me knew my company had important business to conduct with him.

Before I decided whether I was going to wave at him or shrink behind the crowd of bodies, a ghost of a smile touched his lips.

He waved me over. In disbelief, I pointed my finger at my chest as I mouthed "me?" and he nodded. What did he want with me? I looked to Riley for advice and was met with eager shooing motions. Sensing an opportunity to clear up any confusion over this morning's meeting, I worked my way through the crowd to him. The women around him were reluctant to make room, shooting me catty-glares, but I managed to wiggle through an opening.

"Hello Kristen," he said.

He did remember my name. "Hello Mr. Sorenson."

"Please, just call me Vincent. I didn't expect to see you here, but now that you are, this'll be a lot more interesting." He grinned.

I wasn't sure what he meant. Confused by the whole situation, I asked, "What are you doing here, Vincent?"

"Business. And you're going to decide if you want to help me." He gestured to the big guy and his bizarre pet spiders.

Okay . . . that doesn't explain a whole lot.

"I should tell you, Mr. Sorenson. I have a fear of spiders," I said, eyeing the jar.

He leaned close to my ear so I could hear him. "All the better. You asked for my money earlier today, Kristen." His smoky voice was implacable. "I wasn't impressed. Here's your second chance to convince me to trust you with my assets."

Shit. We *did* blow the meeting this morning. I gulped. "What do you want me to do?"

As if to answer my question, the hulk uncapped the jar and picked out a spider with a pair of chopsticks.

The sight of the tiny black creature outside its confines made me panic. I tried to escape but Vincent caught my elbow in a light but secure grip and pulled me to him. "You're fine, trust me. Just watch."

With his hand on the filled shot glass, the big guy placed the spider on the skin between his thumb and forefinger. The spider—

whose backside displayed a red dot—remained surprisingly still, perhaps in as much suspense as I was. Never taking his eyes off the poisonous creature, the big guy slowly brought the drink to his lips, keeping his hand steady, and in one smooth motion downed the contents, flicked the spider off his hand, and crushed the arachnid as he slammed his glass on the bar. The crowd erupted in cheers.

The big guy looked expectantly at me and Vincent. His steely eyes said "your turn".

"You're not seriously going to do that are you?" I blurted without thinking.

His eyes narrowed as he smiled. "I am. And you're going to help me by putting the spider on my hand."

I was about to say "hell no" but thought better when I noticed his probing eyes. "I'm really not comfortable with this."

"Consider it a test. How far are you willing to go to serve my interests?"

I felt my breaths shorten. "Are we talking about money here or poisonous spiders? Because those are two very different things."

"Believe it or not, there's a lot at stake if I don't follow through." He gestured to a pile of documents on the counter. I couldn't read the language, but from the formatting I could tell they were contract documents—so this wasn't just a wager between two inflated egos. "I imagine there's also a lot at stake for you."

"What if it bites you?"

"Let me worry about that. If it does, it won't be your fault."

"What if it climbs up and bites me?"

"I won't let it happen. Trust me, you'll be fine."

This wasn't professional; this was insane. Crazy. I'd never done anything close to this dangerous before. If I had known I'd have to handle deadly bugs to win clients, I might not have taken this job in the first place.

I was stuck between a rock and a hard place: don't do it and for sure lose Vincent as a client; do it and possibly kill both the hottest man I'd ever met and my career. Either way, I was screwed.

I glanced over at Riley and saw her give me a thumbs up.

Damn you, Vincent. I picked up the chopsticks and unscrewed the jar, grimacing as I lowered the utensil inside. When I touched one of the creatures, it moved and I instinctively retracted my hand.

"No way. I can't do this," I exclaimed.

"Giving up so soon? Nothing worth pursuing comes without risk."

Inflamed by his taunting, I tried again. This time the black creature didn't move and I was able to clamp it with the chopsticks. It felt hard and squishy at the same time and when I pulled it out and got a better view of its wriggling legs, it took every ounce of willpower not to throw it across the bar. My hands were trembling and I was afraid I'd drop the spider or worse, rile it up enough to bite Vincent. Then a warm hand around my upper arm steadied me.

"You're doing great. Just relax a little. Focus on controlling your own body, not on what you're holding."

"Easier said than done," I replied, even though his advice seemed to be working.

The next few moments were a blur, but I somehow managed to place the spider gently on Vincent's hand. He downed his drink and went the extra mile by flicking the spider back into the jar instead of killing it.

Once again, the bar roared approval.

Afraid I would have to do it again, I turned to the big guy and was relieved to see him passed out on the counter.

Vincent had won.

Chapter Three

It wasn't long before the ruckus died down. The big guy had woken up, signed the contract, shook Vincent's hand, and left. The crowd had dissipated and Riley was now being entertained by one of the British guys from the expat group. I found myself seated beside Vincent at a cozy table in a secluded part of the bar, alone.

Even with all the alcohol I imagined was flowing through his system, Vincent looked as sober as a judge. Not only were his nerves steel, but so was his blood. I began to wonder if those were the only parts . . .

"What can I get you to drink?" Vincent asked, flagging the waitress.

I considered avoiding more alcohol in case we discussed business, but I didn't want to be rude either. "A mojito please."

The waitress flashed a flirty smile at Vincent before leaving, which made me bristle.

He returned his attention back to me. "I'm surprised. You struck me as more damsel than dame."

The comment was decidedly personal and I felt justified in taking offense. "And you strike me as more reckless than brave. Why were you in a drinking contest with a spider-loving thug?"

His sinful lips curved into a wicked smile. "You can't always judge people by their appearance. Nambe is a real estate mogul. He owns a lot of property in the area including this bar. I wanted one of his private beaches and he set the terms. You'll find the most successful people play by their own rules."

His comment made me recall how far I had just gone to win him over as a client. "Do all your business transactions involve endangering your life?"

"Just the interesting ones. The bite wouldn't have been fatal if I went to the hospital immediately. When you want something bad enough, sometimes it's surprising what you're willing to do." He adjusted his seat and his leg brushed mine sending an unwelcome flutter through my belly.

The waitress returned with my drink and I took a sip, relishing the taste more than I should have. "Does that apply to swimming with sharks and jumping off cliffs?" I said, feeling emboldened by the mojito as well as the other alcoholic beverages I'd consumed since setting foot inside this bar.

"It applies to whatever gives me a thrill. What gives you a thrill Kristen? Besides winning my account."

Unsure if that was a flirtatious line or an accusation, I answered, "Who says that gives me a thrill?"

"It makes you good at your job. Pitch aside, the materials you gave me were polished."

"Thank you." I flustered at the compliment. It was rare to have my work given the appreciation I felt it deserved even by my colleagues, let alone a client.

"What would you do if I chose your company?"

"You're saying after I did all that, you're still not convinced you can trust us with your money?"

"What you did puts Waterbridge-Howser back in the running. After your partner insulted my intelligence this morning I had almost ruled you out."

Crap. "I'm truly sorry about that, it wasn't intentional. We were just trying to be persuasive and it seems we missed the mark."

"Fair enough." He stirred his drink and shrugged. "I'm curious, what are you doing in a bar like this?"

The question sounded like he thought I was here on the prowl— which was not at all the reason. "It was my friend Riley's idea." I pointed a blaming finger at Riley across the bar, who seemed to be too enamored with her company to notice. "She's a little adventurous."

"So are you," he said touching my hand with the tip of his finger. "Do you have a boyfriend?"

"Excuse me?" The conversation had turned decidedly flirtatious and I wasn't sure how to react. I'd never been hit on by a potential client before and there were no company guidelines addressing this type of situation. Regardless of how attracted I was to Vincent, if anybody at work suspected I was mixing business with pleasure, my professional reputation would be ruined. I'd seen it happen before.

"Don't tell me your partner is."

"You mean Richard? He's definitely *not* my boyfriend."

"Good. So you're single." He leaned his breathtaking face closer to mine heightening awareness of him.

I stood my ground. "Maybe I am, maybe I'm not. Either way I'm sorry to disappoint you, but I don't date potential clients," I said, hoping the brush-off would end the personal discussion and we could return to talking about business.

Those seductive lips so close to mine curved into a smile. "Who says anything about dating? I just want to finish what you started this morning."

"What are you talking about?"

"We were here." He gently but firmly took my hand in his and placed it on his chest. The move caught me off guard and all I could do was suck in a deep breath when I felt the sudden warmth of his body and the strong beat of his heart beneath my palms. "Let's move it further." He began to move my hand slowly downward. As my fingertips traced the hard contours at the base of his pecs and the firm cut of his stomach through his shirt, goosebumps ran across my skin and the hairs on the back of my neck stiffened. My pulse quickened and my lips parted to accommodate faster breaths. It wasn't until my fingers reached the base of his stony abs that my mind caught up and I pulled away.

"This morning was an innocent mistake," I shot back, aware I was more aroused than offended by the gesture. "I don't know what kind of girl you think I am exactly, but I don't mix business with pleasure."

"I do." His sexy voice could tear down any woman's defenses. I knew I had to get away, afraid I wouldn't be an exception.

"Good for you. Thank you for the drink Mr. Sorenson but if you'll excuse me, I need to get back to my friend." I rose from my seat with the intention of leaving but turned back to that gorgeous face one last time. "If you're still interested in Waterbridge-Howser, you have Richard's number."

His lips curled into that same wicked smile from earlier. "We'll be in touch."

When I returned to Riley's table, she was by herself.

"What happened to the British guy?" I asked.

"I got bored with him. But nevermind that. What happened with you and you know who?"

"Nothing. It was just a professional discussion. All business." I was trying to convince myself as much as her.

"Yeah, right. You're going to get laid tonight."

I shook my head vehemently. "No," I repeated. "Let's go. I've had enough of this place."

Chapter Four

We had taken off two hours ago from Cape Town International and were heading back to JFK. Riley and I had made the most out of the rest of our stay; we hadn't had fun like that in a long time and I was already dreading returning to work. While I enjoyed working at Waterbridge-Howser, no job beat out long scenic hikes around Cape Town and watching Riley flirt with the locals.

I looked over to see Riley still fast asleep next to me, her head lolling on the backrest. If only I could get a few minutes of shuteye. Riley had tried to prod me about what happened between Vincent and me at the bar, but I left it vague, knowing that she would never let it drop if she knew the truth.

My head still pounded from the celebratory shots she insisted we take for our last "night" in South Africa. She had made some new friends on the beach who took us to the best viewing spot in town, and we'd stayed up all night watching the sun rise over Table Mountain. I had to admit, it was gorgeous, but we regretted it afterwards when we had to pack and head to the airport. Bleary eyed with the beginnings of what I was sure would be an awful hangover, we dragged ourselves to the gate and boarded. Riley had fallen asleep almost as soon as she sat down.

The ding of the seatbelt sign brought my attention back to the folder open in front of me. Richard had sent me an email late the previous night asking me to look over Vincent's file again. He was nervous that Vincent hadn't called us yet, which made me nervous as well.

We hadn't seen any sign of Vincent Sorenson after that night at the bar. When we were exploring the wilderness around Cape Town, I was half expecting him to pop out of a forested area nearby locked in a mortal engagement with a panther, or make a dramatic appearance by falling out of the sky with a parachute. Something death defying. But there was nothing.

That night, Vincent had been so close to me I could smell the masculine scent of whiskey and spice from his clothes. I remembered his mouth lingering close to mine as he trailed my fingers down the chiseled expanse of his torso. I wondered how his lips would feel against my exposed neck. Would his kisses be soft or desperate?

I shook the thought out of my head as I flipped through Vincent's file. He had studied mechanical engineering at Berkeley, though his professors would have said he had majored in surfing, and mechanical engineering was just his pastime. He graduated and promptly took up a life of surfing and seasonal jobs. But a few years later, he designed and built the first prototype of his surfboard camera by himself in his apartment—he seemed like he knew how to use his hands and was obviously into mixing business with the rest of his life.

I recalled the texture of his hands from when he pulled my hand to his chest at the bar. They were neatly maintained but strong and calloused from all his outdoor activities. A slow heat gathered in my core as I imagined him sliding them up my thighs—I had resisted him in Cape Town but I wasn't sure I could resist his intimate touch again.

I shook my head. One encounter with Vincent Sorenson and I was already squirming in my panties. Since when did I start fantasizing about near strangers, and potential clients at that? Besides, anything happening between me and Vincent was bound to be a dead end. Those women around him at the bar were a thread away from having their dresses pooled on the floor. How could I compete with that? Did I even want to? I'd made a mistake with a man like that once, but I wasn't about to do it again.

Riley let out a soft snore, her head rolled with the tilting of the plane and stopped gently on my shoulder. She always made it seem so easy. If she wanted a guy, nine times out of ten, she got him. What would she have done with Vincent? I shook away the thought.

Whatever reason Vincent Sorenson had for not contacting us, I just hoped it didn't have to do with me shooting down his advances. I put the papers carefully back into the folder and tucked them away. Vincent was only a dangerous fantasy that needed to disappear. I leaned my head back and pulled the itchy airline blanket over my head, hoping to get some sleep before we arrived in New York.

***

My legs were rubber and sweat drenched the shirt on my back. I was willing my legs to move but they wouldn't. The air was the consistency of mud. What was I running from?

Run. Just run.

Fear coiled in the pit of my stomach and I wanted to vomit.

Someone was behind me. Blue eyes burning hot and cold at the same time behind thick spectacles. How can he be so fast? He grabbed my arm, twisting it behind me. Pain flashed through my shoulder, but I couldn't open my mouth to scream.

The shrieking of my alarm clock woke me up. I ripped my sheets off, damp with sweat. Damn it, I'd thought I was over that. I shook my numb right arm, aware I must've been sleeping on it all night, and clumsily hit my hand against the nightstand in confusion before I realized the alarm clock had fallen on the floor. Reaching down, I picked it up and squinted at the red letters. 7:00 a.m. I got up and snuck into the bathroom, noting Riley's bedroom door was still closed. She didn't have to get to work until nine, and she usually slept in until the absolute last minute.

My heart rate had slowed to normal by the time I finished my morning shower and dressed myself for work. I took the elevator down, sipping on my breakfast smoothie. Broccoli, oatmeal, protein powder, orange juice, a banana and yogurt: it was the breakfast of champions. Riley introduced me to it as a hangover cure, but it quickly became my go to morning snack. Looking at my reflection in the elevator doors, I decided I'd definitely dressed the part of a professional in my white blouse, a-line skirt, and black heels. Heck, if I had a few million dollars I'd trust myself with the money.

I power walked the streets of the Lower West side until I reached the subway station, only slowing to step over the manhole covers to avoid getting my heels stuck. At the intersection, a herd of commuters merged with me. Men and women in business suits moved in perfect synchronicity, all without any conversation.

That was the strangest thing about New York City I had never gotten used to. People could be right on top of one another but no one ever said a word. It was similar in Boston where I went to college and worked for a year afterward, but before that I lived in Coppell, Texas, where nearly everyone knew your name. You just felt more like a person when people actually recognized your existence.

I still thought of Texas as home, even though I hadn't been back in years. My parents still lived there but we'd been out of touch since I left for college. They were workaholics and expected the same of me—at the expense of my childhood and a real relationship with them. I wasn't bitter, but I also wasn't fond of their attempts to steer my life. They had their own lives now and I had mine.

The waves of commuters swept me along with them into the Bowling Green Station. I supposed ignoring strangers was a coping mechanism when you lived in a city of eight million. You couldn't learn the names of everyone even if you wanted to.

Twenty minutes later, I stepped out of the elevator on the forty-eighth floor of the gleaming steel and glass structure that was home to Waterbridge-Howser. A marble accented mahogany reception desk greeted me. Aluminum letters spelling out the company's name hung tastefully on the wall behind the desk. The conference room to the right was empty, the view of the park filtering through it. Every detail was designed to demonstrate wealth and power. Appearances were important in this business.

I navigated through the cubicle maze to my desk. We weren't packed together as tightly as possible, but it wasn't the open office plan of a design studio either. Tall dividers gave analysts their privacy as they investigated investment opportunities. Some analysts, like myself, were experienced enough to talk to clients directly, answering their questions and handling minor issues so the higher-ups would be free to work on bringing in more business. The managers' offices formed the perimeter of every floor, each one with a window view. The partners of the firm had their own section of the floor, and they only ever emerged to speak to the managers.

I dropped my satchel onto my desk and pulled out Vincent's file before heading through the outer rim of the cubicle corral to Richard's office. His door was half open and he was typing something on his computer.

"Richard, you wanted to meet about Mr. Sorenson?"

"Yes. Come in. Did you look over his file?" he said, not looking away from his screen.

"I checked everything and even reviewed our proposal. Our suggestions were very reasonable based on what we know about his finances."

Richard looked directly at me. "Any idea why he hasn't called us yet?"

In a second of irrationality, I thought about blurting out the details of meeting Vincent at the bar but decided it better if Richard didn't know anything about that. Besides, it was irrelevant. If anything, Vincent would have been more interested in working with us after that meeting.

I shrugged. "I don't know, maybe another firm got to him before us?" I remembered Richard's condescending comments about the "Wave Whisperer" and his assumptions about Vincent's lifestyle that no doubt influenced his approach to the meeting. That might have something to do with the fact that we hadn't heard from Vincent, but I kept my mouth shut.

Richard frowned. "Screw it. Nothing to do now but wait. Let me know if you hear anything."

I took the cue that the meeting was over when Richard turned back to his computer. When I got back to my own desk, I pulled up my email. The first thing that popped up was a message from my cell phone provider informing me I had reached my data limit for the month. *Again?* These cell phone services really knew how to fleece you. I deleted the email and moved on, reviewing work memos and deleting spam.

The rest of the morning bled into the afternoon. After eating lunch and helping another analyst resolve a reporting issue, I came back to my desk to find a note thrown haphazardly over my keyboard.

Kaufman called, have to meet him. Keep me updated if Sorenson calls the office.

Jon Kaufman was one of the larger clients Richard handled. He had a large plastics refinery west of the Hudson and was one of the clients who didn't come to our office. Rather, we went to him. I never met the guy but from the way Richard spoke about him, he was difficult.

I put the note aside and settled into my routine. I had barely gotten into the zone when my phone rang.

"Hey Kristen, I have Mr. Sorenson on the line for you." Our receptionist sounded like she was going to pass out just from the mention of his name.

So we hadn't blown our chances completely. For a moment I considered the possibility Richard had been right. *These guys are fairly predictable.* But there was no way Richard gave Vincent a positive first impression, and if anything saved us, it was probably my stunt with the spider at the bar.

"Thanks, transfer him over." I kept my voice level despite being aware that Vincent had asked for me specifically. I'd told him to call Richard as part of my brush-off. I just hoped his intentions were business.

A beep later and Vincent's silky voice vibrated through my handset.

"Hello Kristen."

Even over the phone, his velvety rasp made it difficult to maintain my composure. I switched the phone to my left hand and wiped my sweaty palm on my skirt.

"Hello Vincent, it's good to hear from you," I said, feeling like I'd just swallowed a cotton ball.

"I've been thinking about our meeting."

Which meeting? The one where I played with his nipple ring or the one where he asked me to mix business with pleasure?

"I'd like to discuss business," he continued.

I exhaled, relieved he wasn't interested in revisiting our personal discussion. Maybe he took the hint. "I'm happy to hear that. When would you like to schedule a meeting?"

"Today."

I laughed nervously. "We might need a little more time to make it out to South Africa."

"I'm at my office in Manhattan. Sixty-five West Fifty-ninth Street. Eighty-second floor." That was just a few blocks away. Of course. He had a media office in Manhattan that produced a popular extreme sports series that was broadcast on multiple cable networks.

"Could we do tomorrow? Richard is meeting with another client until late this afternoon."

"He's not needed. I'll be on a flight to Lucerne tomorrow. It has to be today." His voice betrayed no sense of urgency or need, just a statement of facts.

My mind swirled. Could I take the meeting with Vincent? I had all the paperwork ready; it was in the same folder as the proposal. Richard had let me close some smaller clients before so I knew what had to be done. But what would he say if I went to the meeting without him? I had a pretty good guess of what he'd say if I was the reason we lost Vincent's business. I had to take this meeting, if only to avoid the four letter words Richard would have in store for me if I didn't.

"Yes, of course. How is three p.m. for you?" I asked.

"Perfect. I'm looking forward to it, Kristen."

After he hung up, I let out a long breath, blowing my bangs out of my face. I was going to see Vincent Sorenson again. Although I certainly hadn't forgotten about both our meetings in South Africa, I wasn't sure if he'd been thinking about them at all.

At two thirty, I quickly packed my bag and told the receptionist to tell Richard or anyone else who stopped by my desk that I was going to be at a client meeting.

It was only when I was on the elevator down, the paperwork neatly filed in my briefcase, that I realized what I'd gotten myself into. Vincent Sorenson and I were going to be in the same room together. Alone.

***

Well this is different.

I stood in front of the sleek black reception desk at Red Fusion, SandWork's media arm, trying not to eye the curved adult-sized plastic slide that came from the ceiling and ended just right of where the receptionist was sitting. I smiled at the blonde woman behind the desk. She beamed back at me. Her rows of perfectly white teeth and her sultry figure made her more appropriate for a movie set than an office.

"Can I help you?" she said.

"Hi, my name is Kristen Daley. I'm here to see Mr. Sorenson."

"Of course, he's expecting you. Right this way." I followed her, watching the way her hips swayed in her curve-hugging dress. Though I tried to resist, I couldn't help inspecting my reflection in the glass door to make a quick comparison. Was she one of the pleasures

Vincent mixed with his business? But so what if she was? I had no right to be upset.

The Red Fusion offices were abuzz with activity. An employee sat cross-legged on the carpet, tossing a stress ball at the wall, stopping only to peck furiously at the laptop in front of him. Others were seated around large tables, having animated discussions. It was nothing like the reverential near silence at Waterbridge-Howser.

"Here we are, you can go inside. Vincent's ready for you." The receptionist stopped in front of a frosted glass door. The same glass formed a wall that stretched to either side of the entry.

I nodded thanks to her before pushing open the door and walking inside. Silence greeted me. Whatever the glass was made of, it completely blocked the noise from outside. In the corner was a black leather couch with a small coffee table in front of it. A large desk was set squarely in the center of the room, a metal and glass tribute to modernity. It was a stark contrast to his desk in Cape Town.

Vincent stood by the window, one arm behind his back, looking out. He was wearing a navy suit matched with a grey tie and white shirt. His long locks were slicked neatly back. Unwillingly preoccupied with wild fantasies, I nearly tripped on the rug in front of his desk as I walked closer. My pulse danced in my veins and a flush coursed through my cheeks. If I had fallen on him twice, I would've died from embarrassment.

Blue skies and skyscrapers along Central Park silhouetted his figure. He looked equally comfortable in a suit as he had in shorts and flip-flops.

He turned around, his dark eyes shimmering. "Beautiful, isn't it?"

I looked at his chin, chiseled with perfect angles, as if carved from a slab of marble. My eyes moved up to his mouth, his lips full and soft.

I cleared my throat. "Yes, it is. I've never quite gotten used to the view. Good to see you again, Mr. Sorenson."

"Please Kristen, have a seat." I stumbled to the guest chair in front of his desk while Vincent remained by the window.

I took it as my cue to continue. I set my bag down and reached inside for the glossy documents Richard and I prepared for a follow-up meeting.

Vincent studied me for a moment, his head tilted slightly to one side, as if examining a piece of art. Or his prey. Not knowing what else to do, I unleashed my rehearsed speech. "Thank you for meeting with me again. Waterbridge-Howser will be an excellent choice for your wealth management needs. We offer personal attention as well as products that larger—"

He held his hand up to stop me. "I've decided to go with Waterbridge-Howser." He glided from the window to me, occupying the small space between my seat and his enormous desk. He leaned back and sat on the edge, his crotch inches away from my heated face.

For a moment I forgot where I was or what I was even trying to accomplish. Wait, did he just say he wanted to work with Waterbridge-Howser? I realized my mouth had been hanging open, and I closed it with a snap. Adrenaline surged through my body. I had just closed a big account—this was massive.

"Sir?" I said, ignoring his position so as not to draw attention.

"Please, Kristen, it's Vincent. I let it slide when you called me Mr. Sorenson earlier, but if you're going to call me 'sir' then I'm going to address you as 'madam'. Now let's get back to business."

Vincent Sorenson, eager to get back to business. The irony wasn't lost on me, even in my dazed state.

"I can sign the paperwork today, but there's one condition." He paused. "You must be my point of contact. I'll need a number to reach you at any point in the day."

His dark pupils drew my gaze and I found myself unable to look away. I knew there'd be a catch. "Richard's usually the one who works directly with clients and I'm not sure I have the authority to—"

His expression implacable, he waved his hand to swat away my excuses. "Get the authority. Your partner is insulting and unacceptable. You're smart, ambitious, and not afraid to take risks. It's either you or I walk away."

I blushed at his compliments, although I wasn't sure why he thought I wasn't afraid of taking risks, but I had bigger issues to deal with. Even though this would be an enormous boost to my career, Richard would be offended if I agreed to Vincent's condition. Not to mention the obvious: I'd be spending much more time alone with Vincent. I doubted his true motives, but there was no way I could turn down this opportunity. I'd just have to figure out how to handle the complications.

I released a deep breath. "You're certainly very demanding, Vincent."

"You have no idea how demanding I can be." His eyes traveled up the exposed skin of my legs as if possessing me with his gaze. I crossed my legs to quell the uncomfortable sensation growing between them.

And there it is again, he can turn it on and off at will. Despite the edgy feeling of being this close to Vincent, I had to admire his ability to make anything sound sexual. If he was willing to sign with Waterbridge-Howser based on the misguided belief he'd get into my pants, I wasn't about to stop him. I'd just have to keep him at arm's length.

"Fine, I'll be your point of contact," I said, pulling out a business card from my satchel and handing it to him. "My information is on the card, you can reach me at the office during the day. My Blackberry number is available for *emergencies* as well." I hoped the emphasis was taken.

"Good," he said, pausing as though there was something else he wanted to add before gesturing towards my bag. "Do you have the paperwork?"

I handed him the contract.

"Thank you for deciding to go with us. I'm looking forward to working with you," I said, holding my hand out. He took it and squeezed firmly, the heat of his palm sending tingles up my arm. I didn't know if I was more excited about landing a huge client or Vincent's touch.

Without moving from his position in front of me, he signed and dropped the papers on his desk, rather than returning them to me. "Now that we have the business out of the way, we can get to the pleasure." The last word rolled off his tongue like a satin ribbon, sensuous and inviting.

"I'm sorry?" Heat coursed through my face.

"We didn't finish our conversation at the bar."

"I thought we were quite clear," I said, mouth drying by the second. He wasn't going to make this easy.

He shrugged. "You made it clear you didn't like mixing business with pleasure, so I didn't. The business is done, now it's time for pleasure."

As he leaned closer, his spicy cologne warped my brain into a puddle of incoherence. I froze as a series of lewd images played in my mind. His fingers caught a wisp of loose hair and pushed it behind my ear before trailing down my neck. Instead of pulling away, I closed my eyes and took a deep breath, hoping he couldn't read the desire painted on my face.

"If you read the paperwork, you'll see pleasure isn't part of the agreement," I tried.

Vincent took his hand away from my face, his dark pupils intense and focused. The sudden absence of his skin against mine felt wrong. I craved his touch immediately, but I tried not to lean closer to him.

"Of course not, the contract I signed was business. The pleasure part is just between you and me. Who's trying to mix them now?"

My pulse beat a steady staccato in my ears. Alarm bells ringing faintly in the back of my mind were overwhelmed by the building need radiating between my thighs. His sizable bulge was just a few feet away from me and became bigger every time I looked at it. I drowned in fantasies of being crushed under his chest, his cock pressing against my aching sex.

"Vincent, we can't."

"Why not?"

"I'll lose my job if anyone finds out."

He looked around. "How would they? I checked behind the couch earlier, we're definitely alone."

I had to give him credit for his persistence, but the longer I was in his office the more likely I was to give in. I needed to end this conversation quickly. I couldn't get involved with a man like Vincent.

"That's not the only problem," I blurted. "Just because you're attractive doesn't mean I'm willing to sleep with you."

Some of the intensity left Vincent's face and his mouth twisted into a boyish grin, but he never broke eye contact.

"You're attracted to me and I'm attracted to you. We're getting somewhere."

I flushed with embarrassment. It was an unintentional admission. "No we're not. There's no way I'm having sex with you in your office."

"I can pleasure you in so many ways beyond sex. Let me show you."

A surge of arousal made my body tremble. I had no doubt Vincent knew how to pleasure a woman. A man didn't become that confident without plenty of experience. In fact, he probably used the same lines on the perky blonde who greeted me earlier.

"What about your receptionist?" I snapped, the jealous words escaping my mouth before I had time to bite them back.

He furrowed his brows. "Lucy's a happily married woman and I've never touched her, nor would I ever. What kind of man do you think I am?" His tone surprised me; he sounded almost indignant.

I regrouped. "A dangerous one."

He shook his head and smiled. "I find danger only heightens the pleasure." His stance widened giving a fuller view of that distinctly male area so near my face. I gripped the arms of my chair.

God, he was determined. And worse, it was turning me on more than I'd thought possible. I licked my dry lips, realizing how close he was to me. Vincent tilted his face to the side, a lustful glint in his eyes.

He leaned down and pressed his thumb against my lower lip, dragging it open slightly. All thoughts of pulling away were drowned out by the roaring in my ears.

"This is wrong," I whispered, relishing his touch, my breathing shallow and forced. His beautiful face was close to mine, breath heavy and filled with desire.

"No, just a little dangerous."

His lips crashed into mine, sealing firmly over my mouth. My head swam, dizzy with desire. His tongue flicked against my lips, tenderly at first, then more passionately. I couldn't believe how full and soft his lips were. A soft whimper escaped my mouth.

This close to him, I could smell his unique scent underneath the cologne and feel his body heat. It was driving me wild. I squirmed in my seat, my panties beginning to feel damp already, and tilted my head back so as not to break the kiss. I knew if we stopped, my mind would return to rationality again, and that was the furthest thing from what I wanted.

He straightened, his lips drawing me upwards until I was standing as well. Faintly, I heard a stack of papers falling to the floor. We stumbled over to the leather couch in the corner. Our lips broke contact when I fell backwards onto the couch. My skirt rode up my thighs, revealing a scandalous stretch of skin.

"Gorgeous," he said, fire burning in his eyes.

I bit down on my lower lip as I tried to pull my skirt down to cover myself. Before I could adjust it, he was on top of me, his lips pressing firmly against my vulnerable neck, making me moan. I could feel his erection throbbing against my leg, his warmth seeping through the thin fabric. One hand slid up my inner thigh, and I instinctively spread my legs wider for him, urging him to touch me as my fingers fisted his wavy hair.

An electronic sound beeped from the desk. My eyes shot open and my hands fell from his head.

"Shit," Vincent cursed, running one hand through his hair and straightening his suit with the other.

He walked over to the desk and pressed a button on his phone. "Vincent, your three thirty is here. Should I send him in?"

"Give me another five minutes," he said into the speakerphone before looking back at me. "I'm sorry about the interruption. We can pick this up after work. I'll be done at five."

I stared at my surroundings, lightheaded. My skirt was just inches away from exposing my damp panties. I sat up quickly, smoothing it back over my legs. *What the hell did I just do?* I'd never lost my senses like that before and I was both mortified and furious with myself. This was completely inappropriate and unprofessional.

I got up to leave with what dignity I had left.

"Kristen, are you okay?"

I took a deep breath to control my temper. "This was a mistake Mr. Sorenson. It shouldn't have happened and I apologize for my part."

"Mistake?" His brows furrowed.

"I wasn't thinking clearly and you took advantage of it. We can still move on and pretend like it never happened, or I can transfer you to Richard—" My nails dug into the palms of my hands.

He let out a frustrated breath, shaking his head. "I'm not working with anyone else but you. I thought that was settled."

"Look, I admitted I'm attracted to you, but we shouldn't have acted on it. You're a client for Christ's sake. You caught me off guard and I was confused." I tried to make it sound as convincing as I could, but he didn't look like he was buying.

He stooped to pick up the paperwork and my work bag. As he walked over to me, I scrambled to my feet. My heels felt wobbly, and I took a step back, worried he was going to kiss me again.

He eyed me darkly, "Are you sleeping with anyone?"

He just wasn't going to give up. "No, but I don't—"

"Then there was no mistake. Stop apologizing, and stop denying what happened. We both wanted it." His brows narrowed, his gaze was intense. It was clear we were both exasperated, but for very different reasons. "If you still think you're confused, I'll make you a bet: before this week is done, you'll be touching yourself while thinking about me."

His casual reference to my masturbation routine left me shocked and wordless. Though I was no prude, I hadn't talked openly about touching myself to anyone but Riley and certainly not with any men I'd dated. And I wasn't even dating Vincent!

He watched my shocked expression as if waiting for me to speak, but I couldn't think of a coherent response.

"Right now I have a meeting. What I said earlier stands. If you're not my point of contact, I'm not doing business with Waterbridge-Howser." He gave me the signed contract and guided me to the door, his hand at the small of my back. I didn't have the energy to fight it. "This isn't over Kristen. We'll discuss later."

When I stepped out of the office, no one seemed to notice my shellshock or even pay me any attention. I let out a deep breath I hadn't realized I'd been holding and checked my reflection in the glass wall, one eye trained on the office staff. The collar of my blouse had been turned upwards and I quickly folded it down. I ran my hands over my skirt to smooth out the wrinkles, but my panties were a lost cause. I'd have to pick up a spare on the way back or do without for the rest of the day. As I ran my fingers through my hair, I could see my face was a shameful red in my reflection.

The sooner I got out of there the better. That kiss was a mistake that might cost me more than my career. Now that Vincent had seen the effect he had on me, I had a nagging feeling he wouldn't stop until he had exactly what he wanted.

Chapter Five

I studied my face in the Waterbridge-Howser bathroom mirror again, searching for traces of what happened in Vincent's office. It still didn't look right. For the third time, I wiped off my lipstick and reapplied. It had to look fresh, like I decided to redo it after getting the contract in anticipation of the big celebration. This was a huge deal. I should be happy.

During the walk back to the office, I'd decided I was going to remain his point of contact. Nervous as it made me, landing Vincent would be huge for my career. I couldn't let that opportunity slide. Even if I'd just let something almost unthinkable happen. A client had kissed me, and I had reciprocated. I knew he expected it to happen again, and I wasn't sure I'd be able to resist his potent sexual energy. It was irritating that a bad boy like him could have such an effect on me. Hadn't I told Riley I liked nice and caring guys?

I closed my eyes again. I was still embarrassed. This was a high point in my career, but I felt awful.

I gave my makeup and hair one final appraisal before deciding they were fine. I practiced my celebratory smile but it looked off. I'd never been good at being phony.

The door opened and two first-year analysts walked in. I couldn't wait any longer. It was showtime.

I walked out the door and Richard was waiting for me. "So how did it go?" he asked. His gray eyes were bolts of intensity. How on earth had he made it back from Jersey already?

I took a deep breath, put on my best fake smile, and held up the file. "The docs are signed. Deal's closed. We got it."

His hands shot up in triumph then came down awkwardly into a single clap. He looked torn whether or not to hug me but didn't, instead taking the documents from my hand. I let them go willingly.

He quickly leafed through each of the required signatures as I shifted back and forth on my feet. "See, I told you we impressed him. Carl will be pleased. God I can smell the bonus already. Definite promotion."

I nodded, smile still plastered on my face. The feelings stirring through my body weren't fit for expression. More than anything, I was beginning to feel anger. This should be my breakthrough moment; I'd worked so hard for it. Instead, I was concerned about hiding my relations with Vincent from my employer so I wouldn't get fired.

"You know, I was worried you were in there crying because something had gone wrong," he said, his eyes fixed on the final signature. "I'm surprised he didn't want me there for the signing. Did he say anything important?"

Before I could respond, a shrill voice came from our left. "Did I just hear we got Sorenson?"

I turned and saw the blonde curls and round face of Molly, another analyst. She had been at the company for five years and did good work, but hadn't quite broken through yet. Her voice also carried in a way I didn't think was possible before I'd met her. Not for the first time, I wondered if it could be heard on adjacent floors.

"Kristen and I locked it down today," Richard said, holding up the documents.

"Wow, congrats!" She turned and waved her finger at me. "Now you better make sure you don't let him take all the credit here. I saw you go to that meeting." Molly worked under a different manager and had known Richard long enough that she could get away with such comments.

I barely trusted myself to speak but I had no choice. Still with my best fake grin, I shook my head. "I won't."

"Well I won't stand for it if I hear you did."

I nodded, wanting to put an end to the conversation. While we'd been talking, heads had been popping out of cubicles offering their congratulations. The rest of the work day passed in a blur of emails and catching up on other work. It seemed everyone was excited but me. How could I have let Vincent kiss me?

***

I walked into my apartment emotionally drained; I wanted to collapse on my bed and cry. Riley was sitting in the living room watching one of the housewives shows and eating noodles. She waved when she saw me come in and finished chewing.

"How did it go?" she asked excitedly. I'd texted her on the way to the meeting with Vincent for moral support, but had forgotten about following up afterward. There would definitely be missed messages on my phone when I looked at it.

"We got it," I said wearily.

She screamed in delight, got up, and bounced over in her blue shorts and sorority t-shirt to hug me. I dropped my bag and reciprocated as best I could.

Riley seemed oblivious to my mood. "We *have* to go out and celebrate," she said.

"I don't know. I'm really tired."

"Come on! This is the biggest moment of your career. I would *kill* to have something like this happen at my job."

I looked at her and my shoulders slumped. "Sorry, I just need to wind down with a bath and fall asleep tonight. It was a really big day."

She looked at me and frowned. "Are you okay? Did something happen?"

Maybe someone. I couldn't bring myself to talk about it yet, so I shook my head. "I'm just totally beat. Stressful day."

I felt her gaze linger for a second longer but she moved on. "Okay. But we're celebrating this weekend and I'm *absolutely* not taking no for an answer. We can try that new tapas place. Sangria!"

I smiled. "Sounds like a deal."

Riley nodded and went to the fridge to get what was probably her seventh diet coke of the day. "So what actually happened in the meeting?"

I looked away. "It's kind of a blur. We talked, and after a while he was satisfied and signed. It's hard to remember the details."

"So this means a promotion, right? I remember you saying landing accounts was everything."

"Yeah, I guess."

I'd lied to my roommate. Remembering every second of that meeting was no problem at all. The problem was forgetting.

I went to my bedroom to change into my robe before walking into the bathroom. As I drew hot water for my bath, my thoughts lingered on Vincent. The audacity he had to kiss me in his office had me stuck between upset and impressed. I supposed it was to be expected from an adrenaline junkie like him. Obviously most of the risks he'd taken up to that point had worked out just fine. If this one failed, it was no sweat off his back. I recalled the incident in Cape Town. Compared to being bitten by a poisonous spider, kissing a girl was nothing.

I shrugged off my robe and poured my favorite bubble bath soap under the tap. The cinnamon candle I chose was one of my favorites, and I lit it while waiting for the tub to fill up. Once it had, I turned off the tap and stepped in, submerging myself up to my neck.

The warm water and fragrant scents had an immediate effect on my nerves. I'd chosen bubbles with notes of vanilla, sugar, almonds, and just a hint of musk. The combination was relaxing while making me feel sexy—something I needed because I wasn't getting anywhere with my dating life. Or lack thereof. It'd been a long time since I'd even kissed someone, let alone had to resist a kiss. I'd forgotten these things take willpower.

I leaned back and closed my eyes, feeling the bubbles pool around my chest and neck. This was just what I needed. I wiggled my toes and started a body scan meditation I learned in yoga class, gradually relieving the stress from my system.

As I felt my muscles relaxing, I shifted and realized how sensitive my pussy was. *When did that happen?* I hadn't been this aroused in weeks. Images of Vincent's profile invaded my mind. His arms. His chest. And his waves of blonde hair inches above my face earlier that day while I was sprawled beneath him on his couch, his probing fingers raising my skirt to my hips. He felt even better than he looked.

I was vaguely aware of my hand sneaking toward my aching sex. When the pad of my finger touched my clit, I paused. Masturbating about Vincent wasn't going to make this any better. I needed to forget my attraction to him and think of him only as a client. Maybe I should ask Riley to set me up with a date or two; she'd love the opportunity.

As if seeing other men would solve my Vincent problem. I smiled when I remembered him calling Richard "Dick" at the end of our first meeting. Bad boy or not, he was gorgeous, charming, and had a sense of humor. Forgetting my attraction to him would be like forgetting to breathe.

Maybe one touch. I let my hand graze my clit lightly, stimulating the sensitive nerves there. My breath caught and I tilted my head back. It'd been a few days since I last touched myself, which was normal. But since I met Vincent, days felt more like months. I tried another touch and an unexpected shiver ran up my spine, making me gasp. I'd anticipated a slow build, but after a few light strokes, I realized I was already primed.

He'd bet me I'd masturbate to thoughts of him. The gall of Vincent Sorenson. I always thought I'd be offended if someone said anything so crude to me, but it only heightened my attraction to him, which was annoying. I wanted to resist and prove him wrong—more for my own conscience than his—but I was rapidly becoming too aroused to care. What would it matter anyway? I'd never tell him and he'd never know. He wouldn't have the satisfaction.

Without wasting time, I continued pleasuring myself, increasing both the pressure and area with each stroke until I was gliding up and down my lips in a slow circuit, coming up to my clit and down, easing in and out of my aching sex. Fingers steadily at work, my thoughts went back to Vincent. The fantasy of his strong hands exploring my body with his signature boldness drove me wild. My breath started coming in quicker bursts as I shortened my motion, an orgasm swelling in my core.

My phone rang, interrupting the moment. On the second ring, I realized it was my work phone. At eight-thirty. Nobody called that phone after work unless it was important, and I was expected to answer no matter where I was.

Drying my hands on my towel, I leaned out the tub and reached into my robe—reflecting, not for the first time, on how ridiculous it was I had to take my work phone into the bathroom with me.

Strange. Whoever was calling had an unknown number.

"Kristen Daley," I answered.

"I hope I'm not catching you at an awkward moment." The familiar voice made my pulse leap.

Vincent. I became all too aware of my compromised state with him on the other line. Why did this have to happen to me?

I was tempted to hang up, finish my orgasm then call him afterward with a clear head but I wouldn't know what number to dial. I took a deep breath hoping to calm my nerves enough that my voice would come out evenly. "Mr. Sorenson, of course not. How can I help you?"

"You know it's Vincent," he said, correcting me. "I'm afraid I have a problem."

My heart skipped a beat. There were numerous problems he could have, one of them being regret for signing with my employer earlier today. "What problem are you having?"

He sighed deeply into the receiver. "I haven't been able to focus on my meetings or get any work done. You're constantly on my mind. I need to taste your lips again. Uninterrupted."

I tried to think of something to say, but first had to find the pieces of my mind that had scattered across the bathroom.

"I'm flattered. But that sounds like a personal problem that I can't help you with, Mr. Sorenson."

"Vincent. And tell me if you haven't thought about me as well."

I briefly wondered if my company recorded conversations on this phone but remembered IT telling me they didn't. Regardless, I needed to steer this discussion away from lips and tasting. "*Vincent*, I'm sorry, but this discussion just isn't professional." I didn't understand why it was so hard for him to get that into his head.

"Then let's end it. We're two consenting adults who have a strong sexual attraction for one another. What do we have to do to make this happen?"

A curious bubble swam towards my chest and I popped it with judiciousness. "As an adult, I admit our mutual attraction, but you and I can't happen. Personal relations with clients are forbidden by my employer. If you have a problem with that, speak to the Waterbridge-Howser human resource department."

"I already checked. There aren't any rules against it."

Damn it, he was determined. "There are office politics. I could get fired or dead-end my career—I hope you understand that. You might not have anything to lose, but I do."

"I'm losing my mind thinking about you." The urgency in his voice was surprisingly endearing. It was both unsettling and relieving to know I had such an acute effect on him. "I felt the way you kissed me. You want more."

My hand at my forehead, I closed my eyes and sunk lower into the tub as I tried to control my rapid breaths. "Vincent, it was a heated moment and we both got carried away. That's all."

His voice became dark. "Have you touched yourself yet?"

I hesitated, my grip on the phone tightening. "That's really none of your business." My response came shakier than I'd wanted and I silently cursed myself.

"Already," he purred, the silky vibration raising goosebumps across my skin. "Kristen, let's be reasonable about this. I promise you the real thing is better than whatever you're imagining."

I squeezed my thighs together to suppress the growing need between them and sighed. "Please don't make this so hard."

"I am hard," he grunted then paused as if thinking, and when he spoke next his gruff voice was dripping with desire. "You're naked right now, aren't you?"

My toes curled against the drain cover. *How did he know that?* His ability to sense my arousal through the phone was uncanny, and I briefly wondered if he could also read my mind. "Nice try," I lied, a smile creeping across my face despite myself. "But I need to get going, if that's all."

"God, Kristen. If you're touching yourself right now it's only a fraction of the pleasure I'd give you." He sounded as pained as the throbbing ache growing between my legs. "You're selling both of us short."

His strong words had an even stronger effect on my body. I was afraid I was going to start touching myself again if I didn't get off the phone. The need was becoming overwhelming with him on the other end of the receiver; he was so far away yet so close.

I exhaled deeply, preparing the words I needed to say to him. "As your advisor, I recommend you hang up the phone, then with that same hand pleasure yourself until your arm goes numb or you're satisfied—whichever comes first. Once you've finished, you'll have forgotten all about me."

When he didn't respond, I began to wonder if my brush-off was too harsh. Then he spoke. "I made the right decision to have you as my point-of-contact. You're everything I expected and more. We'll be in touch."

I heard a click then silence. I looked at my phone a second before putting it back in my robe pocket. What did he mean I was everything he expected and more? Was that whole conversation just some kind of weird test? The idea annoyed me further.

I sighed in frustration. The sexy-relaxing combo I'd been working with wasn't going to cut it anymore—all relaxation had gone down the drain with that call. I needed a glass of wine and my bed. It had been a long, long time since I'd been this horny. My entire body felt like a wound spring.

I swung my leg over the side of the tub, intending to get out but gasped at the sensitivity. My sex, forgotten during the heat of the conversation, was swollen with desire. Knowing I wouldn't fall asleep without release, I rocked back into the tub and kicked my legs up. My fingers returned to where they'd been before and I resumed stroking, eager to flush myself of an irritating ache that had only grown worse during Vincent's call.

I thought of Vincent on top of me, the way his strapped arms would look as they braced his weight, the feeling of his rough grip, the raw power of his lithe body stretched out.

My strokes became shorter as my orgasm neared its peak. *You're naked right now, aren't you?* His lurid accusation intensified the stimulation and I increased my pace until the sensation was unbearable. The next second I felt the first shudders of the most powerful orgasm I'd ever had rip through my core. I gripped the edge of the tub to brace myself as I trembled with relief and satisfaction.

After a few small aftershocks, I came down from my bliss. My head was clearer than it had been moments ago and I assessed the situation. There were worse things than having a hot billionaire obsessed with you. If I could keep my actions in check, working with Vincent would be great for my career. On the downside, he was seductive as sin and persistent to a fault. I briefly imagined all the women willing to do anything he asked of them. A bad boy like him could really hurt me, and if anyone should've learned that lesson, it was me.

I got out of the tub and dried off. It was already getting late and I was more than ready to slip beneath my covers to end this exhausting day, but my mind wouldn't stop racing. After tossing and turning in bed for an hour, preoccupied with thoughts of Vincent, I grumbled in resignation.

I reached into my nightstand, grabbed my vibrator, and went for round two.

Chapter Six

The next few days went by in a haze. After the thrill of landing the account, it was back to the normal grind of the analyst life: making reports and parsing data to pass along to higher-ups. I stayed busy in an attempt to stop myself from daydreaming about Vincent. My next meeting with him wasn't for a week, and I didn't want to think about him any more than I had to. Doing so was too distracting and more than a little stressful.

Still, at the end of each day, I was disappointed not to have heard his voice. It seemed like Vincent was going to pursue me harder but maybe he had already found a new distraction. Of course, that would be a stress relief from a professional perspective—and should have been one I welcomed wholeheartedly—but I had to admit his pursuit of me was the most exciting thing that had happened to me in a while. Maybe ever.

Finally, Friday rolled around. When I got home, Riley told me she scored some tickets at work for the Knicks game and asked me to join.

I quickly pulled on a nice shirt and skinny jeans but took longer on the makeup and hair. I was applying the final touches in the bathroom next to Riley who was finishing her makeup.

"So have you seen Vincent since Monday?" she said, touching up her mascara in the mirror.

"Nope," I said. "Our next meeting isn't until next Tuesday."

"Is he still into you?"

"What do you mean?"

"Come on. The question isn't whether he's into you, it's how aggressive he's being about it. You get all flustered every time I mention him, so spill. I know you're hiding something."

"I'm not. You saw him. He's hot. Lots of girls find him hot, and I'm sure he does really well with plenty of them. But we have a professional relationship."

She blinked her eyes a few times and put her mascara away. "Okay, if you don't want to talk about it, that's fine. But he's into you and I know you know."

"Whatever. Who are we meeting again?"

She'd moved onto lip gloss and smacked her lips a few times. "Jen and Steph. They started at the same time I did. I think you've met Jen."

Riley had a lot of friends from work and I'd probably met this girl before even if I didn't remember. I was just happy to be off the subject of Vincent. "I think so. Are we meeting them there?"

"Yeah, and they texted that they left a minute ago. You ready?"

"You know I'm always faster than you. Let's go."

"After you doll."

The seats weren't great, but they were cheap, and more importantly it was a low stress, girls' night out, which was exactly what I needed. We got popcorn and sodas and settled in, flirting lightheartedly with the guys in the row in front of us. Jen and Steph were both fun and inclusive, filling me in when the conversation referenced inside jokes stemming from work.

The three of them had a better rapport than anyone I worked with at Waterbridge-Howser. The work sounded less interesting from what Riley had told me, but at least the environment sounded fun.

Ten minutes into the first quarter, we spotted ourselves on the Jumbotron. The camera lingered long enough for us to wave and cheer enthusiastically. It was funny how excited I was about something so trivial; for the tenth time that night I reflected on how good Riley was being to me. This kind of evening was absolutely perfect. She often knew when I was upset and steered things to my comfort zone when I needed it—and I needed it as much as ever after such a crazy couple weeks. Even though she didn't know all the details, she had a good idea of how I was feeling and wouldn't push the subject further than my comfort level.

During the break between the first and second quarter, we were approached by a balding man in a suit with a nametag that indicated he was a member of the hospitality staff at Madison Square Garden. "DAVE" touched his hand to his earpiece, then looked between me and Riley.

"Excuse me, miss," he said to me, "are you Riley Hewitt?"

Startled, I pointed to my friend. "No, that's her," I said. Riley turned to face Dave.

"Ms. Hewitt, you and your group have been upgraded to box seats, compliments of the house. If you'll follow me."

We all looked at each other in shock. Did we win some kind of random drawing? When Dave indicated he didn't know the details, only that he was the messenger, we briefly discussed it among ourselves. "Why not?" was the verdict. I'd never been in the box seats at MSG—they were super expensive—but it sounded like a blast. After the craziness of the situation with Vincent, my luck was looking up; this night was somehow getting better by the minute.

After a short walk, Dave led us through a private hallway to a double-doored suite. Passing through the threshold, we stepped onto lush carpeting and marveled at the leather couches surrounding a wall-sized TV displaying the game. In the back laid out buffet-style was enough snack food and drinks to stock a grocery store. Our mouths beginning to water, Dave continued the tour by ushering us through a sliding glass entrance to a balcony. He gestured to the rows of seats indicating we could watch the action live if we preferred but we were mainly interested in returning to the food.

He brought us back inside and clapped his hands together. "That concludes the tour. Any questions?"

"Are you sure this is all free?" Riley asked. "Like you're not going to charge my credit card after we leave right?"

Dave smiled. "Somebody's getting charged but it isn't you fine ladies, I assure you." After we indicated we had no further questions, he turned to leave but said, "I almost forgot. You'll be joined later by some Knicks shareholders. I promise, they're wonderful company." He winked then left with a sordid grin on his face.

Oh great. The mystery behind a group of girls receiving too-good-to-be-true box seats became clearer.

Jen huffed. "If this 'upgrade' means getting hit on by a bunch of old guys all night, I'm going to be pissed."

"I don't know," Steph said. "If they're shareholders, they're probably really rich. Let's just take advantage of the free goodies, have fun, then go home."

Jen went to the suite door and checked to make sure it wasn't locked, which thankfully it wasn't. After some discussion and some longing glances at the food, we decided to stay and enjoy ourselves.

We stuffed our plates with nachos, cookies, and other hip-friendly treats and brought them out to the balcony seats. By the time we settled in, the second quarter had already started. The Knicks were losing, but that didn't bother me. I was more of a football girl but crowd energy made watching any live sport enjoyable. Plus, the delicious nachos kept my tummy happy.

A Knicks player threw yet another terrible pass and the other team stole it for a breakaway dunk. The Knicks coach called timeout and slammed his clipboard down, venting his frustration in the form of passionate words and wild gesticulations.

"Reminds me of my boss," Riley remarked.

"Totally," said Jen. Steph nodded in agreement.

"I thought you said he wasn't bad," I offered.

Riley rolled her eyes. "Compared to others, he's not. But he has a habit of always walking by, making sure no one's playing solitaire or checking Facebook. He's a stickler for rules and blows his top when people don't follow them. If I had to describe him with one word, I'd say 'particular'."

Her boss sounded similar to Richard on a bad day. "I'd use a stronger word. 'Anal' sounds good."

A warm hand rested on my shoulder, making my words linger in the air. "Hello Kristen."

I twisted my head to see who it was even though the voice was unmistakable. Vincent, in a crisp white shirt that bolded his dark eyes and slate-gray slacks that hid powerful lean muscles, was preparing to take a seat in the row behind us. The impeccable timing combined with being hit by his intense aura made my nacho-filled stomach drop to the floor.

"Vincent, what are you doing here?" I asked anxiously, unsure which parts he caught of our private girls conversation. *Besides stalking me.*

"You remembered to call me Vincent. I'm touched." He smiled then squeezed my shoulder gently. "I was enjoying the game from the front row when I saw you and your friends on screen. I figured I'd send my regards to my new account manager."

"You're his account manager, Kristen?" Jen asked, surprised.

I looked at her, then Steph, then Riley. Their eyes trained on Vincent were as wide as their mouths, like they'd just seen a god. "Umm . . . yeah. Guys, this is Vincent Sorenson, CEO of SandWorks. He's a new client." I introduced Jen and Steph to him and he shook their hands in turn. They looked as if they were going to melt from his touch and I couldn't help commiserating.

"Although we hadn't been formally introduced, Kristen's already told me about you Riley," he said smoothly, shaking her hand.

She blushed then giggled uncharacteristically. "Kristen's told me all about you as well."

I glared daggers at her, hoping she'd take the cue.

"Good things I hope."

"Only the best," she replied, pointedly ignoring me. "Jen, Steph want to get some more snacks inside?"

I stealthily pinched her hip and she smoothly pulled my hand away without reacting. She was determined to leave me and Vincent alone and I was determined to prevent that. God knows what happened last time Vincent and I were by ourselves in his office. I shuddered to think something similar would happen at this public venue.

"I'll come with you," I said, more as a plea than a suggestion.

"Oh no, I'm sure you guys have *so* much to talk about." She smiled at me then turned to Vincent. "Thank you for the box seats Mr. Sorenson. Hopefully Kristen can show you our *full* appreciation." Her obvious wink made me wince. Then she tugged Jen and Steph inside, the two of them stealing glances at Vincent as they left.

When it was clear we were alone, Vincent deftly hopped over the row and took the seat beside me. He reached back and grabbed two drinks he must've put there before alerting me to his presence and offered one to me.

"A mojito. I know it's your favorite."

Irritated by the charge I got from being so near him, I accepted the drink and took a gulp to calm my nerves. I wanted to be mad at him but couldn't think of a good reason. "See what you did? You scared off my friends." This was supposed to be girls' night out, but with the amount of testosterone he exuded I sensed it had just turned into Vincent's night out.

"They seemed to be having fun." He raised his glass and clinked it against mine. "So do you." His lips curled into a charming smirk and he adjusted his position, brushing his arm against mine. The unwelcome surge over that entire side of my body made me realize how much I missed his physical presence.

I took a sip, then another, debating what to say to him while he eyed me suspiciously, the drama of the game below us all but forgotten. "Do I make you nervous?" he asked.

His relaxed posture and collected demeanor provided a stark contrast to my own composure. "No. Why?"

"You're pounding that drink."

I glanced down at my mojito which was now just ice cubes. *When did that happen?*

His amused eyes were on mine when I looked back up. "I can get you another if you want."

"Are you trying to get me drunk?" I blurted, recalling our last heated conversation in which I was naked and in the middle of masturbating. "I'm not going home with you tonight if that's what you're planning."

"Relax Kristen. You're a beautiful, intelligent woman. I know you can handle yourself." The casual way in which he deflected while complimenting me made me stiffen and when he put his hand on mine, I felt my knees go weak. Good thing we were sitting down."What's really bothering you?"

I placed the drink in the cup holder and pulled my arms across my chest, more to avoid the effect of his touch than to pout. "You. What are you doing here? Are you stalking me?"

"I may constantly fantasize about you but I don't follow you around or have you followed if that's what you're asking."

"So you just happened to be here when I'm here."

"It's the playoffs. As a major shareholder in the team, I have more reason to be at this game than you. Maybe you're the one stalking me?"

His cleverness caused me to laugh and I gained a greater appreciation for his sense of humor. "You wish."

"Maybe you researched my finances, realized my connection to the Knicks, and, unable to resist your intense feelings, showed up hoping to see me. Looks like we both got lucky." He took a sip of his own drink while keeping his dark eyes trained on me.

Even though I'd been plagued with constant thoughts about him throughout the week—some of them including fantasy meetings in his office—I couldn't imagine myself acting on them. "In your dreams, buddy," I said, my tone more playful than serious.

He leaned toward me, his mouth close to my ear and his long velvety hair brushing my cheek. Rather than resisting, I found myself relishing the contact. His scent was different than usual but the signature spice was present and had its usual effect on me all the same.

"You want to know what I dream about? We can make that a reality," he purred.

My body involuntarily shivered at the silky vibration. I admired his graceful tenacity but I had already come to expect that from him. "Sorry, but you're not really my type."

He pulled back but was still close enough for me to feel his radiating heat. I saw his seductive smile widen. "I am. But what do you think your type is?"

"Nice. Sweet. Caring. Not exactly a thrill-seeking CEO."

His smile turned lopsided and he replied, "You'd be bored in a month. I think you want someone exciting who also makes you feel safe. I can do that."

My thumb and forefinger pinched my chin in thought. "Hmm . . . you know that does sound appealing but as enticing as it is, I already told you, we can't happen."

"Professional concerns, I know."

I raised a brow. "So you do listen."

"When it involves your lips, you have my full attention."

The tension in my shoulders relaxed and I felt a crack in my guard. He was both physically beautiful and demonstrating thoughtfulness. It wasn't just the drink and remembering my roommate; he actually listened to my concerns. I decided to illustrate the situation to ensure we were on the same page. "You're Romeo and I'm Juliet. If we get together, bad things will happen."

"Is that it?" He carefully scanned the arena then returned his powerful gaze to me. "Because I don't see your bosses anywhere. I thought a Waterbridge-Howser employee would be a little more creative when it comes to getting what she wants. You certainly strike me as the type."

"What type?"

"A woman who gets what she wants. Harvard for economics? Working at a wealth management firm trying to get ahead when guys like your partner, Richard, are trying to screw you over or just screw you at every opportunity? You have to be both tough and smart to thrive in that environment."

How did he know what I studied in school, or even where I went?

As if reading my mind, he said, "I looked up your background before I signed with your company. Remember, I'm trusting you with hundreds of millions of dollars."

"I thought you made me your point-of-contact just to get into my pants."

"I might be a risk-taker when it suits me, but I'm not a moron. You're an impressive woman, Kristen."

Well at least he knew how to make a girl feel good. And aroused. He shifted his legs closer to mine and in that moment, I could swear the alcohol must've reached my brain because all I could think about was the image of him ripping off those slacks in front of me like a male stripper. "Do you try to have sex with all the other impressive women you meet? Is this a conquest for you?"

He looked at me with surprise. "None as impressive as you."

"Well, I'm flattered." I really was, but my purposeful tone didn't show it.

"I don't see you as a conquest," he added. "But I'd be lying if I said I didn't find your feistiness a turn-on."

I blushed fiercely. "I have legitimate concerns."

"Which brings us back to the topic you didn't address. If all you have are professional concerns, it won't be an issue keeping what we do just between us. We've kissed in my office and you still have your job."

He had a point, but there were other reasons I was resisting him, and I wasn't about to surface those skeletons. "It's a risk I can't take. As deliciously attractive as you are, I want my job more than I want you. I barely even know you. And you barely know me."

"Then get to know me. Give this," he gestured back and forth between me and himself, "a chance."

"What are you saying?"

"A date. If it goes well, let's have more. If not, we go back to a purely professional relationship. I promise, keeping one date a secret won't be a problem." He found a lock of my hair and curled it seductively between his fingers. "What we do is private. My lips are sealed."

As exciting as the prospect of a date with Vincent was, his suggestion seemed inconsistent with his approach. Until now, he only seemed interested in having sex with me. Dating was a whole different beast and I wasn't certain he grasped the significance. "Vincent, as thrilling as a date sounds, I'm not sure you understand what you're proposing. A date isn't sex. And if we went on one—not saying we would—but if we did, I'm telling you upfront we won't be having sex. Maybe not even kissing." The last part was added for emphasis.

I expected him to pull back but without skipping a beat he said, "I'm fine with that."

His response gave me pause. "Did I miss something? I thought you just wanted a quick lay."

"I spend the average week on three different continents so I don't usually have time for a relationship. Hence, the direct approach. You've made it clear you aren't the kind of girl who wants casual relations. I still want to see you. Taking it slow isn't what I'm used to but I can adjust."

"Is your concept of dating just a means to sex? I'm no prude but to me sex is a meaningful act between two people who share a connection. I'm not just going to add an extra hurdle for you to clear.

You just raved about how smart I am and now you're treating me like I'm an idiot."

"Dating is whatever we make it. I want to show you I'm interested in you beyond just sex."

His response was a relief. "Okay."

"Is that a yes?"

Probably the result of the mojito coursing through my veins and Vincent's pheromones swimming in my brain, I heard the words come out my mouth before I had time to process the implications. "Fine. One date."

His stunning features lit up making him even more gorgeous.

"But," I added, cutting off the words lingering on his tongue. "I need discretion. I don't want to worry about my employer finding out about us."

"I agree, it won't be an issue. How's eight tomorrow?"

"In the evening?"

"No, a.m."

"Isn't that a bit early for a date? What do you have in mind?"

"It's a surprise."

My head was spinning. "Okay . . . where do you want me to meet you?"

"I'll pick you up."

I nodded. "How can I know what to wear if you won't tell me where we're going or what we're doing?"

"Nothing fancy, don't worry about it," he said, looking me up and down. "It looks like you know how to handle that anyway."

My face grew hot again. "Thank you."

He leaned close to me, and I felt his breath on my neck and shuddered, bracing for an attempted kiss. "Just be ready at eight. You can do that, right?"

"Yes."

"You don't think I'm going to try to kiss you here, do you? You're underestimating me, Kristen." He leaned back into his chair, grazing my leg with his fingers as he did. His touch sent a jolt through my body, making my breath hitch.

"I can behave," he finished.

I looked at him, breathing in short bursts. I hadn't thought it was possible to look intensely calm before that moment.

"I'll get you another drink."

As he went into the suite he passed Riley on her way out. She bounced down next to me. "So that looks like it went well."

I snorted. "I guess."

"So when's your date?"

I had to work on being less obvious. "Tomorrow."

"Good. If you said there wasn't a date I was going to smack you."

I turned to her. "You do know I'm still allowed to make my own decisions, right?"

Riley cocked her head. "Sometimes you need a little push to make the right one. Where's he taking you?"

"It's a surprise. He wants me to be ready in the morning."

Riley crinkled her nose. "Doesn't sound like the usual, whatever it is. Something tells me he's not the kind of guy to invite a girl to walk around the park."

"No, definitely not."

"It's one date. Worst case scenario, you probably get to do something exotic and fun with a guy who is stunning eye candy."

I swallowed. "Worst case I lose my job."

She laughed. "If bad boys got caught easily, they wouldn't still be bad boys. You'll be fine."

The rest of the game passed in an increasingly tipsy blur. I spent the evening waiting for Vincent to touch me again from where he sat behind me—my shoulder, my neck, anything—but he never did.

As we left the arena, the only thing on my mind was the next morning. What could he possibly have planned that required starting so early?

Chapter Seven

My alarm clock buzzed at 7:00 a.m. I woke up face down on my pillow and promptly chided myself for taking full advantage of the complimentary bar in the suite last night. I drew my comforter over my head, desperate for the extra sleep, when I realized I was going on a date in an hour. A surge of anxiety pulsed through me and I shot from bed, shedding my clothes on my way to the shower. I turned the water on hot, hoping the heavy steam might relax me, but I couldn't stop wondering what a surprise date with Vincent Sorenson involved. Rented out museums? Five-star restaurants? Yachts? I had no idea what I was going to wear.

I lathered up a bar of soap, running it across my torso and down my legs—shit, should I shave? I was planning on wearing jeans but I could hear Riley's voice in my head, berating me for my informal outfit choice; she would insist on a skirt and I would eventually yield. I grabbed my razor and swiped the blade carefully over my legs.

I turned off the shower and grabbed a towel, quickly drying off before rummaging through my closet to find a modest blue skirt and a silken racerback tank top. I threw them on over a matching bra and panties set and walked into the kitchen to find Riley sipping liberally from a cup of coffee and flipping through *People*.

"I'm sorry, did I wake you up?" I bypassed the coffee, already jittery enough from nerves, and poured myself a generous cup of orange juice.

"Are you kidding me? I've been up for an hour, there was no way I was going to miss this."

"Well you wouldn't have missed much, I still don't know where we're going."

She closed her magazine slowly and pushed it away before looking at me in contemplation. "Are you bringing condoms?"

"What?" I asked, the abruptness of the question catching me off guard.

"This," she said, "is why I got up early. You have to think about these things!"

"No, Riley, I am not bringing condoms. It's only our first date. A test date really."

"Well, I commend you. It would take some serious restraint to keep me from tearing the clothes off of a guy like Vincent."

I rolled my eyes over the rim of my cup. "Are you sure you don't want to go on this date for me?"

"Come on, I was kidding. I'm just excited for you," she said. "It's your first official date in—"

"Don't remind me," I interjected, cringing at the thought that it'd been two years since my last relationship and months since I went on anything close to a date.

"You're ready for it, that's all I'm saying."

"Yeah, I think I am," I said softly, remembering my tryst with Vincent in his office, the way I had practically collapsed into him as he kissed me. I couldn't remember a time when things had felt so natural.

"Well, the outfit is definitely cute," Riley said, giving me a quick once-over.

"I thought you'd approve."

"But I hope you plan on using a comb before you leave." She laughed and gestured to the knotted curls my hair had dried into.

I glanced at the clock and darted to the bathroom when I realized I only had a few minutes left to get ready before Vincent was supposed to arrive. I grabbed a brush from the sink and tamed my hair into a stylishly messy bun, finishing just as a knock came at the door. I jumped in nervous anticipation and quickly applied a coat of mascara to my eyelashes.

"He's here!" Riley sang out from the living room, her voice a high trill. She ran into the bathroom and ushered me out, thrusting my purse in my hands. "Have a good time, be safe, and tell me *everything.*"

"I will, I will," I reassured her as I opened the front door. She escaped back into her room before Vincent could spot her in her pajamas.

He stood in front of me, six feet of muscled perfection fitted in jeans and a sleek black sports coat. He gave me one of his lopsided smiles and my heart skipped a beat. "Good morning," I managed, suppressing the bashfulness that had suddenly overwhelmed me.

"You look great," he said, placing his hand on the small of my back and guiding me out of the apartment building. I could feel his fingers gripping at the fabric of my shirt, the familiar gesture sending a flush of heat to my face.

When we got outside we stopped in front of a silver Camry, its square frame and dull paint job suggesting its old age. I'd expected a limousine or fancy sports car, something befitting his wealth. "Is this your car?" I blurted.

"You wanted discretion," he said as we got in.

"Is this the part where you tell me where we're going?" I teased as he began driving.

He shot me a grin. "Do you always make it this difficult for a guy to surprise you?"

"I like to be prepared, that's all."

"It shows. Those charts you put together for our first meeting must have taken some time."

I looked at him, dismayed, as I recalled my disastrous performance in Cape Town. "Turned out to be worth it, I think they were the only redeeming part of our presentation."

"Are you sure that little slip and fall act wasn't planned?"

"I told you it was a mistake, but Richard will probably be implementing it into our future meetings."

"I can't blame him, it was my favorite part."

"So you told me, but I'm not sure I want to be known for groping CEOs." I tried not to sigh as I remembered the firm expanse of Vincent's chest beneath his t-shirt.

"I guess I was just lucky I was there to break your fall." He turned to me smiling, and I practically had to tear my gaze from the curl of his full lips.

"Something tells me you don't trip over your own feet often," I said, distracting myself from the lustful gleam in his eye. "Don't surfers need to have pretty good coordination?"

"In that case, we'll have to work on yours," he said as the car came to a slow stop.

"What?" I looked out of the window, taking in the hazy tarmac of an airport parking lot.

"We can't go to St. Thomas without surfing at least once."

I clenched my jaw to keep it from dropping to my chest. I had to fight the urge to protest, running through all the reasons surfing made me nervous in the first place. But I knew I couldn't sabotage a date with Vincent Sorenson because I was too afraid to stand on a board for awhile. "Is this JFK?" I sputtered as we got out of the car.

"It's a private airport, actually. There weren't any direct flights to the Caribbean so we're settling for something more intimate." He gestured to a small plane in the distance.

I had imagined the yachts and the sports cars, but I hadn't been anticipating a private jet. Maybe Vincent wasn't the bad boy I'd pinned him for. In fact, he was turning out to be pretty considerate. A date on a remote island couldn't have been easy to organize and his little stunt at the Knicks game was more than generous—my friends certainly thought so.

"Well, I do like a challenge," I conceded, deciding if he was willing to make an effort then so was I.

He grabbed me by the hand and pulled me towards the plane. "That's what I thought."

I had just been getting used to the idea of a private jet when I was met with custom leather seats, a glass coffee table, and a suede sofa all situated in the cabin of the plane. True, I hadn't been on a date in a long time, but even if I had been, it wouldn't have been anything like this. Dinner and a movie this was not.

"So much for discretion," I said as I surveyed my surroundings.

"We'll be all alone up here," he said as he turned to me, his eyes falling briefly to the line of cleavage visible at the neck of my shirt before traveling back to my face. I glanced around, looking for a stewardess, but he wasn't lying. The cabin of the plane was empty except for us—it couldn't have been more discreet.

"Is it customary for CEOs to have their own private jets?" I was trying to sound nonchalant but I knew my awe was glaringly obvious.

"I admit, it takes some getting used to." As we settled into our seats he placed his hand on the armrest between us, his long fingers splayed across the leather. I wanted to reach for it, to bring the knobs of his knuckles to my mouth and run my tongue over the shallow lines in his skin. I glimpsed the couch, imagining the small of my back sticking to its leather surface as Vincent leaned over me, the pressure of his muscled frame pushing me deep into the cushions. He would draw my legs around his waist, his hand cupping the space behind my knee as our lips opened around one another. I would grab his lean hips and push myself against him, eager for a friction I hadn't felt in a long time.

"You mean jetting overseas isn't one of your pastimes?" I swallowed, trying to pull myself from my heated reverie.

"SandWorks wasn't exactly handed to me. I spent a lot of time traveling, working paycheck to paycheck, before I thought of the waterproof camera. In fact, that Camry is something of a relic from those days."

"I have to admit, it wasn't what I was expecting when you picked me up."

"I did a lot of traveling in that car, even spent some nights in it," he said. "But when business took off one of the first things I had to learn was how to manage my money."

"Isn't that what you hired us for?" I couldn't imagine him struggling to learn anything. His business savvy had been obvious since the first day we met.

"Yes, but it wasn't always easy to know who to trust in the beginning so I had to rely on myself. Something tells me you never had much of a problem with that, though."

"What do you mean?" I asked, growing defensive at the implication.

"Financial analyst, Harvard girl—your parents must have done well for themselves to be able to send you there."

My home life wasn't a point of conversation I enjoyed but I didn't want him thinking I hadn't worked hard for my success. "My parents put a lot of pressure on me to do well, but they couldn't afford private school. I left Texas with some savings from summer jobs but I had to work my way through college; I didn't pay off my student loans until I landed a job at Waterbridge-Howser."

"Texas? I knew I could detect an accent."

"So could everyone in Boston, I spent a lot of time trying to hide it but I guess I got tired of pretending it wasn't a part of me."

He turned to me, his gaze smoldering. "You're a walking contradiction."

"Excuse me?"

"You say you don't like to take risks, but it couldn't have been easy starting a new life on your own."

I had never considered myself adventurous, my own parents thought it was irresponsible of me to uproot my life, but Vincent seemed unconvinced.

"You're not exactly easy to figure out either. Vagabond turned CEO? I didn't see that coming."

He gave me one of his sly grins. "You can't be prepared for everything, Kristen."

A few hours later we landed, the white beaches and swaying palm trees greeting us from the airplane window. We made our way through the small airport to the rental car area. Vincent picked out an Aston Martin convertible, which surprised me probably more than it should have considering I'd just stepped off his private jet. I dealt with wealthy clients on a daily basis and I had some vague idea of the luxuries they could afford, but I'd never actually been wealthy myself—seeing what Vincent's money could buy had thrown me off a bit.

The drive to the beach served well to distract me from my nagging fears about surfing—the breeze whipping my hair, the taste of the ocean's salt lingering in the air, and the rolling hills that surrounded us were impossible not to notice. But as we approached a wood slatted surf shop edging the beach, the creeping fear I'd felt earlier came back full force.

"I have to admit, I'm kind of nervous about this," I confessed as we got out of the car. "Jellyfish, sharks . . . you hear horror stories, you know?"

He took my hand, gripping it reassuringly. "Don't worry, I'm not going to let anything happen to you."

Vincent was right, he had been surfing for years, and I really didn't have any reason not to trust him—with my safety at least.

"But you can't surf in that," he said, gesturing to my skirt and blouse. "We'll need to get you a swimsuit."

After trying on a few swimsuits in the dressing room, I decided on a black halter top bikini with single string bottoms.

My heart nearly sank to my stomach when I caught a glance of the total price of our surfing gear—between new swimsuits and surfboards, Vincent had spent more than Riley and I spent on restaurants in a month.

After I had changed, I met Vincent by the water and was nearly floored by the man who stood waiting for me fitted in nothing but a pair of white boardshorts that clung loosely to his hips. My eyes lingered on his six-pack, the taut ridges of his abdomen leading down to the sharp, downward angle of his pelvic bones. I swallowed as I noticed the nipple rings glinting from his chest and among the various tasteful tattoos around his right arm and chest there was a blackened outline of a diamond on his rib cage. I wondered about its significance; Vincent might have been a risk taker but there always seemed to be a purpose behind everything he did.

I stumbled in the sand, wrestling with the side of me that was salivating over his edgy look and the side of me that was a little intimidated. I'd never been with a man who took so many risks with his body, but I'd also never been with a man who defied all of my expectations. Not to mention a man who was so irresistibly attractive.

His lips slowly curved into a smile as he eyed me up and down. "I like the swimsuit. Ready?"

I had to force my gaze to meet his. "Ready as I'll ever be."

We waded into the ocean, the shallow waves leaving rivulets of water trickling down Vincent's bare chest. When we were waist deep he dropped our surfboards by his side and turned to me.

"The most important thing to understand is you have to control your board, you don't want to find yourself overwhelmed by the force of the wave," he began. "So lay down on your stomach and put your hands here."

I did as I was told, sliding my stomach across the board's waxy surface.

"Now press your hips into it." Without warning he gripped the soft curve of my hips and pushed against them, the callouses of his fingers working against my skin. The way he effortlessly maneuvered my body until it was in the correct position made me think I wasn't the first woman he'd taught how to surf.

I tried to bite my tongue but I was determined not to be just another one of Vincent Sorenson's conquests. "How many surfing lessons have you given?"

"A few."

"Mostly female clientele?" I shot, the words coming out before I even had a chance to consider them.

He pulled his hands from my hips, the heat of his skin lingering where his fingers had been, and I instantly regretted my presumptuousness.

"Are you trying to ask me how many girls I've brought here?"

I sat up on the board, straddling it to keep from falling over. His eyes wandered to the water lapping over my clenched thighs. "I just want to know what this is."

"This is a date, Kristen. Not a ploy. The only lessons I've ever given were just that—lessons."

I averted my gaze. "It's not your conventional first date, that's all."

As my board began to drift, he pulled it closer, his fingers brushing the flesh of my inner thigh. I shivered at the contact and considered maybe it wasn't anger I was feeling but jealousy. If Vincent's touch could send me into a fit of desire then I could only imagine what he'd made other women feel, ones who didn't demand first dates.

"What are you used to?" he asked.

"What most people are used to—dinner, movie. I guess I haven't gone out with enough CEOs."

"Who have you gone out with?"

I shifted away from his touch, growing uneasy at the one question I refused to breach. "No one serious," I said as I leaned forward on the board so I was laying on my stomach again. "Am I doing this right?" I asked, determined to change the subject.

"Move further down the board and keep pressing your hips into it."

I wiggled down the board and awkwardly extended my abdomen but I was too flustered by the thought of my messy dating history to focus on my form. Suddenly Vincent was behind me, his hands settled into the groove of my hips as he pulled my body toward him. I wished desperately I was wearing a t-shirt, a wetsuit, anything to lessen the direct contact between us. I couldn't distinguish between the water and the dampness that had been growing between my legs since I first caught sight of him on the beach.

"I can't—" I began to protest, too overwhelmed by a foreign desire to think about surfing technique.

"You can. I'm right here." He slid his hand to the small of my back and pressed. My pelvis pushed into the board, the vague contact with my clit sending a heat into my belly. I chided myself for my desperate arousal—I wanted to take things slow, especially with Vincent, a man who was too busy continent hopping to commit.

I pushed myself up again, distraught. "I have no idea why you like this sport so much," I said, trying to blame my agitation on the lesson. I teetered on the board as I tried to gain my balance and he clutched the top of my thighs to keep me steady.

"Haven't you ever had an adrenaline rush?" he asked, moving his hands further up my thighs until they were dangerously close to the heated space between my legs. I looked at him, his eyes wild with anticipation, the tendons of his neck taut as he clenched his jaw. "Your body becomes attuned to every sensation, your energy peaks—"

"It's addicting," I breathed.

"Don't you want to feel that way?" he asked as he drew his face closer to mine, our lips brushing briefly. I could taste the salt that had caked to his mouth.

"And if I fall?"

"It won't hurt."

I pulled away from him, afraid if I let him any closer I'd lose my bikini, and paddled toward the shallow waves in the distance.

We practiced surfing well into the afternoon but Vincent proved more of a distraction than a help—the pent up sexual energy I had felt during our lesson still lingered within me. When my arms were too weak to keep paddling, we left the water for the beach. As I set my surfboard in the sand, Vincent reached out and gently grabbed my left hand, pulling it close as if to inspect it.

"How did you injure your pinky?" he asked, sitting down next to me. Being so close to him on the sand made me pine for the cooling effects of the water. "You've been holding it out all afternoon."

I pulled my hand away, instinctively clutching my finger. "I'm a little accident prone, tripped and fell a few years ago and sprained it."

"Accident prone? You were pretty good on the water."

I practically scoffed, I'd been falling off my surfboard all afternoon. "I don't think surfing is my true calling. It's a little too rough for me out there."

"Sometimes rough is good," he said as he lifted my hand to his mouth and kissed my pinky, dragging it across the full line of his bottom lip. I looked up at him, the sun catching the amber of his eyes, and I could hear the rapid beating of my heart in my ears. I still didn't understand how one look from him could throw me so off balance. I glanced around the beach, making sure we were alone.

"You're covered in sand," he said, wiping the grainy pebbles from my palm. "We should rinse off."

I did feel the need for a shower after all our time in the water so I agreed.

He stood and reached his hand out to me, pulling me up and into him. My hands grasped at his bare chest as I tried to gain my balance. His skin was warm and slick with a layer of sweat, and I couldn't help but imagine running my tongue down the firm ridges of his abdomen. It had been two years since I'd slept with a man and I could feel my neglected need hitting me full force.

I tried to pull myself from his grasp, afraid the friction of our bodies would overwhelm the rational part of me, but he grabbed me by the waist and pulled me closer. The quick pulsing of my heart seemed to take up between my legs as he leaned forward and took my face in his hands. As he pressed his lips into mine, working my mouth open with his tongue, my knees buckled and I grabbed his bicep to keep myself steady. I could hear his heavy breathing, feel his warm exhales against my cheek as our tongues moved over one another. It was true it had been years since I'd been with a man but I'd never been so consumed by a kiss and I was worried I wouldn't be able to control myself if I let it continue.

"Where are the showers?" I asked, breaking away. I was desperate for a reason to distance myself from him—what would he think of me, better yet what would I think of myself, if I had sex with him when I'd demanded a date to avoid sex? But without a word he lifted me onto his waist, my legs wrapping instinctually around him, and walked us toward the showers.

"Put me—" I began but he cut me off with another kiss, his mouth pressed so urgently against mine that my lips tingled. I ran my fingers through his hair, pulling lightly, as the hard cut of his pelvis rocked against my clit while he walked. I clenched my thighs around his torso to keep myself from grinding shamelessly against him, wanting to feed the desire that had begun pulsing faintly between my legs.

He put me down as he turned on the shower and before I had time to get my bearings, I felt his hands running down my back and across the waist of my bikini bottom. He reached up and loosened my hair from its ponytail, the heavy, damp locks falling down my back as he rinsed the sand from my body.

"What are you doing?" I asked, trying to avoid his touch. I immediately berated myself for getting caught up in the moment—I didn't need casual sex, especially with someone who was used to getting what he wanted from women. I had promised myself I wouldn't get involved with another man too quickly, and here I was about to strip naked on the first date.

"I'm cleaning you."

"I can do it myself," I insisted.

His hands stopped their merciless roaming but lingered in the middle of my back, his fingers batting at the loose strings of my bikini top. He looked at me, the water running over the sharp bridge of his nose and down to his lips. "Why're you so afraid to ask for help?"

"Because I don't need your help." I tried not to acknowledge the muscled torso, wet and glistening, just mere inches from me.

"I want to make things easier for you." He slid his fingers beneath the strings of my bikini top and I could feel him wiping away the coarse sand stuck there, his fingers moving toward the side of my breast. I felt my nipples harden from his touch, barely concealed beneath the thin fabric of my suit.

"I just think it would be better if we take things slow," I breathed.

"Is this slow enough?" His hands creeped toward my chest, the cool tips of his fingers sending goosebumps across my skin. Just as he was about to cup my breast, he shifted quickly, trailing his fingers lightly down my torso. I groaned in a frustrated desire, wanting him to pinch my nipples between his fingers, take them between his teeth and bite gently.

I reached out to him in spite of myself. My fingers traced the raised edges of a tattoo on his shoulder. "What does this one mean?"

"It's sanskrit for 'balance.' I'm a hard worker, Kristen, but I believe in rewarding myself." I could feel the bulge of his stirring package beneath his board shorts as he moved closer to me.

"And these?" I crooned as I fingered his nipple rings.

"Something of a souvenir from Fiji."

"You couldn't just get a t-shirt?" I leaned into his chest and took his nipple between my fingers, pinching the cool metal ring lightly.

"I wanted something a little more interactive," he moaned as he grabbed a handful of my hair.

"I knew I felt something hard when I fell on you in South Africa." The aching throb between my legs had become nearly unbearable and all I wanted to do was pull his board shorts from his hips and take him in my hands. But things were already going faster than they were supposed to and I would have no one to blame but myself if I gave into Vincent and ended up getting hurt.

"What about you, Kristen? Any piercings you're hiding from me?" The tone of his voice and the ceaseless roaming of his hands suggested he had every intention of finding out unless I put a stop to things.

I tore away from him, mustering all of my willpower to deny my desire. It was hard to ignore just how sexy Vincent was, and I wasn't sure I believed those surfing lessons he was giving were innocent. It seemed like a flawless plan—the minimal clothing, maximal touching and his persistent charm, any woman would succumb to the seduction. But I wasn't looking for seduction and if that's all Vincent was interested in doing then it was better I walked away from our date with my dignity still intact, something my last relationship had taken from me.

Not wanting to cause an argument or dredge up my relationship history I flashed him a doe-eyed look and stepped out of the shower's stream. "Nothing worth pursuing comes without patience," I teased.

His shoulders dropped in obvious disappointment but the toothy smile on his face left me hopeful that maybe sex wasn't his only motive. "I guess that means you want to see me again."

"Maybe," I said playfully as I left the stall, "but you'll have to let me off this island first."

I made my way to the women's bathroom and slowly peeled the soaking swimsuit from my body, taking my time as I tried to decompress from the shower. It was ridiculous to try and convince myself I didn't want Vincent. But whisking a woman off to an isolated island for an afternoon had raised some red flags. Although no one had ever planned such an elaborate date for me, I was starting to think Vincent knew the rules of seduction far better than he knew the rules of dating. I didn't want to give up on him but I couldn't let my body get the best of me next time.

Once I had changed and fixed my hair into a loose, damp braid I left the bathroom to find Vincent leaning against the convertible, the deep tan of his skin standing out against his white t-shirt.

He leaned down and kissed me before tugging lightly on the braid. "You look beautiful," he said.

I blushed, conscious my makeup had washed off and my hair was a mess. "You don't look so bad yourself."

"Are you hungry?" he asked. "All that time in the water wore me out." He shot me a suggestive grin and I knew he wasn't just talking about the ocean.

"I'm starved," I said, but I knew no amount of food could quell my appetite.

Chapter Eight

By the time we boarded Vincent's plane, it was evening and I was physically drained. After the hours of surfing, we tried out a Caribbean barbeque place with amazing burgers then drove around the island sightseeing until the sun set. It was a romantic, memorable first date and I found myself hoping it wouldn't be our last. I'd expected him to be his usual charming and seductive self all day, but he was surprisingly attentive and caring, showing he'd listened when I'd told him about taking things slow. He suggested we stay the night—in separate rooms of course—but I wanted to avoid the possible implications. Resisting him in the public shower was hard enough; sleeping in the same hotel with beds conveniently nearby might've been too much for my resistance if he decided to be seductive again. Instead, I'd fallen asleep on his shoulder on the flight back. When he dropped me off at my apartment, we exchanged a chaste goodbye kiss. He promised to text me tomorrow and I promised to tell him what I thought about a second date. I trotted to my room and plopped on my bed, exhausted from the day's activities.

**

Monday morning felt better than it had since as long as I could remember. With everything I did with Vincent over the weekend, it seemed like forever since I got the chance to sleep in. Which is why I took full advantage of the opportunity on Sunday. Except for exchanging a few flirty texts, the day had been uneventful but relaxing. Not that being involved with Vincent Sorenson wasn't thrilling enough, but the lazy Sunday was just what I needed to re-energize.

I'd told him I needed more time to think about seeing him again but it was more to save face than anything else. If I was honest with myself, the idea of secretly dating a gorgeous client was thrilling, but

I'd been careful not to reveal that to Vincent. I also found myself wanting to know more about him. He wasn't the surfer bum that Richard pegged him for nor was he the cold, calculating businessman typical of individuals his stature. He was something in between. Steadfast in pursuit but adaptable. Charming yet respectful. In other words, complex.

Next weekend seemed interminably far away. What would we do on a second date? Where did we stand? All I knew was I already felt safe with him, which was both comforting and unnerving. I hadn't felt that way in a long time with anyone; I'd even begun wondering if I could trust a guy again.

I recapped my date to Riley expecting irrational excitement, but her reaction was subdued. She announced she was coming down with a cold, her throat's scratchiness since coming back from Cape Town an advanced indicator. Before leaving for work, I told her I'd stop by a Duane Reade to pick up orange juice and cough medicine. If she needed anything else like blankets or a humidifier, she could just text me.

I arrived at work a little earlier than usual, eager to start the day. The morning passed in a blur of investment research and excel sheets. It was rare that coworkers didn't stop by to chat but I supposed it was just one of those busy mornings. I was about to head to lunch when Richard made an unexpected appearance at my cubicle.

"Hard at work, I see." His voice didn't contain its usual confidence bordering on smugness.

"Just finished the ROI projection charts for the Sorenson account and about to head to lunch. Need something?"

He sighed heavily and I leaned back in my chair preparing myself for some bad news. There was no way the firm had found out about my trip with Vincent already. "I came to tell you that you've been promoted."

"What?" This was good news. I had been promoted only six months ago, which earned me the privilege of working under Richard in the first place. Now I was promoted again? Richard had been right, landing the Sorenson account did have its perks.

I beamed. "This is great! It's just like you said. So are you going to buy that new convertible you've been talking about?"

"No." He sighed again, rubbing his temples with his fingers. His jaw was working overtime. "*You* have been promoted. Not me. I also found out Vincent specifically listed you as his point of contact. Did you know about that?"

I gulped. Richard was upset with me and I had to diffuse the situation. Complete honesty wasn't the answer. "He mentioned the possibility, saying he was impressed by my work. But I didn't know he would go that far."

His eyes narrowed. "What did you tell him and what did he say when he handed you the signed documents?"

"I just went through the standard follow-up pitch and he stopped me before I could finish. He said he liked my work and wanted to sign the papers. I gave them to him and didn't really look too hard after he signed."

He opened his mouth to say something but shut it, his mind seemingly deep in thought. He grumbled something under his breath and left before I could question the situation or offer words of consolement.

I tried to put Richard's frustration into perspective. Despite him being ten years my senior, my promotion brought me to the same level as him. No longer a meager 'analyst', I was now a 'client acquisition manager' that would be reporting to Richard's boss, Carl Stansworth, directly. I figured Vincent's request for me to be his point-of-contact was the reason Carl promoted me, but I wondered why Richard wasn't promoted. Richard certainly did his fair share of work, which meant either the company wasn't doing well enough to promote him or Richard wasn't on Carl's good side. I figured it was the latter. Whatever the reason, the situation made it look like I stole his client lead. I was concerned about rubbing Richard the wrong way, but there wasn't much I could do about the circumstances.

I skipped to lunch and returned to my desk with a newfound passion for my job. My fingers a whirlwind at the keyboard, I felt at peak productivity, churning page after page of reports and analyses.

It was approaching the end of the workday when my purse chimed with the sound of a text message. I reached inside, flutters in my stomach, figuring it was another flirty text from Vincent. I was already thinking about him so often since our date it was difficult to concentrate on anything else, and the frequent communication wasn't helping. I wasn't sure how long I'd be able to resist him if we kept this up.

I discovered the text was actually from Riley. Maybe she needed something else from the store.

Hey someone stopped by asking for you.

Not what I expected, but okay. Using my thumbs, I typed a response back to her. *Did he have dark eyes, sexy blonde hair, and abs to die for?*

A moment later the chime sounded. *No. Didn't get his name.*

So it wasn't Vincent. He probably wouldn't have dropped by anyway knowing I would be at work. I also wasn't expecting any packages . . . who could it have been? I was in the middle of preparing a response when I received another text. Riley must have accidentally hit send early on the last one.

But he had gorgeous blue eyes, brown hair, and rimless glasses.

Suddenly, the office spun, coming choppily like a film with missing frames. My pulse leaped and I felt an immediate tightness in my chest. I tried to breathe but couldn't. The familiarity of the experience made me realize I was having a panic attack. I stared at the words, reading and rereading them, hoping they'd change.

Blue eyes. Brown hair. Rimless glasses.

There was no mistaking it. *He* had shown up at my doorstep. How did he find out where I lived? Why did he show up now? Should I call the police? Run? Stay at a hotel tonight? For how long? A flurry of questions and actions raced through my mind. And none of them seemed good.

In the midst of the chaos, my phone chimed again. Hands trembling, I checked the new message, fearing the worst.

The sight of Vincent's text grounded me in reality. *I'm aching for you. When can I see you again?*

I recalled how safe I felt around him. That was the one thing I desperately needed right now and only he could give it to me. Not knowing what else to do, I decided to see him tonight, be with him.

Tonight. Your place. Can you pick me up after work?

I waited anxiously for his response. A few seconds later, it came.

What happened to slow? :)

I'm not promising anything. Can't a girl come over just for fun?

Of course. We'll hang out.

Spotting Vincent's car pull to the side of curb, I checked to make sure nobody I recognized was around. Once I confirmed that none of my coworkers would suspect Vincent was taking me to his place, I hopped into the passenger seat.

His peacock blue shirt showcased his trim torso and his tailored black pants matched his expensive shoes. The effect was striking, and for a moment it felt surreal that a guy like this was picking me up from work.

"Hey." I smiled at him.

He shifted the car to 'park' and leaned over, kissing me as if starved for the taste of my lips. His raw hunger for me was intoxicating. Hesitant at first, I easily succumbed to the sensation, running my hands through his long blonde locks and reciprocating. I enjoyed the soft feel of his mouth and his surprisingly fresh masculine scent.

Once our lips broke contact, he spoke. "Hello, Kristen."

Hello to you too. "Sorry to give you such short notice."

He placed his hand on my bare knee, the warmth from his skin a welcome sensation. "Anytime you need anything, don't be afraid to tell me. I can be accommodating."

"Thank you." I considered for a moment if I should tell him about my ex-boyfriend showing up at my apartment, but I didn't want to freak him out. People typically didn't unload their baggage onto someone else when they've only been on one date. I hadn't told anyone about my ex's dark side before, not even Riley. But then again, I hadn't had to. "So how was your day?"

"Went from good to great." He grinned as his hand began lightly brushing my leg below my skirt. "How about yours?"

"Not bad."

His sharp eyes studied my features carefully. "You seem kind of tense. Is everything all right?"

I hesitated. "I got a promotion today, thanks to you."

"Congratulations. You deserved it," he said. "And I'm not just saying that because I like you. You're a rare talent."

I blushed. "And you're quite the seducer. You sure know how to flatter a girl."

"Not flattery. Honesty. And I'll take that first part as a sign of affection."

The sound of my stomach grumbling betrayed my hunger and Vincent must've heard it. "What do you feel like eating tonight?" he asked. "I'm planning on cooking for us."

"No preference," I answered. "You don't have to go through all that trouble though, I was just thinking we'd go to a restaurant or get take out."

He shook his head. "I'm taking you to the best restaurant in the city—my kitchen. Tonight's an opportunity to impress you with my culinary skills."

"Expert surfing instructor, now a master chef." Also, billionaire and sex god, but I figured those were already obvious. "How many surprises do you have?"

Those sinful lips forming a smile made me feel a sudden ache between my legs. "Oh the things I'll show you, Kristen."

Just as my thoughts began to turn naughty, a mental shopping list interrupted them. "I almost forgot, I need to pick up some medicine for Riley. Do you think we could get that first?"

"Of course. We'll stop by the grocery store," he said, pulling away from the curb to join the flock of cars in traffic.

If picking me up from work was surreal, grocery shopping was an illusion. I was cautious at first that someone might see us, but caution turned to laughter as we roamed the aisles for items. Two weeks ago I was rebuffing Vincent's advances, and now we were picking out food to cook for dinner like an established couple. It was a domestic experience that felt bizarre but natural. I hadn't been looking for anything serious or Mr. Right or even much of anything, and there I was with someone who felt like all those things. I hadn't expected Vincent to be this way but then again he'd been constantly surprising me.

By the time we left, I felt a lot better than when he had picked me up from work. With half a dozen bags loaded into his trunk, he drove while I played the role of navigator, directing him to my apartment.

When we neared my place, all humor and playfulness evaporated from my system, replaced by the anxiety from earlier. He turned to me and smiled as he stopped the car in front of my apartment building, putting the emergency lights on. "I can park. I'm curious to see your place."

"It won't take long, I'll just be a minute," I said, hopping out. I didn't want to risk him running into my ex, if he was still around. Things would go from bad to disastrous. "Keep the car running."

He seemed a little confused but then nodded. "I'll be waiting."

As I scaled the wooden steps of my building's stairwell, I couldn't help checking over my shoulder every few steps or being wary of dark corners. I breathed a sigh of relief when I reached my door without incidence. When I entered the apartment I found Riley in a robe on the sofa watching television, a box of tissues next to her.

"Brought you some stuff," I said, handing her the orange juice and Dayquil.

"Thanks, you're the best." Her voice was nasally and she blew into a tissue to clear her nose.

"Do you have the flu? Should I take you the doctor?" I put the back of my hand up to her forehead to check her temperature.

"Nah, I think it's only a cold. I just need to keep blowing my nose every few minutes."

"Glad to hear it's not serious."

She looked at my shoes which I hadn't taken off like I normally would when I entered the apartment. "You going somewhere?"

I suddenly felt guilty for bailing on her. "Riley, I'm going to stay at Vincent's tonight."

Her eyes grew wide. "Oh, congratulations! I'm glad to see you're finally coming out of your dating shell."

"About that . . . I need to tell you something." I waited until she gave me her undivided attention. "Don't open the door for anyone. Especially if it's the guy who came by earlier. Whatever you do, don't let him inside."

Her brows furrowed. "Who is he? Should I be worried?"

"He was someone I dated before I moved here. Don't worry, he only cares about me; he won't do anything to you. I'll tell you more about it some other time. But keep your mace handy just in case."

"Whoa, whoa." Her hands made shoving motions in front of her face. "You can't just say 'keep your mace handy' and dash out. What's going on? Do we need to call the cops?"

I shook my head. "We can't call the police. It's complicated." As reluctant as I was divulging details that had haunted me for the past two years, I briefly told her about Marty and how he hurt me. How he was the reason I moved from Boston to NYC in the first place. I didn't have the time or desire to elaborate on sordid details, but she deserved some sort of explanation.

She looked at me with concern as if I was the sick one. When I didn't explain further, she sighed and said, "Okay, Kristen. You can tell me the rest later. I'll keep an eye out."

"Thanks for understanding, Riley."

"When are you coming back?"

"Maybe tomorrow. I'll bring you some more goodies."

She sniffled. "All right, stay safe."

"I will."

I went to my room and quickly changed out of my work clothes into a comfy pair of jeans and a light blouse. I packed an extra set of clothes and my toothbrush into a night bag.

When I finished packing, I waved to Riley and left the apartment, returning to Vincent's Camry.

"Is your roommate all right?" He sounded as concerned about Riley as I was. "I can drive her to the hospital."

"I appreciate the thought, but she just needs sleep and vitamin C."

"You're not sick are you?"

"I don't think so."

Before I could react his lips were on mine again, this time parting my lips with his tongue. He probed my mouth with slow licks of his tongue against my own. Caught up in the heated embrace, I momentarily forgot my concerns.

"Good," he said after our mini makeout session ended. "I'd hate to miss work because I couldn't stop myself from kissing you."

The engine started and we headed toward his place. It was only a few blocks away but with the rush hour traffic in Manhattan it would take us twenty minutes.

We stopped at a red light. I glanced out the window and saw someone on the sidewalk with brown hair and rimless glasses. The hairs on my neck stiffened. It looked like him, but wasn't. Fidgeting in my seat, my hand began rubbing my pinky again.

"Something wrong? You look nervous." Vincent's voice startled me.

I shook my head. "I guess I'm just looking forward to seeing your place."

He grinned. "That makes the two of us."

We pulled into his underground garage complex that resembled ones built for malls. It was filled with exotic cars. With my minimal knowledge on the topic, I was only able to identify a half dozen Lamborghinis and Corvettes but I was still impressed by the eye-catching designs of the ones I couldn't name. After a few loops to the lower levels, we found an empty spot and parked.

Still in awe, I asked, "How many people live in your building? There are a lot of expensive cars here."

He smiled. "Just a few tenants. Most of these are mine."

"Oh." Realizing he could've picked me up in any of these much nicer, much more expensive cars, I had a greater appreciation for his being discreet about our involvement. The Camry was far less luxurious than the Lamborghini.

We stepped into an elevator and Vincent inserted a key into the control panel. The trip to his floor was both faster and quieter than I anticipated. I'd expected a hallway leading to his front door, but when the elevator opened I saw a grand piano and a pair of sand-colored plush sofas around a glass coffee table on dark hardwood flooring illuminated by elegant accent lighting—we were already in his living room. We were on the south side of the building, but the spacious layout enabled sight across the apartment to the north side windows where I could see the Chrysler building as well as the rest of Manhattan. One step out the elevator and I realized the entire building floor was his apartment.

"Impressive," I said, slack-jawed.

"Glad you like it," he said smoothly, leading us deeper into the living room.

I set my bag on the floor and took a seat on his couch as he carried the grocery bags into the kitchen. He returned with a glass of white wine wearing slippers instead of his black loafers.

"Should I take off my shoes?" I asked, not seeing the pile of shoes I was accustomed to seeing when entering my apartment. Instead, there were a bunch of modern abstract statues on display, making this place seem more like a showroom than a personal living area.

He eyed my flats. "You can just put them next to the couch, make yourself comfortable."

In the middle of taking my shoes off my stomach growled again, which was his cue to begin washing vegetables in the kitchen.

"What are we eating?" I hollered. We'd picked up a lot of things, some serious and some just for fun, like a box of Teddy Grahams. It was probably more than we needed and I wasn't sure what he planned to cook for dinner and what he planned to save in the freezer.

"It's a surprise."

"Do you need any help?" Not that I was a great cook myself, but I could at least cut vegetables.

"There's not too much prep work. It'll just be a few minutes. Feel free to look around and make yourself at home. "

Looking around was exactly what I wanted to do. "Are you sure you don't want to give me a tour? I might see something embarrassing." I cringed at the thought of Vincent seeing my bedroom. He'd find papers littering my desk and undergarments hanging on chairs and strewn across the floor. It wasn't that I was messy; I just had my own organization system.

"Like what?"

"Oh I don't know. Underwear, stuffed animals, porn, sex toys."

He was silent for a moment. "Just don't look too hard then."

I couldn't tell whether that was a joke or not but decided I didn't want to ask. As I went from room to room, I noticed everything was neatly arranged and clean, far from your typical bachelor pad. I wondered if he had a maid keep his apartment tidy or if he did it himself. Knowing him, it was another line on his already impressive résumé—accomplished housekeeper. I took a moment to muse the fantasy of him being a manservant.

When I found his office, I spotted documents on his desk that were thoroughly highlighted and marked with detailed notes. Curious, I sifted through them and recognized they were the ones I gave him during our first meeting. I put a lot of work into those documents. He must have thoroughly studied them before deciding to choose my company as his wealth management firm and making me his point-of-contact.

At the beginning of my self-guided tour, I couldn't help making comparisons between Vincent's living style and Marty's. They were both neat and meticulous. But towards the end I found some movie posters of martial arts films from the 80s. That cheesiness was decidedly not like my ex.

By the time I circled back to the living room, fascination with Vincent preoccupied my mind. Besides the posters and getting to see his wardrobe of suits, I was disappointed not to find many more personal items. It seemed as if he had moved in recently. He did mention traveling multiple times per week, so maybe he kept the family pictures somewhere else.

He had an elaborate kitchen though, fit for a top chef. I was pulled toward the food by the wonderful smell.

"Have a seat in the dining room. I'll bring the dishes out," he said untying his apron and hanging it on a nearby rack. He was still in his work clothes, but traded black loafers for sandals.

When I took a seat at the table, there were already two glasses of white wine set out with the tableware.

"Something fresh and light." He entered with two plates in hand.

I smelled the mouthwatering scent before I saw it. Linguine al dente with shrimp scampi. The presentation was immaculate. "My favorite seafood dish. How did you know?"

"It's my favorite as well. I guess our tastes match."

"Maybe with food. But I think we differ on the decor." I gestured to the Bruce Lee poster sitting in the corner.

"It's an old keepsake." He smiled and handed me my plate of shrimp and noodles. "Try this. Tell me if I got it right."

I took a bite then had to take another one. "Wow this is delicious. Where did you learn to cook so well?"

"When I was right out of college I surfed a lot with a few of my buddies. We had seasonal jobs and worked just enough to support our lifestyle. To save money, we'd buy food for the group and I ended up being the one to cook most of the time; the others weren't very good at it." He laughed.

"I can see why they wanted you to cook." I scarfed down another bite. "That wasn't too long ago if I'm not mistaken. So what's it like to go from that kind of lifestyle to this in only a few years?" I gestured to the lavish apartment.

"It's been a rollercoaster ride. Perfect for a thrill-seeker like myself. Now, instead of being responsible for cooking for a group of guys, I'm responsible for thousands of employees. The stakes are different but fundamentally it's the same."

"Do you still keep in touch with those guys?"

"We try to get the group together at least once a year. Everyone's busy these days, not just myself. A few of them even have kids." He laughed and shook his head as if remembering something ridiculous. "If you knew them back then, you would think they were destined for life-long bachelorhood."

The obvious inquiry was on my mind. I didn't want to ruin an already wonderful evening, but I knew it would bother me if I didn't ask. "And how about you?"

He paused for a moment which made me almost regret asking the question. "Being a bachelor has its benefits. I travel a lot and do a lot of thrill-seeking activities. Being unattached makes it easy to do those things. But I'm thinking it might be more enjoyable to do things with someone you care about."

"Makes sense."

"How about you? The life of a single-female wealth manager, meeting rich, handsome clients seems appealing."

"I haven't really given much thought to settling down. I hadn't really even given much thought to dating in the past few years. Been mainly focused on my career."

"Are you saying I'm special?"

"Don't get a big head, Mr. Iron Chef," I teased. "You're persistent. I'll give you that."

"That's not the only thing that's big right now," he said, his hand settling on my thigh and rubbing slow, suggestive circles with his thumb.

Unsure if I was ready for things to progress further, I tried to change the topic. "What are we having for dessert?" I asked, more as a joke than a serious question. The exquisite dinner he prepared was more than satisfying, and his domestic skills scored major points in my book.

He didn't answer, but smiled and went to the kitchen. I waited a beat, not sure whether I was supposed to follow or remain seated. When he came back he had in his hand a red cloth napkin. "I want you to taste it. But you're going to need to put this on first."

"A napkin? Messy desserts don't sound like your style."

His smiled widened. "Try again, beautiful."

I examined the napkin again, noting that it was folded twice over into a narrow band suitable for wrapping and tying. "Umm . . . a magic trick?"

"Blindfold."

"I think I must've missed a part of our conversation."

"You're going to put on this blindfold and I'm going to feed you the dessert."

"Why do you want me to put on a blindfold?" I'd never done this before and I was a little anxious.

His grin was both mischievous and seductive. "It'll help you isolate the sensations in your mouth."

"Can't I try it without the blindfold first?"

"If you want to taste my dessert, you're going to have to follow my rules. Trust me. Just like you did in Cape Town."

"You haven't been planning this have you?"

"From the moment you pinched my nipple, a lot of things have gone through my mind. This could have been one of them." I could hear the amusement in his voice and wondered what other ideas he entertained that day. "I noticed you've been tense since you left work. I want you to forget about the stress."

He moved my chair—with me in it—from the dining table and placed it in the open area nearby. He came up from behind me and brought the blindfold in front of my face, preparing to place it over my eyes. My pulse quickened at the thought of having my eyesight taken from me. The last time I trusted him, I ended up holding a poisonous bug. "You're not going to put a spider in my mouth are you? Because if so, I can't continue with this," I asked, half-serious.

"Don't be silly. If anything, you'll be begging me to continue." The dark warning sent a shiver of arousal through me.

He put the blindfold on and tied it firmly behind my head. It was tight enough not to shift around but loose enough to be comfortable. I tried reaching out to touch him to ensure he was still there; he took my hands and gently placed them on my thighs. "Hands in your lap, until I say otherwise."

In complete darkness, I felt uncomfortably vulnerable. I'd never done anything like this with anyone before. Was I ready to trust him this much? I sensed him leave the room for a moment to go to the kitchen. All I could do was wait for what he would do next.

Then his footsteps returned and stopped in front of me. "Open your mouth."

Here it comes, I thought. I tentatively obeyed, unsure what was coming. What was he going to feed me? The sound of a metal clink made me think of a belt buckle. Surely not . . .

"Wider."

I wasn't sure if I should have; I probably should've asked him what he was going to put in my mouth. Instead, my lips stretched wider, compelled by the authority in his voice.

"Be careful with your teeth. I don't want you biting me."

What? Before I could protest, something slowly entered my mouth and sat heavily on my tongue. It tasted sinfully sweet and creamy.

"Close."

Without needing be told, my lips instinctively wrapped around it and tightened, suckling the decadent chocolate from his finger.

"Taste good?"

My murmur of approval sounded more like a moan. As he slowly retracted his finger, I took my time licking the tip, wanting to savor every last bit. I heard him stifling a groan when he finally pulled away. It was one of the most erotic sounds I'd ever heard, and I desperately wanted to remove the blindfold to see his expression.

"That was just the first bite." His voice registered lustful amusement, his mouth close to my ear. "This time, I want you to really focus on the pleasure in your mouth. Block out everything else." I felt him brush my hair intimately behind my ear then his tender lips were against my cheek. "Like this," he whispered, his mouth trailing gentle, sensuous kisses to my ear, drawing soft moans from my lips. "And this." He pinched my earlobe between his lips and pulled the sensitive flesh into his mouth, sucking it with just enough pressure to make my legs quiver and sex clench in heated anticipation. There was no way I'd be able to block out the sensation of those lips on my body. And I didn't want to.

"Ready?" he asked.

I wasn't but I wanted another taste of the dessert to heighten the pleasure from his kisses. "Yes," I breathed.

Eager, I opened my mouth again. Sweet cream brushed the tip of my tongue and I tried to lick it, but it pulled out of reach. When I sensed him bring it back, I stuck out my tongue to try to taste it but it retracted, teasing me. The next time he touched my tongue, I playfully nipped at his finger.

"You're so feisty," he murmured into my neck then bit the skin playfully, sparking a dangerous current of desire. I wanted to grab his hair and pull him in further but was aware I needed to follow his rules.

"That's because you're teasing me."

"Am I? Tell me what you want," he purred against my neck.

"I want to taste it in my mouth."

"What do you want to taste?"

"You know what."

"Tell me."

"Your finger."

"Good." He slowly moved his finger into my mouth and I swirled my tongue around it. "That's it. Just like that." His voice was oozing with desire, which only increased the growing ache in my sex.

"Are you focusing on just the sensations in your mouth?" he asked, his tongue making slow, sensual licks along the throbbing vein in my neck while his finger was still in my mouth.

"Mmhmm," I lied.

His breathing was as labored as mine. Suddenly, his lips and finger pulled away and I began to think I had done something wrong. Then his mouth was on mine. I parted my lips for him and his tongue slipped inside, the tip tasting of rich, creamy dark chocolate. The taste of his mouth mixed with chocolate was overwhelmingly sensual. I reached up and ran my hands through his silky hair, grabbing and pulling his mouth deeper into mine, all resistance and restraint gone. I didn't care for his rules anymore. I wanted him so badly it was physically painful.

"No hands," he grunted, soft lips becoming rough. I could tell he was trying to act upset because I'd broken his rule and the thin veil masking his desire only intensified my yearning for him.

Suddenly, he wrapped one arm around my torso and the other behind my knees. He lifted me into the air like a bride, mouth never leaving mine. We must've entered his bedroom because the next thing I knew, silk sheets hit my back. Hot with need, I parted my legs to accommodate his hips pushing between them.

My hands tightened, craving the feel of the hard muscles of his back. His hips against mine, I felt the solid weight of his erection through his pants press against my stomach.

"You feel that? That's how much I want you."

"I feel it." My voice trembled with desire sensing what was coming.

He ground his erection against my sex in slow, firm circles. Even through the layers of our clothes, the pressure and friction sent currents of pleasure, fueling my hunger for direct contact. "Tell me what you want," he whispered hoarsely.

"I want to feel you inside me, Vincent."

He grabbed both of my hands and raised my arms over my head, pinning them with one firm hand while the other skillfully unbuttoned my jeans. "Keep your arms here, Kristen. Otherwise I won't let you have it. Understand?" Only a slight waver in his tone betrayed the steely control he projected.

"I want to feel you though. I want to see you," I protested, not understanding why he was torturing me with desperate need. He'd wanted this ever since our first meeting and now that he had me dripping with desire, he was taking his sweet time. I needed him inside me. Now.

"Nothing worth pursuing comes without patience," he said, throwing my own words back at me, inciting frustration that only intensified my arousal. His tone softened. "Clench the pillow behind your head if you need to. I promise, this will be worth it."

I grumbled approval, so horny I was afraid I was losing my mind.

I wiggled my hips to aid him as he gracefully slipped off my jeans along with my panties. A moment later, I heard them thud in a faraway corner. "God, Kristen. Your cunt is so beautiful."

His filthy words sent fresh juices to my aching sex. I crossed my legs, embarrassed of what he might see. Although I'd shaved recently, I was self-conscious about him viewing such a vulnerable area of my body.

He parted my legs with firm hands. "Don't hide such a beautiful thing from me. I want to see it. I want to see everything. Show me."

I'd always been a little shy being nude in front of a man, but compelled by the urgency in his tone, I did as he asked. Somehow he had the ability to make me feel beautiful.

Then I felt something slowly enter me. A finger.

"So wet. So soft. *Damn it.*" He growled, as if straining to hold back a primal desire threatening to consume him. His mouth was close to my pussy, his hot labored breaths brushing my clit. I imagined him staring at me, dark eyes inflamed with lust, watching as he pushed his finger into my eagerly awaiting slit. If only I didn't have this blindfold on, I could see his gorgeous face.

He thrust his finger in up to the second knuckle, and I bit my lip, trying to hold back the moan building inside my throat. It'd been so long since I'd been touched, I was afraid I'd come from that single motion alone.

"You're already close aren't you?"

I nodded painfully, fingers desperately clutching the pillow, perspiration misting my skin.

His finger resumed thrusting in and out, twisting as it did so. First slowly, then faster. His pace increased edging me closer to my impending climax.

"Oh my god, I'm coming."

The orgasm slammed into me, shattering my senses. I arched into his hand and my sex clenched his finger.

Before I could fully recover, I felt sensation against my clit.

"No, Vincent. I'm too sensitive."

His expert tongue lapped hungrily at the hood, periodically dipping into my cleft and nuzzling my clit with his nose. After my mind-blowing orgasm, I didn't think my body could take anymore.

"So good. So sweet." He groaned as he devoured me, sending my head spinning. I writhed on the bed and released my grip from the pillow behind me. I reached for luscious locks, pulling his tongue deeper into my cleft as I bucked my hips. I'd never experienced such brain-sizzling oral pleasure before.

"It feels too good," I moaned.

"I've never been this hard before," he growled. "I want you so bad."

"Take me," I cried.

His head moved away and I heard buttons scatter as he ripped his shirt. His belt buckle and pants soon followed. I knew he freed his cock because there was a dull skin-slapping sound as it hit my stomach. I reached to touch it, to feel its scorching heat and pulsing energy. It was heavy and long enough to accommodate both my hands.

"You don't know how much I've thought about those hands wrapping around my cock." His voice was desperate and needy. I squeezed him and he released a pained cry.

"Can I take the blindfold off?" I pleaded.

"Yes. Take it off. Everything off."

With one hand, I pulled away the folded napkin and I gazed at what was in my other hand.

"Jesus, you're big."

My gaze snagged on the hard tapered lines of his pelvis. And ripped. My gaze trailed from his hips up and across steely abs and chiseled pecs pierced with silver rings to his breathtaking face, dark eyes flushed with desire. I'd seen him in his swimsuit before, but now he was completely nude, radiating raw sexual energy that stole my breath.

"I can't fight it anymore, Kristen. I need to be inside you."

He reached into a bedside drawer and produced a small packet. I released my grip as he roughly took his member in his own hands and wrapped himself before guiding it to my entrance. I sucked in a deep breath preparing for his size. Although I used a vibrator, Vincent looked bigger than what I was used to. I anticipated he'd impatiently thrust to the hilt, but he took his time, slowly parting the folds with the head. With how wet I was, he was easily able to slide in. He stopped when the tip was fully inside and pulled back with the same patience, slowly stroking my walls with just the head, cycling sensations of emptiness and fullness again and again. The teasing was agonizing.

"Deeper," I begged.

He pushed deeper, unhurried, every ridge of his heated flesh firing nerves I didn't realize I had. My mind swam in the experience.

"Faster," I panted.

"You said slow."

I began to regret having said those words to him during our date in St. Thomas, but then his pace quickened. I gripped his backside and pulled, aiding his thrusts as I bucked forward for stronger penetration. It'd been so long since I had sex that the pleasure from Vincent moving inside me was almost unbearable. Consumed by desire, our mouths and bodies wrestled in primal lust, cries of pleasure echoing throughout the apartment.

"You're making me lose it, Kristen. I can't stop."

His thrusts became more urgent, more desperate as did my moans. Then I felt him jerk and the first wave of heat poured into me. He released a strangled growl the moment I clenched around him. He collapsed into me as my world went dark again for a moment. We laid there for a spell, neither of us speaking, just the sound of our heavy breaths and heartbeats filling the silence.

"You're incredible," Vincent said, lifting his face to look into my gaze.

I smiled, staring back into those dark eyes brimming with warm affection. "I was thinking the same thing."

"I thought I was going to die there for a moment."

"I'm not sure I haven't."

He smiled and kissed my cheek. "You're still here. With me."

Chapter Nine

We were standing among the impressive marble pillars of the library, looking out at the red brick buildings of Harvard Square. It was autumn and the red and yellow leaves fluttering down beneath the waning sun made a picturesque setting for a stupid argument about a post on my Facebook wall.

"Just tell me who he is!" the man yelled, his brown hair combed just above his bright blue eyes perfectly, as always. Together with his rimless glasses, he resembled a J Crew model.

"He's a friend from a class. It's nothing!"

It was the third time we'd fought that week. We were never a couple that fought a lot, but for some reason we'd been getting into more and more arguments recently. A year older, he'd graduated before me and gotten a job at his dad's law firm in Boston. Since then, he'd visited me regularly on campus, which I was grateful for, but knowing I was surrounded by other attractive guys my age seemed to make his jealousy worse.

He looked around. "You swear it's nothing?"

I hated having to deal with this part of our relationship. We'd been through this argument before—some guy waving at me or saying hello, sharing class notes, or asking if I wanted to go to a social event—and every time it ended with tears and hurt feelings. For both of us. It got to the point where we decided to share phone, email, and Facebook passwords.

"Oh my god, yes."

He took another look around and held out his hand, pinky extended. "Fine. Pinky swear."

Childish as it was, I was glad to be done with the argument. The past few months he'd been flipping out over every single guy who even looked at me, and it was a problem. I hoped I had at least avoided anything more extreme. But when I looked at his cold blue eyes, I was unsure. I glanced around sheepishly, but the campus was mostly deserted, finals having ended weeks ago.

I held out my pinky and intertwined it with his, hoping the action would appease him. His eyes flashed and he yanked me to his chest, twisting my finger savagely. I gasped, the full weight of the dread I had been carrying for weeks finally rising to the surface of my mind. As the pain erupted, hot tears flooded my eyes. My other hand shot up to pry my injured hand away from him, but he was too strong.

"Don't ever lie to me Kristen. Never. Do you understand me? Never."

My world blurred as tears poured down my cheeks. I tried desperately to scream for help but as I opened my mouth, his hand shot up to cover it. The world went gray.

I woke up screaming. A bundle of nerves, it didn't help I couldn't recognize my surroundings. Where was I?

"Kristen," a familiar voice said, "it was just a dream. You're okay."

I turned to Vincent beside me. His face was full of concern and his hand was wrapped gently around my shoulder. Realization swept over me. He was mostly right, it had been a dream. Not *just* a dream, but I was safe for now. I turned to him.

"That must have been a bad nightmare. Do you remember it?"

I remembered it in more ways than one. It had been the breaking point with Marty. Our relationship had seemed good for a long time, but when he started getting abusive it got ugly fast. That had been over two years ago.

"Vincent, I think—" I faltered. There was no need to unload this story on him right now. I barely knew him; I had been handling Marty on my own for two years without any issue, I could keep handling him for a while longer.

He pulled me tightly against his bare chest. The warmth and hardness was immediately comforting. "It's okay. Take a minute. You're safe here."

I traced my finger around one of his nipple rings. They were starting to grow on me. Again, he was right. I did need a minute because my heart was pounding. The more I thought about it, the more I couldn't believe Marty had actually shown up at my apartment.

He began stroking my hair down to my nape. Slowly I felt myself relaxing. Vincent was really being amazing about this. It would have been easy to wake me up and then roll over, dismissing my unease, but the way he was holding me close and comforting me was perfect.

"What was your nightmare about?" he asked.

I thought about telling him, but I just couldn't. It was too early in our relationship, or whatever it was we were doing. If I told him, he would probably feel like I was unloading way too much baggage way too quickly. He was already treating me differently than his other women. I didn't want to push it.

"Nothing," I said.

"You were thrashing around pretty hard for a dream about nothing."

"I just mean I don't remember."

He said nothing for a few minutes, continuing to stroke my hair. Finally, he spoke. "If you don't want to tell me, just say so, but please don't lie to me. I hate being lied to."

"Okay, fine, I don't want to tell you."

"Why?"

"Because this is our second date and things are already moving fast enough as it is."

"The more you build this up the more I want to know. I want to be close to you. I thought that's what you wanted. Not just casual dating and sex."

I said nothing, thinking. It was sweet that he wanted to be close to me, but this was just too soon. Maybe I could just make something up. It would be lying again, but at least this situation would be resolved.

"There's no point in obeying people's arbitrary rules about dating or anything else, really," he said. "You either feel safe with someone or you don't. It doesn't matter how long you've been together."

I took a deep breath. "You really think for yourself, don't you?"

"Telling people where to go with their arbitrary rules is one of the biggest reasons I am where I am." He pulled me in tighter. "Which, I might add, is a pretty amazing spot right now."

I smiled, but continued to say nothing. Could I really trust him not to run away when he found out about my past with Marty? He was saying all the right things, and I really didn't have a reason to believe he was lying, but it all seemed too good to be true. My cautious side was blaring for me to slow down.

And yet, I probably wasn't going to get a better chance to tell him about Marty than this moment. If he reacted badly, at least I would know that he was asking for me to tell him.

I pulled gently away. *Here we go.* "My ex-boyfriend showed up at my apartment today."

He scrunched his brow. "Does this have something to do with your dream?"

"It was about him."

He nodded, eyes still squinting. "So you still have feelings for him?"

I shuddered and he squeezed my shoulder. "No, no. Nothing like that. It's just—"

I faltered again. He looked at me, concern etched on his face. I started to cry and had to take several deep breaths to calm myself down enough to speak. "He was kind of abusive," I managed.

Vincent's mouth thinned to a tight line, and I saw his jaw working. He inhaled sharply, features shifting in a way I'd never seen before. Would he think I was weak or, worse, helpless because I had been abused?

"What do you mean, kind of?"

When I didn't say anything he shook his head, "It doesn't matter, where does he live?" His eyes were alight with violent promise.

"No—I mean—I don't know. Don't hurt him Vincent, it's not worth it."

"You let me decide whether it's worth it or not."

I started crying harder. This wasn't the reaction I was expecting. Vincent looked like he was ready to pound Marty's head in. It was sweet that he was feeling protective of me, but getting violent wasn't going to help anything. I hated violence.

When he saw me crying the hard lines in his face melted. He was breathing fast, but the fire in his eyes was mostly gone.

"I'm sorry. I didn't mean to upset you. What did he do to you, exactly?"

I shook my head. "Please don't make me go into details. I'm through with him and he can't hurt me anymore." How would I explain getting caught in a relationship with a man who had borderline personality disorder? How he was so sweet at first, and very attentive, but then would snap at a moment's notice? How he managed to hold it together for the outside world, but not with me? How it felt to beat yourself up over wanting to leave someone who had a legitimate mental illness they couldn't really help?

"Okay, okay. You're right. No need to dig up the past." He didn't say anything else, and I was grateful that he wasn't pressuring me any more about this even though I could tell questions were running through his mind.

I put my ear back down onto his chest and draped my arm over him. After a moment, he hugged me close, his hand resting on my hip. "I haven't spoken to him in years and somehow he knows where I live. It's unsettling."

"What happened when he came to your apartment?"

"Riley answered the door, and he told her he was looking for me. She texted me his description and I recognized it immediately. When I went to check on her I told her not to answer the door again."

"It sounds like he might be dangerous. You should stay here with me until we get this worked out. Or I can put you up in a hotel."

This was moving way too fast. I hadn't told him about this so he could fix the problem for me. "No, Vincent. I can't ask you to do that."

"You're not asking, I'm offering."

I said nothing.

He sighed. "Fine. No hotel then. I'll get you a security team. I know a couple of guys at Blackthorn Security, you'll barely notice them."

I shook my head.

"Think about it." He looked intensely at me for a moment before speaking again. "Can you go to the police?"

"I doubt it. They wouldn't do anything in Cambridge."

"Figures. They're never good for anything. What's his name?" When he saw the look on my face he continued, "I won't do anything to him, I promise."

I wouldn't have told him, but the solemn look on his face comforted me. Vincent wasn't the kind of guy who made promises lightly.

"Martin Pritchard. I called him Marty."

He nodded slowly. "Where did you meet him?"

"We dated all through college. He started out being really nice, but gradually got more and more possessive and jealous."

"Did he hurt you?"

"Please don't." I took a deep breath, trying to quell the nausea I had begun to feel as I recalled my dream.

Vincent said nothing and we sat in silence for a couple minutes. "Please let me get you a security team. You'll barely notice them, and they could save your life."

"Vincent, I told you this because you wanted to know, not so you could solve this problem for me. I can deal with my own issues." I was scared of Marty, but I really didn't want to seem weak in front of

Vincent, like a woman who needed saving. What if I counted on him and then he disappeared? I would only have myself to blame.

His jaw was working again, but he didn't say anything for a minute. "Fine. Do you at least have some way to defend yourself if he tries to attack you? Mace, a knife, a gun, anything?"

My head spun at the thought of owning a deadly weapon. What kind of person did he think I was? "No. Why on earth would I own a gun?"

"Let's get you something tomorrow. Not a gun, but something."

I shrugged as hot tears began budding up in my eyes and running down my cheeks. He was listening, but he sounded very worried about this. I already regretted telling him. He wasn't running away, which was good, but I didn't want him to feel obligated, or like I was too weak to deal with this on my own.

Arm still around me, he rocked me onto my back so he was over me, brown eyes searching mine. "Kristen, I'm glad you told me about this. We can handle it however you want, okay?"

I nodded, though the tears were still coming thick. As the burden of the whole situation began to lift off my shoulders I realized how stressed I had been.

Vincent kissed away the tears rolling down my cheeks with soft little pecks. The way his muscles bulged as he cradled my head in his arms felt comforting. I really didn't want to deal with this right now.

"Let's forget about this for now," I said. "We can go to the store tomorrow like you suggested. I'd prefer not to think about it anymore tonight."

"Okay." He continued kissing away the tears on my face, sprinkling in kisses on my forehead.

I shifted and felt his cock through his underwear with my leg. Even when he wasn't hard, the size of his package was impressive.

He wasn't aroused, but I was getting to be. I needed a distraction from this situation. I had an idea of how I wanted to distract myself as I reached down to grab him through his underwear.

"I think I know how I want to handle this," I said.

He looked uncertain. "Are you sure? We can just go to sleep if you want."

"I don't. I want you inside me. I want my mind off this." I peeled his underwear down his legs and free of his feet. He didn't resist.

As soon as I had, he wrapped me up in his muscular arms and kissed me passionately on the lips, his hand moving down my torso to my panties as I stroked his cock. The way he responded so quickly to my touch heated my core.

"I can do that," he whispered into my ear, his hand hovering over my aching sex. "Let's take our time."

Our sex was slow and deeply passionate. Vincent kept himself close to me, cradling me chest to chest as he moved in and out. When we came together, it was the closest I had ever felt to another person. Afterwards, he took care of the condom and came back to scoop me up across his lap.

"That was incredible," he said.

"I agree. I'm exhausted." I was in a serious post-coital bliss, actually.

He took a deep breath. "Kristen," he said, "I will never let anyone hurt you."

It was touching that he was still thinking about the situation with Marty. "You don't have to protect me, Vincent."

"You're not asking me to, but I will."

I scooched up so my hand rested on his chest and looked into his earnest face. It was at that point that I realized that I really believed it when he said it. Maybe Vincent was my type after all. As I closed my eyes and snuggled closer into his embrace, the last image I saw was the light of my cell phone, the only light in the room. It burned for a second against the backs of my lids then slid away, leaving me to bask in the warmth of the moment.

Chapter Ten

I woke up cradled by a pair of tan, muscular arms and sighed contentedly. This time I knew immediately where I was: Vincent's bedroom. He was playing big spoon to my little, and as I lay there reminiscing, the previous twelve hours played through my memory in a pleasant haze. Vincent had, on balance, been very supportive about the situation with my ex-boyfriend Marty. I hadn't wanted to talk to him about it so early in our dating—I hadn't even told Riley until yesterday—but after seeing how it worked out I felt much better.

Turning over, I took in his handsome face breathing slowly and smoothly. His distinctive masculine scent was becoming familiar, which was both comforting and a major turn on. He slept like a man without a care in the world, and yet I knew anybody running a business as large as his had plenty to worry about. I admired his ability to deal with stress.

Over his shoulder I read the bright green digits of his alarm clock: it was only six-thirty. My mind immediately went to dirty places; my sex drive had always been mediocre at best but now it was through the roof.

I ran my hand down his sculpted abs toward the impressive cock below and was pleasantly surprised to find him hard. He had morning wood. It was difficult to take credit for turning him on while he was still sleeping, but wrapping my hand around him even through the soft cotton of his boxer briefs still made me wet. I softly ran my fingers up and down his shaft, eager to pull him out of his underwear.

He stirred. "Feel something you like?" he grunted sleepily. His eyes were half open and he looked sexy as he wiped them and yawned like a lion.

"I was feeling jealous of whoever was turning you on while you slept," I said coyly.

"You shouldn't be. You've been the only woman in my dreams for a while now."

I giggled, unsure if his claim could possibly be true. He knew what to say to make me feel special, at least.

"Nothing like the real thing, though." He kissed me on the forehead and moved his arm under me, cupping both buttocks through my underwear. "I like the way you look first thing in the morning."

I was sure my hair was a total mess, and my makeup was probably all over the place, but I blushed at the compliment anyway. Vincent, with his wavy hair and manly stubble, was built to look amazing right out of bed. I was jealous of how effortless it was for him to look as enticing as he did.

Leaving his erection for a moment, I planted my hand on his hard stomach and scooted myself up to smooch him on the lips.

He kissed me back more passionately than I'd anticipated, his tongue probing against my mouth. I broke the kiss and started another, this time ready, and our tongues wrestled playfully. I could see myself waking up to this on a more frequent basis.

Smiling against his mouth, I reached down toward his waist and slipped my hand beneath the elastic band of his underwear to grip the throbbing head of his cock. He was so hard I shuddered, imagining how he would feel inside of me. My pussy ached in anticipation of the way it would stretch around him.

His grip on my butt tensed before he picked me up and turned me onto my back, never breaking our kiss. Only once I was down did he grab the hand holding his cock and pin it to the bed.

He leaned down and nibbled on my ear, his hot breath tickling me. "I have to get to work," he whispered.

My heart sank. I'd been looking forward to one more round of sex before I had to return to reality. "Okay," I said.

When I moved to sit up, he smiled and easily pinned my shoulders down to the bed with his free hand.

"I said I have to get to work. You stay put."

Before I could answer him, he moved lower until his face was between my legs. I half straightened in surprise, ready to tell him he didn't have to do that, but quickly threw my head back on the pillow. My fingers gripped the sheets as the sensation of his tongue fluttering around my pussy radiated through my body.

He looked up at me and grinned.

"You remember me telling you that you have a beautiful cunt last night, right? Because it's gorgeous and glistening for me right now."

I closed my eyes. "It wants you inside," I said, not wanting to see the expression on his face. Talking dirty still made me feel uncomfortable but it was rapidly becoming second nature.

His hands left my legs and I felt the bed bounce up. "Keep your eyes closed," he said. I heard footsteps, then the sound of a wrapper being torn. "You like the suspense of not being able to see, don't you?"

I nodded and waited for the bed to bounce again with his weight.

Instead, his strong hands grabbed my thighs and he pulled me across his smooth bed sheets until I was on the bed's edge, legs high and spread. Exposed. He entered me swiftly, throwing me off balance. I opened my eyes afraid I was going to fall. I found his face and was comforted to see him smiling and holding me steady.

"You should trust me more," he said, thrusting slowly but steadily. "I told you I have a million ways to make you feel good and better."

He kissed me then scooped me up. I threw my arms around his neck and my legs around his waist as he placed one knee on the bed and then the other, all the while inside me. The muscles in his shoulders and back bulged. It was amazing how strong he was.

Once he had lowered me back onto his soft sheets, he began to move in and out quickly, building an even rhythm. I relaxed, slipping into a trance, my mind free of everything but the sensation of his body against mine, his cock inside me pushing against the walls of my sex. The heat in my core radiated out into a blanket of sensual pleasure.

"You're so snug," he said, pumping.

He continued to move in and out of me with a steady rhythm. My climax was coming fast and I felt my muscles contracting in anticipation. He moaned in response and began thrusting harder, causing me to move my hips against him. Sex with Vincent was like nothing I'd ever experienced. It was exhausting and yet I wanted more and more.

"You're close, aren't you?" he said. "Come for me, Kristen. Now."

He thrust to the hilt and the orgasm slammed into me. My muscles tightened to their limit before my core burst and pleasure wracked my entire body. The sensation was at once too much and not enough; I moaned and thrust my hips out toward him, wanting to take all of his impressive length. I clenched around him and his cock jerked, which made me squeeze harder.

When my quivering had finally wound down, he gave one more mighty thrust then closed his eyes. Convulsions seized his lithe body as he came, the condom filling with his hot seed. I watched his face, fascinated, hardly believing I could make him feel such a strong sensation. It was an unfamiliar power trip.

"Damn it," he growled, pulling out of me and tying off the condom. He threw it in the trash and plopped down on his back, scooping me up after a second to my new favorite spot on his chest. "How am I ever going to get you off my mind when we have sex like that?"

"And why would I want to be off your mind?" I said coyly.

He gave me a small smile. Then his eyes glazed over as if he were looking off to the horizon. The subtle change in his demeanor was jarring. This must be another one of his sudden shifts. I didn't want to leave the bed and end the moment, much as I knew I had to, but I could tell for him the moment was already gone.

"Busy day?" I asked, raking my fingers up and down his chest.

Unmoving, he said nothing.

After a moment, I tried again. "Vincent, where are you?"

He shook his head as if warding off an unpleasant thought and looked down at me. His face was another derivative of charming Vincent. The man I'd been with earlier was gone.

"Sorry," he said. "Lots of work to do. Coffee?"

I hated that he could do that. How could he go from having passionate sex to being all business so quickly? Maybe it was something you had to put up with when you got involved with a man who ran a global empire, but it still bugged me. I nodded because I didn't trust myself to speak.

When I walked into his kitchen I was greeted by the sight of Vincent making an omelet in his light blue underwear. His impressive bulge strained against the pima cotton even when he wasn't hard, and it left little to the imagination. With the way the morning light was pouring in his window, the scene looked like something out of a magazine ad—selling anything, so long as it included him.

It was a great recovery. "I didn't realize breakfast was being served with coffee," I said.

"Three egg omelet with red and green peppers, onion, jack cheese and ham. I hope that's all right. I'm a big believer in putting good things into your life if you want good things to come of it."

"Wise words." I wondered if Vincent thought of me as a good thing. Or if I thought of him as a good thing. We hadn't known each other very long; we were still getting to know one another. A good thing could easily turn into a bad one as I've figured out from experience. People can be surprising.

He winked. "And yes, you count as a good thing."

He flipped my omelet deftly onto a plate already containing sliced melon and strawberries and set it on the counter. Pouring me a fresh cup of coffee from a french press, he continued. "I have to go to Rio tonight. I'll be gone the rest of the week, but we need to keep in contact every day, especially since your ex found out where you live. Are you sure I can't put you up in a hotel or get you a guard?"

I took the coffee mug from his hand and took a sip, savoring the complex notes. It was so much better than the coffee at the office. "No," I said. "None of that will be necessary."

He nodded. "Okay, but after work we're going to the store before I leave and getting you some protection. Mace, at least. Something else as well. Maybe a gun."

I was touched he was so concerned about Marty, but I thought he was overreacting. We weren't dealing with a serial killer here. "That's fine, but I really think mace will be enough. I don't need an assault rifle or anything."

"Eat up, we do need to get to work soon," he said. "Want me to drop you off at a nearby subway station or at your building? I mean, you know, discretion and all."

"My building's fine," I said. The drop off would be quick enough and Vincent had tinted windows. It wouldn't be an issue to hide him taking me to work from my firm.

He shrugged. "Great. Remember, we need to hit the store after work, so no staying late."

I nodded. This swerve between business and affection was going to take some getting used to, but I could probably manage.

***

After getting dropped off in the high style of Vincent's old Camry, I walked into the office for my first day as a Client Acquisition Manager. Moving my things from my cubicle to my new office took up the first half of the morning. The office was going to be pretty sparse for a while, but it was mine. I was excited.

I planned on starting on some work on Vincent's account before lunch. I looked for the manila folder containing Vincent's signed contract along with other information about his assets but couldn't find it. I realized I must have left it with Richard. I'd have to get it from him.

My office was toward the end of the hall, which meant I had to walk almost the length of the floor to get to Richard's office. When I got there, I knocked and saw he was on the phone. He glanced at me briefly before gluing his eyes back to the screen.

I waited.

He was on the phone for almost ten minutes before he ended his conversation and got off. Still not glancing at me, he finally spoke. "Yes?"

I took a deep breath. "I think I left the Sorenson files with you. Can I have them?"

He continued typing. "You know those are with records by now."

"Okay, but I also know you made copies. Can I have those?"

He looked around before finally gracing me with a glance. "Listen, I'm very busy. Go down to records and have copies made there."

So this was how it was going to be. I understood his annoyance, but he was being a jerk about this. I knew he had to have copies of the file in his office somewhere. He would've had them immediately, and he was so organized it would take him seconds to locate them.

"Richard—"

"I'm busy. Go down to records to get your files."

"I know you have them here somewhere. I'm happy to—"

"Is there anything else? For the hundredth time, I am very, very busy today."

I took a deep breath to calm myself. "No, that's all."

The right thing to do was let him be angry and not feed into it. Still, it hurt that he was being so rude to me. Maybe he was trying to keep me down even though we had the same title. Regardless, I'd have to put up with it for as long as I could.

I went down to records and wrestled with them to get the documents I needed. When I got back to my desk I found I'd received an email from my new boss, Carl Stansworth, asking me to drop by when I had a moment. "When I had a moment" really meant I needed to get there ASAP because he had a small opening in his schedule and wanted to see me during that time. I checked the timestamp and saw it had been sent eighteen minutes ago. That meant I didn't have long; guys like Carl booked themselves pretty full. I gathered up my stuff and rushed out of my office.

On the way to Carl's office—which occupied a corner on the opposite side of the floor from mine—I checked my phone and saw I had a text message from Vincent.

Hope your morning has been going well. Mine's been going steadily downhill.

Thoughts raced through my mind. What could have happened? I texted back asking what was wrong.

My phone buzzed again.

I'm not in bed with you right now, mostly.

Blushing furiously, I tapped out a quick reply.

This is a work phone! We have to be more discreet than that!

I shoved the device in my jacket pocket as I came to Carl's office. The door was closed. My phone buzzed as I looked around for his secretary. Spotting her, I walked over. "Carl asked me to drop by a minute ago. Do you know when he'll be free?"

As I waited for her to finish typing, I glanced down at my phone to read Vincent's message.

Fine. Your performance managing my assets this morning was exemplary. I have ideas for some new positions we could take that I want to share at our next meeting.

"—was your name, honey?" I snapped to attention, feeling the heat in my cheeks again as I worked to push Vincent's message from my mind. She must have been asking who I was so she could buzz Carl. I needed to focus at work or else my performance would suffer at the worst possible moment.

Before I could respond, I heard Carl's voice from behind me.

"Kristen, come on in." I turned to face him and he nodded at my phone. "Impossible to get away these days, right? I admire you young people for being so good at managing all these devices. I want to throw mine through the window once or twice a day." His green eyes twinkled behind gold framed glasses. The way his face wrinkled when he smiled combined with the white hair on the sides of his head—he was bald on top—showed his age, but he owned it and generally exuded an air of happiness.

I shoved it into my pocket and laughed politely. "That would be a pretty serious liability if it hit someone."

Carl chuckled as he led me into his office. "You could have been a lawyer if you weren't doing this. Maybe you should talk to them; they're the ones making me mad enough to throw the thing half the time."

I did my best fake smile. He sat down and motioned for me to take the seat across from him.

"So," he said, clasping his hands on the desk, "Vincent Sorenson. First of all, congratulations on landing that one. Tough prospect. Second, what's your plan to keep him?" He smiled and looked at me expectantly.

I wished I had been given more time to research what to do with Vincent's account before talking to Carl about it. Since I hadn't had enough time, I decided to stay vague. "Well, the bond market has some pretty promising sectors, so I'm thinking we can start there."

He nodded. "Sure. The thing is, a guy like that is going to want big returns. He's used to taking risks and reaping the rewards."

I bit my lip. He had a point. "True, which is why I also wanted to suggest a plan targeting BRIC assets. There's more risk there but those economies have been performing very well for a while and I think he'll be interested in the international flavor."

His eyes widened and he held out his fingers. "I think Brazil is the only one with surfing out of those, right? Russia definitely not, and I'm not sure about India but I know I'd only go surfing off the coast of China if I wanted to commit suicide by pollution." He laughed. All anyone at the firm seemed to know about Vincent was he was rich and enjoyed surfing.

"Do you surf?" I blurted.

He laughed even harder. "It was a hypothetical. Can you imagine me surfing?"

I shrugged and wracked my brain for a useful nugget from the research I had done on Vincent's company before the pitch. "Actually, India has lots of great surfing, and his company has been targeting China as a new growth market. Apparently there are people going out on the water there, though I imagine they're avoiding the river mouths."

Still chuckling, Carl nodded. "Shows what I know about that stuff. I like this BRIC plan. Focus on that, and present the safer bond strategy as a backup if you need it. We're going to get some analysts working under you, but that will take a while because people are wrapping up other jobs, so for now you're going to be on your own. Knowing your work ethic, I'm sure you won't mind the longer hours in the interim."

I nodded, eager to get back to my desk and see if this plan was even remotely viable. This is what happened when you weren't prepared: you had to make stuff up and it might not work out.

"Anything else for me?" he asked.

I shook my head. "No. I do think Vincent will like this BRIC plan. He's actually flying to Rio tonight for a product launch."

He furrowed his brow. "How do you know that?"

Great question—how did I know that? Beyond the truth, of course. This whole seeing a client thing was going to keep me on my toes.

"I saw a news story about it," I said, scrambling. "I have Google Alerts set up for his name and his company. Just saw the story before I walked over here actually." It didn't explain why I knew he was flying over tonight, but hopefully it would be enough of an answer for him not to push me on it.

It was. He shook his head. "It's been so long since I was an analyst, I feel out of the loop. Great to see young blood getting their feet wet. I'm predicting great things from this account, Kristen." He stood up and I did the same before he motioned me to the door. "I have a lunch meeting now, but keep me posted on how things are going and let me know if you need anything."

With another nod, I left.

I was taking deep breaths to stop myself from hyperventilating all the way back to my office. When I got there, I closed the door behind me and sat in the dark. Meeting with Carl would have been stressful in itself, but adding in the situation with Vincent made it even more so. Thankfully, it seemed to have gone well. Carl liked me, which was more important than Richard liking me, since Carl was my new boss.

I knew better than to go to Carl about anything Richard was doing unless it was absolutely necessary. Bosses were a lot like clients: they wanted you to make their lives easier and make them money. Giving Carl a situation to deal with was the best way to make sure he liked me less.

Other than losing him money. That would be worse.

I got up and flicked the light on in my office before checking my phone. No new messages. I tapped out a belated reply to Vincent's earlier message about taking up new positions at our next meeting.

Probably not our next meeting, right? I don't think they will let us fool around at the store.

Seconds later, I got a reply.

Oh right, I meant in my daydreams about you. Make sure you get out of work as close to 5 as possible. It might be a little tight to catch my charter down there.

I suddenly felt bad. He was so busy and I was burdening him. Even though he was still doing his best to squeeze me in his schedule, I was definitely making his life more hectic. This shopping trip was probably going to work out, but I almost wished I had kept my mouth shut about Marty. It was hard to argue this wasn't a negative element in whatever was going on between us.

I sat staring at my phone, thinking of what to text back, but there was nothing to really say. The best I could do was apologize when he arrived, because he wasn't going to take no for an answer at this point. Once he set his mind on something, he followed through. Getting me protection items was evidence of that.

The rest of the day passed in a swirl of research and note taking. It looked like the BRIC strategy would be doable, to my relief. I could start preparing materials for my next business meeting with Vincent soon.

First though, there would be another non-business meeting.

At 4:59, I packed up my stuff and left the office earlier than I had in months. I knew Vincent would be waiting for me in his Camry by the time I got down.

***

"I thought we were going to the grocery store to get mace," I said as I stared at a sign with a rifle and knife crossed over one another like crossbones. Bold letters read 'Army and Navy Surplus'. The towering brick facade was almost as intimidating as what I imagined they sold inside. Vincent had driven us to the outskirts of the city on the pretense that there was an awesome grocery store there with lots of free food samples. But as I looked at the barren strip of highway to my right and the stretch of farmland to my left I knew we were miles from any grocery store.

"I knew you would've protested to coming out here, but I wasn't going to take no for an answer. You need to protect yourself, Kristen."

He was right, I would have protested—we hadn't even gone inside yet and I was already itching to leave. Having weapons lying around my apartment was only going to make me more nervous about Marty making a reappearance. If I admitted to myself that I needed protection then I was also admitting that he was a legitimate threat to my safety, and I didn't want to revisit that thought.

"Martin probably realized it was a bad idea to stop by my apartment," I began, trying to convince him that the trip was unnecessary. "I bet he's already gone." I knew Vincent felt strongly about my safety but I was determined not to be treated like some damsel in distress.

He turned to me, his lips set into a thin line. "This is about more than that. You're a young woman living in the city . . . I need to be sure that no one can hurt you."

"Vincent, you can't save me from everything."

"I can try."

I nearly blushed at his sincerity. Maybe I wasn't ready to face the severity of the situation I was in, but Vincent was—I'd never seen him so persistent, and he certainly didn't have anything to gain from bringing me here. My earlier fears that my relationship history had lessened his feelings for me were quickly dissipating.

Still, I tried to imagine what we would find in Army and Navy Surplus that would be of any use to me and came up empty—I envisioned gun-lined walls and cases of sharpened knives. I'd never so much as used a sling shot, let alone a real weapon.

"Well, you should know that I've never fired a gun or anything before," I admitted bashfully.

Vincent took me by the hand. "Let's look around first. We'll find you something you're comfortable with."

I rolled my eyes as he ushered me through the entrance to the store, but I wasn't going to argue with him since we were already here.

The inside resembled a massive warehouse and I was immediately hit by the sight of military accessories—army jackets, yucca packs, deactivated hand grenades, and antique first aid kits were only a few of the items that decorated the storefront. Beyond us lay conveniently labeled aisles for "cooking," "outdoors," and "defense." I swallowed a hard lump as I considered the last one.

"Some of this is just for show," Vincent said, gesturing to a set of novelty dog tags. "The stuff we're looking for is locked in display cases near the back."

As I fingered the length of an empty bullet casing poised on a nearby shelf I wondered why Vincent knew so much about this place, down to its very layout.

"Have you been here before?"

"Just a few times. When I was living from place to place after college I needed supplies I could rely on, things that wouldn't break down. I got so used to shopping at places like this that I guess I never broke the habit."

It was hard to imagine Vincent roughing it after having seen his house, but I knew he hadn't always lived a privileged lifestyle.

"I also learned that you need to be able to defend yourself," he added.

"What did you need to defend yourself against?"

"Nothing serious. People would sometimes try to take advantage of us, steal from us, because we were young and seemed vulnerable. It's funny, even when you become successful you find yourself dealing with the same thing."

"I guess I was young and vulnerable, too," I admitted, thinking of how clueless I was when I began dating Marty. "Just in a different way."

"Now you won't be." He put his hand on the small of my back and urged me forward. We made our way toward the defense section, bypassing a few shoppers, but the place was nearly empty.

As we approached the back of the store I spotted a glass display case that stretched at least ten feet across. Its shelves were illuminated from below so that the items crowded onto them seemed to glow.

A middle-aged man came out from a door behind the case, cleaning the barrel of shotgun with a rag. He had thinning grey hair cropped short to his head. He wore a forest-green jacket overloaded with pockets. A gray shirt underneath covered a paunch belly draping slightly over a pair of army cargo pants. His arms were so muscled that he seemed to be walking with his chest permanently puffed out.

"Can I help you?" he asked in a distinctive accent as we approached him. The name tag pinned to his t-shirt read "Darryl."

"We're just looking for some protective equipment," Vincent answered.

"This is the place for it. What kind of protection are we talking about?"

I wondered how many different things you could defend yourself from, but the length of the display case suggested there were plenty.

"Something she can use if she finds herself in . . . a bind." His mouth twisted. Vincent was taking the threat of Marty very seriously.

Darryl's eyes widened. "A bind, huh? I've got just the thing. Give me a minute." He disappeared behind the door he came out of earlier, leaving Vincent and me alone.

"Maybe I should just leave town with you," I teased as I turned to him, leaning my hip into the display case. "He can't find me if I'm not here, right?"

Vincent seemed to stiffen at the mention of his trip but quickly reached up to cup my chin in his hand, gently running the pad of his thumb across my jaw line. "You can't put your life on hold because of this, Kristen."

"I know," I sighed, leaning into his touch. "A vacation just sounds nice right now."

"The trip is going to be anything but vacation."

"What are you doing in Rio?" I asked as I realized that he hadn't told me much about the details of his trip.

"We're throwing a launch party for a new product," he said, dropping his hand from my face.

"What kind of product?"

"We're releasing a new surfboard in South America and there's a big party to publicize it. There's going to be famous stars, business people, media—the usual."

Thoughts flooded my head of the women surrounding him at the bar in Cape Town. I'd wondered why he hadn't told me about the party earlier, but I tried to chalk it up to distraction. After all, I had given him a lot to think about. "Sounds like vacation to me."

"In this business even parties are work."

I was just about to ask him for more details about what kind of people would be there, worried that a launch party in Brazil would be as wild as it sounded, when Darryl reemerged. He had a silver revolver in his hand that looked like he reached into a television and pulled it out of a Dirty Harry movie.

"This is a Ruger SP101. It'll take some getting used to especially with your small hands. I'd take it out to the firing range a few times to get a handle on it and build up some callouses."

I shot Vincent a doubtful look but he gestured for me to try it. Really?

Darryl placed the gun in my outstretched palm and I had to use my other hand to help support the weight.

"How does it feel?" Vincent asked.

Like I'm holding a bowling ball.

"I'm not sure this is going to work," I replied.

Darryl wrinkled his brows and scratched his chin. "Okay, I got something better." He went into the back room again and reappeared. This time he was carrying a large, steel tube with a trigger attached to its bottom.

"This is an M1 rocket launcher," Darryl said, his voice raising an octave with excitement. "It'll obliterate any 'binds' you might find yourself in. Try it out, see how it feels."

Darryl thrust the rocket launcher into my hands before I had a chance to protest. I stood, awkwardly bearing the heavy weight, unsure how I was even supposed to hold it. I unwittingly laughed from the overkill.

"I'm not sure I can fit this in my purse," I joked.

"How about something a little more discreet?" Vincent asked, taking the rocket launcher from my hands and setting it on the display case.

"Well, we've got these over here." Darryl scurried over to the end of the case, beckoning us to follow him with a frantic wave of the hand. He pulled a knife from its shelf and unsheathed it, revealing its thick and serrated edge. "This"—a wide and crooked smile spread across his face—"is an OKC-3S Bayonet. This is a real bang for your buck, multi-purpose, you know, not just for defense. But if that's what you're looking for, a defense weapon, this will get them every time." He thrust the handle of the knife at me, his own fingers digging into the blade.

"Try it," he insisted.

"I think I'll just . . . look."

He shrugged, as if to say suit yourself. "If you're looking for discreet, this is it." He stuck the knife back into its sheath and slipped it into the hip pocket of his cargo pants. "Can't even see it."

"Don't you think this is all a little overkill?" I asked to both men. They both looked at me, surprised.

"You can never be too prepared, honey," Darryl said.

Vincent nodded.

Ugh. Men.

I exhaled heavily, which seemed to make Vincent come to his senses.

"It's a beautiful knife," Vincent said, his charming business persona taking over. "But I think we're more interested in something like this." He pointed to a row of silver necklaces spread across the top shelf of the case, a different pendant attached to each chain. The quaint pieces of jewelry looked out of place next to the weapons that surrounded them.

"Ah, these are very popular," Darryl said as he set the knife down next to the rocket launcher, much to my relief.

"A necklace?" I asked, turning to Vincent.

"Not quite."

"Which one are you interested in?" Darryl asked.

Vincent looked at me contemplatively, as if considering which pendant would suit me best, before turning back to the case. "That one."

Darryl pulled one of the necklaces from the bunch and held it up, a small heart-shaped locket spinning from the chain. He showed me the bottom of the heart which contained a small hole.

"You can insert a mace cartridge into the back," Vincent said, taking the necklace from Darryl and laying the heart flat on his palm. He flipped it open to reveal a small canister, its nozzle situated into the hole.

"You just squeeze the heart in the center to shoot the mace." He draped the necklace around my neck and fastened it.

I looked down at it, afraid to even touch it for fear of setting it off inside. "I don't know, Vincent. What if someone knocks into me and it goes off?"

"There's a safety switch," Darryl cut in. "See the small button on the side? You have to slide it down to be able to use it. If you're in trouble you won't have to reach into your purse, these necklaces are one of our best sellers because they're so convenient."

"Kristen, if someone attacks you, you'll be able to defend yourself without inflicting any real damage to them. All I want is to be able to protect you, and this is the only way I know how. I can't always be there." He reached out and touched the pendant, his fingers brushing against my exposed clavicle. The gesture was tender and so were his words. If it would make Vincent feel better knowing that I could defend myself then I didn't see the harm in wearing the necklace. In fact, the idea of having something so accessible already felt like a small comfort to me.

"All right, I'll take it," I said.

"We'll get one for Riley too," Vincent said.

"Riley already has her own."

"But is it a necklace? It'll be more convenient than whatever she's carrying around in her purse."

It was a good suggestion. Although Marty had been cordial with Riley the first time he stopped by, I knew his mood could escalate, and quickly. I didn't want her to be collateral damage.

I nodded in agreement.

"I also think you should have something else, just in case the mace isn't enough," he added.

"I've got just the thing," Darryl said, reaching below the display case. I imagined him pulling out a flamethrower or a chainsaw so I was almost taken aback by the simplicity of the small rectangular device he set in front of us. "It's a taser. If the mace doesn't subdue him, this will. Guaranteed."

I picked it up and pressed its button, jumping as a bright blue electric current ignited at the taser's end.

"This seems dangerous."

"It will hurt someone, no doubt. But not permanently," Darryl assured me.

"It'll be a last resort item," Vincent said. "Just keep it in your purse."

I could think of a million ways something could go wrong with the necklace—I could forget to wear it one day, it could break, or get ripped from my neck. Having a backup plan couldn't hurt.

"Better safe than sorry," I conceded.

Vincent smiled and pushed the taser and necklace toward Darryl. "And a few extra mace cartridges," he said. "So she can practice."

I turned to Vincent as Darryl rang us up. "Well, if Marty does show up he'll be sorry," I tried to laugh off my unease.

"He can't hurt you now, Kristen. I won't let it happen." He reached out and brushed the hair from my face, and I found myself wishing he didn't have to leave town—the mace and the taser were helpful, but neither of them could make me feel as safe as Vincent did.

Vincent paid for the items, by his insistence of course, but at least this time they were cheaper than a day of surfing. As we left the store and approached his car he put his arm around my shoulder and pulled me into him. "You know, I think that rocket launcher suited you."

"I could barely hold it!"

He leaned me against the driver's side door; his hands settled into the groove of my waist. "You've handled more powerful things."

"Powerful, yes," I teased, rising up onto the tips of my toes to bring my mouth close to his. "But not as big."

His hold on my waist tightened as he gripped at the fabric of my shirt, balling it up in his fists as if he wanted to tear it from me.

"I've never heard you complain." He planted a hard kiss onto my lips and I almost dropped my shopping bag, the sensation of his skin against mine sending a wave of desire through me. Worried that other shoppers might catch us in our heated embrace, I broke away from the kiss.

"Too bad it's not big enough to reach from Brazil to New York City," I said.

"What's your schedule like tomorrow?" he asked as we got into the car.

"I'll be pretty tied up all day. I have a meeting with Carl and then I need to review some things on your account. Why?"

"Just because I'll be in South America doesn't mean I don't want to see you, what about video chat tomorrow night? How's seven?"

I leaned close to him, breathing in the sharp scent of his cologne. "It's a date."

Chapter Eleven

Vincent swung by a Duane Reade so I could grab Riley a few more cold remedies and then dropped me off at my apartment. I hated to say goodbye so suddenly but I knew he needed to get to the airport to catch his flight.

I climbed the flight of stairs in my apartment building to my floor and saw two guys carrying boxes into the apartment across from me. One was tall and leanly muscular with a striped shirt stretching against his torso that seemed two sizes too small for his build. The other was short and stout with broad shoulders and bulging biceps. The odd duo reminded me of Mario and Luigi.

A CD fell out of the box the short guy was carrying and I stooped to pick it up.

"Here, you dropped this." As I held out the cd, I looked at the cover. There was some weird picture of a sphinx—head of a man, body of a lion—except the head was female and the body was a motorcycle. The title read "Born This Way by Lady Gaga".

He set the box he was carrying on the floor inside, smiled, and took the CD from me. "Thank you so much. Can't imagine going for long without these catchy tunes." His smile widened and he offered his large hand. "Bernie."

I shook it. "Kristen."

He gestured to his tall friend who was unpacking kitchen items. "And that's Kurt."

"Hello." I waved. "Welcome to the building."

Kurt smiled and waved back. "Are you in the unit just across from us?"

"Yep, the one with the blue 'home sweet home' doormat in front."

"Great to meet the neighbors!" He grinned.

After exchanging pleasantries, Kurt and Bernie returned to their business, but not before inviting Riley and I over for dinner sometime after they'd finished settling in. They seemed like a nice couple.

I opened my front door to find Riley curled up in a blanket on the couch, a steaming mug cupped in her hands. At least she was sitting up, a noticeable improvement from the last few days.

"Vick's vapor rub, moisturized tissues, and cough drops— strawberry flavored, of course." I set the bag of items on the dining room table along with my bag of protective gear and flopped onto the couch beside her.

"You're the best," Riley said, her voice still nasally. "But I still wouldn't sit too close, I don't want to get you sick. Vincent would probably never forgive me if a cold kept you from seeing him."

"Actually, he's leaving for Brazil tonight for a launch party." I tried to keep my voice even, not wanting to betray the jealousy that was lingering faintly in the back of my mind.

"So that means I can cough in your general direction?" she joked.

"No," I rolled my eyes. "But it does mean I'm staying in. And I need your help with something if you're feeling up to it."

"Okay. What's going on?"

I wrung my hands nervously, knowing that if I told Riley about the mace and taser I'd have to tell her about Marty, too. But she deserved to hear the truth, especially if there was a chance that she'd have to deal with him again. "I remember you had mace when we were in Cape Town and Vincent just bought me some. I was wondering if you could show me how to use it?"

"Mace?" she asked as she set her mug down and turned to me. "Is this about your ex?"

"Yes. I haven't heard from him since the day he stopped by, but I just wanted to be prepared."

"Prepared for what, Kristen? You still haven't told me what happened with him."

I hesitated, but the idea of finally revealing my past to Riley brought with it a sense of relief. "I met Marty in a business finance class," I began. "I was a Junior and he was a Senior. We flirted a little but it wasn't until he was my TA the following year that we really hit it off."

"Your TA, huh?" she teased. "Ms. Harvard Grad sleeping with the teacher, I almost don't believe it."

I shot her a wry side glance, but I had to admit that Riley knew how to make a difficult situation bearable.

"He was only a year older than me," I said. "Not to mention gorgeous, smart, and completely charming. All of the girls in my class had a crush on him." My stomach churned at the thought of Marty at the beginning of our relationship—the romantic dates, the small but sweet gestures, the intimate conversations. That version of him seemed so distant from the guy he turned into.

"So why exactly are you afraid of him? You practically fled the apartment the other night."

"Things were great between us for the first few months. He seemed like a catch. But when the pressures of post-college life started getting to him he became jealous and possessive." I swallowed a hard lump as I recalled the scathing names he called me, the minor but frightening ways he would grab me when I challenged him.

"I know that's not healthy," Riley said, cocking her eyebrow. "But it doesn't exactly make him dangerous. What aren't you telling me?"

I sighed and looked Riley in the eye, preparing to admit to her what I'd been hiding for so long. "Marty has borderline personality disorder, but I didn't discover that until a year into our relationship. He could turn from charming to vicious in a matter of seconds. He would call me names if he thought I was flirting with another guy, sometimes he'd get aggressive—"

Riley threw the blanket from her shoulders, seemingly agitated. "Aggressive? Are you saying he hit you, Kristen?"

"No, he never hit me. But . . ." I held up my crooked pinky finger.

She reached for my hand frantically and squeezed it gently with her own. "Oh my god, Kristen. Why didn't you tell someone?"

"He comes from a powerful family. I couldn't tell anyone about it. Not even the police. So I left . . . changed my address, found a new job, and hoped he'd move on. But somehow he's found me, and I'm not sure what he wants."

"Well now I feel like a complete jerk for pushing you to date, I had no idea you were dealing with this."

I smiled at Riley's concern, feeling I had made the right decision by telling her. "How could you have known?"

She looked up at me and twisted her mouth as if she had something she wanted to say but was afraid to say it.

"You can ask me anything, Riley. It's fine."

"How did you deal with it? It must have been scary . . . being with someone who could turn on you at any second."

Silence settled over us as I considered her question. Had I dealt with it? I'd been pretty much avoiding the thought of Marty since I left Boston and even now, with the possibility of him in my city, I was still trying to push the memory of my relationship with him from my mind.

"For a long time I tried to act like it wasn't a big deal, like maybe it was a phase. But after the pinky incident I left as fast as I could and I guess I haven't really dealt with it, not until now."

"Have you told Vincent?"

"Yeah, and then he hauled me out to the middle of nowhere to buy me mace and a taser."

"A taser?" Her eyebrows shot up. "You'll definitely have to show me that."

"Don't you think it's overkill?"

A seriousness settled over Riley's face as she scooted closer to me. "This guy could come back, Vincent just wants you to be safe. And so do I."

"Then maybe he shouldn't have jetted off to Brazil." I felt my cheeks grow hot with embarrassment as I realized how childish I sounded.

"Isn't he just going for business?"

"Cape Town was business, too, but you saw him at the bar . . . women flock to him." I tried not to picture bikini clad models latching onto Vincent's arm and feeding him drinks all night.

"But Vincent doesn't flock to other women. Kristen, the guy bought you a taser."

I laughed as my hand instinctively wandered to the necklace he'd put on me earlier that day. Riley was right. I'd never seen Vincent so attentive or concerned as he was when we were at the army surplus store—it felt good to be with someone who cared about my safety instead of threatening it.

"Will you show me how to use this?" I said, eyeing the necklace between my fingers.

"That's the mace?"

"He got you one, too." I walked over to the dining room table and pulled the extra mace cartridges from the bag as well as the necklace we had picked out for Riley, a star shaped pendant dangling from the end.

"This is definitely more convenient than that bulky brick I've been carrying around in my purse!" she said as I handed her the necklace.

We left the living room and stepped out onto the balcony so we wouldn't chance inhaling the spray. After Riley showed me how to insert the cartridge and where to press in order to set it off, we practiced shooting mace at a potted plant. After a dozen or so attempts, we both felt confident in our accuracy and quickdraw. We also felt sorry for the plant.

Although the practice was a much needed tension reliever, I couldn't believe I was in this position again, only this time I was actually preparing for Marty's possible attack instead of ignoring it.

"Are you okay?" Riley asked, seemingly sensing my unease.

"I just can't believe this is happening." I looked out over the balcony at the glinting lights of the city in the distance, wondering if Marty was still out there.

"We're doing this to make sure he doesn't hurt you again." She put her hand on my shoulder and I nodded, acknowledging her concern. "But we probably shouldn't test out the taser." She laughed.

I smirked. "We wouldn't want you couch-ridden again."

"Speaking of couch-ridden, I should probably rest."

"Me, too," I said as I realized how exhausted I was. "It's been the longest day."

We went inside and each disappeared into our rooms. I took off the necklace and placed it on my bedside table, still nervous that I might accidentally set it off in my sleep, and hid the taser in my closet. I would tackle that one another day.

As I climbed into bed, I found myself thinking of Vincent's trip to Brazil and realized that I no longer felt so nervous about it. I couldn't deny that he was attractive and that other women would always respond to that. But for the first time since Marty showed up I didn't feel so scared. In fact, I felt in control.

Chapter Twelve

I tried not to let my nerves get the best of me when I got to work the next day. I wasn't sure what my meeting with Carl was for, only that he wanted me in his office at noon. The morning went slowly, my anticipation of the meeting causing me to look at the clock every few minutes. The dragging time made it hard to push thoughts of Vincent's business trip from my mind. I hadn't heard from him since he left. I knew he was busy but he could've at least managed a text.

Although I had Vincent to thank for the greater sense of security I now felt with my mace and taser on hand, I couldn't shake the lingering sense of jealousy I felt every time I thought of the launch party. Bikini clad models would no doubt be there to show off the new surfboard, and there would certainly be no shortage of alcohol. Vincent said it himself—he wasn't used to taking things slow, and he definitely wasn't used to commitment, how could I compete with models when I was on an entirely different continent?

I tried to distract myself with work—skimming the accounts of a few potential clients and answering emails throughout the morning. When it was finally noon I made my way to Carl's office, stopping in the bathroom to make sure I looked presentable, before giving a light knock on the door. A low voice called from behind it, telling me to come in.

I opened the door and stepped into his office. It was almost as impressive as Vincent's—a view of the Hudson River Park served as a stunning backdrop for plush leather office chairs, a glossy hardwood desk, and chrome fixtures that gave the space a classic but contemporary touch. Carl was poised over an open file, a silver pen flicking quickly across the pages inside.

"Good afternoon Mr. Stansworth."

Carl immediately looked up from his work and gave me a smile, a refreshing change from Richard, who could barely tear his eyes from his phone. His remaining gray hairs were neatly combed. Although he had crow's feet beneath his eyes, he was sprightly and kept in good health. "Afternoon Kristen, why don't you take a seat?"

I sank into the black cushioned chair across from his desk, the nervous energy I had worked up earlier hitting me full force as I contemplated why Carl had called the meeting. Had Richard complained about my performance? Did Carl know about me and Vincent? I'd never forgive myself if I'd let an attraction ruin my career.

"You're probably wondering why I've asked you into my office this afternoon," he said as he carefully capped his pen and set it aside, focusing his attention on me.

I swallowed and tried not to betray my panic as I answered him. "Yes, sir."

"Well, I'd like to start off by saying that you've done good work on the Sorenson account." A warm smile spread across his face as he spoke. I breathed a sigh of relief as I realized that I wasn't going to be demoted or, worse, fired for dating a client. "We knew he would be difficult to land, but you did it."

The nervous energy I had been feeling earlier began to dissipate with Carl's encouraging words. It felt good to be recognized for the work I'd done, especially without the assumptions that my "feminine allure" had anything to do with it. Still, Richard was integral in researching Vincent and formulating our strategy for our first presentation—I really couldn't have done it without his help. "Thank you," I said. "But Richard did a lot of work on that account, too. I can't take all the credit."

"Richard played his part, but you closed the deal. That's what matters on an account like this, so congratulations. You earned that promotion."

"Thank you Mr. Stansworth."

"And that's why I've asked you in here today, I was hoping you could give me your opinion on a prospect we've been trying to land for a few weeks now."

I hoped I wasn't blushing, but I was flattered that Carl trusted me enough to consult me on a pitch I wasn't even assigned to. "Who's the client?"

"Michael Cohen, are you familiar?"

Anyone who worked at Waterbridge-Howser would recognize the name; in fact, most of the firms in New York City had been trying to take him on as a client ever since he dropped Ellis-Kravitz as his wealth management firm two months prior. "Of course," I said. "He owns the most profitable industrial machinery company on the East Coast and is looking to expand cross country. I thought he had already decided to go with Waterbridge-Howser?"

"So did I, but we recently found out that he took a meeting with Watson-James. We're scheduled for a follow up pitch tomorrow but I think we need to rework our strategy—clearly it didn't work the first time."

I hadn't reviewed the materials, and I was worried that I wouldn't be able to suggest anything useful. "I'm not sure I can be of much help," I admitted.

He opened a desk drawer below him and rummaged around for a minute before producing a thick manila folder. "I wouldn't have asked for your help if I didn't think you were capable, Kristen. Just take a look at this file," he said as he handed the folder to me. "These are the documents from our initial meeting with Cohen. I'd like to hear any ideas you might have on a new approach."

I browsed the contents of the folder, comparing the initial proposal to the limited knowledge I had of Cohen's company. Feeling emboldened by Carl's confidence in me, I decided to point out the first inconsistency that I saw, hoping not to step on any feet. I took a deep breath, formulated my thoughts, and spoke. "The initial approach was strong, the emphasis on his expansion is key. But I think you might benefit from a broader focus on the strongholds he already has on the East Coast. Especially with the risk he's taking by expanding, we need to reassure him of the solid platform we can build using his current assets. I think we need to show him that we're invested in the business he's already built, not just his potential for the future."

Carl twisted his mouth in apparent consideration, and I began to worry I'd insulted him. I wasn't used to being consulted on large accounts; Richard was more of a delegator, leaving me to deal with prep work like charts and graphs rather than formulating strategy.

"Where do you think we can best incorporate that information into the follow-up pitch we already have?" Carl asked.

"In my opinion," I began, clearing my throat nervously, "it should be the first thing you emphasize. It will show him that you respect his company and also make for a smoother transition into the points on expansion."

He shook his head slowly. "Watson-James is known for tradition. Cohen probably met with them when he realized our approach was future focused. Great catch, Kristen. You may have saved yet another account, keep it up."

I tried to hold back the beaming smile that was threatening to creep across my face as I handed the folder back to him. "Thank you Mr. Stansworth, let me know if there's anything else I can do for you."

I left Carl's office feeling more confident in my job than I ever had while working for Richard. Instead of treating me like his inferior or some prop, Carl treated me like his peer. I had to admit that I'd learned a lot from Richard—mostly by figuring things out on my own—but I had a feeling that working with Carl would be far more hands on. I couldn't help but think that, although I'd earned my new position at Waterbridge-Howser through hard work, my new career success wouldn't have been possible had I never met Vincent.

As I approached my desk I felt my phone vibrating in my pocket. I pulled it out to look at it and my stomach did a flip when I saw who it was from: Vincent. We'd been seeing each other for a few weeks now, but I still found myself getting excited every time I heard from him.

All work . . . I'm ready for some play, still on for Skype at 7 your time?

I was relieved to know that he was thinking about me despite how busy he must have been with the launch party. My earlier jealousy was starting to seem irrational—if Vincent wanted casual sex he could have it. It certainly would have been easier than dating, but he was cutting time out of his schedule for me. He was adjusting.

I typed a response. It's a date, but there might be a little work involved.

Only for you. Talk later.

I smiled as I put my phone away. Vincent might have been a bad boy once, but it seemed that things were changing.

***

On my way home, I ran across Kurt, who was on his way to pick up take-out from a Chinese restaurant nearby. We exchanged a few pleasantries. I told him I worked for a wealth management firm and he told me he worked security. I wasn't sure what that meant exactly but it wasn't hard to imagine him being a bouncer with his height and muscles.

When I got inside the apartment, the air was hotter than normal. Riley was laying on the couch as usual but in her work clothes, her bag next to the coffee table. It looked like she plopped down as soon as she made it inside. Must've been a hard day at work.

"Yeesh, why is it so hot in here?" I asked.

"The air conditioning is busted and it's like ninety degrees outside. Thank goodness for global warming and summer, right?" Riley replied, eyes closed and back of her hand resting on her forehead.

"I feel like we should be getting a tan in this heat. Are they going to fix it?"

"Yeah, I called the landlord. He said other people complained and he has a guy already working on it."

"That's good news." I slipped out of my shoes and put on some slippers. Moving on, I asked, "Did you go to work today?"

"I was feeling well enough to go in around noon. But I'm definitely sleeping early tonight. My head's still congested."

"I'm glad to hear you're better."

"How was your day?" she asked.

"Nothing too exciting. I had a meeting with my new boss. Carl's much better than Richard—who by the way is starting to be a pain in the ass. He thinks I stole Vincent from him."

"I saw you hold a poisonous spider." Her hand leaped from her forehead to point at me. "You definitely deserved Vincent more than he did."

I shrugged. "He doesn't know that though. And I'd like to keep it that way." I dropped my bag beside the kitchen table.

"So, other than work." She straightened herself on the couch and brushed her strawberry-blonde hair behind her ears. Her blue eyes looked at me carefully. "How are you doing?" she asked delicately.

I leaned against a kitchen chair and shifted my feet. "I'm okay. It's been on my mind but I feel a lot better and safer since Monday. Vincent's been out of town but he's checking up on me regularly, which is nice."

"That's good to hear, Kristen. I'm really happy for you. It sounds like Vincent really cares about you."

He'd been unexpectedly supportive since I told him about Marty. Any other guy would've probably made an awkward excuse to avoid me and I wouldn't blame them. Most people were busy battling their own problems; they weren't going to fight somebody else's—no matter how good the sex.

"I think I really care about him."

She smiled. "As you should. How did things go at his place?"

I felt my cheeks blush. "It was good. He made dinner for us. I found out what an awesome chef he is."

"A great cook as well? God, I'm not even going to lie to you, Kristen. I'm so jealous."

I laughed. "Thanks, I guess."

"So." Her eyes turned wicked. "Did you get some action?"

I smiled bashfully and tried to look away from her curious eyes.

She beamed and pointed her finger at me again. "I knew it."

I recounted the rest of the night at Vincent's place to Riley, only leaving out the most intimate details—which were the ones she wanted to hear most. I could trust her not to tell anyone, but I didn't feel ready to have a detailed discussion about my newly invigorated sex life. I was still trying to wrap my head around it. After over two years without sex, I'd just had it three times with nipple-pierced bad boy Vincent Sorenson. Blindfolds and multiple orgasms? What could I make of that?

Besides being the best sex of my life.

Riley seemed satisfied with the rundown even without the graphic details. I knew she'd probably prod me again about it later and I'd end up telling her more.

By the time evening rolled around, the heat had died down. I still didn't hear the whir of the air conditioning but at least the temperature outside had cooled enough to be bearable.

I'd wanted to change into something lighter but only had a pair of pink athletic shorts I had from high school that were clean. I ended up keeping my work blouse on and tying my hair in a ponytail as I carried my dirty clothes to the laundry room located in the basement of our building.

As a precaution, I brought my necklace and hid the taser within the pile of clothes. If Marty decided to show up and hurt me, I could easily subdue him or at least keep him at a distance long enough for me to call the police. That's if he decided to hurt me. He'd hurt me in the past but I still didn't know why he was showing up at my doorstep now. Was he here to say he changed? Did he want us to try again? He hadn't left a message with Riley or given any reason for his surprise visit. He had just asked to see me. The mysterious circumstances worried me.

After putting two loads through the washer and dryer, I was relieved I didn't have to use the protection items. There hadn't been anymore Marty incidents since Monday and I was hoping it would stay that way. By the time I got back to the apartment with the last batch from the dryer, the air had cooled. It was still warm though and I brought a glass of ice water into my bedroom for refreshment as I folded my laundry on my bed.

Riley had moved from the couch to her room, following through with her plan to sleep early.

I'd just finished folding the last garment when my laptop chirped. A window popped up indicating there was a Skype video call from V. Sorenson. I took a seat at my desk and clicked "accept". Moments later, Vincent's stunning face appeared on my computer screen. He was thousands of miles away but now right in front of me. I missed his spicy scent but just seeing him still had a strong effect. Sometimes I hated technology for making my life more complicated—emails, social media, always being connected to work—but this time I loved it.

I turned the volume high enough to hear Vincent but not enough to wake up Riley in the next room. She was a heavy sleeper and I doubted even a blow horn would wake her.

Vincent was in a gray dress shirt without a tie and the top button undone. His face had a bit of evening stubble. The ruggedness contrasting with his elegant attire was startlingly attractive. He looked tired from a long day but seemed excited to see me.

I smiled at him. "Hey," I said cheerily.

"Hey," he responded with enthusiasm of his own. "Can you hear me? Is the video coming through?"

"Crystal clear. Your handsomeness is transmitting in its full high definition glory. Am I coming through for you?"

He smiled. "Yes, but nothing can compare to the real thing. How are you, Kristen?"

"Good, just finished some laundry. How about you? How's your trip going?"

"Not bad. Business as usual." He paused for a moment. "I've missed you."

I blushed. The words weren't unexpected but it was still surprising to hear them out loud. "I missed you too."

His dark eyes were scanning my surroundings. "You've got a nice bedroom. I like the stuffed animal in the background."

I laughed. I'd seen it so often, I'd forgotten it was there. I got up from the desk and went to retrieve the stuffed bird from my bed to give Vincent a better look at it. And an explanation for why a grown woman in her mid-twenties had a kid's toy.

"I also like those shorts," he said. "I couldn't agree more."

I turned back to Vincent. "What do you mean?"

"It says 'juicy' on the back."

"Oh God." My face heated. "I didn't have anything else to wear. I got these when I was in high school. A lot of girls wore them at the time and I caved to peer pressure. I should've thrown them out."

He grinned. "I'm glad you didn't. Suits you well."

Hoping to move on to a less embarrassing topic, I picked up my bird and brought it back to the desk. "On the other hand, I'm never going to throw this out."

"Why do you have a plush penguin?"

I squeezed the soft rainbow beak, posing its adorable face for Vincent. "It's a puffin. It looks like the offspring of a penguin and a parrot if they ever mated. I used to be obsessed with them when I was like five. My parents got me this during a trip to the museum.

That was back when I had a better relationship with them. I'm not as into puffins now but this guy still has a lot of sentimental value."

"I can see why you like it. It's cute."

"Well I'm glad you and Mr. Waddles get along." I wiggled its nubby feet at Vincent. "His approval of you means a lot to me."

Vincent smiled in a way that was both charming and cute. If only I had a plush version of him to snuggle with on nights when he was away on business.

"Spunky on the outside, soft on the inside. You're quite the combination."

He continued as if another thought just occurred to him. "I know I've said this before. But thinking about you is making it difficult to concentrate on business. I don't expect you to understand but it's hard to focus on work when you've got an erection."

"Well. . . I don't know what to say." I really didn't because I'd never had an erection before but I could at least imagine the dilemma. I offered the first suggestion that came to mind. "Why don't you just watch porn like a regular guy?"

His brows knotted and his lips frowned. "Wouldn't work. You make porn look bad." He opened his mouth to say something further but closed his eyes and sighed deeply instead.

"Something's bothering you. What's wrong?" I asked.

His elbow on the desk, he ran a hand through his wavy hair but stopped halfway so that he rested the side of his head in his palm. He looked weary. "I wished we didn't have sex."

Nerves shot through my system and my grip on Mr. Waddles tightened. Why would he say such a terrible thing? Was it because I dumped my baggage on him and now he regretted being involved with me?

"What? Why?"

"Cause it made me want you more. I can't stop thinking about it. You in a blindfold. Your gorgeous body. . . It's so damn frustrating being so far away from you."

Relief washed over me like a cold shower in this summer weather. "You scared me for a second there. I thought you were going to say you didn't like the sex."

"I don't like how much I liked it. I'm dangerously close to cutting this trip short to come back to Manhattan. I'm not sure how much longer I can go. I think I might be addicted to you."

I felt his pain. Over the past two days, I'd constantly thought about him and our multiple sex sessions at his place. It had been distracting—something I welcomed given the drama of my ex lurking in the background; Vincent was a much needed diversion. But most of all, it made me realize how far I'd fallen for him in such a short time. It was frightening and thrilling—knowing he was feeling the same way about me made it less scary.

I had an idea.

"Maybe this will help," I said as I placed Mr. Waddles on the far end of the desk away from me. I released my hair from its ponytail and let my locks drape around my shoulders. I shook my head to give my hair the voluminous and sexy look I'd seen in commercials. Then I smiled seductively at him.

He straightened in his chair. "You have my attention."

I undid the top button of my shirt then the next two, enticing him with a view of my black bra beneath and an eyeful of scandalous cleavage. The nurturing side of me wanted to heal his pain.

"Mmmm," he murmured.

"Like what you see?" I teased. His desire for me always gave me a thrill.

He nodded slowly. "I want to see more."

I looked down at my chest. My breasts were nearly fully exposed. For some odd reason, I'd thought the ample skin I was already showing would be enough for him. But Vincent wasn't like any other men; I'd forgotten whose sex drive I was dealing with.

"I'm not sure," I said, hesitantly.

He smiled wickedly. "Let me see those gorgeous tits."

Showing cleavage was one thing, exposing full-on nipples was another. I couldn't help recalling a spate of stories in the media recently about a misbehaving senator sending naked pictures of himself to his mistress and those images getting leaked on the internet. I wasn't a senator, but I still had a reputation I needed to protect. The bad part of the internet was anything that got on there would be around forever.

I glanced at my door handle. Riley was likely in dream land and even if she wasn't, my door was still locked. I didn't know how safe it was on Vincent's end. "What if someone walks in on you? Or how do I know you're not recording this? I don't want my chest all over the internet."

"I'm in my hotel room right now. No one's coming in. Trust me, I'm not going to record this but every inch of your beautiful skin is going to be seared into my memory." His finger touched his temple. "I'm going to keep the image of your luscious breasts all to myself."

"I don't know. . . I'm not in the habit of doing internet camera shows. The idea makes me feel a little vulnerable."

His brows narrowed into sharp lines. I knew that look. It was the same one he got whenever he was in the middle of conducting serious business. He was thinking. Hard.

"Here, I'll expose myself. We'll both do it. I'm trusting you not to record this. I have a lot to lose if this gets out."

I thought about what the headlines would say: Billionaire exposes penis to wealth manager. Cock grows while stock shrinks.

Exposing himself was a huge risk for him, which demonstrated how much he wanted to see me naked. Even for a risk-taker like Vincent, I realized this kind of vulnerability meant a lot.

"Umm. . . okay I guess. You first," I said, unsure whether he was bluffing or serious. If he didn't do it, I wouldn't either.

The corners of his lips curved upward. "A dare? I usually go by 'ladies first' but you've given me something to work with so I'll make an exception."

He aimed the camera down to his lap, where I saw the front of his slacks tented. He was hard already? Just from that small amount of skin I showed him? My belly fluttered at the sight of the bulging fabric. Was he really going to do this?

I watched with bated breath as one of his hands gripped the black belt at his waist while the other tugged on the silver buckle to loosen the tightness. The leather arched into his palm and with a controlled jerk he drew two elegant prongs from their fitted holes. He pulled the tapered end of the belt through the rigid frame of the buckle, the band first being resistant but then sliding easily, yielding to the demand of his fingers. A few more inches, and the belt wrapping his powerfully trim waist was freed. He released the two separated ends and let them hang lazily in his lap. He wasn't exposed yet but I still felt the familiar tingles of excitement laced with arousal ripple through my body.

I marveled at how such a small gesture could inflame my senses. I wouldn't have believed it if not for the pulsing between my thighs reminding me how turned on I was becoming.

His hands were working quickly and my mind and body needed time to catch up with each titillating movement.

Once he unhooked the clasp on his slacks, he moved his fingers to his fly and paused.

"I know how you like it slow," he purred.

He slowly drew the zipper down and peeled the flaps of his pants back, exposing his dark boxer-briefs. Here it comes, I thought, my pulse beating quickly. He reached into the front opening, curled his fingers around the bulge hiding beneath, and pulled his cock into plain view. He released his hand and it stood erect on its own, the bulbous tip staring back at me, flushed with anger.

My hand flew to the base of my neck and my breath caught. How could a cock be so savage-looking and beautiful at once? And why was I getting so turned-on just by the sight of him?

I'd watched soft-core porn on a few occasions. While it was nice, it never became a habit. I didn't think the visual stimulation was strong enough. However, watching Vincent undress and touch himself could change that opinion.

He raised the camera back to his face. "Your turn, Kristen."

I gulped. He'd followed through on his part so now I had to. I started to wish the glass of water I'd brought to my bedroom had been spiked with alcohol. Prickles ran across my skin. Was it getting hotter in here again?

Nervously, my hands moved to the next button on my shirt and were preparing to undo it when he interrupted me.

"Do it on the bed."

Okay... sure...

Pliant to his command, I straightened from my chair and padded softly to the bed. I tried a few different seductive positions, but couldn't figure out one that I felt was both comfortable and sexy. I'd never done this before and it turned out to be harder than I anticipated. "How do you want me?"

"Kneel down on the bed with your knees apart. Straighten your hips. Don't sit back on your heels."

His instructions were oddly detailed and precise. I briefly wondered if he'd done this cyber-show thing before and if so, with who. But the impatience in his words didn't give me a lot of time to think, instead they spurred my actions. He knew what he wanted from me and I was eager to please him.

I unbuttoned the next button, then the next. I wasn't sure if I was doing it in an alluring way or not but I saw the desire in his face grow after each button was freed.

"You're so beautiful, Kristen," he said, as if reading my insecurity. "You have nothing to be self-conscious about. Everything you do is sexy."

Finally I pulled my blouse away from my chest and then off my shoulders, intending to slip the garment from my arms.

"Easy. Take your time," he said in a low rasp, eyes intense and unblinking. "Let me enjoy you."

I slowly finished removing my shirt and dropped it to the bed beside me. My pulse was beating rapidly and my stomach was a bundle of coils. I was still in the kneeling position he liked but now only in my bra and shorts. How far was this going to go?

"You're making me so hard, Kristen."

Wasn't he already hard? How could he be even harder? Curious to see my effect on him, I asked, "Can you show me?"

He aimed his camera downward and I saw his cock again. It was somehow firmer, longer, and more savage-looking than before. A faint trace of precum made the tip glisten. A surge of arousal ran through me.

He then adjusted the camera and scooted his chair backward so that both his face and lap were on screen.

"Can you see it? Can you see how hard you make me?" he growled. He brought one hand down to his lap and fisted his member. He began slowly stroking himself, eagerness making him forget to lube his palm. I was shocked he was masturbating in front of me. This wasn't just a camera show anymore; this was turning into cyber-sex. Fast.

I'd always thought the idea was silly—two people telling each other what they'd like to be doing to the other and each performing the action on themselves. It seemed more masturbation than sex, which didn't seem very appealing. But the deepening ache in my loins disagreed.

I'd never watched a guy jerk-off before and the sight of Vincent doing it, made me a little curious and a lot aroused. Although his strokes were slow and short, he was rougher with himself than I would be with him.

"I can see it."

"Touch your tits as I touch my cock. Make me harder."

Emboldened by the sight of his arousal, I began rubbing my breasts over the bra for him, pushing them up and squeezing them together in suggestive motions. It felt natural and sexy.

He grunted approval.

I reached across my chest and undid the clasp. I pulled the bra off and laid it gently on top of my blouse but covered my breasts with my hands.

"No hands, Kristen," he commanded, impatience and lust dripping from his voice.

I was getting into this, not just turned-on but also having fun. I was doing something risky I'd never done before and I was beginning to see the appeal. It was making me bold in a way I'd never expected. Having Vincent giving me orders for his pleasure made me want to do the same for him.

"You first, Vincent. No hands."

"What?" He continued pumping himself while drinking in the sight of me.

I wagged my finger playfully at him. "You heard me. No touching yourself until I say so."

His fist stopped its motions and he furled his brows. "Why?"

I smiled. "I want to tease you like you enjoy teasing me."

"Are you trying to kill me?"

My smile widened. "You're so melodramatic."

"Damn it Kristen, you can't expect me to watch you touching yourself and not allow me to jerk-off. That's like putting a bone in front of a dog and asking him to sit still. It's cruel."

I was amused by his analogy. The image of Vincent Sorenson on a leash at my beck and call certainly had its appeal. "Be a good boy and you'll get your reward. Okay?"

He grumbled then sighed heavily, his cock still hard as ever. "I don't like it... but fine. I'll do it for you."

"Thank you." Seeing him comply, I slowly removed my hands from across my chest, allowing my breasts to be fully exposed to the camera.

His jaw clenched and his cock twitched making me both fascinated and aroused by his male anatomy.

I began rubbing my breasts in circles, taking time to caress the hardened tips. I was feeling desirable from the yearning in his gaze.

Spotting the glass of water by my bedside, I reached over, pulled out an ice cube, and watched his eyes widen. The cold sensation between my fingers felt good in the warm air. I raised the cube to my chest and sucked in a deep breath when the cold touched my nipple. A surge of arousal heated my core and I squeezed my thighs together. I slowly circled the ice around the hardened tip, relishing the frigid bite on my fevered skin.

Vincent was chewing his bottom lip so hard I thought he'd draw blood. "You're so seductive, Kristen. I'd give my own two thumbs just to taste you."

He clenched his fists by his side, straining against the desire to touch himself. His discipline was admirable and his desperate desire was making me scorch.

"I want my tongue and mouth all over your breasts. I want to nibble gently on those hardened tits," he grunted. "Pinch them for me."

I placed the ice back in the glass and did as he asked, imagining Vincent's sinful mouth in place of my hands. Soft moans escaped my lips as I pinched my nipples and tweaked them a little roughly like I knew he would do if he were here. It was the perfect mix of pleasure and a slight edge of pain.

"You're doing so well," he said, voice straining with lust.

"So are you," I cooed, seeing his palms on his thighs, fingernails digging into the skin in resistance. His usual calm expression looked tortured.

"You don't know how difficult this is for me."

"Never had to wait for something you wanted?"

"Never wanted anything so damn much."

Still in the kneeling position Vincent liked, I slipped my fingers into the waistband of my shorts and slid both the shorts and the panties underneath down. I had to lean back to kick them off giving him a full view of myself, which I knew he appreciated. Fully naked before the camera, I resumed the familiar kneeling position.

"Your body's driving me insane."

"What would you do if you were here? Right now?"

"I'd use my tongue to take care of that throbbing clit of yours. It needs special attention."

I began rubbing easy circles around my clit with my fingers, imagining Vincent's expert tongue on that sensitive spot. "Feels good, Vincent."

"I can imagine it. The sweet taste of your cunt on my lips." He licked his lips decadently. "My mouth's watering just thinking about it. That's what you do to me, Kristen."

"Mmhmm. . . I like your mouth on me. It feels so good." I increased the pace of my fingers on my clit.

"You're so greedy. I see it in your eyes. I know you want more. Put two fingers inside yourself. That's my tongue burying inside you."

Without skipping a beat, I obeyed his command, thrusting two fingers into my wet, aching sex. "Ohhh, Vincent." My other hand began rubbing my breasts. It was as much for his pleasure as it was for mine.

I wasn't sure how long I was going to make him wait to pleasure himself. He looked like he was about to explode in more ways than one.

"You can touch yourself now, Vincent," I said, breaths uneven. "I think I've teased you long enough."

He gritted his teeth. "No. You need to come first. I have to see the look on your face when you come thinking about me. You're going to come first, then we're going to come together."

"Yes," I breathed, feeling my orgasm approaching dangerously fast. I hadn't even had one yet and he was telling me I was going to have two. I would've doubted my body could manage such a feat if Vincent hadn't made me come twice in quick succession Monday night. The idea of having two orgasms made my mind swirl and the pleasure from my fingers intensified.

I stared into his gaze, mesmerized by what I saw. He wasn't just drinking in my image with those intense brown eyes; he was ravaging me in his thoughts and I could almost feel it.

"I'm getting close, Vincent," I panted.

"I see it. Do it. But don't close your eyes. Watch me as I watch you come."

My fingers found a sensitive spot deep inside. They focused on that one area, increasing their pace as pleasure ripped through my body. I could feel myself approaching the edge fast, the force from Vincent's gaze pushing me to a perilous cliff.

"Oh God!" My hand gripped my breast as my orgasm slammed into me. I watched him through tear-filled eyes; watched his dark gaze burrow into mine, his pained expression turn desolate. I heard him release a strangled cry as a bead of semen erupted from the tip of his cock. I thought he would reach to shield it but his hands remained obediently on his thighs. Left untouched, the cum trickled along the underside of his erection. It wasn't a full release, but it was more than just precum.

It then occurred to me that he'd come without any touch—just the sight of me was enough.

"Jesus, Kristen. You see what you do to me? You see what you do to my god damn cock? You make me lose control."

Still a little blurry-eyed, I said, "I see it, Vincent. It's so hot. It's making me want to touch myself again." While still in my post-climax bliss, I began to rub my clit again. It was a little numb but it still felt good and the pleasure was getting better by the second.

He growled approval. "Don't stop. I'm going to touch myself now. I'm going to imagine that sweet cunt of yours wrapping around me tightly." He took his right hand and gathered the cum along the underside of his member and swirled it around the length of the shaft and the surface of the head for lubrication.

"This," he said holding up his hand, fingers together and half-way curled with thumb across the top, "Can't compare to you. But we're both going to use our imaginations. Watch yourself sit on my lap. "

He slowly brought the tunnel he made with his hand down to his lap where it hovered right above his erection. I watched with heated anticipation as the soft but firm opening gave a little as he slid his fist over the head, wrapping the girth tightly. The explicit image made my body recall how it felt to have him enter me for the first time. The size and fullness was mind-scrambling.

He wrapped his fingers around his member and began smoothly stroking himself while bucking his hips forward with each movement to penetrate the tight enclosure.

The detailed visual made it easier for me to imagine myself spread across his lap, eagerly bouncing up and down as I savored the delicious experience of being impaled by Vincent. I timed the thrusts of my fingers into myself with his strokes, making the situation seem more real.

As the pleasure grew, my knees began to fatigue so I leaned back, supporting my weight on one elbow with my legs spread wide.

"I like that position even better." He grinned.

He continued pumping his cock at an insistent but leisurely pace, both of us enjoying the physical pleasure and visual stimulation. Our breathing was stuttered and we were both sweating.

I was starting to feel a bit lightheaded from the heat and dizzying eroticism so I reached over to my nightstand to take a sip from my glass of water.

"Getting hot?" he growled.

"You know it," I panted, fingers still working inside my pussy. "Air conditioning broke earlier today."

"What if you took some of that water and poured it on yourself?"

I giggled at his distinctly male suggestion. "And get my bed all wet? I'm all for your creative ideas but I think that one's a little impractical. I don't want to sleep in soggy sheets."

"It combines my two favorite things. Water. And you."

"I'm sorry. What can I do to make it up to you?"

"Surprise me."

I thought about what else I could do to stimulate him. Then I remembered I had my vibrator in my nightstand. Nobody except Riley knew I had it but after seeing Vincent pleasure himself, I felt comfortable showing it to him. I leaned over and pulled the smooth silver rod out.

I held it up for him. "This is smaller than you. But we'll both use our imaginations," I said, mimicking his words.

His pleasure-tortured expression became laced with fascination.

I switched the toy on and brought the buzzing tip to my entrance. Immediately, the vibrations on my sensitive folds surged through me, fueling my arousal. I used it to massage my clit for a little while then eager for a feeling of fullness, I thrust it inside myself. My head tilted back and I moaned. Cries of ecstasy escaped my throat, some coherent, some not, but I was sure I heard Vincent's name several times.

"I guess this means I win the bet," he said with dark lust, breaths heavy and fist pumping hard. Beads of sweat dotted his brows and a few strands of his wavy hair were matted to his cheeks. "You're masturbating while thinking about me."

"If you recall, I never took that bet," I replied, barely able to catch my breath or my mind for that matter. I licked my lips because all the moaning had made them dry. "And if I did, I would've lost anyway when you called my work phone that day."

"I knew it." His mouth curved into a wicked smile. "Your voice gets this tiny rasp when you're turned-on."

My face grew shamefully hot but embarrassment wasn't enough to stop my hands from shoving the vibrator in and out of myself. If anything, it fueled the heat burning in my core. "No it doesn't."

But then I heard it.

"Just like that." He laughed. Then abruptly groaned from the stimulation. "Just like that. . ." His voice trailed off in a whispered moan.

The erotic sound of his cries vibrated through me making me tremble and clench tighter around the silver cock inside me. Like before, I timed the thrusts of the toy with Vincent's strokes. The pleasure was stronger than it was when I was using my fingers and I could already feel myself approaching another climax.

"Come for me, Kristen. I'm right there with you."

Vincent's strokes grew frantic and urgent and so did my thrusts. It was just me before, but now we were both now edging toward a cliff.

"Kristen, you're making me lose it," he cried.

The vibrations from his voice combined with the vibrations from the toy drove me over the edge. "Vincent, I'm coming!"

"Fuck Fuck Fuck."

Right before my world darkened, I saw him desperately try to cup the tip of his cock with his hand and semen bursting violently from the gaps between his fingers onto his lap and keyboard. He howled a choked cry of both pain and relief as my eyes rolled back into my head from my own orgasm. I heard his heavy panting and soft groans through my speakers as I laid on the bed, feeling like I couldn't move.

After a few minutes, he spoke. "Jesus, Kristen. I need to get a towel because of you. Maybe a new laptop."

I'd recovered enough energy to prop myself halfway up. My limbs still felt wobbly but I was eager to look at him. I smiled. "I'm sorry. I guess I owe you one."

"Don't be. I'd buy a new laptop every day if I could see you touching yourself."

"You're so sweet." I grinned.

"I don't think Mr. Waddles approves of me anymore after what I had you do."

I laughed and glanced at the plush puffin on my desk where I left him. Lifeless eyes hid recent trauma. "He'll get over it. I enjoyed it. You might say I found the experience thrilling."

Vincent winked at me then got up from his chair to grab a towel. I got a peek at his firm backside which made me consider going for round three, but my boneless body protested. I went to the bathroom and quickly washed up. Moments later, Vincent returned to the screen in his boxer-briefs and began cleaning up the evidence of our session.

"So have you done this before?" I asked as I tugged on fresh pajamas and took a seat at my desk. "You know, this whole cyber sex thing?"

"This was a first for me. I wouldn't take a risk like this unless it was worth it."

"You could've fooled me, it sounded like you knew exactly what you were doing."

"Sometimes you just follow your instincts," he said, smiling.

A yawn bubbled up to my mouth and I tried to stifle it with my hand.

"Are you going be able to sleep?" he asked. "I would've liked to be there to keep you warm, but unfortunately we're apart."

"I appreciate the thought but I don't think I'm going to have any trouble falling asleep tonight." My hand covered another yawn. "I think you wore me out."

"I told you I can be very demanding."

"If only I'd known what you meant back then at your office."

"Would you still have agreed to be my point-of-contact?"

The corners of my lips rose. "I would've thought twice if I knew I'd be masturbating on camera for you a few weeks later. I don't think I would've been so keen on that idea."

"It's a good thing you didn't know then." He gave a sly grin then continued. "I can see that you're tired. We'll have plenty of time to catch up this weekend."

I touched my fingers to my lips and then kissed the camera with it. "Night, Vincent."

"Goodnight, Kristen."

Chapter Thirteen

After the intense video chat session the night before, Thursday was remarkably uneventful. Vincent had been tied up with business all day and night so we didn't Skype again. He said he'd make it up to me by taking me somewhere special this weekend. After flying on his private jet to St. Thomas, I could only imagine what "special" meant.

Friday rolled around and I was excited because Vincent was returning to Manhattan. I'd been busy with research on a new lead for Carl. It was a woman who had recently made a fortune from creating a shoe that could easily change from heels to flats. It was one of those genius ideas that makes you slap your forehead and say, "Why didn't I think of that?"

I didn't slap my forehead though, instead crinkled it as I diligently researched her background. If there's anything I've learned from my time with Vincent, it's that successful people win by playing by their own rules. I was too busy trying to follow other people's rules to make up my own. And I was okay with that, for now.

I looked at the extra duffel bag I had set next to my filing cabinet. This morning Vincent had texted me saying he was going to pick me up after work and I should pack a swimsuit and extra pair of clothes. It probably meant we were going somewhere tropical again. Of course, I didn't complain.

My eyes were on the clock on the lower right corner of the computer monitor, watching the last few minutes of the work day tick by painfully. I felt like a kid waiting for recess. In addition to the items Vincent asked me to bring, I packed something extra. Sexy lingerie.

I waited for him at the usual spot behind the office building as he pulled his Camry to the curb. I opened the passenger door and hopped in.

He smiled and I smiled. We locked eyes then locked lips in a passionate embrace. We both missed one another and the kiss said it better than words ever could.

"You ready?" he asked. He was wearing a t-shirt and khaki shorts like the first time I met him in Cape Town. I'd almost gotten used to seeing him in a dress clothes so the effect was striking. Definitely sexy casual.

"So ready."

He flicked the heart-shaped pendant around my neck. "I like how it looks on you."

I glanced down at it. The deadly weapon looked rather cute. It certainly matched my outfit. "I've gotten a few compliments so far. You have good taste."

We drove off and I settled into the feeling of being physically next to Vincent again. I watched the buildings and people pass by outside the window and periodically stole glances at Vincent's beautiful features.

"Not going to ask me where we're going this time?" He smirked.

"I figured it's somewhere with water. But I'm eager to be surprised."

"Seems like I'm rubbing off on you."

"Maybe." I grinned. "Although I'd much prefer you rubbing on me."

It was his turn to grin. "Don't worry. I assure you there will be plenty of that this weekend." He gently patted my thigh to console me.

Before long, we arrived at the airport and stepped out onto the familiar tarmac. Hand-in-hand, we boarded his private plane.

The pilot was the same middle-aged gentleman who flew the plane when we went to St. Thomas but this time there was also a flight attendant. She was an elderly woman who introduced herself as Nancy and ushered Vincent and me to a row of three seats in the rear cabin. We had rows of seats in front and back of us which provided a bit of privacy while the space between rows were big enough for ample leg room. After stowing away our bags, she took a seat at the front cabin near the cockpit, preparing for departure.

During take-off and twenty minutes into the flight, Vincent's hand seemed to never leave my leg, heating my thigh and running light touches along the skin with his fingertips.

My gaze was fixed out the window watching as the city below us became tinier. It was still hard to believe I was going for another weekend trip via private jet.

"Like the view?" Vincent asked as he caressed my thigh, his voice silk and his scent delicious.

"I like the feel as well," I said, eyeing his hand petting me.

"You remind me of a cat. Feisty at first but once you earn their affection they can be very receptive. Plus, you like birds."

"I'm flattered. Didn't figure you for a cat person though." I looked at him curiously. "Cats are great but I think I'm more of a dog lover. I had a yellow labrador when I was growing up. They're loyal, obedient, protective, always smiling at you." I touched the tip of his sharp nose with my finger and he smiled at me. "You remind me of a dog."

"I guess that's fair." His forearm rested over mine on the armrest and he began massaging the sensitive skin between my fingers with his own. "But don't expect me to hump your leg."

I laughed. "I wouldn't put it past you."

"I wouldn't put it past me either." He pinched the bottom edge of my gray pencil skirt. "Especially when you're wearing a skirt like this. I don't know what your bosses are thinking allowing you to wear something like this to work."

My face heated. "It's a typical work skirt, Vincent. Are you saying the dress standard for women in the professional world is unacceptable to you?" I teased. "Maybe they shouldn't allow men with your libido to go to work with women around."

"I don't care what other women wear. I care what you wear and if anyone else is thinking about these legs." He affectionately patted my thigh with his palm.

"Well then," I said, raising my brow at him. "You'll probably be pleased to hear my new client lead is a woman."

His hand on my leg tightened. "Only if you don't plan on pinching her nipples."

"Oh?" I said curiously. "I would've thought that would be a turn-on for a man with your sex drive."

"Turn it around. Have her pinch your nipples, then it'd be different."

I frowned. "How is that any different?"

"You'd be the one moaning."

Shock hit my system followed by a heated ache. Vincent was already a walking sex magnet but the time I spent apart from him made him like a sex vortex. This was going to be a long plane ride.

"Don't worry. The only client nipples I've pinched are yours and I plan to keep it that way."

"Hopefully it's not the last time you pinch them."

"So you like me pinching your nipples? I thought that was only something women liked to do and men were indifferent to."

"I like it. Gives me a charge."

I laughed. I could imagine most guys being embarrassed about admitting they enjoyed having their nipples tweaked but Vincent was very comfortable with his sexuality—at least in front of me. The confidence was alluring.

I lightly squeezed his nipple between my fingers and he made a soft groan. "You've opened my mind."

"Well maybe I can open you to other things as well. . ." His hand ventured between my thighs and began creeping up beneath my skirt.

I didn't resist but when his hand came dangerously close to my pussy, I nervously scanned the cabin. "Vincent, we don't have privacy.

There's the pilot and the flight attendant at the front of the plane," I said, gesturing toward the cockpit. Peeking my head over the row of seats in front of us, I could see Nancy seated near the emergency exit reading a magazine.

"So?"

"So, I don't want to do anything that would embarrass us."

"I'm not embarrassed."

"You're not embarrassed if Nancy sees us—you know. . ."

"She has grandchildren." He leaned closer so that his lips were grazing my cheek while he spoke. "She knows what happens between two people when there's sexual attraction this intense." His hand slipped further up my skirt and brushed over my panties against my clit.

I desperately sucked air into my lungs to stop myself from moaning.

"Are you embarrassed? Of us?" he whispered.

My eyes darted to the front of the cabin. Nancy was still reading her magazine. "A little embarrassed of doing this in public. But I do like you touching me."

"Relax, Kristen," Vincent said softly. "We both know this flight is too long to go without us touching one another. We won't get caught if we're careful. We just have to keep quiet."

His hand found an opening in my panties and his fingers slipped inside. He ran one probing finger along my cleft, sliding up and down slowly. Insistent pressure fired raw nerves on sensitive flesh. I hadn't felt his touch in a week but the need was so great it felt like months.

I licked my lips.

"Just say the word, and I'll stop," he crooned. His finger found my entrance and dipped inside.

I bit my bottom lip. Stopping was the last thing I wanted. If anything, I was about ready to join the mile-high club.

I tried bucking against his fingers but the seat belt restrained my movements. Moving my hips forward gained slightly more penetration. But it wasn't enough.

Vincent kept his thrusts at the same depth.

"More," I breathed.

His thrusts became deeper and more insistent.

I tried stifling the moan threatening to burst from my throat but Vincent's hands were too confident, too skilled. I wasn't going to hold on. The last of my will broken, my fingers curled around the ends of the armrests. Eyes closed and head tilted back against the headrest, my mouth opened to scream.

Vincent's lips sealed over mine and I moaned into his mouth. His tongue dipped in, giving slow licks against my own, pacifying my quivering tongue.

The intercom buzzed. "Passengers, we're at our cruising altitude. You can remove your seatbelts now," the pilot said.

The lighted seat belt sign dinged then turned off.

I unbuckled myself and was preparing to thrust my hips into his hand when he grabbed me by the shoulder and spun me around so I was laying flat with my back across the row of seats. Before I could protest, he had my wrists restrained above my head with the seat belt straps. A position I was intimately familiar with since the night at his place.

With a grunt, he pulled off my skirt and panties along with it, discarding them beneath the seats in front of us. I gasped in horror, realizing that I'd never put them back on in time should someone stop by to check on us. They were as good as thrown out the emergency exit.

He dipped his head between my legs and went to work on my throbbing clit with his tongue. Soft flicks combined with fast and slow movements.

My breathing became rapid and shallow. I curled my toes and struggled against my wrist restraints, fighting off the cries of pleasure threatening to escape my mouth.

While his tongue continued firing sensitive nerves, he began thrusting his finger inside me. His slow back and forth thrusts became fast twisting and crooking motions. His fingertip found a delicious spot and I shuddered.

Next thing I knew, he placed his other hand on my pelvis below the belly button and pressed inward firmly. The pressure on that part of my body was unfamiliar.

"What are you doin—" I asked, but his actions answered before I could finish the question.

My hips instinctively curved upward under the force of his hand and his insistent fingers massaging a sensitive spot inside me hit a bullseye.

"Oh shit," I cried, pleasure tearing through my body. I closed my eyes and bit down hard on my lip to stifle another outburst. My hands fought against their restraints but it was deliciously futile.

How the hell did he do that? Vincent apparently knew my body better than even I did.

He gripped my thighs roughly and whispered gentle hushes into my pulsing clit. "Shh. . . quiet. . . so good," he groaned softly. Then he buried his face in my cleft, tongue penetrating my folds and nose rubbing my clit. He growled hungrily into my depths, tongue dipping in and out greedily, leaving no nerve untouched. "So fucking good," he bellowed, the low vibrations rumbling through me, making me clench all over to stop myself from shaking.

I was careening dangerously toward a second climax. Just a little more and he'd push me over the edge.

Then his tongue stopped.

"Keep going," I whispered fiercely.

He pulled his head up from between my legs and looked at me, wagging his finger. The gesture seemed oddly familiar. "Uh-uh."

My body was still hot and thrumming madly. "Please Vincent, I need release."

He smiled from leg to leg. "Payback, Kitten. For the Skype session. You'll have to wait."

I was too frustrated and horny to consider the implications of him calling me a pet name for the first time. He pulled away and I tried to rub my thighs together to finish what he started, but he caught my ankles with a firm grip. "Patience. I don't want you spoiling your need. I have a lot more pleasure for you tonight."

I groaned. I'd never wanted to climax more than I wanted to now. Never experienced the thrill of sex in public, of riding the edge of being caught and getting away with being bad. Never been driven to such desperate heights of pleasure. Never been denied the release raging in every bone in my body. And I never imagined uttering the words that were flying off the tip of my tongue. "I'm not a baby, Vincent. I know what my body needs. And it needs a thirty-thousand-feet-in-the-air sky-shattering orgasm right about now."

His expression softened. "I was too harsh. I left you too high. I'm sorry, Kristen. Let me help you come down slowly." He released my ankles and dipped his head back down between them. He gently tongued my clit and folds, easing the ache he had left there.

I moaned softly and closed my eyes at the delicious sensation.

A ding sounded and a light came on above our heads. I quickly realized I must've accidentally hit the flight attendant button with my hands. I heard Nancy close her magazine and begin walking toward the rear cabin. Panic swept through me. I was naked from the waist down and there would be no way I could pull my skirt and panties on in time even if I could slip my hands from my restraints.

Vincent moved from between my legs and casually reached into a drawer beneath the seat. Nancy rounded the row in front of us just as Vincent pulled a blanket over me, covering me from the waist down.

"How are you two doing? Can I get you anything?"

Vincent sat coolly in his seat, my feet resting on his lap beneath the blanket covering us.

"Kristen had to lie down because she's not feeling well. Do we have anything that'll make her feel better?"

"Oh my dear. Your face is all red. You look like you're burning up. I'll get you some water and motion sickness tablets."

"Thank you," I said, holding my hands behind my head, hoping my hair hid the fact that my wrists were bound together with seat belt straps.

By the time Nancy returned, I had slipped on my skirt and panties and sat back up.

"Oh you're looking better already. Here's the water and tablets."

I popped the tablets in my mouth despite not needing them and took a swig of water. "I'm feeling much better, thank you Nancy."

"My pleasure. Can I get you two anything else? More blankets?"

"We're good for now. Thank you," Vincent said. Nancy returned to her seat near the cockpit where she resumed reading her magazine.

Vincent turned over to me. "Who's the one not being careful now?"

"That was an accident."

"You going to make it until we land?" he asked, hand possessively caressing my thigh again.

"It's not like I have a choice do I? Unless I want to appear airsick again."

"It'll help if you try to get some sleep. I have a feeling you won't be getting much of that once we arrive at our destination."

Chapter Fourteen

I managed to catch a light nap before we landed. Once the plane came to a stop, I stepped out into a cool breeze and seventy-degree weather. It was approaching evening but the sun was still out, illuminating the small airport and tropical scenery in the distance.

"We're on an island in the Caribbean called St. Lucia," Vincent said, hand at my back ushering me toward the terminal.

"Seems you're fond of the Caribbean."

"It's close to New York City where I spend a lot of my time nowadays. But this isn't our final destination."

This place seemed as good as any for an ideal weekend getaway. "Where are we going?"

"It's close by but we'll have to take a boat from here."

We hopped into a rented jeep and took a short drive to a harbor.

Vincent led us to a sleek boat with white hull and red trim. Letters along the side read "Pier Pleasure".

"Clever name," I commented.

He smiled. "Took me a while to come up with it. It was either that or 'Playbuoy'." He nudged me gently to indicate he was teasing.

"Glad you didn't choose the latter."

I didn't know anything about boats but I could tell it was built for speed. The controls didn't appear complicated—it wasn't much more than a throttle and a steering wheel—but the boat had a very big, very loud engine. The way we shot out as soon as I had put my life vest on and sat down next to Vincent told me handling this thing wasn't a job for amateurs.

He slowed the boat to a cruising pace as we headed off toward an island in the distance with the sun setting in the horizon casting red and orange hues on the deep blue waters. I wondered what he had in store for us tonight.

The boat came to a stop and he tied it to the dock jutting out from the shore.

"So what is this place?" I asked as I stepped off the boat onto the wooden planks.

"It's my private island."

"You own an entire island?"

"It's not that large, just a few miles in each direction. Not big enough for a runway. It's my personal spot to get away from everything."

First St. Thomas then St. Lucia. I was starting to see a pattern. "So what do you call it? St. Vincent?"

He laughed. "That's actually the name of a real island just south of here. The people on St Lucia call this place "île aux oiseaux", which is French for "Bird Island". There's a lot of pretty, exotic birds that live here."

"Interesting."

"Unfortunately, there aren't any puffins."

"That's a deal breaker," I teased.

His lips curved into a grin. "You're high maintenance. But worth it."

"I was just kidding," I said, playfully nudging him. "I really appreciate everything you've done. Surprising me on our dates. Being discreet, being supportive. I want you to know that all those things mean a lot to me."

His grin widened. "So have I changed your opinion about me?"

"What was my opinion before?"

"You tell me."

I sighed. "Okay, I'll admit I thought you were a bit of a sex-crazed playboy who was more hands-on with his recreation than with his business."

"And now?"

"The sex-crazed part hasn't changed."

"Maybe it has for you." He winked.

"Maybe," I mused. "I will say I've wanted sex a lot more in these last few weeks than in the past few years—possibly ever."

"Good, 'cause we'll be having plenty this weekend."

"Okay." I smiled. My response sounded a little odd to my own ears considering I'd rebuffed his sexual advances only weeks ago but a lot had changed since then. I had no intention of taking my response back.

He led us across the beach to a path leading into the forest. Fortunately I only packed a small bag so it was easy to carry, otherwise it'd be ridiculous rolling luggage across sand and dirt. After walking for fifteen minutes, tall trees swishing in the breeze and birds chirping all around us, we reached a small cabin with smoke billowing from the chimney. The setup reminded me of an old fairy tale involving bears—except my hair was brown. If I saw a bowl of porridge inside I'd probably make Vincent eat it.

He opened the door and gestured inside. "Ladies first."

I stepped inside and was hit with the spicy smell of wood. It was like the spicy scent I loved to smell on Vincent but stronger. The exterior looked rough but the interior was refined with smooth hardwood floors, elegant furniture, and a stone fireplace at the back that was already lighted. The cabin was small and cozy with various pictures and objects lining the shelves to each side of the fireplace. It felt more like a home than his condo in NYC.

"Quite a setup you have here," I said, admiring the surroundings.

"Welcome to my home." He dropped his bag on the brown couch in front of the fireplace and looked at me for my reaction.

"It's beautiful and quaint. Did you build it yourself?"

He laughed. "Although I would've liked to, it would've taken forever. I had it built a year ago when I purchased this island. I come here often but when I'm away, I have someone come by and maintain the place or prepare the place before I arrive."

"You sure know how to vacation."

I wanted to look around the cabin more, particularly at the pictures he had, but Vincent wrapped his arm around my shoulder and said, "Come on, it's getting dark. I want to show you something."

I put down my bag next to his on the couch and followed him out of the cabin. He led us further into the forest and we eventually popped out onto another beach. There was a tent set up with standing torches lighting the path around it. When we got closer, I could see it was some sort of Arabian-looking tent with lush reddish-lavender drapery. It was open on the side facing the ocean, giving a scenic view of the rolling waves along the shore and the small silhouette of other islands in the distance. Inside was a blanketed floor and a sea of cushions with middle-eastern-inspired geometric designs on them. There was a fire pit in the center and a hole in the roof above it.

"Private island, romantic tent—I can see how this would be a hit with the ladies."

"Since you're the first lady I've shown this place to, you tell me. Am I getting lucky tonight?"

"Unless you tell me this is all fake and I'm actually on some kind of twisted reality show, you are definitely getting lucky tonight."

"Not going to play coy?" He grinned. "I like how you know what you want."

We took a seat on the soft blankets and just as I was about to relax, my stomach growled.

Vincent laughed. "That's a familiar sound."

"I can't help it. Sometimes my body just does what it wants."

"You have an amazing body." He reached over to an ice chest and opened it to reveal an assortment of meats and veggies inside. "Let's feed it."

We cooked shish kabobs over the fire and ate to our stomachs' content. By the time we finished, the sun had gone down and only the dim glow of the moon and the torches nearby provided light.

"I'm stuffed," I said patting my belly.

"Any room for dessert?"

"Does it include blindfolds?"

He smiled and shook his head. Then he pulled out a bowl of strawberries from the cooler along with a bottle of chocolate syrup.

"Yum yum," I said, licking my lips. "Chocolate-covered strawberries are always a good choice."

He picked a plump one up by the stem and doused the tip in rich chocolate. "Open wide."

I closed my eyes and opened my mouth wide.

"You're closing your eyes, Kristen. You don't have to."

"I want to, though. You taught me to isolate sensations and I like that."

I could hear him smile. Then I felt the strawberry enter my mouth and I bit into the soft flesh.

"Mmm. So good," I murmured between chews.

We took turns feeding one another with strawberries and before long, we had finished the batch. Vincent put the bowl back in the cooler and said, "It's dark. We should head back to the cabin."

He twisted at the waist to reach for the cooler lid and I tugged on his outstretched leg. "Wait, there's something else I want for dessert."

He gave me a puzzled look as I crawled toward him. Snaking between his legs, I grabbed his waist and began unzipping his shorts.

"What are you doing?" he asked, as I pulled down his zipper and kissed the bottom row of his stone abs. The muscles beneath were hard but the surface of his skin was softer than I'd expected.

"I want to taste you, Vincent," I purred.

He gripped my shoulders firmly but gently. "We're out in the open. Someone might see us."

Fingers in the waistband of his boxer-briefs, I paused. "I thought you said we were alone on this island."

"We are. But we're exposed. Ships pass by here. Let's go back to the cabin."

I yanked his pants and underwear down, freeing the stiff erection I knew would be there. I playfully slapped his cock, causing it to wobble side to side and making him groan. "You're not afraid of having sex on your plane with a flight attendant twenty feet away but you're afraid of having sex on your private island with no one around. Gimme a break."

"It's riskier here. They could snap photos and it'll be in the tabloids. I don't want you to have to deal with that."

"It's dark. I doubt there are ships and even if there are, I doubt they'd see us." His cock rested heavily on his belly and I licked the underside from the base to the tip.

He groaned, the vibration making my nipples tighten. His hands around my shoulders constricted. "Your employers could find out if there are pictures," he said, voice strained.

"They won't."

"Let's just go—"

I took him into my mouth, sucking his heated flesh vigorously like the most decadent lollipop I'd ever tasted. He gasped and groaned painfully, growing harder by the second. I scarcely registered his hands moving from my shoulders to my hair, conveniently pulling strands away from my face as I went down on him; I was too busy enjoying the fierce throbbing sensation in my mouth. It wasn't the first time I'd given oral, but it was the first time I'd given it to Vincent and I wanted it to be memorable for both of us.

I began rolling my tongue over the tip as I sucked him greedily.

"Oh. No. Kristen," he cried, biting off the words.

I gripped his hips and pulled myself deeper then shallower then deeper again in a smooth cadence, enjoying the hard fullness of him in my mouth. Saliva covered his cock making it slick and harder to grip. My lips tightened, clenching him stronger and with more pressure, each milking stroke tighter than the previous. Each of his male groans came more anguished than the last, turning me on intensely.

"Fuck, Kristen," he snarled. "Fuck it all."

His grip on my hair tightened and he began short hasty thrusts into my mouth, deeper than I had been taking him, but not far enough for me to gag. With his hand behind my head, gently guiding me and his hips pumping softly but urgently, I could feel him growing hotter, his need growing more desperate. The warm taste in my mouth became faintly salty, a distinct trace of his arousal. I thought he'd climax at any moment and I was ready to take him.

All of him.

He pulled me away, my lips making a popping sound when they released suction from his cock head. "I need to taste you," he growled.

In a frenzy of lust, he laid me on my back and tore off my shirt along with my skirt and panties, tossing everything behind him. Out of the corner of my eye, I saw my clothes accidentally land in the fire pit and burst into flames but heated lust overrode rational thought. If I had to walk around naked on Vincent's island, so be it.

Chest heaving, I spread my legs and he promptly positioned himself between them. He dipped his head and took one aching breast into his mouth, sucking and licking around the tip. He lightly pinched the tip between his teeth and pulled firmly. I gasped at the sensation, the ache in my chest traveling down between my thighs and making me clench my legs around his waist.

I saw him reach for the syrup and shake the bottle impatiently. He turned the nozzle upside down and began squirting chocolate across my chest. I gasped at the cool sensation. The first squiggles of chocolate were done haphazardly across my chest then he slowed down, making careful spirals around each tender breast. After putting the finishing touch on each tip, he cast the bottle aside and took a moment to admire his work.

With one finger, I swirled the chocolate around each tip, watching his eyes darken with lust.

His hands began plumping each breast. He dipped his head again and pulled one mound into his mouth, lapping up the chocolate, running long, easy licks along the syrup lines.

"Oh Vincent."

I arched my chest into him, relishing his hot mouth against my cool skin. He flicked the tender tip of my nipple with his tongue sending a heated shiver along my spine. I tilted my head back and moaned.

He ran patient but urgent kisses from my chest down to my thighs. Then he attacked my clit, flicking it with the tip of his tongue then lapping it with the full surface.

He lifted his head and pierced me with his dark gaze. "You've had this coming, Kristen," he growled. "You're too damn sexy."

Vincent reached into his pocket for a condom and quickly wrapped himself before his hips slammed into me at full force, penetrating me to the hilt, making me slide backwards on the blankets. I arched into him feeling too full and yet craving more at the same time. I watched the area where we were joined as he pulled back, every vicious inch sliding out, slick from my own wetness. I lifted my legs, spreading them further, encouraging him back to me. With only a primal grunt as warning, he drove forward again, entering me to the base, his balls slapping against my bottom. My fingernails dug into the sculpted flesh of his back and my teeth bit into the hard muscle of his chest. He cried wildly like an animal lost in heat.

"God, Kristen. You're too much."

I tried but couldn't form any coherent words. Only fervent moans tumbled from my trembling lips.

"I'm going to ravage you until our bodies can't move."

His filthy words sent me soaring; his thrusts sent me rolling like the waves on the shore. "Yes, Vincent," I cried desperately. "Take me. Take it all."

He pounded into me and I bucked into him. If a ship passed by and saw us, I didn't think I'd even care.

"I'm lost, Kristen. So. Fucking. Lost."

Passionate moans and painful cries filled the cool night air and the chatter of wildlife in the trees seemed to ebb and flow with the rhythm of our feverish bodies. We tumbled across a sea of blankets entwined at the hips, scattering pillows, chocolate syrup, and sand in every direction, making a mess of a carefully prepared arrangement.

The stars idly watched as we put on one hell of a show for them.

Chapter Fifteen

I woke up in daylight surrounded by warmth. Every muscle in my body felt sore but in a good way. A familiar spicy scent tickled my nose and I realized Vincent was holding me in his arms tight against his chest, his calm breaths against the back of my shoulder and the morning breeze a feathery touch to my skin. Though no longer hard, he was still inside me. We were wrapped in layers of velvety blankets beneath a purplish-red roof under a dazzling blue sky. The fire in the pit had gone out. Was this another dream?

I shifted my naked body in his arms to face him and studied his stunning features. His dirty-blonde hair was disheveled. Traces of dry chocolate hung at the corner of his lip. I wiped it off with my finger and sucked the pad.

His eyes opened slowly, blinking a few times then revealing those dark irises I'd become so fond of.

"Hey," I said softly.

His lips curved up lazily. "Hey."

"It's morning."

He rubbed the drowsiness out of his eyes. "Did you sleep well?"

I nodded. I hadn't even remembered falling asleep. I couldn't remember ever being separated from Vincent's body last night. Had I fallen asleep with him inside me?

He yawned like a lion waking from slumber. "How do you feel?"

"Like I'd been thrown around by a tornado. You?"

He smiled. "Like I was in a fight with a panther." He twisted his head to look over his own shoulder. There were long red streaks marking his golden skin.

I gasped and began lightly massaging around the wounds, hoping it would help with the pain. "I'm sorry. I didn't realize I was scratching you."

"I didn't either." His lips gently kissed the tip of my nose. "Definitely feisty."

"I got carried away. I didn't know I had that side of me. I promise I'll be more careful."

He kissed my forehead. "That's going to be hard because I intend to bring that side out as much as I can."

"But I hurt you, Vincent."

He nuzzled his cheek against my head. "You make me feel alive."

I curled up into him, kissing his neck, inhaling his scent into my lungs. He was almost too good to be true.

"By the way, I'm sorry about your clothes," he said.

"It's all right. They were in the way. I won't miss them."

"We'll get you some new ones once we get back to the city."

"That sounds fun."

"Speaking of fun," he said. "I was thinking we'd explore the island today and do some birdwatching. You interested?"

I voiced my excitement for the activity, my adolescent interest in birds recently reignited.

After cuddling in front of the waves for a while, we decided to head back to the cabin. Vincent put his clothes back on and I had to make do with a blanket in place of the garments that had been destroyed in the heat of last night's passion. We rinsed up, put on fresh clothes, and ate a light breakfast of eggs and toast in the cabin.

I was perusing the pictures next to the fireplace while he went to find a set of binoculars. The first few seemed to be of him and his surfing buddies on various beaches across the world, grinning and showcasing their abs and surfboards. There were one or two women in the pictures but it was clear each was the significant other of one of Vincent's friends. A few other pictures showed Vincent shaking hands with famous people. It was obvious they were taken at events or parties. My eyes halted on a picture of just two people on a beach. It was Vincent smiling with his arm around a stunning brunette. Her straight silky hair framed sultry dark eyes and full lips. Her body in a bikini was elegant like a model's but she also had curves in all the right places. She was beautiful—much more so than me. My chest tightened with jealousy. Who was she? One of Vincent's ex-girlfriends?

Vincent returned to the living room with a pair of binoculars around his neck. "Found 'em."

"Great," I said. "Hey Vincent, who is this in this picture?"

He came to my side in front of the row of pictures. "Oh, that's Giselle, my younger sister."

Giselle. The name was pretty. I felt my chest relaxing, knowing she was Vincent's sibling.

Vincent had a sister? How come I didn't know that. Come to think of it, I didn't know much about his family even from all the research I'd done. There just wasn't a lot of information available. "I've seen a lot of pictures of you when I was researching your background. But how come I've never seen her in any of them?"

"Most of the pictures of me out there were taken when I was out in public. Some with my approval, some not. As you might've guessed by now, I like to keep my private life—well, private. That's why I was concerned about ships seeing us last night."

"Oh." I'd forgotten how famous Vincent was since our involvement. Our frequent interactions made him flesh and blood, real. It was easy to forget he was often under a watchful eye by the media.

"Your sister's very beautiful."

He paused, eyes seemingly far away, deep in thought. It was the same look he had when I first told him about Marty. "She's a good girl. I'd like you to meet her sometime. I'm sure you two would get along well."

I wondered what Giselle was like. Was she basically a female version of Vincent? Perfect and charming?

"Come on. Let's do some spying." Vincent put his arm around my shoulders and we headed out into the forest like a pair of adventurers.

The rest of the morning passed in a flurry of bird sightings—ones I'd never seen before or seen only in nature magazines. Vincent played tour guide, giving me details about the different species on his island. We traded off on the binoculars and I whipped out my phone periodically to take pictures.

We were hiding behind a bush, the sun bright overhead, when I spotted a familiar bird perched on a tree branch. "Whoa, that looks like a puffin but with a big 'ole beak."

Vincent laughed. "It's a toucan. Like the bird from those Fruit Loops commercials. Except this one is a Keel-billed Toucan."

We watched it groom itself, using its beak to preen its breast feathers. With its brightly colored coat and distinctively shaped head, it looked majestic.

Vincent pointed and I saw another bird on a branch behind the grooming one that looked to be of the same species but considerably larger. The big one was closely watching the smaller one, bobbing its head up and down, shifting from side to side on the branch inspecting the smaller one from every angle. The grooming one didn't seem to notice the sketchy behavior.

"What's that bird doing?" I whispered.

"The one grooming is female and the other is male."

The female toucan continued going about her business while the male silently hopped from branch to branch, edging closer to the female without her noticing. The female turned her head to preen at the feathers on her back and I thought she'd spot the male, but the male cleverly jumped to another branch out of sight as if anticipating her movements. Before long, the male made it to the same branch as the female, inched closer, then suddenly jumped on top of her. The female squealed and fluttered her wings but the male kept her steady with his strong claws.

"Whoa," I said, my finger clicking the shutter on my cell phone camera. "Is that big bird humping the little one?"

"It's called a cloacal kiss," he said. "Birds have an orifice on their backside called a cloaca for reproduction. They touch their cloacae together and the male deposits sperm into the female. In some species, it only takes a few seconds."

"Sounds kind of anticlimactic," I mused, snapping another picture.

"I guess it depends on the birds. I'm sure it's that way with some humans as well." He grinned.

"Not with us. It's a very long and hard process." I turned my camera to snap a picture of him.

He smiled. "With lots of climaxes."

"For sure. At least on the female's end."

"The female is what's important. The male has to win her over."

"Like some kind of challenge?"

He shook his head. "Because she's worth the pursuit."

"You could always try sneaking up and mounting the female like the birds do." I pointed to the toucans. The female had calmed down and become receptive to the male humping her.

"You think that would work?"

I smiled mischievously at him. "Catch me and find out."

He wrapped his arms around my waist and I playfully struggled to get free though I knew it was futile. "I got you."

"No fair," I said. "You have to give me a head start. Close your eyes and count to a hundred."

"There's steep slopes and sharp rocks on this island. I don't want you getting hurt."

"You're sweet, Vincent. But I think my fragile female body can handle a frolick in the woods."

"Okay, Kitten." He smiled, releasing his hold on me. "I'm game." He cupped his hands over his eyes then started counting.

I dashed off, zipping through the dense trees and hurdling over small bushes. I could hear the sound of his numbers growing distant.

"One hundred," he said, voice faint. "Here I come."

A few minutes later, I heard his footsteps crunching against leaves nearby and I ducked behind a large brush. I thought he'd find me but he walked right past the brush, calling out my name. I picked up a small branch from the ground and threw it in a different direction. He headed off toward the sound of the branch thumping against the ground and I had to keep my hand against my mouth to stop myself from laughing. I was amused I could outsmart billionaire Vincent Sorenson.

Once he was out of sight, I made my getaway in the opposite direction. I was having fun eluding him. I hadn't played coy last night, but today was different.

I'd planned on setting out in one direction but a series of large trees and shrubberies caused me to make several small, winding detours. After a while, I wasn't sure if I was still going in the same direction. Eventually, I realized I had no idea where I was going. I started to head back the way I came but stopped at a large scraggly tree, it's branches resembling gnarled tentacles—the distinct appearance was very memorable. If I was tracing back my steps, I should've spotted this tree before. Why hadn't I seen it before? Where was I? Vincent had said this island wasn't large but it seemed pretty big. I couldn't get a decent sense of my bearings because the thick foliage prevented seeing very far. I was starting to suspect I was lost.

I heard a rushing sound in the distance and having no better option, decided to track down its origin.

I came into a clearing and realized I was staring at the base of a waterfall. Water rushed from fifty feet high down to a large basin below that streamed out in rivulets to what I imagined was the Caribbean Sea at some point.

In awe, I stepped closer and perched on a smooth rock beside the edge of the pool and stared at the clear water below. There were a few colorful fish swimming that resembled Koi but smaller. I got on all fours and bent low to dip my hand in the water to try to touch one of them.

"Nice view," a voice said behind me.

Huh?

Strong hands gripped my waist from behind and a hard surface bumped into my backside.

I gasped and nearly fell into the water but the hands kept me stabilized. I twisted my neck to see Vincent behind me, his hips flush against my buttocks.

"You found me," I cried.

He smiled. "If you're ever lost, I'll find you."

Eager for a dip in the cool water, I pulled off my shirt and the rest of my clothes. "You haven't caught me yet," I said, jumping into the water nude to swim away from him. The basin was shallower than I expected because I was able to touch the floor with my toes when the water reached my nose.

Mischievous smile on his face, he removed his own clothes and cannonballed in after me.

I swam toward the base of the waterfall and almost made it there when Vincent caught up to me. He gripped my waist and turned my body to face him then he kissed me deeply.

Laughing and smiling, we swam to the base of the waterfall and behind it. There was a small enclosure in the rock like a shallow cave, large enough to comfortably fit two wet bodies. Vincent picked me up out of the water and sat me on the smooth stone ledge then gripped the edge beside me and pulled himself up.

"This is a hidden spot on my island," he said, the steady sound of water splashing in front of us. "You'd almost found it on your own."

"Are you secretly a pirate? And you keep your treasure back here?"

He raised his hand to my face and brushed his fingertips along my cheek. "You're my treasure."

I blushed. "You're always so smooth," I said softly. I reached to brush a wet strand away from his eyes so I could better appreciate the full handsomeness of his features.

His dark gaze intensified and his voice lowered intimately. "I may not be a pirate, but I'd still like to plunder your booty."

"Wow. So corny." I laughed. "I think I might have to take back what I just said."

"Couldn't help it. You made it too easy." He grinned. "But seriously, you have a very nice bottom." His hand reached around my waist to cup the back of my thigh and I leaned backward against the cold stone and lifted my leg to allow him to cup my buttocks. The stone was hard, but the position was comfortable.

"I guess that answers that then," I said.

He positioned himself between my legs and shifted over me, nipple rings dangling above my breasts. Water trickled down his bare torso forming droplets at the base of his abs that fell onto my sex. "Answers what?"

"The question of whether you're an 'ass' guy or a 'tits' guy."

"Why does it have to be one or the other? I like both. And everything around and in between."

I shrugged. "Don't ask me. I don't make the rules."

He squeezed my butt cheek and his lips curved upward. "Then let me show you how I break them."

He tilted his head and his mouth sealed over mine. His tongue slipped inside running long leisurely licks along my own tongue.

I could feel his thick member growing warm and stiffening against my thigh. My sex responded in its own way.

He brushed my wet hair away from my forehead and planted his lips there. "I like your head. It's beautiful, smart, and has wonderful thoughts."

"I'm flattered," I hummed. The water crashing around us contrasted sharply with the coziness of this little cave.

He moved slightly lower. I closed my eyes and felt his supple lips delicately kiss my eyelid. "Your eyes. Vivid and sharp."

I murmured approval, enjoying the tender words and intimate gesture.

He kissed my mouth again. "Your lips. Soft and firm."

My breathing quickened and I could feel my body throb against the wet stone.

He moved to my chest, sucking tender flesh into his mouth causing me to arch my back and moan softly. "Your breasts. Shapely and alluring."

I reached to tenderly touch his cheek and he kissed my hand. "Your hands. Warm and gentle."

He trailed light kisses down to my bellybutton. "Your stomach. Grumbles when it's hungry."

I giggled.

Then his head went between my legs. "Your cunt. Sweet and greedy." He kissed my clitoris then flicked his tongue rapidly against it. I exhaled deeply and licked my lips. Vincent was an expert at oral stimulation and I'd welcome his mouth there any day.

I thought he'd remain there but he pushed my legs back with his hands and went even lower.

His lips kissed at sensitive skin and I puckered at the sensation. "Your ass. Round and juicy."

Then I felt something soft and moist nudging the entrance. It was unexpected and I didn't have time to prepare myself. "What are you doing, Vincent? I've never—Oh!"

His tongue brushed light circles around the rim, wetting the entrance with his saliva. I'd never tried anything back there before not even on my own. I'd been curious but I was too afraid it would hurt.

"Vincent," I breathed, unsure if I wanted him to continue despite the pleasure rippling from where his tongue contacted my skin.

"Relax, Kitten. I've got you."

I wiggled my legs and tightened my core as Vincent steadily explored my bottom with his tongue and lips. Eventually, I finally relaxed. That's when his tongue was able to slip inside. His finger entered my pussy at the same time and I crossed my legs together tightly to control the pleasure. My feet found the low-hanging roof of the cave and I was able to press my toes against it to keep my legs up.

"Feels too good," I moaned. I bucked my pelvis into his finger and into his tongue. Each movement left me feeling full on one end and empty in the other. The seesawing pleasure coursing through my body was driving me over the edge. My hips became more desperate, my cries of lust more profane.

"You're making me so hard," he grunted.

He added another finger into my pussy and rammed me faster. I shattered on the rocks like the water crashing around us. My feet lost their grip on the roof and my legs came down, resting on Vincent's sculpted shoulders.

"I want you inside me, Vincent," I panted, eager for that feeling of fullness only he could give me.

He frowned. "We have to go back to the cabin. I didn't bring any protection with me."

I swallowed hard before speaking. "I'm clean, Vincent. Are you?"

His brows narrowed. "Yes but—"

"I trust you. I'm on the pill. Do you trust me?"

His eyes lit. "Yes."

"Then let's do it. Here. Right now."

"Are you sure? I want this Kristen, but I don't want you to have regrets."

I nodded. "I'm sure. I want this. I want to feel you inside me with nothing separating us."

"Oh Kristen."

He tilted his head and sealed his mouth over mine.

I reached for his erection—which was as hard as the stone against my back—and used the swollen tip to rub against my clitoris. He groaned into my mouth.

I aligned the tip with my entrance and he slowly entered, allowing me to savor the feeling of every bare inch spreading my throbbing sex. Deeper he dove, stretching sensitive flesh, firing raw nerves in his wake, leaving me mindless and breathless.

"You feel so good," he cried, his mouth trembling by my ear.

His thrusts were so deep. My body felt impossibly full. I gripped the muscles of his back tightly but careful not to scratch him with my fingernails this time. "Vincent, you're so hot inside me."

"I can feel my blood rushing," he groaned. "It's because of you, Kristen."

Our bodies were so close, his hard pecs flat against my breasts. I could feel his heartbeat through his chest, the strong beats vibrating through me, making my own chest beat harder. "I want you so bad it hurts. Don't stop."

He drove into me. Again and again. Shaky breaths escaping both our lips each time he hit the back of my sex. "I can't stop."

Our wet bodies collided over and over again. Our mouths and tongues twisted and tangled in clashing harmony. He plundered my depths and took what he wanted. I opened myself and gave him everything he desired, lost in senseless pleasure.

His thrusts became more urgent, his expression more desperate.

"I'm coming, Kristen," he groaned painfully.

"Come inside me, Vincent." I dared him with my hips and coaxed him with my fingers digging into his firm backside.

"Oh fuck!"

A wave of heat seared my insides as I felt him violently spurt inside me, filling me to a depth I'd never felt before both physically and emotionally. He continued pumping his hips, shouting curses, emptying more of himself. I clenched around him, squeezing every last drop of desire out of him and into me. I wanted him. All of him.

He collapsed on top of me, panting, surrendering. I enjoyed the feel of his weight against me, crushing me tenderly.

***

Once we were back at the cabin, we decided to take Vincent's boat over to St. Lucia to grab lunch and basic supplies for the cabin. After our morning activities, I was as relaxed and happy as I could remember. Being with Vincent was both comfortable and exciting at the same time. I could scarcely believe how well things were working out between us.

We walked from the cabin to the beach and boarded the Pier Pleasure. He was wearing a light blue linen shirt with the top few buttons unbuttoned and gray shorts of a similar fabric, with flip flops and Oakley sunglasses completing the look.

Untying the boat from the dock, the muscles in his arms and chest bulged beneath his shirt. More and more, watching him do any physical activity made me think of the way he looked naked.

After starting the engine, Vincent directed us on a beeline straight for the main island. He looked confident and collected piloting the boat, taking the waves in stride. As the wind and ocean spray blew through his wavy blond hair, he resembled something out of a movie. His face radiated focused intensity directed toward the task at hand; he was soaking this experience in and making sure we didn't have any mishaps.

For all that, I was white-knuckled next to him. He hadn't gone this fast our first time, and it felt pretty close to out of control to me.

This was worse than a New York City taxi. I didn't know how fast we were going but it felt like a hundred miles per hour easy.

I had to ask. "How fast are we going?" I yelled over the wind.

Rather than respond immediately, Vincent gave the wheel a sharp turn. I screamed as the boat veered to the left and rolled in the same direction. For a second I thought the boat would flip, but it stabilized, and I was surprised at how exhilarated I felt as I settled into feeling the movement. Before we had even completed a circle, I realized I was having fun. Vincent's addiction to this kind of adrenaline rush was making more sense the longer I knew him.

Once we were pointed back at the island, Vincent eased the throttle down to almost nothing. "What did you say?" he asked, smiling.

It took me a minute to remember what that question had even been. "How fast was the boat going earlier?"

He shrugged. "Probably forty or so. I wasn't paying close attention. Nothing too crazy."

I had driven at a higher speed on the highway, but traveling on the water felt much faster than going a similar speed on land. "It felt crazy to me."

"Have you done much boating before?"

I shook my head. "Nope."

He nodded. "It's like a lot of things. At first it seems totally out of control, but most things that seem dangerous usually aren't too bad when you're with someone who knows what they're doing. Fact is, you'd have to be a really bad driver to flip this boat in these conditions."

"And you know what you're doing?"

"Most of the time, anyway."

As I wondered what that meant, he kicked the throttle up, and the boat raced off toward the main island.

I didn't know anything about boats, but even I could tell Vincent's was the nicest by far out of the half dozen I saw in the small marina we navigated into. The water was clear down to the sand below as we walked down the long pier to the beach. I could even see some fish congregating around the wooden pillars of the pier. A few dozen people were milling around the strip; it contained a single restaurant, a general store, a surf shop, and not a lot else. Past the palm trees and vegetation there were some houses further inland, and the occasional car or truck drifted by.

The warmth of the white sand between my toes was a pleasurable contrast to the ocean spray moments earlier. Vincent seemed to be surveying the beach as we stepped off the pier, but after a moment he turned to me.

"I hope you like seafood," he said, "because that's all there is to eat here."

I looked around. "I'm guessing it's fresh."

He smiled. "Just caught. Let's grab a table."

We walked over to the restaurant, Isabela & Antonio, and took a seat at one of the two tables on the covered patio. The establishment was owned by a husband and wife, both of whom were in their fifties and appeared to live on the second story of the building. Isabela took our order: I got the mahi mahi with mango salsa and Vincent asked for peppercorn crusted swordfish.

"Do you eat here often when you're down on your island?" I asked, once she had gone back to the kitchen.

Vincent nodded. "Antonio keeps it simple, but he's a great cook, and you can't beat the quality of the fish. I also buy from the local fisherman and cook myself at the cabin, but I like to support them any time I come over."

"It doesn't look like they have much competition."

He looked back toward the kitchen. "That's true, but people here tend to take pride in their work for its own sake, especially people like those two who weren't born here. You don't try to make a life in a place this remote because you're lazy, that's for sure."

I knew enough about Vincent's background to know he valued people who worked hard. You didn't get to where he had gotten without that kind of work ethic. I was the same way, though I wasn't quite as adventurous about going out on my own. "So far you've had very good taste. I'm excited."

He smirked. "Good. I like it when you're excited."

I blushed. He had been showing his affection a lot lately. "I'll bet. So how long have you been coming down here?"

"Years and years. I was coming here way before I bought the island. Surfing is good on the other side of the island. Too calm on this side."

Calm was good from my perspective. "I like this beach."

"Sure, and the conditions on the water are usually great for the boat."

"You're always looking for a little extra excitement, aren't you?"

"Usually. Not so much since I met you, though. You're a handful."

I laughed.

A minute later, our food came. Vincent was right: the preparation was simple but the ingredients spoke for themselves, which was the opposite of a lot of the food at restaurants in New York. I hadn't realized how hungry I was after our morning activities, but as soon as I smelled my food I realized I was starving. We both inhaled our meals. Isabela came with the check, Vincent paid, and we were soon making our way to the convenience store.

"We just have to pick up some odds and ends for the cabin," he said. "It's hard to get used to not having the basic necessities right around the corner when you're used to the city, but around here you have to."

I shrugged, contemplating the food in my belly. I wasn't ready to get back on that boat just yet. "No problem. I bet you're already thinking about flying around in your boat."

"I'm thinking about doing something in the boat, that's for sure." He winked.

My cheeks warmed. Could he really be in the mood again after yesterday and this morning? We'd certainly be exposed on the boat. But the rocking from the waves would be an interesting element. At this point, I knew if he came onto me, I would probably end up going along with it. He hadn't been wrong when it came to finding ways to pleasure me so far. I was still contemplating as we walked into the store.

The general store was surprisingly packed with merchandise, all at an eye-popping markup. When you're the only store in town, I guess you can charge what you want. Vincent picked out some toiletries and other necessities while I followed behind. He was a very efficient shopper. Within minutes we were at the checkout line. I was spacing out musing on the color labels of the liquor collection behind the counter—there was a very heavy rum focus—when a stunning blonde woman came in wearing a red bikini and stopped at the edge of the counter.

She had long, wet blonde hair and the definition of a beach tan—there was even sand still clinging to her torso. She had ample breasts, curvy hips, and a flawless complexion. Her six pack was so defined I wondered whether she was a fitness model. In fact, the more that I looked at her, the more I thought she must be an athlete of some kind.

When I turned my attention back to the counter, I saw the effect she was having on the men in the store, the clerk behind the counter included.

And Vincent. He turned his attention toward her like a shark smelling blood.

Jealousy stirred in my stomach. Working at a desk in the city didn't exactly let me compete on the body front with a woman like that.

The man at the counter cleared his throat. I thought he was going to point out some version of "no shirt, no shoes, no service," but he just said, "Hello, Ariel."

She had a model's smile, and she used it here. "Hello, Emilio."

Then she caught a glimpse of Vincent and beamed. "Vinny! Oh my gosh, you're here."

"Ariel, what a surprise." He smiled.

"I can't wait to straddle your newest board." She laughed.

Vincent shifted. "You'll have to let me know what you think. What are you doing in St. Lucia?"

She pushed her hair back over her shoulder and tossed her head. Every movement she made irked me. "Surfing is doing a photoshoot on this side of the island. You know, because of the sand. Not that I need to remind you how nice the sand is over here." She winked.

I looked up at Vincent's face. He appeared slightly flustered and he averted his gaze. Calm and collected Vincent losing his composure? How could she have such an effect on him? My jealousy worsened.

Ms. Photoshoot stepped closer to Vincent. I put my arm around his waist to remind him that I was still here. It made me angry he was ignoring me in front of this gorgeous woman. Didn't he realize he was making me jealous?

Vincent shook his head as if he were in a trance. "Sorry, bad manners. Ariel, this is Kristen. Kristen, this is Ariel Diamond."

He didn't even introduce me as his girlfriend. Reeling, I felt I should speak. "So are you a model?"

Ariel laughed in a way I found patronizing. "I'm mostly a surfer, but I do some modeling work, as well as riding Vincent's board every chance he gives me." She turned head and shoulders toward Vincent, as if I didn't exist. "Which, again, hasn't been enough lately, Vinny. When am I getting my personalized new toy."

He laughed. "I'll look into making sure you get it when I get back to work."

Another perfect smile tore its way through my ego. Who was this woman that was expecting a personalized surfboard from Vincent's company? Did she and Vincent have some kind of past he hadn't told me about? She was acting super familiar with him, and he wasn't shy around her either.

"Good," Ariel said. "Done any surfing lately? Or have you been hunkered down in that awful office of yours?"

My mind recalled the surfing lessons Vincent had given me on our first date. I hadn't been very good, but it had still been a fun day, especially in the showers afterward. That had been an important day for our relationship.

"Not really. We'll have to get together some time to do it properly."

I couldn't believe this.

Ariel continued. "Good, I'm holding you to it. You're always so much fun. Anyway, I have to get back to the set soon. Let me know about that board."

"Will do."

She left us to finish her shopping and Vincent checked out while I continued feeling invisible. It was unbelievable how small he'd made me feel. The way he interacted with Ariel made it seem like he didn't want me there. There were some ways I just didn't fit into Vincent's lifestyle, and one of those was doing extreme sports activities he loved.

We were both quiet on the walk back to the boat. I wondered whether I would ever be enough for Vincent. We were barely into our relationship—or whatever it was we were doing—and already I was seeing holes.

As he untied our boat, his shirt slipped exposing more of his torso, including his diamond tattoo. It couldn't be a coincidence the symbol coincided with Ariel's last name. Was that for her? I decided I needed to ask him about his relationship with her, whatever that was, but the boat ride back to his island wasn't the place to do it. As the wind blew against my face, I thought about how I was going to broach the subject.

Chapter Sixteen

By the time we returned to the cabin and unpacked the items we bought, it was almost four o'clock. Vincent and I spoke little from the time we left the dock until we had finished putting away supplies. He seemed distant in a way he hadn't been since we'd been seeing each other, and it worried me. I took a seat at the dining table as he was beginning to busy himself in the kitchen.

"Vincent. We need to talk."

He looked up from the vegetables he was chopping and squinted. "Is something wrong?"

His obliviousness was amazing. The anger that had been bubbling up under my skin was ready to spill over. "That wasn't okay."

"What wasn't?"

"Don't play dumb. Every second you were talking to Ariel Diamond you were wishing I wasn't there."

Vincent took a deep breath, put down his knife, and sat next to me at the table. "That's not true. I'm very glad you're here."

I crossed my arms. There was no way he was getting off easy on this one. "Don't try and smooth talk your way out of this. Who is she?"

"She told you, she's a surfer. She's a world-class surfer, actually. Big name in the industry."

"Okay. And?"

"My company sends her free products for testing and endorsement. So that's what you heard when she was talking about sending her the new board."

"Okay, that explains that. How about 'Vinny?'"

He said nothing. His thousand yard stare reminded me of the way he looked in the store.

"Well?"

"You're getting way too upset about this."

I hated the way he was deflecting. The more he stalled, the more I realized something was up. "Am I? Have you had sex with her?"

He flinched. "Why would that matter?"

"Because I'm asking. You have, haven't you? Why didn't you tell me?"

He threw his hands up. "Because it's not important! Do you really want me to run down a list of every woman I've ever slept with?"

Thinking about the length of that list made me nauseous. I was sure he had slept with many, many more people than I had. Still, that wasn't what this was about. "No, I'd rather not think about that. But were you going to wait for me to bring it up before you told me anything about your relationship with her?"

His jaw worked, but he remained silent. I could tell he was going through the options of what to say in his mind. After several minutes of waiting for him to speak, I felt like I needed to move the conversation along.

"Okay, you're clearly not being forthcoming about this, so I'm just going to ask you: is the diamond tattoo on your chest for Ariel? Or is that just a weird coincidence?"

His mouth formed a thin line. He took several deep breaths, then put his hand on the table. "I should start at the beginning: it makes me feel old to say this, but I've known Ariel Diamond for thirteen years. Since I was a teenager."

I nodded. That was longer than I had known anyone except my parents.

He watched me for a minute, but I wasn't saying anything. He continued. "We met while I was in college. She was part of the crew I surfed with in California while I was in school and then after. You could say we kind of came up together. So I've known her for her whole career, and she's known me for mine."

"And you guys dated?"

He nodded. "Yes. Eventually we started dating. I got the tattoo for her when I was twenty."

"How long did you date?"

"A few years. It was up and down. We aren't really compatible, though I fought against that at the time. The only thing we really have together is surfing."

"So you loved her?"

"I definitely thought so at the time."

The next question was one I wasn't sure I would get an honest answer to. "Do you still love her?"

He shook his head firmly. "No. We still have a friendship, but I moved on a long time ago."

I had my doubts. He had a tattoo devoted to the woman. She was more than just a flame he had moved on from. "Really? Why didn't you get the tattoo removed?"

"Why would I? It's not like I'm on bad terms with her. We're just not right for each other as romantic partners. That doesn't mean we can't be friends."

I thought about my only real ex. Marty. We weren't exactly on the best of terms. The idea of being friends with someone you were once romantic with seemed pretty foreign to me, but it worked for some people. "So when was the last time you guys were intimate?"

He shrugged. "I don't know, five or six years?"

The way he was so casual about sex was often a turn-on, but right now it made me feel pretty insignificant. I had to keep the conversation going or I knew I'd dwell on it. "So all that innuendo from her was just joking around?"

"She was probably trying to get a rise out of you. I'm sure she knew we were together so she was probably testing you by seeing how you would react if she flirted with me."

Did he just say we were together? It didn't feel like it, especially after he'd let Ariel test me like that. Did I want to be with someone who would let me squirm?

"Are we together? Because I felt invisible while you were talking to Ariel, and it's even worse if you were conscious of the fact she was trying to do that."

His eyebrows shot up. "Felt invisible?"

"Please. You didn't even introduce me as your girlfriend." Granted, I wasn't sure whether I was his girlfriend. We hadn't talked about what our status was as a couple, or even if we were a couple.

He let out a deep breath and grimaced. "Sorry, that was an oversight. I was surprised and not really thinking."

That was a non-answer. "But you knew she was testing me and you just let her keep going. Why did you do that?"

"What did you want me to do? The way she was doing it, I would've had to say something very awkward and it would've made things uncomfortable for everyone. What she was doing was pretty harmless."

"It wasn't harmless to me! And why did you disregard the surfing we did on our first date when she asked?"

He blinked. "I didn't. I said 'not really', which was true given what she asked. From what I remember, I was a lot more focused on you than I was on the surfing during that date. "

"So you can't actually have fun surfing with me because I'm not good enough?"

"I had a great time and I think we could have fun doing it again."

If we ever went surfing again. "You're not bored with me?"

He looked up and shook his head. He was getting frustrated. "What have I done that makes you think I could possibly be bored with you?"

I started to tear up. I said something that had been in the back of my mind for a while. "You can't surf or do a lot of the other thrill-seeking stuff you love so much when you're with me."

"Kristen, I'm a big boy. If I didn't think we were compatible, or if I was getting bored, or anything like that, I would just tell you. The fact is I don't feel that way. Compatibility is much more complex than shared hobbies. And a relationship is much deeper than thrilling moments. We haven't been together long, but you and I both know we have great chemistry. I'm still crazy about you, and you're still the only woman I want or need."

Warmth spread from my face around my entire body. It felt good to hear those words. Even after the day before and that morning, seeing him with Ariel had shaken my confidence in how attracted Vincent was to me. If you had shown me a picture of Ariel Diamond when I was doing my initial research on Vincent, I would have said they were a perfect match. But that was before I knew him. There was more to him than he let on to the public.

"Promise?" I asked.

"Yes," he said, smiling, "I promise."

I beamed. Vincent, as if coming to a sudden realization, jumped up and went to the counter. By the time I turned around to track him, he had a camera up and snapped a picture.

"Perfect. I'd been meaning to get a good picture of you as a keepsake." He looked at his handiwork on the camera's screen. "Take a look. I think it's a great shot."

He came over and handed me the camera. He had caught me smiling wide and staring right at the camera. I was a little teary-eyed but I still looked happy. He was right, it was a perfect shot. Candid but well-framed. A professional photographer would be proud.

"I'm getting two copies. One for the cabin and one for my condo. You don't mind do you?"

I shook my head. I pondered the significance of my portrait sitting next to his cherished photos including the one with his sister. Mine would be the only one with a single person in the photo.

"I'd get one for my office desk. But I don't want to put your job in jeopardy if your employer finds out we're together."

Night fell and we curled up outside in the beach tent watching the stars, which were much more numerous than they were in New York, where you were lucky to see any. I had put on the black lingerie

I brought and we had sex that night but it was more slow and intimate than the lustful frenzy the night before. My clothes weren't torched and there wasn't any chocolate involved. Vincent came once again inside me and we cuddled afterward for the remainder of the night, sharing tender kisses and small irrelevant details about our lives.

The next day was spent packing up for travel and then traveling. It had been a mostly relaxing trip, and as we landed at JFK, I wished it could have lasted just a little longer.

Chapter Seventeen

By the time the cab dropped me off at my apartment, it was almost eleven p.m. Exhausted, I walked in and found Riley watching Keeping Up With The Kardashians. She was drinking a diet coke as always and wearing yet another pink and blue sorority t-shirt and shorts combo from when she was in college.

Riley paused her show and got up off the couch. "You're back! I didn't know if you'd be home tonight. How was the trip?"

I put my stuff down on the counter and opened the fridge hoping for something to eat. Thankfully, there was some string cheese that was mine. I grabbed it. "It was good. He has a private island with a cabin that we stayed at. The entire area is gorgeous."

"A private island? Are you fookin kidding me?" Riley took a seat on a stool in the kitchen, where I was standing. "I'm so jealous. Look at that tan you're getting with all these trips. I need to find myself a billionaire to jet me down to the Caribbean on the regular."

I looked down at my forearms. It hadn't even occurred to me that I would be tanning, but I was getting some pretty good color. "Dating a billionaire has its perks, I have to say."

She laughed. "Things have been quiet here."

I unwrapped my string cheese and pulled off a strand to eat. "You seem to be feeling better at least," I said, chewing.

She nodded. "That I am. Better to be bored than sick. So how is Vincent, anyway? Have you two had the talk?"

"The talk?"

"You know, boyfriend/girlfriend, that kind of thing. It's getting to be about that time, right?"

Could everyone see through me this easily? How would I ever keep dating Vincent a secret when people could read me like a book? I needed to remind myself to never, ever play poker. "We did, actually."

"Oh yeah? How did it come up? Did you start it?"

I grimaced at the memory of the previous afternoon. It had ended well, but there were some bumps. "Kind of. We actually had a bit of a fight beforehand. While we were down there we ran into an ex-girlfriend of his."

My roommate's eyes widened. "On his private island?"

I shook my head. "No, we were on a bigger island nearby grabbing lunch and supplies for the cabin."

"Oh okay. That sucks. Was she hot?"

I threw my hands up. "A little sympathy would be nice!"

She shrugged. "I'm finding out how much sympathy you need. Judging by your reaction I'm guessing she was a knockout. Sorry, that sounds brutal."

I grimaced. "She's a pro surfer. She was down there modeling, actually."

Riley's eyebrows shot up. "Did she flirt with him?"

"Oh yeah. Vincent said he thought she was testing me."

It was her turn to grimace. "How did he react?"

Remembering Vincent's reaction, or lack thereof, to Ariel's flirtations brought a fresh bubble of nausea to my stomach. "He went along with it. Didn't seem to think it was a big deal."

"I can see why you had a fight. What's this surfer chick's name?"

"Ariel Diamond. And yeah, but the talk we had about it ended up being good."

While I was talking, Riley had whipped her phone out and was tapping and swiping at the screen. Her mouth made an 'O'. "Look at those abs, Jesus. I'm really sorry Kristen, having a girl this hot hitting on your man had to be excruciating."

I snatched her phone from her grasp. "Riley, you're really not helping!"

She tried to grab her phone back, but I pulled it away. "I'm just getting a grasp of the situation, Kris! Give me my phone back. I promise I'll stop checking this girl out."

I shook my head. "You haven't even listened to the part that was good yet."

She made one last attempt to grab her phone away, but I was too quick for her. Finally, she put her hands in her lap. "Okay, fine. So this borderline sea nymph with abs out of an anatomy textbook shows up. Then what happens?"

I snorted. She was going to be petulant about this. "Fine. here's your phone, but no more comments about how hot Ariel is, okay? Or her body."

Riley smiled and took the phone like a child receiving candy. "Thank you. So you ran into this woman and then what?"

"Well, we were in this little general store and she comes in. Everyone is staring because she's wearing a bikini." I watched my friend carefully, but she had a better poker face than mine. "She walks up to us and calls him 'Vinny' like they were lovers."

At this, Riley laughed. "'Vinny?' Do you call him that?"

"No! I don't think it fits him at all."

She shook her head, still laughing. "Me neither."

I told her about their dating history, leaving out the part about the tattoo. Riley nodded attentively. "So it sounds like they're just friends now, right? Obviously their personal connection is helpful professionally, but he's not actually into her now."

I tapped my finger on the counter, thinking whether I should spill about the tattoo. "Well, there is one weird thing. He had a tattoo of a diamond on his ribs."

I watched Riley process for a second before her mouth dropped. "Wait. Is it for her?"

I nodded. "He got it when he was twenty."

Her mouth puckered as she considered. "He's like thirty now, right? That's a long time ago."

"Thirty-one, yeah. He says there's no reason to get it removed because they're still friends. It's not like things are ugly."

"That's fair, actually. If he still loved her but couldn't be with her, it would hurt to look at that thing every time he had his shirt off. I know when I've a bad breakup I have to get rid of everything that reminds me of the guy."

I rubbed my pinky. Sometimes you can't get rid of every reminder.

"I guess you have practice," I said.

Riley smiled. "I even throw out the underwear I'm wearing when we break up."

"What?"

She half smiled. "Sorry, TMI?"

"Good lord, yes! Why on earth would you do that?"

She closed one eye, chuckling. "Do you really want to know?"

I thought about it, but shook my head. "You're right, I don't."

She continued laughing for a minute before getting a hold of herself. "Anyway, he has this tattoo. You said there was a good part."

I told her about how Vincent had assured me, as well as the picture he took. She was impressed that he would want a photo of me for his cabin and condo. Seeing how she reacted to the story made me feel better about my reaction to the situation. It had been a bit of a shock to see him around Ariel, but all in all things had ended up in a good place.

"Well that all sounds good," she said. "I'm super happy for you. How's the other part of your relationship going?"

"Which part?"

"The sex, silly."

I blushed. Riley's mind was never far from the gutter. "It's going well."

She waited, her blue eyes urging me to go on. "'It's going well?' You can't date a man that gorgeous and leave me with that. I'm watching reality television and chugging diet coke over here."

I shrugged. It wasn't something I liked to talk about, even with Riley.

"You were on his private island. If you stayed inside and did missionary before bed, I'm going to smack you."

More heat rose to my cheeks as I thought about how far from reality Riley's insinuation was. I knew she was trying to get a rise out of me. She knew being so blunt about sex would throw me off balance. "We didn't stay inside all day, I'll say that. But that's all I'll say."

Riley jutted her lip, pouting. "Can't you throw a girl a bone?"

She was doing a good job of looking pathetic, but I held strong. "Sorry. I just don't like to talk about that stuff. You know that."

She sighed, shoulders slumped. Sitting in her sorority outfit with her blonde hair in her face on a kitchen stool, she looked almost comical. "Fine." she said after a moment. "But things are going well, all in all?"

I took a deep breath of my own. "Yeah. The thing with Ariel was scary, but the scariest part was realizing how much he's beginning to mean to me."

"Sounds like you're getting serious pretty quickly."

"I guess so," I said, surprising myself with the note of sadness in my tone.

"Is he feeling the same way?"

Was he? He had told me he was crazy about me, and being in a picture in his cabin was a nice gesture, but I just had a hard time completely trusting him. He was gone so much in so many different places, and I knew the effect he had on women. On the other hand, he really hadn't given me any reason not to trust him. Maybe it was something that would just take some time.

"He did say he was crazy about me," I said. "I don't know how much more he can do to make me know how he feels."

"The island trips are also nice. Have you thought about dropping the L-word yet?"

Panic shot through my system. Had I already fallen in love with Vincent, after years of being uninterested in men? "No. That seems pretty sudden, doesn't it? It hasn't been that long."

Riley got up and grabbed a glass of water. "It is what it is," she said. She took a sip. "No need to rush it. I was just asking. Anyway, I should probably get to bed. See you tomorrow."

I wished her good night and took the seat she had been occupying moments earlier. Did I love Vincent? Things had been moving so quickly I hadn't even paused to consider my feelings. Time was passing, though. Whether I liked it or not, my relationship with Vincent couldn't stay at the same place indefinitely.

***

When Vincent and I had landed at JFK yesterday, he'd told me he had to do a quick turnaround before he traveled back down to Brazil. He would be back as soon as he could, and would be sure to let me know. Even flying by charter as he did, I couldn't understand how he could keep up his schedule. It sounded exhausting spending so much time in so many different places.

Monday morning found me in a very familiar place: in front of my work computer. Though the office was something I was still getting used to. I spent the morning sorting my inbox and reading through the long list of office memos waiting there. While I wanted to get to work on the more interesting task of creating Vincent's investment plan, if I didn't get through these emails now they would just build up and become unmanageable. It was an important part of my job to make sure I didn't miss any communications that could be vital.

My diligence paid off when I saw an email from Carl sent ten minutes before I arrived in the office. The message said to meet him in his office at ten. He had an interesting opportunity on a potential client that he wanted to discuss. I set an alert on my calendar for the meeting and hurried through the rest of my messages.

The meeting was upon me before I could get started on the work for Vincent. I grabbed a notepad and hurried across the floor to Carl's office. This time, his door was open, though he was on the phone.

He waved me in, and I stepped inside, waiting just in front of the door. "Ted, I've got a meeting. We're going to have to continue this at lunch. Yep, got it, 12:30. Usual spot. See you then."

He hung up and turned to me. "Kristen, thanks for dropping by. Shut the door and take a seat."

I did so. Carl shuffled through some papers until he found the file he wanted. While he wasn't a Luddite, he had more of a preference for dealing in paper than most of the people at the firm. It was why I was taking notes on a notepad rather than my laptop. Paying attention to little details like that was important at Waterbridge-Howser.

He clapped his hands together and rubbed them together, staring me over his glasses. "First off: Sorenson. I haven't heard anything bad, which from my perspective means things are good. Am I right?"

I nodded. "Things are going great. Lining up the last bits of the strategy and I'll be ready to present soon."

"Great. That's a tough client, so stay on your toes, but so far it sounds like you're doing the business. Good work."

"Thank you." I smiled. Carl understood that part of being a good boss was making sure people felt appreciated when they were doing their job well. Every little bit helped.

"You deserve it. As always, let me know if I can do anything. Anyway, I brought you here because I have an interesting prospect I think you would be perfect for. Do you think you can fit another pitch into your schedule?"

Working on another new client pitch would mean many days of very long hours on top of what I was already doing for Vincent. However, as the pitch with Vincent had shown, working on new business was the best way to get bonuses and promotions. I had just received a promotion, so this probably wouldn't mean another one, but it would be another drop in the bucket for my next move. With Vincent gone as much as he was, it wasn't like I had anything pressing going on in my personal life. As I thought about it, the distraction would be welcome.

"Of course," I answered.

"Great. You're going to have an analyst working with you on this one, which should ease the burden timewise a bit. The prospect is a woman who has leveraged her fame as a fitness model by selling home fitness equipment."

Did he say fitness model? My chest tightened. However unlikely it was, I had to be sure. "Is the prospect Ariel Diamond?"

Carl frowned and looked at the file. "No. Her name is Selena Richards. Who is Ariel Diamond?"

Relief swept through my body from my chest outwards. I thought of a suitable lie to tell about Ariel. "A professional surfer I learned about while doing research for the Sorenson account," I said. That was mostly true, depending on your definition of research. "She does some fitness modeling too. Sorry for interrupting."

"You do have a good grasp of that account." He chuckled. "I have to say, it's impressive. You're really on top of that guy."

I blushed, but he was looking back at the file and didn't notice. After he had finished giving me the details about Selena Richards, he left me with instructions to get a plan of action and some materials to him by the beginning of the next week. I walked out of his office excited at the chance of another sizable client.

After I got back to my office, I texted Vincent about the news. A few hours later, he replied.

Sounds great. Will have to tell me more when we talk next. I will try to call this week.

Disappointed I wouldn't be able to talk to him that night, I texted back.

You can't get away tonight even for a little bit?

It took another fifteen minutes for him to respond.

I'll be lucky to sleep tonight, sorry. As soon as I have free time, I'll call.

Frustrated, I put the phone on my desk and went back to my work. It wasn't like I didn't have plenty to do myself. Vincent had said from the outset that he was a very busy man who usually didn't have much time to give for a real relationship. I had brushed it off then, but maybe that was a deal breaker for me. Being in a relationship with a man who was constantly continent-hopping meant spending a lot of time being basically single. That hadn't been a problem before, but now I realized I might be getting attached.

The rest of the work day passed in a blur, then the rest of the work week. The weekend passed without a call from Vincent. Whenever I texted, it would take him so long to text back that a conversation was hopeless. Another work week went by until it was Friday again. I had stayed late on Thursday working on the Richards pitch, so when my phone buzzed half an hour early on Friday morning I was upset. I picked it up and saw it was Vincent.

Happy to finally hear from him, I picked it up and answered. "Hello," I said.

"Hello, beautiful. Sorry to call so early. This is the first time I've had any free time at all in a couple weeks." He sounded exhausted.

I rubbed my eyes, trying to wake up. "I was beginning to think you'd forgotten about me. Is everything okay?"

"Just about. I'm in Lisbon right now, actually. Flew in a few hours ago. I don't know if I mentioned I was coming here."

It was a little disappointing that he hadn't told me he was traveling, but I guessed it didn't matter. As I sat up in bed, I realized I was feeling a little nauseous. "You didn't. What are you doing there?"

"More meetings. We're making a push in the European market with some of our surf swimwear."

"Sounds like life's been pretty crazy."

He sighed. "This is fairly normal to be honest. Like I told you, I'm all over the place pretty often."

My nausea was getting worse. Had the Chinese food I'd eaten for dinner the night before been bad? Maybe I just missed Vincent that much. I hoped I wasn't getting sick. Working on a pitch while you were ill was a good recipe for misery. "When do you think you'll be back?"

I heard another man's voice on Vincent's end. He cursed. "I'm sorry Kristen, I have to go. The materials for my next meeting aren't ready, apparently. I'll let you know when I'm back in New York when I have a better idea. It's going to depend on how the meetings here go. Sorry again. I'll be in touch soon."

My heart sank. Vincent's schedule was really putting a strain on our relationship. I had taken the amount I was seeing him before for granted, and even that hadn't been much. "Okay. Bye."

He hung up. I looked down at my phone and saw I still had another forty minutes before I had to get up. As I shifted to plunge back into my pillow, I felt a fresh wave of nausea. Fearing I was going to vomit, I got up and sprinted to my bathroom. I barely made it.

After that, I did feel better. I went and grabbed some soda and drank it slowly in the kitchen. The nausea seemed to have gone away almost entirely, so I decided I'd still go to work. What to do about Vincent was another story. It wasn't really his fault he was so busy, but I still felt more than a little neglected. Even though I wasn't sure exactly what else he could do, I needed to talk to him about it.

If we were going to be a couple, we wouldn't be able to keep it secret forever. Vincent had correctly said that having relations with clients wasn't expressly forbidden. I didn't want to broadcast our relationship to the whole office, but we could risk a nice dinner in the city. It would show how much I cared about him. Whenever Vincent did return, I resolved to invite him out for a good steak. My treat.

He ended up calling a couple days later. Apparently the response in Lisbon had been mediocre. It wasn't the end of the line for the venture, but he would be returning to New York for a few days to work with another team on how to proceed. When I told him I wanted to take him out, he sounded genuinely excited. He would be getting in late Friday morning, and we were going out Friday night, despite my protests about jet lag.

Finally, Friday evening came. Despite my busy schedule, I had managed to make time to buy a new dress for the occasion. It was a ruched sheath in black, cut slim to hang against my hips. With black stilettos, red lips, and my hair curling just right, I felt as sexy as I ever had going into a date. When I stepped out into the kitchen to show off to Riley, her jaw dropped.

"Look at you, sexy girl! I bet his mouth will be absolutely watering."

I beamed. "Thanks. Are you going out?"

She nodded. She was wearing a very short, shiny blue dress that made me guess she was clubbing. "Yeah, me and the girls are going prowling tonight. I'm actually going out to grab some early drinks at Jen's before we get dinner and go dancing. Who knows, maybe I'll snag my own billionaire. Where are you two headed?"

"Strip House. After all these Caribbean weekends I figure I can treat him to a nice steak."

Our door buzzer went off. I looked at the oven clock: seven on the dot. Harried as he probably was from traveling, he was right on time. After saying a quick goodbye to Riley and grabbing my clutch, I hurried down to meet Vincent outside.

He was leaning against a streetlight post, looking at his watch like he was posing for a picture. He wore a black button down with the sleeves rolled up and black pants. His skin had the golden color of a man who had been spending a lot of time in a tropical climate. Our days apart had already caused me to forget just how attractive I found him. The way he stood there, I had half a mind to invite him up to my apartment so I could get my hands on him immediately.

He looked up and straightened. I watched him take in my appearance for the evening. Moving his eyes from my legs up to my eyes, he smiled. "Hello, Kristen."

I beamed. "Hello, Vincent."

"I like the outfit." He stepped toward me and bent down to whisper in my ear. "It'll look even better pooled on the floor."

I pressed my cheek into his chest. "I think you're right. But we need to get ourselves fed first."

He took my hand. "Where to?"

"I made reservations at Strip House. It's nice out, so I think we should just walk."

Vincent looked around, then shrugged. "Lead the way."

We made it to Strip House twenty minutes later, holding hands the whole way. The restaurant was decorated in an 1890s bordello style, with red wallpaper and low lighting. The Zagat Guide had been right: this definitely felt romantic and even a little naughty. I was very pleased with the selection.

Vincent looked around and took everything in. "Nice choice," he said. As the hostess took us to our seat, he slid his hand down my back, fingering the band of my underwear through my dress.

I shuddered at the intimate gesture. Thoughts of how the evening might end sent a surge of heat through my body. Every touch he gave me merely made me want him even more. The way I craved him bordered on scary: I had been working for the past two years to be a very self-sufficient person, but there was no replacement for his hands on my body.

We took our seats and ordered quickly. I got a bottle of malbec to split between the two of us, and we both ordered steak. Vincent looked more relaxed than I had thought he would. Yet again, I was impressed with his ability to switch between modes seamlessly.

We made chit-chat until the wine came. I had decided I wanted to wait until I had a little liquid courage before I brought up the topic of his schedule. There was still no answer popping out at me as far as what he could do, but I thought having the fact that it was bothering me on his radar wouldn't hurt. If he got offended about it, then maybe, as much as it hurt, having him out of my life would be for the best. Some kind of balance between work and life was important to me in whoever I ended up with. As crazy as it sounded to me, I realized that thinking about him in those terms wasn't too far-fetched. Of course, that was just my perspective. I wasn't sure if he felt the same way.

Once the wine came, I took a big sip. When I looked at Vincent, I could tell he was watching me carefully. He knew me well enough to know something was up.

"So," I said, gathering myself, "how was your trip?"

He scrunched his eyebrows. "Fine. Business. Is there something you want to say?"

I took a deep breath. "You were gone a long time."

"I know. It was exhausting."

"Is that normal for you?"

He chewed his lip. "Yes and no. It happens. When you run a business, sometimes you just have to be the person to handle things."

"Can't you just delegate to someone else and fire them if they do it poorly?"

A fire broke out behind his eyes as he continued to work his jaw. "I could, sure. I could do whatever I wanted."

The intensity with which he had begun to speak startled me. I knew I could guess the answer to the following question, but I asked anyway. "So why don't you?"

"Because there are a lot of people whose jobs depend on my company being good at what it does, and I owe it to all of them to make my company the best I can make it."

I found myself nodding before I realized it. It was a more altruistic answer than I was expecting.

"Besides," he continued, "I'm thirty one. Not exactly pushing retirement age. As successful as I've been, I still have ambitions to push the company further."

That was closer to the answer I had guessed. "Where do I fit into these plans?" I asked. Tears fought to come out, but I held them back. I didn't want to be crying for this conversation, especially in public.

His expression softened. "I'm still figuring that out. Believe me, it's not absent from my mind."

"These past two weeks were very hard for me. I felt like I was just another thing on your todo list."

He sighed. "Kristen, I told you at the Knicks game that I'm a very busy man."

"I know. And I brushed it off at the time. But it's becoming a problem for me." I was still holding on without crying, but I didn't know how much more of this conversation I could take before the waterworks started. It was strange not being able to control my emotions better in public.

He took another deep breath. His thin lips and squinting eyes signaled to me he was thinking hard about what he was going to say next. I waited. Finally, he spoke. "I just need some time to figure out how to make it work. You're important to me. I think I've shown you that so far. Even if I'm not perfect, I want to make this work, and I tend to get what I want when I put my mind to it." He smiled. "Just please be patient. I'm working on it."

It was as good an answer as I could expect. A smile crept over my faith. I was relieved that he hadn't gotten too defensive. He was right: we hadn't been dating that long. I couldn't expect him to change his lifestyle overnight. If he was working on it, that was enough.

I heard his phone buzz. He reached into his pocket and checked his phone quickly before looking up at me. "Sorry, that's set to only vibrate when it's from an important number. But tonight's just between us. It can wait. I'm leaving this here while I go to the men's room so you don't think I'm sneaking away for business, okay?"

I was surprised at the way his brown eyes searched my face. His expression showed how seriously he was taking our conversation. I nodded my assent. "Thank you for listening to me," I said. "It means a lot."

I could see him relax as he smiled. "I'm trying. Be right back."

Sure enough, he left the phone next to his silverware. I watched it, musing on how many people must be trying to reach Vincent at all hours around the world. That he was the nexus of such a huge enterprise was amazing. Sure, I had to keep my work phone on me at all times, but that was mostly to answer to my bosses. When people went to Vincent, it was because they had decided he needed to know something. He wanted that communication.

His phone flashed—though it didn't vibrate—and despite my instincts toward respecting his privacy, I looked. What kinds of things were people sending to Vincent at all hours? I thought it would probably be something almost indecipherable to me: earnings reports, internal memos, or something similar. Instead it was a text message. I read the name upside down and felt my throat tighten up.

The text was from Ariel Diamond. I reached across the table and snatched up his phone to read the message properly.

Hey Vinny! Had so much fun riding your COCK ;-)

My stomach dropped. My mouth tasted like acid. I wanted to throw the phone across the room. The wine along with it. The room felt as though it were turning like Vincent's speed boat. I felt so sick I thought I might vomit in the restaurant.

He fucked Ariel Diamond while he was on his 'business' trip.

Mixing business with pleasure. I was almost more angry at myself for being such a fool than at him. How could I have fallen for his stupid charming words?

I inhaled a shaky breath and got up from the table. Vincent could get this bill without a problem. In fact, he should. I wanted nothing to do with him.

Tears flooded my vision as I left the restaurant.

I was too shocked to feel anything but numbness. How could he do that to me? After he had reassured me so convincingly that he didn't have feelings for Ariel anymore, he had sex with her. Just like that. It probably didn't even mean anything to him. Maybe he didn't have feelings for her and just had sex with her because he thought he could get away with it and needed a stress reliever. What were the chances I would find out, after all? I was all the way back in New York, trusting that he wasn't calling because he was too busy. With work, of course.

I found a cab and got in. Minutes later I was at my apartment. I gave the driver a twenty dollar bill and didn't wait for the change. Vision still blurry with tears, I unlocked my apartment door and stepped inside. The place was empty; Riley must've already left with her girlfriends. I briefly entertained the idea of joining them but thought better of it. Being around people wasn't what I needed right now. For now, I just wanted to be alone in my bed to cry.

My phone had been vibrating in my purse the whole cab ride home. I didn't dare look at it. Vincent surely had some brilliant excuse for that message, but I didn't even want to hear his voice right now. As I replayed our relationship in my head, I couldn't believe how foolish I had been. Of course a risk-taking billionaire like him wouldn't want to be locked down with someone like me. I was too safe, too boring to satisfy his needs. Sure, sometimes he wanted someone safe to come home to, but that would never be enough.

He would always want more.

My phone buzzed again. Annoyed, I pulled it out of my clutch. Sure, enough, it was Vincent. He had called ten times and sent two text messages. I didn't read them before I hit the phone's power button. Maybe I never would. I could have Riley turn on my phone and delete them for me.

A fresh wave of nausea and tears overtook me. I lay down on my bed and cried as hard as I ever had. Each sob shook my body so hard it was painful. At times it was hard to catch my breath, but still it kept coming. I just couldn't believe he had done that. How could he? Right when I had finally opened myself up, he had stabbed me square in the back and twisted the knife for good measure.

Dimly I heard a pounding at the door. He'd followed me home. I sat up and looked at the makeup smudging my pillow. Great, another piece of laundry.

I probably looked like a raccoon. Even so, I couldn't have him pounding on that door forever. My neighbors would file a noise complaint against me. I went to the door.

"Go away," I yelled. "I can't even look at you right now."

The pounding stopped for a second, then became a knock. I was surprised he hadn't yelled back. Typical Vincent, to have a measured response at a time like this. Where previously I had admired the way he could control himself, now I was thinking he might be some kind of robot.

Maybe he would go away if I just screamed at him to his face. I opened the door, and was greeted by a man that wasn't Vincent.

My head felt like a helium balloon. The blue eyes behind the man's rimless glasses sparked with an angry intensity I'd thought I'd left behind.

It was Marty.

Chapter Eighteen

It was my first day of class for Econ 102. Junior year. I'd made it this far, busting my ass semester after semester, camping out in office hours, staying up late nights, living off of caffeine. Somehow I'd survived.

I thought getting into Harvard was the hard part and the rest was grade inflation, but the classes were actually pretty tough. Of course, others cruised by on raw intelligence and superhuman brains that soaked up lectures like a sponge soaking up water. Unfortunately, I couldn't do that. I was the exception. Which meant I spent my first two years making closer friends with textbooks than I did with real people.

The lecture room was large enough to fit two hundred students and it was nearly packed. Among the sea of bodies, one caught my eye. Actually, one caught the eyes of the majority of the females in the room: bright blue irises, tousled brown hair, high cheek bones, and chic glasses sitting atop a sharp nose. He looked like a male model from a J.Crew catalog except he wasn't digitally enhanced—he was real. His features were sculpted with precision and economy. Fitting. Considering the subject matter of the class—and considering he was seated in the front row, which meant he was the teacher's assistant.

I took a seat in one of the middle rows and waited for the professor to start the lecture. I could already tell this was going to be my favorite class of the semester.

***

"You know, out of over a hundred students, you're probably the only one who comes to my office hours regularly," he said with a heart-stopping smile.

I'd found out his name was Martin Pritchard. A senior economics major. Brilliant, insightful, and devilishly good-looking. It took an extraordinary amount of willpower not to get distracted by those vivid blue eyes that somehow seemed to burn hot with intensity and cold with calculation at the same time. A lot of girls had come to Martin's office hours during the beginning of the course in hopes of snagging a lay. They giggled, flitted their hair, and batted their eyes. Once they realized he was only there for academic concerns—not sexual ones—they lost interest.

He was sitting across from me in the TA office, trying to help me understand the latest assigned readings. Just the two of us.

I blushed and looked down at my notebook filled with scribbles about minimum wage laws and Nash equilibriums. I had no idea what any of it meant.

"I need the extra help. This stuff is kind of hard for me."

"You ask great questions. Ones I'd expect to hear from students from the more advanced econ classes." He grinned a perfect set of teeth. "I think you're just detailed in your thinking. Learning is a lot like putting together a puzzle. And different people have different sets of pieces. The ones with more pieces take more time to put it together, but once they do, it's a bigger picture."

I smiled bashfully, averting my gaze to my notes then returning it to him. "Thanks. I never thought of it that way."

He tapped his head. "Big picture."

We both chuckled then smiled at one another. It was definitely a shared moment and I didn't know what to say to follow it, which is why I was glad he ended up breaking the awkward silence.

"Hey," he said brightly. "There's a presentation by Gary Becker today in Lowell Hall. You wanna go?"

At the risk of sounding ignorant, I asked, "Who's that?"

"A famous economist known for the 'rotten kid theorem'. He's my favorite." Martin beamed. I loved how he got excited about economic topics and renowned economists during office hours. His energy was infectious—even making me excited about the stuff from time to time.

I wrinkled my brows. "What a great name for a theorem."

He chuckled. "Great name for a great theorem. Imagine a bad brother takes pleasure in harming his sister. If the parents say they'll give more inheritance money to the child who needs it more then the bad brother will want to help his sister do well so that he will end up getting more inheritance. His welfare has become dependent on the welfare of his sister. You can turn a bad boy into a good one with the proper incentives."

My brows scrunched further, pondering the example.

Martin shrugged then winked. "Maybe he's not famous enough."

I laughed. "It sounds interesting." And like a chance to hang out with a gorgeous guy. Besides, it wasn't often I got the chance to do leisurely things. "Sure, I'll go."

***

We began seeing more of each other. First neutral social events, then it became increasingly clear that we were dating. We'd been seeing each other for a few months when we walked by the gymnasium and Marty suggested we try out the swing dance club.

"A guy wanting to go dancing? I don't know, I'm not a very good dancer."

His full lips curved into a wicked grin. "Are you saying men can't dance?"

"Isn't that the stereotype?"

"Isn't it also the stereotype that girls are good at dancing?"

"Touché."

He put his arm out for me to grab and I took it gracefully. "Shall we?" he said.

I was surprised to find he wasn't only smart and handsome, but also a good dancer.

224 | Priscilla West

We spent the evening with our bodies close to one another, laughing and working up a sweat. I tripped over my feet and stepped on his multiple times but he didn't seem to mind. He helped show me how to do the basic moves and even convinced me to let him swing me around his waist.

It was the most fun I'd had in college to date.

**

"I've never done this before, Kristen. Have you?" His body was tense as he hovered over me on my bed in my dorm room. I had taken his shirt off and it was now lying on the floor where I'd thrown it. The surface of his sculpted torso was smooth and it was a major turn on to see it so up close. I'd been surprised to find he was amazingly fit for a nerdy teacher's assistant. A regular routine of swimming and dancing will do that to the body.

His chest was heaving as he tried to control his breathing.

I smiled. "If you're asking if I'm a virgin, I'd have to say no. I had a couple boyfriends in high school."

"I see." He averted his gaze from mine to look down at my chest, where he often liked to look. I didn't mind. In fact, I liked the way it made me feel desirable. He was usually so confident and in control but now in this intimate moment, he was vulnerable.

"Is that a problem?"

"No. . . I just never had a girlfriend before you. I'm kind of nervous."

I squinted my forehead.

"You look surprised."

"I am. I thought you'd have an extensive dating history given how smart and gorgeous you are."

He looked at me with those vivid blue eyes. "I don't trust others easily. I usually don't get too close to people."

"You trust me?" I gently pulled off his glasses and placed them on the bedside stand. His eyes became radiant.

"I trust you, Kristen."

"We'll go slow Marty. We'll take our time." I pulled one dress strap off my shoulder. I took his hand and placed it on my breast, releasing a slow breath as I felt the warmth radiating from his skin.

His cheeks flushed. It was so adorable to see him this way. "Kristen, I—I think I . . ."

"What is it?"

He shook his head. "Nothing. You're just so wonderful. The most amazing person I've ever met."

I smiled. "Even more amazing than Gary Becker?"

"A hundred times more amazing."

I tugged his brown hair and brought his lips down to mine. We made love that night for the first time.

***

Marty punched a fist-sized hole in the drywall of his apartment.

I was frightened. I'd seen small glimpses of his temper over the past few weeks—small outbursts over seemingly trivial things other people did—but I wasn't too concerned. I attributed it to stress. He was a TA and had a heavy course load after all. But his reactions had never gone this far.

"Marty, calm down. It's not a big deal."

"It is a big deal. How could he do that? Doesn't he have a conscience?"

"You're overreacting. He didn't mean it. He didn't see you coming so he accidentally opened the door and hit you in the face."

He sighed and rubbed his nose, which was beginning to swell up. He sat down on the brown suede couch next to me with his head in his hands.

"Why do you get so upset?" I asked. "Have you been stressed lately?" I began stroking his back gently. It was as much to soothe him as it was to soothe myself. I was still shaken up by that punch.

"No, I'm fine," he grumbled.

"Talk to me, Marty. You're not telling me something."

He didn't answer for a moment, preferring to rub his temples to calm himself. "I've never told anybody about this . . . sometimes I just get really angry. My mom was a bit harsh on me when I was growing up."

"What happened?"

He let out another long sigh. I could tell he was debating whether to say what was on his mind or not. "She was a drug addict." The words lingered in the air for a moment. "Even when she was pregnant with me, she was snorting cocaine. She says she's clean now but I know she still drinks a lot."

My heart ached for him. I knew what it was like to have a bad relationship with your parents. How it affected your social skills and your ability to relate to other people. You couldn't escape it no matter how far you ran. For me, moving from Texas to Massachusetts wasn't far enough. I thought I had it bad but it sounded like Marty had it even worse.

"I'm sorry to hear that," I said, continuing to rub his back to soothe him. "I didn't know."

He brightened unexpectedly. "Don't worry about it. It's in the past." He touched my cheek and kissed me. "I know I have a short fuse sometimes but I'm working on it. And you make me want to be better."

***

"Are you taking your medications?" I asked Marty. We were sitting in a secluded alcove of the Houghton library trying to study.

He had another bad episode recently when he punched a second hole in his wall because a professor criticized a point in one of his essays. The first hole had only been patched two months ago. We'd done it together with some do-it-yourself spackle from a nearby hardware store.

During that time, I'd recommended that he should see a therapist. He was reluctant at first but I finally convinced him to do it. After a few sessions, they told him he had borderline personality disorder, which meant his emotions were amplified and he was very impulsive. He could switch from extreme elation to extreme anger or depression quickly. All from a small trigger—slight criticism, a misunderstanding, etc.

His condition was both good and bad. The times he was happy, he was really happy, which made him the best person in the world to be around. He could brighten your day even if you had just attended a funeral that morning. That was part of the reason girls—and even some men—were attracted to him like moths to a flame. He just had that kind of energy.

But the times he was unhappy, he was awful to be around. It was like a black cloud loomed over his head, tainting everything around him. He would rant and rave, exhibit bitterness, paranoia, and sometimes become physically violent—but he had never hurt me. I had a hard time believing such a wonderful person could become so terrible so quickly. It made me nervous that he could switch between the two extremes in a heartbeat.

Dr. Perkins had prescribed him medication that he was to take regularly. It was supposed to regulate his mood fluctuations. Make him more balanced like the average person. Less volatile.

"No. I can't think straight when I'm on them. I have to write this paper that's due tomorrow."

I felt extremely frustrated. "Do you care about me Marty?"

"Kristen, I care about you more than anything else. You know that."

"Yeah, Marty. I know. But you understand how it affects me when you don't take your meds right? It makes me scared." Tears began welling in my eyes. I didn't want to cry, but it was so frustrating not being able to get through to him. He needed help and I felt helpless in aiding him.

"Shh, shh." He put his arms around my shoulders and rubbed my arm up and down. "I'm sorry, Kristen. I'll take them."

I wiped tears from my face with my hand. "Are you going to your sessions?"

"Yeah I am . . . just not in the past few weeks."

"You need to go to your sessions," I said, trying my best not to sound like I was nagging.

"I know, but Dr. Perkins is a dolt. She doesn't understand me. I'm not getting much from talking with her."

"She's supposed to be one of the best therapists on the east coast for treating your condition. Please, Marty. Won't you do it for me?"

He took a deep breath then relaxed his shoulders. "Okay. I'll do it for you."

***

I'd just gotten back to my dorm room from a party to find Marty sitting on my bed waiting for me, his mouth a thin line. His apartment was further away from campus than my room so we'd been spending a lot of time at my place. It made sense for him to carry my extra key.

The first words out of his mouth were an accusation. "You don't care about me Kristen."

I didn't take to that greeting well. "I do, Marty. Damn it. I do."

"Then why did you go to that party when you knew it would only make me jealous?"

"God. I just went with some girls. They were nice enough to invite me. It's not like I have a lot of other friends here. I invited you but you said you had too much work to do."

"I know. I just hate the thought of other guys making a move on you. You're so beautiful. It drives me nuts to think you'd leave me for someone better. Someone more handsome and charming."

"I'd never cheat on you Marty. You have to trust me."

He grumbled then softened his voice. "I do trust you."

***

It was spring break and I didn't really want to go home to see my parents so I went to Marty's instead. He'd said they had a large house and his parents would be excited to meet me. His dad, Charles Pritchard, was a founding partner at one of the most prestigious law firms on the east coast so his family was financially very well off. It'd been a week since I arrived at the Pritchard household located on the outskirts of Boston and things weren't quite what I expected.

I was standing next to Marty in the living room. We were planning to go out for a dinner date but the car was gone and the other two cars were in the shop.

"Where's Dad?" Marty asked..

"He's out late again," Mrs. Pritchard said. She was sitting in a recliner aimed at the big screen TV but the TV wasn't on. She had a half-empty bottle of amber liquid in her hand. Even in her disheveled state, Melody Pritchard was a knockout for her age. Radiant blonde hair, hourglass body, and the face of a Victoria's Secret model. I could see how Marty got his good looks. She lived up to the "trophy" part of trophy wife for sure. "Probably at work banging the secretary." She brought the bottle to her lips for a long sip. "Nobody loves me. Not your father. Not you. My own son doesn't love his mother."

"I do, Mom. You know I do."

"I raised you. I gave you my tits to drink from. You made them saggy and ugly. That's why your father is cheating on me. Because I'm no longer pretty enough for him. How can I blame him for wanting other women?"

"No, Mom. Dad's just busy with work. He's not cheating."

She took another drink. "Men are all the same. Liars and cheaters. Isn't that right Kristen?"

This was awkward. Super awkward. What was I supposed to say to that?

". . . I don't know Mrs. Pritchard. Marty hasn't cheated on me. At least not that I know of. . ." I looked at Marty warily. He gave me a sympathetic look as if to say "I'm sorry you have to deal with this."

Mrs. Pritchard huffed then took another sip and gestured the bottle at me. "I like you. You're a good girl. I'm glad Marty met you." She turned her attention to Marty. "You be good to Kristen. She's such a nice girl. A real sweetheart. Don't you cheat on her like your no good father cheats on me."

"I'd never do that, Mom. I'm good. Just like you raised me."

She nodded. "That's right. You're a good boy, Martin. My son."

Mr. Pritchard didn't get back with the car until midnight that night. We ended up ordering delivery pizza and watching mindless action movies in Marty's room. I faintly heard Mr. Pritchard and his wife arguing downstairs but most of it was drowned out by the explosions and gunshots blaring from the TV.

***

"What do you think about the idea of having kids someday?" Marty asked, his hands behind his head. I was leaning against his chest still coming off the buzz of a recent orgasm.

We'd just had angry make-up sex after having a heated argument over someone—a guy—leaving a benign comment on my Facebook wall. We fought, I ended up deleting it, then we humped like rabbits. It was becoming a more frequent occurrence.

I laughed and looked up at him. "Aren't we jumping the gun here a bit? I haven't even graduated yet."

He smiled. "Just a hypothetical question."

"I don't know. I haven't given it too much thought. Kids are cute when they're babies but even then they're a handful. I can't imagine how rough it'd be when they become teenagers. I'm not sure I'm fit to be a mother. Lord knows I haven't had a good reference."

"I think you'd make a great mom."

I laughed again. "That's quite a compliment. Care to provide some reasons to back up your claim Mr. Know-It-All?"

"You're very caring. Compassionate. You know what not to be like."

"Doesn't mean I know what to be like."

His smile widened and he winked one blue eye. "I have faith in you. You're a quick learner."

He was poking fun of me so I tickled his ribs because I knew he hated that. "How about you? What do you think of being a dad?"

"I'm looking forward to it someday, definitely. Settle down. Be a good father. I'd spend a lot of time with the kid and give a lot of attention, that's for sure."

"You're not going to be busy all the time like your dad?"

"I'd try my hardest not to be. I definitely don't want to be like that."

I began to think about what it would be like raising a kid with Marty. Just keeping our relationship on the tracks was hard enough because of his condition, I couldn't imagine what it would be like if we added a child to the mix.

"You're thinking about something," he said. "What is it?"

I shook my head. "Oh it's nothing."

"C'mon, you can tell me." He stroked my hair gently. "Don't worry, you're not going to upset me."

"Okay," I said softly. "I was going to ask if you were worried about your condition, if it'll be passed on to the baby."

He paused to think about it. "Supposedly, part of it is genetic so it's possible it could be passed down. But it's definitely not certain."

After a moment he smiled. "If it happens, you can be there to keep us both in line."

***

"Why would you drop out of law school?" I asked.

We were in my apartment in Boston. I'd already graduated and been working at a financial company for a few months. Marty was going to Yale Law School in Connecticut but had shown up at my place unexpectedly. We'd been on and off for close to a year now. Things started getting rockier after he went to law school. Every time I'd break up with him, he'd apologize profusely and promise to change. I'd forgive him and we'd try again. It was complicated between us.

This was one of our off cycles.

He shrugged. "It was pointless. I hated it."

"But you were going to work at your dad's firm right? What's he going to say?"

"He can go screw himself," Marty huffed. "That's all he cares about: his law firm. He'll probably be pissed and cut me off financially but whatever. I'm sure I'll find something else to do."

"Marty, it doesn't sound like you've thought this through. You're over halfway done. Why not just finish it?"

"It's stupid. I never wanted to do it anyway. My dad just forced me to do it. Having his son go to the top law school in the country makes him look good. He doesn't really care about me."

"You're upset, Marty. Let's think about this."

"No one cares about me. Dad's never around. Mom's a mess. You're all I have Kristen."

I inhaled air into my lungs to compose myself. "We can't keep doing this, Marty. It's getting tiring. We go through the same thing over and over again."

"I'm tired too but we love each other too much." He stared into my eyes. The intense gaze from those blue irises bore through layers of doubt and uncertainty. "We both know we'll never be over."

***

I shoved clothes and items into my luggage in a hurry. My pinky still hurt, which made it difficult picking things up with my right hand. I needed to get out of here. Get out of Boston.

Thankfully I didn't have much stuff. The apartment had been fully furnished when I moved in. All my essential things fit into two large suitcases—at least they did after I smooshed everything together. Everything else I could leave behind.

As for the email and Facebook passwords, I'd have to change them when I got to New York.

I needed to start over.

Chapter Nineteen

The pounding at my apartment door became a quiet knock after I told him to go away. The controlled response irritated me. How could Vincent act so cool after I'd just found out he cheated on me with Ariel? That asshole had some nerve showing up at my doorstep. I was going to open the door and scream at him. He was a wolf in sheep's clothing and he'd fooled me.

The worst part though—he wasn't the first.

I twisted back the deadbolt, but purposefully left the chain lock in place. Vincent wasn't coming inside—not unless he begged. And even then, probably not. I opened the door a crack and glanced at the man standing on my welcome mat.

I froze.

It wasn't Vincent at the other side of the door.

Piercing blue eyes. Square, rimless glasses. Tousled brown hair parted down the center.

It was Marty.

My hand instinctively leaped to the heart-shaped necklace around my neck. How could this be happening? I'd been so consumed with Vincent and work lately that I nearly forgot he had shown up at my apartment a month ago when only Riley was home.

"Kristen! I'm so glad I found you. I've been so worried." The familiar crisp, masculine voice flowed over me, halting my breath. He placed one hand over his heart while keeping the other one behind his back. He was wearing a black v-neck over jeans that led down to brown suede boots. The casual, laid-back appearance contrasted sharply with my reaction to seeing this man on my doorstep.

"Marty?" I wanted to shut the door, to run away, to change addresses again. Maybe change my name this time. But I couldn't move. My hands and feet had turned to ice.

"Wow, you look amazing." He smiled as his eyes scanned up and down my body. "Even better than I remember. I don't know how that's possible."

I became acutely aware that I was still wearing the hip-hugging black dress I'd worn to dinner with Vincent. My hair was still styled but my makeup was a mess after crying over Vincent's infidelity.

"H-How did you find me?"

"When I went to your place in Boston, I found out you weren't there. I didn't know where you went until I typed your name into Google recently and found this address."

That's insanely strange. I regularly Googled myself to make sure my new address never showed up on the internet for that very reason. I knew my company never posted specific employee information on their website. Had I slipped up somehow?

He continued. "I want to say I'm so so sorry for everything I've put you through. I know why you left in such a hurry and I can't blame you."

Tears caught in my throat as I recalled the traumatic moments of my pinky being twisted. A flood of conflicting emotions confused me. Fear. Relief. Pain. Hope. Good and bad memories flashed through my mind. Office hours. Swing dancing. Nights we made love. Days we screamed at each other. His fist going into the wall. We'd been together for two and a half years and I thought I'd locked away those memories in some dark recess of my brain but all of it came crashing down on me now like an avalanche.

"I know I can't ever take things back. I should've called but I knew I had to tell you this in person."

My grip on the necklace tightened. He was right. He shouldn't have just shown up on my doorstep unannounced. Not the first time. Not like this. I glanced warily at his other hand, which was still behind his back. I clicked off the safety on my mace necklace preparing for what he might do after what I was about to say to him.

"Marty, you shouldn't be here."

His blue eyes shifted. A subtle cover slid over them that changed their appearance to pleading. "I'm sorry. I'm so so sorry. I've been working on myself. I've been seeing Dr. Perkins. I haven't given up on us."

"That was two years ago," I stuttered. "I've moved on. I needed to start over."

A flinch in his features betrayed frustration. For a brief instant his eyes flickered intensity. It was the same look as when he punched a hole in his apartment wall. But as soon as it appeared, it disappeared. "Don't give up on me, Kristen. We've been through so much together. We've shared things we've never shared with anyone else. Don't throw that all away."

"You threw it all away. After what you did to me . . ." My hands trembled and my legs felt weak. I staggered against the wall for support. My body burned and my skin prickled. I could feel my heart beating rapidly. I wanted to shout, cry, push, shove, and throw my hands up in defeat all at the same. It was a strangely familiar feeling. Like I had sunk back into an old routine I'd learned to break.

And then I realized: after two years, we were arguing again.

"It was out of line, I know. I won't do it again, I promise. I've been working on myself these years we've been apart." He smiled in frustration. "You've got to listen to me."

How many times had he made promises before? He'd always broken them. He wouldn't take his meds. He wouldn't see his therapist. I'd wanted to believe in him time and time again. A part of me even wanted to believe him now. That he'd finally changed for better. But instinct won out. "No, Marty. No."

"Please, Kristen," he said softly. He pulled his hand out from behind his back. Surprised, I took a step back. In his hand was a bouquet of blue flowers. "I brought you these. Bluebonnets, your favorite."

I was shocked. He'd remembered an offhand comment I'd made when we had visited the botanical gardens while we were still dating.

He'd asked me which flower was my favorite and I'd said the bluebonnet because it reminded me of Texas and the color matched his stunning blue eyes.

My heart stopped in my chest. The anger, frustration, fear—all of it disappeared for a moment.

He stepped forward and extended his open palm through the narrow opening of the door. I could've shut the door before, but now if I tried it would mean shutting it on his hand.

"I'll never hurt you again," he said softly.

"Marty, I—"

His fingers nearly touching my hand at my necklace, I became painfully aware of my pinky throbbing. I didn't know what to do. It was happening all over again. The helplessness. The frustration. The desire to please. The hope that things would be different this time. The fear that they wouldn't be.

Then his fingers touched my hand. The next moment happened too quick for me to process. When my brain caught up, I saw Marty toppling across the floor. A short but muscular body in a striped polo had tackled him to the ground scattering blue flowers across the hallway.

"Bernie!" I screamed, recognizing his orange tan.

Where did he come from? What the hell was he doing? What was going on?

"Get off me!" Marty cried as he struggled to free himself from Bernie's bearhug from behind.

The two men rolled across the dusty hallway carpet, wrestling for dominance, kicking the ground, kicking the wall, crushing flowers in their wake. Bernie slid his bearhug high and managed to wrap his arm around Marty's neck for a chokehold. Marty grasped at Bernie's arm trying to pry it away but the arm was too strong and muscular; within moments, Marty's face became red from lack of circulation.

Growling and gritting his teeth, Marty pushed himself off the floor with Bernie still on his back hovering a foot off the ground.

Marty threw his back against the wall, slamming Bernie so hard it felt like the whole apartment building shook. It was enough to loosen Bernie's grip and Marty took advantage of the opportunity. He adjusted his chin and bit down on Bernie's forearm causing Bernie to release the hold. Marty staggered away but not before kicking Bernie in the face, making him reel backward.

"You fucking moron, messing with me," Marty cried, gasping for air. He faltered on his feet fighting against dizziness to regain his balance while Bernie leaned against the wall recovering from the damage he'd taken, spitting out blue petals from his mouth—and a tooth—in the process.

A tall man with long, toned arms swiftly moved behind Marty like a ninja and grabbed one of his arms and pulled it behind his back while twisting his wrist. It was professional, like something a police officer would do. How did Kurt know how to do that?

I unlatched the chain on the door and rushed into the hallway—not caring about how I looked.

"Stand back, Kristen." Kurt yelled. "We're not going to let him hurt you. We're here to protect you." Kurt pushed Marty down onto the ground and Bernie jumped on top of Marty's back to hold him still with his weight.

"W-what?" I stammered. I had no idea what was going on. It was all happening too fast.

"Kristen, I wasn't going to hurt you!" Marty shouted from his face-down position pinned beneath Bernie.

"He wasn't going to do anything," I cried.

"It's our job—" Kurt tightened Marty's arm behind his back, making him yelp. "To protect you."

I shook my head in disbelief, frantically trying to grasp the situation. "I don't understand."

"Please. Get back inside the apartment Ms. Daley," said Bernie whose nose and mouth were bleeding from Marty's kick.

"Why? How did you know my last name?"

I was about to ask more questions when I heard footsteps bounding up the stairwell. Had somebody in one of the other apartments heard the commotion and reported it? Was it the police?

An imposing figure in elegant dress clothes appeared at the top of the stairs. His breathing was fast and his dark eyes were fierce.

Vincent. He looked as if he had come straight from the restaurant where I left him.

Noticing me along with the commotion nearby, a grave look swept over his features. He dashed down the hallway toward us, his black loafers thumping like hooves against the dingy carpet.

"Vincent!" I cried. I was surprised by the relief I felt at seeing him.

Vincent stopped in front of us, his face marred with concern. He gently gripped my shoulders. "Kristen, are you all right? Are you hurt in any way?" His usual composure in dangerous situations was gone.

"I-I'm fine, Vincent. But it's crazy. There's a fight . . . I don't know what to do. I'm scared." Everything was happening so fast, I couldn't form the proper words to explain. Even if I could, he wouldn't believe me. How could I explain that Marty had shown up unexpectedly with flowers and then my seriously muscular neighbor who likes Lady Gaga tackled him thinking he was going to hurt me? Even I'd have trouble believing me.

I was glad Vincent was here now though. Once again, I became aware of how Vincent made me feel safe. He'd put an end to this drama.

Vincent turned his gaze to Marty being held on the ground. Marty was still struggling, cursing. Vincent's jaw became tight and his eyes a blazing inferno. "You think you can use fear to control her? I'll show you fear." Vincent clenched his hands. "Bring him to his knees," he said.

Kurt and Bernie brought Marty up to his knees while continuing to restrain him. Marty tried to resist but Kurt tightened the hold on his arm. As Vincent stood in front of Marty kneeling, I could tell that they had similar heights and builds. They glared at each other fiercely like two wild lions ready to fight over a female. The similarity between them was jarring.

"What are you doing Vincent?" I cried. Vincent ignored me. His focus was solely on Marty.

"You son of a bitch." Vincent pulled his arm back and swung, landing a clean blow across Marty's cheek. Marty's glasses flew off his head and slammed against the nearby wall. I thought I heard somebody's bone crack. I wasn't sure if it was Marty's jaw or Vincent's knuckle.

"What are you doing?" I screamed.

"Why'd you hit me you piece of shit? I'll fucking kill you," Marty yelled.

"You think you're tough beating up women?" Vincent snarled.

He took another swing with his other hand, landing a blow on Marty's other cheek.

"You just want to control her. You have no right."

"Fuck you. You don't know shit about me!" Marty cried.

Then Vincent began kicking him in the stomach.

"Go to hell," Marty panted in between blows.

"You don't care about her. You never did."

I'd never seen this side of Vincent before. He punched Marty again and again as if possessed. I watched in horror as a realization swept over me: Marty was going to die.

I leaped in front of Vincent to shield Marty. Vincent pulled his punch back as I wrapped my arms around him and buried my face into his chest.

"Stop Vincent! Please, god. Stop. You're going to kill him!"

His body tensed. His arm raised up to strike. I closed my eyes and prepared myself for the worst. Then suddenly I felt his body relax. Vincent's arm slowly came down to his side.

"You come anywhere near Kristen again and I'll fucking kill you."

"You want us to take him away, boss?" Kurt asked.

Boss? Why did Kurt just call him boss? How did he know Vincent?

"Wait." Vincent gently gripped my waist and moved me to the side. He stepped toward Marty and grabbed him by the hair lifting his head to stare into his eyes. "Tell me you understand."

Marty gurgled something incomprehensible, his eyes half-dazed.

"Nod your head if you understand."

Vincent released his grip on Marty's head and Marty nodded faintly.

"Take care of him," Vincent said to Kurt.

Kurt nodded and stooped to pick up Marty's glasses. He and Bernie dragged Marty off by the arms toward the stairwell. Marty put up no resistance this time, his feet dragging along ground.

I couldn't believe what Vincent just said. Were they going to murder Marty in cold blood? Frantically, I asked, "You're not going to kill him are you?"

Vincent looked at me intensely; his brows narrowed into sharp lines frightened me. "Of course not. That was never going to happen. They'll patch him up and send him away, and then I'll have them keep an eye on him to make sure he never comes back. Kurt and Bernie are pros. You're safe now."

"You almost killed him! What the fuck is wrong with you?" I began to pound on his chest with my hands, tears forming in my eyes.

He gripped my arms firmly and stared deep into my eyes. The blazing inferno from earlier was gone, replaced by an equally fierce tenderness. "I needed to make sure he wasn't going to hurt you again."

"But—"

"Look, let's go inside before the neighbors call the police. I'll explain everything."

I was still shaking when Vincent put his arm around my shoulders. He ushered me inside, stepping on blue petals in the process.

242 | Priscilla West

I entered my apartment with Vincent's warm arm around my shoulder. My eyes stung with tears. Thoughts raced through my mind in a swirl. I was flooded with questions.

He gestured to the couch to have a seat but I turned to him as soon as he closed the door behind us. "What the fuck was that Vincent?" I spat. "Why were my neighbors going badass commando on Marty?"

His calm facade had returned and he reached out to wipe the tears from my cheek. "They were the security team I hired to keep an eye on you."

My world spun. I could feel the blood draining from my face. I no longer knew what was real and what wasn't. "You hired a security team?"

"Yes, to watch over you. To keep you safe."

The neutral tone of his response infuriated me. "What the hell? I thought you were half-joking about that."

His expression became unexpectedly dark. "I'd never joke about something like that."

"We talked about this. I told you I didn't want one and you agreed to that. That's why we went to Grandpa Rambo's store on the outskirts of town for mace. You didn't listen to me. You lied to me."

He grimaced. "I did it because I care about you Kristen. It was for your own protection."

"My protection? God. What's wrong with you? This isn't the wild west, Vincent. Seriously, you almost killed a man today."

His mouth was a thin line. "Maybe he deserved it."

"Jesus, I feel like I don't even know you. One minute you're nice and charming, the next you're a violent psychopath. You and your security team beat up a single man like some kind of goon squad. I was expecting the couple across the hall to maybe ask for a cup of sugar every now and then, not turn out to be fucking mercenaries."

His features twisted in pain. "Please, Kristen. I'm sorry. I did lie to you but please understand I had to ensure your safety."

"Keeping me safe is one thing. wailing on Marty like some kind of mobster is another. That crossed a ton of lines. Why didn't you break his legs with a baseball bat while you were at it? Or better yet, cut off one of his fingers. How do I know that's not what's happening right now?"

"I know it seems extreme but believe me, it was necessary. I've seen guys like him before. I know they don't give up easily. I wouldn't have gone that far if I didn't think it was necessary."

I put my hands on my hips. "You've seen guys like him before? Where? Some TV show?"

Vincent sighed deeply. "My sister Giselle had an abusive boyfriend. That's how I know."

I grunted in frustration. He was dropping bomb after bomb on me, destroying pieces of reality I thought I had a hold on. "Okay. Why didn't you tell me about this?"

"I didn't feel comfortable talking about it. And I didn't know if I could trust you before."

"Trust me?" I threw my hands up. "I told you secrets about myself I hadn't told anyone and you were holding back on me. What better time were you going to get to tell me than that night in your apartment when I spilled to you about Marty? But no, you didn't trust me, even after I took such a risk by trusting you, Vincent. How is that supposed to make me feel?"

"I was focused on your problem, Kristen. I wanted to keep it about you."

"Showing me you understood would have been about me, Vincent. Holding out on me while you made plans about my privacy is about you."

"You're right, Kristen. It was selfish. I'm sorry I didn't see it that way before. I was trying to do what I thought was best. Hopefully you

244 | Priscilla West

see that, even if you disagree with my actions." He gently rested his hand on my shoulder.

Despite enjoying the sensation, I shrugged it off. "I don't trust you now though. You lied to me. You fucked Ariel Diamond. You cheated on me. At least Marty never did that." I tried shoving him away but he was like a wall. Instead it was me that fell backward. He grabbed me before I could fall on my ass.

"Hang on, Kristen. Listen to me," he growled, raising the hairs on the back of my neck. "That is all a mistake. The text you saw from Ariel wasn't what it looked like."

"How gullible do you think I am? What else could it mean? It was pretty clear: she liked riding your cock," I spat. The words tasted like battery acid coming off my tongue. I regained my footing and pushed out of his arms. He stepped forward and pulled my waist to him demonstrating his persistence. I knew I wouldn't win a battle of wills with him so I let it pass.

"She meant my surfboard. The new product my company launched—which is why I went to Brazil. It's called the Shuttlecock." He articulated his words carefully but assertively.

What. The. Fuck.

The room spun. "You're lying," I said uncertainly.

"No." His voice softened and his eyes carried the tenderness they had earlier. "I'm not lying. I'm sorry you saw that, but Ariel was just being flippant in that text like she usually is. It's her personality. You saw how she was when you met her. I'm sure she had no idea you'd be seeing that message. Even she's not that much of a trouble-maker."

A wave of embarrassment washed over me. I'd run out of the restaurant upset over a misunderstanding. Realization that my actions must've seemed absolutely childish to him made me pissed off. At him.

"'Shuttlecock?' You have to be kidding me. That's the stupidest name I've ever heard."

He allowed himself a smile. "You thought 'Pier Pleasure' was pretty clever."

"That at least makes sense. Shuttlecock makes no sense."

He took a deep breath and sighed. "You're right, it's dumb. But it's edgy and it's selling well. As you can see, people love making cock jokes."

I took a step back and folded my arms across my chest. I eyed him sternly. "So you didn't have sex with Ariel?"

"No. God no. I haven't even seen her since the time we ran into her on St. Lucia. I told you we're just friends and have been for years. I'd never cheat on you Kristen. Now that would be stupid. Unbelievably stupid."

My arms tightened. "I don't know if I can believe you."

"It's true. There's not much I can do to prove it so you're just going to have to trust me."

"I've trusted you all this time. But now with the whole security team thing, you going psycho, Giselle, and everything else, I don't know what to think. What else are you hiding from me?"

"Ask me anything. I'll tell you."

I clenched my jaw. "But I don't even know what to ask, Vincent. You can't do that—put the blame on me for not asking the right questions."

"No, Kitten. That's not how I meant it."

After lying to me, he was still calling me Kitten? Give me a break. "Don't call me that. You've lost that privilege."

He exhaled heavily and gestured to the living room. "Okay, let's sit down on the couch, cool off, and talk."

Because my feet were getting tired, I begrudgingly obeyed. Once we were seated, I ran through in my mind what I had just learned, deciding what to ask. There were so many pieces missing that needed filling in. I decided to start with the first question on my mind. "So what happened with Giselle?"

He shifted in his seat beside me. "She was in a relationship with someone she met in college for two years. Jim. No one knew she was suffering. There were small signs like arguing but it seemed normal—couples usually have fights every now and then. It wasn't until I saw her bruises that . . . that I decided I needed to intervene. I made sure he got the message." He sighed.

"I'm sorry about what happened to your sister, but in this case you took it too far. Way too far. You didn't have to break Marty's face. He wasn't going to hurt me."

"What did he want?"

"He said he just wanted to talk."

Vincent's eyes narrowed as he ground his teeth. "I wouldn't believe him. That's a classic trick they use. He hurt you before. That's enough to establish that he's dangerous."

"He said he was sorry and brought me flowers. He just wanted to apologize."

"You don't know that Kristen. Kurt and Bernie were watching. If they made a move, it meant they thought you were in danger."

"You don't know either. He was just extending his hand to say sorry. Last time I checked that wasn't a felony."

He looked at me probingly. "Why are you defending him?"

"Jesus, Vincent. Can you be any more insensitive? I'm not defending him." My eyes began tearing again. "Don't treat me like I'm a helpless victim. I can't stand it."

"My team will make sure you won't be."

"Why aren't you listening to me?" I screamed. "Get rid of them! I hate the idea of being watched and monitored."

He kept his gaze firmly on me as I broke down. "Kristen, he might come back. You have to take this seriously."

"You nearly killed him for bringing me flowers, Vincent! I doubt he'd be coming back. I think he 'got the message'."

He quietly handed me a tissue. I took it and wiped my eyes, pulling mascara off in the process. I knew I looked like a mess but I didn't care.

"I don't like it. I want you to feel safe. If he does come back, you'll be completely exposed."

I closed my eyes for a moment and forced out a shaky breath. "Right now, I'm more afraid of you than I am of him."

He narrowed his brows. "You don't mean that."

I looked at him directly. "I do. You don't know what it's like watching your boyfriend nearly beat your ex to death. I'm scared of you and what you're capable of."

Vincent staggered back for a moment, no doubt reeling from my response. "All right, fine. I'll get rid of the security team. I'll tell them to put a tracking device on his car so we can monitor his whereabouts." He stared into my eyes. "But you should know that I'd never hurt you."

"You already have. Maybe not physically like Marty did, but you hurt me emotionally. You betrayed my trust."

"Okay. How can I make this right?"

I shook my head. "I don't know if you can."

"I really care about you Kristen and if you need space, I can do that." He got up from the couch. "But if I had to choose between us breaking up and you being safe, without a doubt I'd choose the latter. I wouldn't be able to live with myself if you got hurt and I had the ability to prevent it. I'd even lie to you if it meant saving you from harm."

"You can't do that. You can't take away my choice from me. I'm a grown woman who can make her own choices balancing her privacy and her safety. You made it your choice."

"It's what happens when you—" He cut his sentence short. "When you really care about someone. If you're asking if I'd do it again. I'll tell you right now: I'd do it in a heartbeat."

After he left, I locked the door. Then I went to my room to cry.

***

I'd cried until I felt nauseous from everything and vomited. It was incredible the police didn't show up. The commotion from the fighting, shouting, and cursing was probably heard on multiple floors. I didn't know my other neighbors on the floor that well but I knew they were in their mid-twenties. They were probably out clubbing. It was Friday night after all.

I walked from the bathroom to the kitchen to get a cup of water. It was past midnight and I was exhausted from the evening's events. I couldn't wait to fall asleep and block everything out until tomorrow. During a long sip of water, the front door unlocked, opened, and clacked against the chain lock.

"Kristen? You left the chain lock on. Open up."

I nearly choked on my water before I recognized the voice.

"Riley, is that you? Are you by yourself?"

"Uh yeah, duh. Were you expecting someone else?" She jiggled the door again but it wouldn't budge. "Are you naked right now with whip cream on your nipples waiting for Vincent to show up? Is that why there are flower petals all over the doormat?"

I breathed a sigh of relief. Typical Riley. "No, I'm not naked," I hollered. "I'll open the door." I went to undo the chain. Once she was inside, I redid the chain.

The short blue dress she went out in was rumpled and there were drink stains on it. She must've danced pretty hard, even if she'd gotten in early. "So how was dinner?" she asked.

I groaned. "Bad."

"Bad? Or badass?" Riley said, her mood chipper as she flung off her shoes into the corner.

When I didn't respond, she looked at me and studied my face. "Whoa Kristen, were you crying? Oh my god, what happened?"

I told her about how I saw Ariel's text message during dinner with Vincent and how I ran home and then Marty showed up.

Riley dropped her bags, gripped my shoulders, and shook me. "Are you okay? Did you call the police?"

"No. Kurt and Bernie tackled him. Turns out they were Vincent's security team he assigned to watch over me."

She squinted. "You mean the gay couple across from us?"

I wasn't sure about the gay couple part. In fact, I didn't know what to believe about Kurt and Bernie. They could've been Navy SEALs or trained killers for all I knew. "Yeah."

"No way." She put her hand up to my forehead to check my temperature.

"Yes way. They restrained Marty and Vincent showed up and beat the shit out of him. I thought Vincent was going to kill him."

Riley gasped. "Wow! I'm sure he was just protecting you though, right?"

"Yeah, but it was way overboard. Marty wasn't even doing anything threatening. We were just talking outside my door when he was tackled."

Her voice lowered. "But he could have done something. It can happen in a split second."

I shook my head. "Still. You don't go as far as Vincent did. He was punching and kicking Marty so hard I thought he was going to die. Plus, he lied to me. He asked me before if I wanted a security team and I told him no and he ignored my answer completely. It makes me feel so small and powerless!" I began to cry.

Riley pulled me to her and hugged me. "It's okay. You're safe now."

I sobbed into her shoulder. "I don't know what to do, Riley."

"Are you afraid Vincent's going to hurt you?" Her words were careful.

"No, I don't think he'll hurt me. But then again I didn't know he was capable of what he did to Marty. I don't know if I can trust him. I don't know what to think."

"You said he cheated on you with that chick Ariel, right? Then fuck him. Let him go surfing with sharks and have his dick get bitten off."

"I saw a text from Ariel saying she enjoyed riding his cock—and I freaked out. But Vincent explained that she was referring to his company's new surfboard called the Shuttlecock."

She pulled back and looked at me. "Are you serious? You have to be kidding." She laughed. "That's hilarious. What a clever name."

"No it's not! It's stupid."

"A shuttlecock in badminton moves back and forth through the air—kind of like how a surfboard moves across a wave. Plus it has the word 'cock' in it. You have to admit that's pretty genius marketing."

Apparently I wasn't the target audience. "You're the worst."

She laughed. "Aw, I'm sorry Kris. I'm listening." She led me by the hand and we took a seat on the couch.

Riley whipped out her phone and began pecking at it. "Looks like there really is a surfboard named that. It's got rave reviews already. People are saying they love the handling but the best part is the name. So I don't think he was lying to you. It was just an innocent misunderstanding."

"He lied about the security team though. And he acted like a psycho. He told me it was because his younger sister Giselle had an abusive boyfriend and he beat that guy up."

"Sounds like he's a knight with shining abs."

Her tone was starting to piss me off. I needed my best friend to take me seriously. "Or a guy with a temper problem. I never knew Vincent had that side to him."

That wiped the smile off her face. "Stop it. Vincent's totally different from Marty. He had a good reason for doing what he did.

Marty hurt you before and I can see why Vincent reacted the way he did. Hell, if I was here when Marty showed up, I'd probably mace first, ask questions later."

She put her phone back in her pocket and rested her hand on my knee. "Give Vincent a chance. He's not perfect. You showed him your baggage, now he's shown you his. Take some time to think about it."

That was a good point about baggage. "I get where Vincent's coming from, but I don't know if we're going to work out. There's so much drama in my life—Vincent, Marty, work stuff. I really wish things were simpler. I don't know if I can handle all the chaos right now. I'm pretty close to a total breakdown."

Riley looked at me searchingly. "Are you thinking of breaking up with Vincent?"

I sighed. "Maybe. Or at least taking a break from our relationship."

She took my hand gently in hers. "To me it sounds like Vincent really cares about you. And I mean really. He got you a freaking security team. And from what you've told me over the past few weeks, you really care about him too. Am I right?"

"Of course I care about him."

"This is only your first fight as a couple, right?"

"Well, it's our second. The first one happened after I met Ariel. This one is much bigger."

"So it's your first major fight. That's pretty normal considering how long you've been seeing each other. I usually have major fights in the first few weeks."

"The circumstances aren't normal at all. Lying about security teams and mauling exes isn't normal."

"Lies are pretty common, Kris. People have been forgiven for far worse lies than covering up an attempt to be overprotective against a psycho ex-boyfriend."

I rolled my eyes. "That's a strong case."

Her blue eyes became serious. "Kristen, you've always been afraid of consequences since I've known you. You're afraid of getting hurt and that makes perfect sense given what you've been through. Your relationship with Vincent is a risk for sure. He could hurt you emotionally but you could also hurt him. But what relationship isn't a risk? Sometimes you have to take a risk because the reward is worth it."

I groaned. "You sound like Vincent talking about risk-taking."

She smiled. "Do I? Have you considered that maybe Vincent sounds like me?"

A grin spread on my lips. I didn't know how she did it, but Riley always knew how to make me smile in the worst circumstances. "He definitely does not sound like you. You've got a dirtier mind."

Her smile turned wicked. "And proud of it. So are you going to be okay? Or do we need to go to Savage Hunks to cheer you up? They're still open at this hour you know."

The last thing I needed right now was to see more muscled men causing a commotion. I needed peace tonight. "As tempting as that sounds, I think I'm okay now. At least a lot better than before."

She squeezed my hand. "I'll be here for you, whatever you need."

I squeezed her hand back. "Thanks Riley."

***

I didn't have work the next day since it was Saturday. Thank goodness because I didn't think I'd be able to get any work done with everything spinning in my mind. Although I had been exhausted the previous night, I still had difficulty falling asleep.

Unfortunately, that didn't stop me from waking up at the usual seven. Habit can be a bitch sometimes.

I immediately checked my phone and realized I had turned it off the previous night. Remembering why I had done so, I chose to leave it off. Still groggy but unusually hungry, I decided to start the morning with a big breakfast of eggs, bacon, and sausage, hoping the meal would help me fall back asleep.

Fortunately it did the trick. I ended up sleeping well into the afternoon. I woke up and immediately went to the couch to veg out in front of the TV. There was a lot on my mind and I wanted to drown it out, which is why I tuned into Bridezillas—my guilty pleasure. Except I felt no guilt watching it, only pure unadulterated pleasure.

Just when a bride's grandmother said she looked like a slut in her chosen wedding gown, I heard a rustling across the hall. I looked out my peephole and saw Kurt and Bernie moving boxes from their apartment. I'd barely gotten to know them and they were already moving out. Bernie's face was looking a lot better without all the blood, although it was a bit swollen. His deep tan made it less noticeable, though.

I thought about stepping out to say something to them but everything I could think of sounded awkward: "Thanks for beating up my ex-boyfriend yesterday . . . I think? How do you two know Vincent? So . . . do you guys tan together?"

I ended up watching them for a few minutes then returning to my show.

They didn't have much stuff, so after a few hours, I heard them finish and lock up. I spent the rest of the day vegging out on the couch, thinking about my situation.

I was still upset with Vincent even though I knew he cared about me and I cared about him. It only made it that much more painful that he lied to me. There were trust issues Vincent and I had to work out and that would take time and effort.

Then there was the issue of work. Carl was feeding me opportunities and I'd been snapping them up, which made me busier and busier. Vincent seemed to be in a similar situation with his company occupying most of his time the past few weeks.

Even though my employers hadn't found out about my relationship with Vincent, it was still becoming a problem. It needed

254 | Priscilla West

work and neither of us had the time to do it—at least not without making significant sacrifices.

When the latest episode ended with the bride literally pulling chunks of her own hair out, I came to the conclusion that I was going to take a break from my relationship with Vincent. I couldn't keep going with things the way they were. If I didn't make a change, I would lose my mind.

***

On Sunday afternoon I finally gave in to turning on my phone. I was going to call Vincent and tell him we should take a break. Closing my bedroom door, I picked up my phone from the nightstand and turned it on. There were a bunch of unread text messages—some of them new and some of them from Friday when I ran out of the restaurant.

I ignored the messages and called him.

He answered on the first ring. "Kristen?"

His silky voice had its usual effect on me even though I knew to prepare for it. "Vincent . . ."

He released an audible exhale and I could picture his chest lowering from the release of air. "I'm so glad to hear your voice. I thought I wasn't going to hear from you again and that scared me."

"Hey Vincent. Listen . . . I need to tell you something." I had to push this conversation forward before Vincent's persuasive hold took effect. Otherwise, I'd begin doubting my decision. Fortunately, it was much easier to resist him on the phone than in person.

"Wait. Just a moment." I heard some mumbling in the background. "Shit. I'm sorry, Kristen. I have a meeting right now. But whatever you want to tell me sounds important. Is it an emergency? Can I meet you later? I'll try my hardest to be done by six."

"You're at work on a Sunday?"

There was another mumble in the background. "Yeah, sorry. We have a lot going on over here right now."

I breathed deeply, reaffirmed in my decision that we were both too busy to make this work. "I'll drop by your office at six thirty then."

Meeting him at his office as opposed to his place or my place would make it easier to leave after the discussion. It would've been easier just to tell him over the phone but I supposed it was more appropriate to handle this in person.

His voice brightened. "Can't wait to see you then."

"Bye Vincent."

When evening rolled around, I gingerly stepped out my front door in jeans and a t-shirt. It'd been nearly two days since I left the apartment. I made sure to pack my taser in my purse before I went over to Vincent's office in case I ran into any more trouble along the way.

As expected, the commute downtown was less crowded than usual since most people weren't working. High-powered CEOs were one of the exceptions. I made it to the Red Fusion offices to find a few people crunching on their laptops. I was about to ring Vincent when an employee who recognized me from before kindly opened the glass door. I thanked him and he promptly returned to his desk to work on his keyboard. Knowing the way to Vincent's office, I walked down the hall and stopped in front of his door. This wasn't going to be an easy discussion, but it had to be done.

I took a deep breath then went inside.

Vincent was at his desk, brows furrowed and typing furiously. He was in his usual elegant New York attire: white shirt with red-striped tie and black pants. When he saw me—those dark brown eyes piercing me like arrows—he stopped working and smiled. "Kristen."

"Hey," I said, returning his smile. I kept one hand in my jeans and waved at him with the other.

He glided around the desk and hugged me tightly, the squeeze making my legs turn to jelly momentarily. As always, he smelled wonderful. The spicy scent tickled my nostrils as well as other parts of my body. He kissed me on the forehead then the tip of my nose. "I'm so glad you're here. I thought you'd call so I could let you in."

"I was going to when one of your employees let me inside," I said as he led me by the hand to his leather couch in the corner. I was reminded of the first time I entered this office intending to make another case for choosing Waterbridge-Howser as his wealth management firm but wound up almost having sex with him instead. That was a distressing time in my life but not quite as distressing as recent events.

"I got you these." He reached for the coffee table and handed me a bouquet of red roses. There was a card attached with a small puffin on the front. It looked rough, like it was drawn with crayons by a child.

"Did you draw this picture?" I asked.

"Yeah, you like it?" He sounded proud of his work.

I had to stifle a laugh. A smile broke out on my face despite myself. "Let's just hope the inside makes up for it."

The card read:

Kristen, I'm sorry. I messed up. I lied to you and didn't respect your choices. Give me a chance to make it up to you.

Yours, Vincent

"This is really sweet, Vincent." I took a whiff of the roses and savored the fresh fragrance. The gesture touched my heart but gifts could only go so far.

"I'm glad you like it." He smiled, his boyish grin making my insides mushy. "So what did you want to tell me earlier today? It sounded important."

I carefully put the items on the seat next to me and exhaled, gathering up the courage to tell him what I'd planned on saying. "I want to take a break."

His smile faded and his dark eyes studied me. "What kind of break?"

"A break from us."

"Temporary or permanent?"

"Temporary. For now at least. My life is too crazy at the moment and I'm sure you're really stressed out as well. It'll be good for both of us."

His gaze narrowed. "The only time I'm not stressed is when I'm with you."

I looked at him skeptically. "What about your work? You've seemed pretty worried about it the last few weeks."

"Work is work. I can manage it, especially when I'm thinking about you. It helps to have something to look forward to."

"I thought you said I was a distraction?"

"That was when my priorities were different. Seems so long ago. Now work is the distraction."

"And I'm your main concern now? Is it because of Marty?"

"It's because the way I feel about you. You're more than a concern. You're a part of my life."

"You've been so busy lately. I've hardly seen you. I don't feel like I've been that big of a part of your life."

I expected him to have some kind of charming response but instead, he bent down and casually slipped off each of his black loafers, leaving him in his black socks. He set his shoes near my feet. Then he started slipping off my flats.

"Uh, what are you doing?"

He managed to slip off one when I pulled my legs away.

"I sincerely hope that you're not expecting us to have sex on your couch. I know you're all for 'finishing what we started' but roses and a cute card aren't going to cut it."

His expression was unreadable. "Give me your feet. I want to show you something."

"What for?"

"Trust me."

Sensing he didn't intend for us to have sex, I gingerly scooched my legs back and offered him the foot with the remaining shoe. He gently removed it and inserted my feet in his loafers.

I felt the lingering warmth of his feet on my own. I looked down and was fascinated by the maleness of the shoe. The texture of the leather was smooth and glossy but the slight crease near the toes and various small nicks gave it a rough, unrefined edge. The shape narrowing sharply at the toes seemed to point forward like a general points his hand to rally an army's charge. I imagined Vincent wearing these in a variety of scenarios: walking to high-powered meetings, standing in front of a podium giving a company-wide speech, bending down to pick up a quarter. My drab flats looked feminine and dainty in comparison.

I wiggled my toes inside, probing the empty space between the inner lining and my feet. Although comfortable, the loafers were much too big for me. They might as well have been clown shoes.

"Now close your eyes for a moment."

I did as he asked, expecting further instructions. After an awkward minute of not receiving any, I opened my eyes.

Vincent looked at me expectantly. "Well?"

"Well what?"

"What do you feel?"

I wiggled my toes again. "Umm . . . a soft insole? I don't know. What am I supposed to feel?"

"You're supposed to feel the muscles in your legs tensing, blood coursing between them, your cock getting hard like steel."

"Um, what?"

"You experience an intense attraction to Kristen. You were thinking about product strategy before but now your thoughts are turning dirty. You can't think straight. All you can think about is when you're going to see Kristen again. And if anyone hurts her, there will be hell to pay. Then you realize she's what you want. All you've ever wanted." He put his hand on my leg, the warmth seeping through the denim to my skin. "When you put yourself in my shoes. That's what you feel."

"Oh."

"Now imagine feeling that all the time. During meetings; on the plane; while you're eating . . . You see now how you're a part of my life?"

I nodded. "You make a good point."

"Do you still want to see me?"

Vincent's charm was starting to take its effect on me but I still had reservations. Maybe I'd built up resistance to him from all our time together. "I don't know. Yes and no."

"What are the reasons for 'yes'?"

I put my finger on my chin and thought about it. "You make a mean omelette."

"That's it?"

"Umm . . . Shrimp pasta as well. Also, you've shown you really care about me. Taking me on trips, carving time out of your busy schedule to be with me, being concerned about my safety."

"And the orgasms?"

"They're a nice perk but I think I could go without them and be okay."

"Then I have room for improvement. Okay, what are the reasons for 'no'?"

"I don't know if I can trust you."

"You've trusted me in the past."

"That's true."

"The bar in Cape Town, surfing, being discreet about our dating, blindfolds, cybersex, sex on my plane . . . am I missing anything?"

"Not that I can think of."

"And I messed up by getting that security team. And for not telling you about Giselle's ex-boyfriend, which you must admit is not a complete breach in trust. More like a half-breach."

I mused about it. "All right, I'll give you that."

"Also the Ariel text message was a misunderstanding so that doesn't count."

"It pissed me off so I'd say that's a half-breach."

"Fine. Even so, it's six in support of trusting me versus two in support of distrusting me. I'd say the odds are in my favor."

"In terms of numbers, maybe. But numbers are soft when there's feelings involved."

"Do you still have feelings for me?"

"Yes. I do. But I still think we should take a break."

He tried inserting his feet into my flats but only managed to squeeze a few toes inside.

"That's not what your shoes are telling me."

"Oh?" I became curious. "What are they saying?"

"They're saying life is crazy right now. I don't know what to do. I want to figure things out on my own because I'm a strong, independent woman. I want to prove it to Vincent and to myself. But I do know that Vincent really cares about me. He's always had the best intentions for me. And I really care about him. As much as I try to say otherwise, I really don't want to be apart from him."

I laughed despite myself, tears welling up in my eyes. He was so sweet. "My shoes talk too much."

He smiled and cleared his throat, but I could tell he was affected too, his eyes betraying him with a glisten. "Come on Kristen, give us a chance. We both have crazy lives but it doesn't mean we should fix things by ourselves. It might be easier. But if we make it through this together, we'll be stronger. If we make it through this alone, we'll just be better at being alone." He touched my cheek tenderly. "Let's work this out together."

He gently brought my head into his chest. I grumbled but didn't resist because it felt too good, too comforting. The distress I felt over our issues seemed to magically disappear when he held me. I realized how much I loved his touch and being with him despite our problems. It was worth taking a chance. Vincent was worth it. Even if it meant risking getting hurt.

"Fine," I muttered. "We'll do this together."

He exhaled in relief and kissed my head. "Can I call you Kitten again?" he asked, nuzzling his cheek in my hair.

I tried to think of a response that didn't make it seem like I totally forgave him. "As long as you let me call you Vinnie the Pooh."

He laughed, the throaty sound flowing over me. "That's the first time I've heard that one."

I looked up at him. "What other ones have you heard?"

"Vin Diesel. My Cousin Vinny. Vitty Cent. Vincent van Gogh . . ." He started grinning.

I giggled. "Those are pretty good but I think your drawing skills need a little work for that last one to work."

"You got me." He smiled. "I made that one up a while ago and tried to get people to use it but it never caught on."

I giggled again.

"But none of those names were as clever as yours." He bent and sealed his lips over my mouth. Our tongues slowly, tenderly probed one another until the need to breathe interrupted them. "You can call me whatever you like."

"I'll probably stick with 'Vincent'. I think it suits you best."

"Vincent it is then, Kitten. Listen, my sister Giselle is having a birthday party for her son next Saturday. Do you want to come with me?"

Vincent at a birthday party for his nephew? I had to see this. It would also give me the chance to meet his sister, Giselle. I recalled the picture he had of her in his island cabin, the two of them smiling on a beach together. I hadn't met any of Vincent's family before and I was more than curious to see how he would act around his sister.

"Sure. Am I going to see you before that this week?"

His face softened. "Not this week, sorry. Flying out tomorrow morning until Friday. I will call you every night, though. My schedule can slow down, Kristen, and it will. It's just going to take some time."

"Okay. I'll look forward to those calls, then."

"Me too."

Chapter Twenty

Sure enough, he called me every evening that week. The work week was otherwise pretty boring—fleshing out Vincent's BRIC strategy and continuing research on Selena Devries—but I began to look forward to talking to him every night so much that the days flew by. I appreciated that Vincent was making an effort after the events the previous weekend. Seeing the way he had been so violent with Marty had shaken my confidence in him, but his tender side was still there. It would be interesting to see how this would continue at his nephew's party.

Saturday morning finally came. Vincent picked me up from my apartment in a silver Aston Martin at nine in the morning. Traffic getting out of the city was a drag, as usual, but we spent the time chatting idly. It was an important step for us to build our relationship back up after it had been badly shaken with our fight. The whole day was important for that reason.

We arrived a little after ten-thirty and pulled up in front of a tidy suburban ranch-style home. The lawn was freshly mowed, and there were balloons on the mailbox announcing a birthday party. We parked on the street. Vincent had brought a birthday present wrapped in balloon wrapping paper, and I handed it to him as we got out of the car. We walked down the street and up the driveway to the house.

"So your nephew's name is Brady?" I asked Vincent, reading the sign on the mailbox.

Vincent smiled and grabbed my hand. The present was in the other. "Yup. He's turning three today."

"Did you pick out his present, or did your secretary Lucy?"

He scoffed. "I would never delegate such an august task. I picked this sucker out online months ago."

His mock offense at my question surprised me. "What is it?"

"This awesome train," he said enthusiastically. "The TrackMaster 500X. It makes twelve different sounds and has an automatic headlight for tunnels."

"Tunnels?"

"Blanket forts, tunnels, wherever it's dark. Point is, the kid's going to be an engineer like his uncle. He loves trains."

I nodded. Vincent was very enthused about this party, especially blanket forts. To be fair, I remembered loving making blanket forts as a kid. My inner child was in line with his inner child on that point.

"Who wrapped the present?" I asked, eyeing the perfect bows.

He laughed. "You caught me. That task I did delegate. It looks good though, right?"

I nodded. "Yeah, I think she deserves a bonus."

"I'll take it under consideration."

We made it to the porch, where we were already able to hear the high-pitched screams of a child running around and playing. The door was unlocked and Vincent stepped inside the house unfazed by the noise. I followed after.

We were greeted in the foyer by a blond, slim woman standing around five six. She had her hair tied back in a simple bun and wore a well-fitting dark blue blouse with black pants. By my first impression, she looked slightly younger than Vincent. I eyed the plate of snacks she was carrying: apple slices with peanut butter. My stomach growled.

"Hello, stranger," she said, smiling at her brother. Her voice was warm and confident. I could see the resemblance between her and Vincent both in appearance and in the confident way she carried herself.

After beaming at her brother for a moment, she turned to me. "And you must be Kristen."

She extended her hand and I took it. Her handshake was firm. "You're Giselle."

She smiled warmly. "As well as 'Mommy' and 'Mrs. Harper.' I'm glad you two could make it."

"Wouldn't miss it for the world," Vincent said.

The child causing all of the noise behind Giselle spotted us. His dark brown eyes opened wide and he tottered over wearing his cone-shaped birthday hat, followed by a man with black hair and a bright smile. "Uncle Vincent!"

Vincent squatted down on his heels and gave Brady a big hug as the man following him took his place beside Giselle. Seeing Vincent in his blue jeans and white polo shirt in this family setting revealed a new side of him. "Hey buddy, how's it going?"

"It's my birthday!" Brady apparently hadn't quite learned volume control yet.

Vincent didn't even flinch at his nephew's high-pitched screaming. "I know. I got you a present!"

The boy screamed in delight. The little guy was super cute and very excited, if a little loud.

Vincent stood back up and shook hands with what I assumed was Giselle's husband, eyeing him firmly. "Good morning, Rob."

Rob returned the gesture. "Vincent."

Vincent put his arm around me. "Rob, this is my girlfriend Kristen. Kristen, this is Giselle's husband Rob."

"Good to meet you," Rob said. He had kind, gray eyes, and looked to be a similar age to Giselle. His build was smaller than Vincent's, but I thought he and Giselle made a cute couple.

Rob reached down and patted Brady on the back. "Brady, this is Kristen. Say hello."

Brady ran up and wrapped his arms around my leg, gripping the fabric of my jeans. "Hi Kristen."

Brady was too cute. I squatted down as Vincent had. "How old are you?" I asked him. I wanted to show Vincent that I was comfortable with children too.

Brady looked at Giselle and then back at me.

"Tell him how old you are, Brady," Giselle said.

He looked at me a little longer and appeared to decide I was okay, to my relief. "I'm three," he squealed.

"Good job!" Giselle said.

Emboldened, he grabbed my hand. His cute little fingers wrapped around one of mine. "Let's go play trains!" he said enthusiastically.

I smiled and followed him. Vincent stayed behind to talk to his sister and brother-in-law.

As Brady led me to his play area, I looked around at the house and all the little touches Giselle had put on her home. Lamps, candles, vases, mirrors: everything was in good taste and combined attractively. It was hard to imagine a life where managing the household was a significant part of what you thought about. Riley and I looked after ourselves, but we were pretty low-maintenance and kept decorating simple.

When we got to his play area, the floor was littered with an array of trains, train track decorations, and even a stuffed conductor. A train track in a big figure eight was spread amidst the chaos. Vincent was right: Brady loved trains. As clean as the rest of the house was, Giselle had clearly decided that Brady's play area was a place where messiness could reign.

I got down on my knees to be down on Brady's eye level. He eyed me earnestly. "Which one?" he asked.

Scanning the floor, I took a red train in my hand and put it on the track. Brady hit the switch on the control center at the track's control house and the train zoomed around. He laughed approvingly.

"Which one for you?" I asked him.

In response, he got up and ran over to a shelf where a child-sized blue conductor cap was hanging on a hook. He picked it up and threw it sloppily on his head before tottering back over. He plopped down next to me and picked a black train to put on the track.

Brady wanted to play with me, but once he started he was in his own little world, watching the trains. After a minute of watching him I heard a familiar voice behind me.

"I got him that cap," Vincent said. He took a seat next to me and watched Brady maneuver his train in silence. A warm smile was on his face the entire time.

Brady played with his train for a while longer before he noticed Vincent had taken a seat at the play area. When he saw Vincent at last, his brown eyes lit up anew.

"Uncle Vincent! Which one?"

Vincent picked out a yellow train to add to the track. Whether it was the train track itself or playing with Brady, he was enjoying this moment in a playful way that I hadn't seen before.

"Hey buddy," Vincent said after a moment, "why don't we build a tunnel for our trains?"

"Yeah!" Brady yelled.

I watched as Vincent got a chair from another room and returned with a blanket. He put the chair at one end of the figure eight, and Brady helped him with the blanket as well as he could. Soon they were racing the trains under their makeshift tunnel.

Brady's enthusiasm for the whole activity was infectious. I could tell Vincent was getting into it, and soon enough so was I, watching the trains fly by faster and faster. Vincent was in the middle of talking to Brady about changing the track to take better advantage of the chair when Giselle came into the room.

"Looks like you guys are having a blast," she said.

Brady was very excited. "Trains!" he yelled.

"I see that. Kristen, do you want to help me finish frosting the C-A-K-E? I think the boys are occupied for a while and Rob just went out to grab some last minute party supplies before Brady's friends come over."

I looked up and sensed a hint of seriousness beneath her innocent veneer. "Of course," I said. "You two will be okay without me, right?"

Vincent looked up from instigating a train crash. "I think so." Brady was too engrossed to notice us.

"Okay," I said. "Be back soon." With that, I got up and followed Giselle into the kitchen.

Giselle's kitchen was a total disaster, which was to be expected when you were throwing a birthday party for a three-year old. Various kitchen implements were strewn across the granite countertop, and a metallic mixing bowl was sitting next to a fresh and delicious smelling round yellow cake. She walked over to the bowl and began stirring the contents inside.

"Have you ever baked a cake before?" she asked over her shoulder.

I wasn't very good in the kitchen. It was one of my failings: I had always been too busy with school and then work to learn how to cook well. I was mostly good with a microwave and doing basic things on a stove top, like warming up soup. Baking a cake from scratch was beyond me.

"Not on my own, no," I said. "The most I've done is bake a cake out of a box with my mother, but that was years ago."

She flashed a quick smile over her shoulder as she whisked the frosting. "Neither had I, until I had to bake a cake for Brady's first birthday. It was hilariously lop-sided, but thankfully one-year olds don't notice that kind of thing."

"It looks like you've gotten pretty good," I said.

"I'm trying, anyway." She waved me over. "Well, even if you haven't done this before, I'm sure you can give it a go. Just try and coat this evenly with frosting. I'm going to work on the blue frosting for writing happy birthday."

I took the plastic frosting spreader from its place on the counter and went to work. It wasn't very different from spreading peanut butter and jelly on a sandwich, which I was a pro at. I quickly got into a rhythm of taking a gob of frosting and smoothing it out on the cake.

Giselle watched me work for a moment and then set to work on the colored frosting. "So you've been seeing Vincent for a little while now?" she asked.

"That's right."

"How did you two meet?"

I laughed nervously. Apparently Vincent hadn't told her much. I decided to be truthful since the cat was out of the bag anyway. "To be honest, it's a bit scandalous."

She stopped whisking. "You weren't married or something, were you?"

"No!" I cried. "Why? Do you think Vincent would do something like that?"

"I don't, but people have a way of surprising you sometimes."

I knew all about that, but I had forgotten what Vincent told me about her history. I wondered if he had told her about the situation with Marty. That was a private thing: the only people who knew about it were Vincent and Riley. Well, and Kurt and Bernie. It still upset me that he had done that. That had surprised me. As sweet as he had been all week, I still wasn't over it.

"I guess that's true," I said. "Anyway, we actually met through work. I work for a personal wealth management firm and head up his account."

She turned and looked at me. "Good for you! I hope you're reining him in somewhat. Every time he travels I worry he's going to have some horrible accident with all the risky sports he's doing."

"Oh, you too?"

She let out a short laugh and shook her head. "He seems to like you. I haven't met a girlfriend of his before."

Here was another surprise. The fact that Vincent had never introduced a girlfriend to his sister, who he was obviously close to, made me feel special. My mind shot to Ariel Diamond. If his sister had never met her, maybe things weren't as serious between them as I had thought, even if the tattoo was strange.

"Not even Ariel?" I asked, before I knew the words were out of my mouth.

Giselle stopped whisking the frosting for a moment, but continued. "No, not Ariel. That was a different period in Vincent's life. And mine, really. We didn't talk much while he was dating her."

"I see."

"He's much more family oriented now than he was then."

"Oh?"

"Ever since our parents died. He grew up after that."

I stopped in place. Vincent's parents were dead? He had never talked about them, but then I rarely talked about my parents and they were still alive and kicking back in Texas. How had it never come up that his parents had already passed away? Did he just not care?

I began spreading the frosting again. "I didn't know your parents had passed," I said quietly.

It was her turn to put her whisk down. "Oh, sorry. I guess it's been so long. They passed away nine years ago."

So Vincent must have been very young. Younger than I was as I stood in that kitchen. Even though I didn't talk to my parents much and didn't rely on them financially at all, I couldn't imagine them being gone.

"Wow, you two were young then."

"I like to think thirty is still young!" she said, laughing.

My cheeks flushed. "That's not what I meant!"

"I know, I know. It was way too young to lose our parents. Vincent took it very hard. It actually turned out to be the beginning of his success."

"What do you mean?"

"After they passed away, he finally got his act together. He developed the camera a few months after the funeral. It was like he was possessed. We were both staying at our parents' house for awhile after the accident and living on the small inheritance we got. He would be working twenty hours a day for weeks on end, out in the garage and on the computer and on the phone. It was a transformation. He went from being a slacker with potential to someone who was totally obsessed."

The tone in her voice had changed. Her words took on a strange sharpness, like she was trying to cut them into me and make sure they sunk in. She obviously admired Vincent very deeply. This wasn't a connection that was for the sake of appearances: Vincent meant the world to her. Listening to her talk about him, I could see why.

She continued. "Any time he wasn't working he was saying he was going to take care of me and of us. To a twenty year old it's pretty weird to have your surfer brother tell you that he's going to take care of the family. It sounds like wishful thinking from a guy who's just grieving for his parents, but Vincent really changed. He became this very intense person who found success everywhere he looked because he wouldn't accept failure. He was selling that camera in three months and had it with retailers soon after, and he just built and built. Everyone underestimates him because of his appearance and his hobbies, but he just keeps plowing forward."

I had researched the story of Vincent's company from a financial perspective, but I hadn't given thought to what it meant on a personal level to grind out so much success. Giselle had seen it first hand. In a way, I was almost jealous.

"It sounds like you admire him," I said, simply because I hadn't spoken in a while. We had both stopped with our frosting duties.

She nodded. "Then he changed again when Brady was born. Before that, he was on a path where it was nothing but business and intensity, but you can't be intense with a newborn. Vincent makes sure my son has the best of everything. Vincent set up Brady's college fund the day after Brady was born, and has done so much research on camps and things to send him to."

She shrugged, laughing. "I'll get these emails at two a.m. saying 'it's your kid but I just want to tell you I'm happy to pay to send him to this camp when he's old enough' or 'do you think Brady would like this? I can get it delivered this weekend.' Never mind my son, it's a full-time job keeping up with Vincent!"

Before today, I would've had a hard time imagining Vincent being so focused on a child. He was always so busy either with his business or doing crazy recreational activities. Having a kid was a lot of responsibility. It was almost in complete opposition to his lifestyle. "It sounds like he practically treats Brady as his own kid."

She shook her head. "He knows the limit. The way he gives me options is always a one-off. He doesn't argue with me or nag me or anything like that. He cares tremendously about his nephew and has an unusual capacity for helping out, so he's taking advantage of that. Plus as you've seen, his gifts for Brady aren't outrageous. I think Brady will become conscious of how much money his uncle has very slowly." She took a taste of the frosting. "Put it this way: it's a good parenting challenge to have."

"What does Rob think?"

"He's supportive. Vincent and him get along well. My brother takes the protective older sibling thing very seriously."

I knew more about how protective Vincent could be than I wanted to. "I bet."

Giselle turned and looked at me intently. I did my best to keep a poker face and concentrate on spreading the frosting, though I could see her out of the corner of my eye. To my relief, she finally went back to her own frosting job.

"Anyway," she said, "Vincent's wonderful with Brady. Like another child. I hope he can have children of his own soon."

I dropped the frosting spreader on the counter and it tumbled to the floor. Embarrassed, I scrambled and picked it up. Was she suggesting what I thought she was?

She stopped whisking again and squinted, smiling quizzically. "I didn't say he's in a rush!"

I washed it off in the sink before wiping up the frosting on the floor. "Sorry, I'm just a little clumsy."

She stood with her arms crossed, watching me again. "That's okay, accidents happen."

Her sleeves were rolled up, and as I was looking at her trying to judge her expression my eyes fell to some peculiar scars on her forearms. Were those cigarette burns? Nothing in the house smelled like cigarette smoke, so I was guessing she wasn't a smoker. Maybe she had been one in the past, before Brady. Or maybe it was something more nefarious.

She seemed to notice I was looking at her arms and rolled down her sleeves before turning back to work. "Anyway, I do hope things work out between you two," Giselle said. "I would love it if Vincent has finally found someone to share his life with."

I let the question of her arms go and flashed a smile fit for a job interview. "So far he's been pretty great."

I heard their footsteps a second before they burst in. There was a crash at the kitchen door, then the knob turned and Brady came in giggling, with Vincent close behind.

"Hey buddy, come back. Where are you going?" Vincent cried.

Brady made a beeline straight for me and threw his arms around my right leg. "Kristen," he screamed, "Come play trains!"

I looked at Giselle, who was smiling. "It looks like I'm being summoned," I said.

"I think so. You guys have fun, I can finish up here."

The three of us went back and played trains until the cake was ready. By that point, a couple of Brady's friends had come over with their parents, and Vincent and I were nearly forgotten. The party ended up lasting until seven o'clock. By the time we left, I was as tuckered out as the kids. I slept in the car the whole way home.

Chapter Twenty-one

Sunday was a blur of errands and getting my life in order. Seeing Vincent in a family environment was a serious eye-opener. After the way he had handled Marty, I was afraid I was dating a hyper-logical man with the emotions of a caveman. But now, seeing him with Brady, it was clear he had a lot of love in his heart. That made me feel good.

Monday morning I dragged my feet out of bed and lurched my way to work. As I stepped off the elevator on the forty-eighth floor of the tall, glass building housing Waterbridge-Howser, I started feeling dizzy. I had a rough night trying to sleep and only ended up getting a few hours. When I got to my office, I put down my bag and walked right back out. I needed caffeine. Badly.

I went to the common kitchen area with my cup. When I smelled the coffee pot, it made me nauseous.

"Man, who made the coffee this morning? It smells terrible."

An analyst named Sam was also in the kitchen; he was busy slathering a bagel with cream cheese. He took a bite of his bagel then a sip of his mug. "Hmm tastes fine to me. I don't smell anything unusual."

"You don't smell it? It smells like dirty feet and tires."

"Maybe you got a super sniffer."

"A what?"

"You know, like someone who has super sensitive taste buds except with smell. I saw it on an episode of Law & Order. When the police dog was unable to sniff out drugs from a crime scene, they brought in this guy who was a super sniffer."

Suddenly curious that I might have a superpower, I asked, "Did he find anything at the scene?"

He nodded vigorously. "He sniffed out this scent that the dog wasn't trained to detect. It was some weird chemical that led the police to this abandoned paint factory where they found incriminating evidence."

"Interesting."

"See if you can sniff my deodorant." He lifted up his armpit and I noticed a faint sweat stain on the shirt fabric. Fortunately he was several feet away.

"I can't smell anything from here."

"Maybe you're not a super sniffer then."

"Yeah, I don't think I have that ability. Otherwise, I would've probably figured it out earlier."

He took another bite of his bagel. "Could be you're pregnant."

I nearly dropped my empty mug but caught it at the last moment. "What?"

He finished chewing. "When my wife was pregnant, she couldn't stand certain smells. Like coffee and the smell of the grocery store."

I laughed nervously and batted my hand at the notion. Sam shrugged and went off to his own desk to do work or perhaps ponder the mystery.

I remained in the kitchen. What if I really was pregnant?

The past couple weeks raced through my mind. I'd vomited twice. The first time I'd attributed to bad Chinese food. The second time happened because I was distraught over Marty showing up and the argument with Vincent that followed. Surely it wasn't morning sickness . . .

My hand flew to cover my open mouth when I realized something: it was almost a week now that my period was late.

Oh no.

During lunch, I made a trip to Duane Reade and picked up a pregnancy test. When I got to the family planning aisle, I felt like I was walking into a sex shop looking over my shoulder every second like I was about to do something scandalous. I found what I was looking for and tucked the box under my arm until I reached the register. After paying, I hurriedly put the box in my purse hoping no one saw me buy it.

When I got home, I spotted Riley in her usual spot on the couch watching TV. I set down my tote in a kitchen chair and headed for the bathroom with the test box in hand, careful to keep it hidden from Riley.

I locked the door and stared at the box for a moment. The picture on the front showed a woman smiling brightly. I glanced in the mirror and saw that my expression looked nothing like that.

I took out a strip and followed the directions, my hands trembling the entire time.

It would take a few minutes before the results showed. I closed my eyes and started a countdown in my mind, dreading to see the result.

Deep breaths, Kristen.

Finally, five minutes had passed. I looked down at the test in my hand.

Pink line. I was pregnant.

I dropped the test on the floor. My hands were shaking. This had to be a mistake. No way I was pregnant. I'd been on birth control. Even though Vincent came inside me when we were in the Caribbean, there was no way he got me pregnant. It didn't matter how potent his sperm was, it couldn't beat birth control . . . right?

I took another one.

Five excruciatingly long minutes later, I looked at it.

Pink line again.

Shit. Shit shit shit. Shit. Fuck.

My world was coming apart. This can't be happening.

I frantically examined the box, hoping to find a warning about its inaccuracy.

"Over 99% accurate. Take comfort in knowing your results."

I stepped out of the bathroom and went to the living room where Riley was sipping a diet coke.

"Riley, I need to ask you something." I tried to keep my voice as calm as possible for someone who just discovered they were pregnant.

She put her drink down on the coffee table and turned her attention to me. "Sure, what is it?"

"Is it possible to get two false-positives on a pregnancy test?"

"Huh? Why are you . . ." Her eyes widened. "Oh my god. Are you pregnant?"

I tried holding the tears back but they started flowing against my will. "I just took a test and that's what it said."

"I thought you were on birth control!"

"I was, I mean, I am. I just—I don't know how this could have happened."

"Oh Kris, you know that even the pill isn't one-hundred percent effective."

I nodded. "I mean, I knew that as a concept, but I never thought that I'd be the tiny sliver of a percentage that it would fail for!"

Riley studied my face, probably discerning that congratulations weren't in order. Her tone became serious. "What are you going to do?"

I started crying harder. "I never planned for this. Vincent and I never talked about it. We've barely even known each other for two months!"

Riley came to hug me and rub my back. "It's going to be okay, Kris. You have options. It's not the end of the world."

"I don't know what to do."

Her voice was soft. "Are you considering getting an abortion?"

"I don't know. What other choice do I have? I'm not ready to be a mom. I thought I'd be into my thirties before I considered having a baby. I don't even know how Vincent would react if he found out."

"Are you going to tell him?"

"Should I?"

"You should. He has a right to know. He is the father right?"

I wiped the tears from my cheek. "Unless my fingers have started magically producing sperm, yes. Vincent's the only one I've had sex with."

"Okay. How is your relationship with him going? You said you two made up right?"

"Yeah, we did."

"Good. That should make it easier to tell him. Have faith in him, Kris. Didn't you say he adored his nephew?"

Giselle's stories about Vincent's emails in the early morning hours enthusing over activities and programs for Brady ran through my mind. "He does. I think he might actually be too intense about it."

"What do you mean?"

"I don't know, his sister made it sound like he's borderline obsessed with the kid. Sends her emails at two in the morning with camps and stuff his nephew can go to when he's old enough."

Riley nodded. "That sounds very sweet. It sounds like he would be a great dad."

"I don't know Riley, liking kids is not the same as wanting one of your own."

"That's true. He's a busy CEO and lives a fast-paced lifestyle. But liking kids is certainly a positive sign."

"Or what if he really does want a child and I don't? What if I just don't want to be a mom yet? I could get an abortion and not tell him. Wouldn't that be easier? If I tell him, and we disagree, this could destroy our relationship. Then it would have been easier just to not tell him, and maybe we can have a baby years from now."

She sucked in a deep breath. "I think you should think hard about whether you want to get an abortion. My mother had an unplanned pregnancy and almost got an abortion. I'm glad she didn't, otherwise I wouldn't be here."

I could feel my face grow hot with embarrassment. "Riley, I didn't know . . ."

"It's okay. We all have secrets Kristen." She squeezed my hand. "Just don't make a quick decision. Think about it. I think I would tell Vincent. If you make this decision by yourself, it's going to be a strain on your relationship for the rest of the time you're together. I mean, it's pretty dishonest."

She made a good point. If Vincent couldn't trust me to talk to him about something this important, that said bad things about the health of our relationship as a whole. Still though, it was just so much to deal with. "You don't think I'm too young to have a child?"

Riley shook her head. "You're twenty-five. A lot of women have children at that age. When people are as young as we are, typically money is a big concern, but that's obviously not the case here. You have a great job and Vincent is loaded."

"That's part of it though, Riley. I can't have a baby fathered by my client. That's beyond scandalous. If I decide to have this baby, my time at Waterbridge-Howser is done."

"I thought you said they had no policy against it!"

I sighed. "Official policy is one thing. Shoving it in the company's face by taking maternity leave to have a baby fathered by a client is another. It's practically proof they got the client because I had sex with him. Other wealth management firms could use that against them every time they make a pitch. The wealth management business is pretty conservative."

"So they would fire you? Isn't that illegal?"

"They might if they could figure out how to get away with it, or they would force me out slowly. It doesn't matter. If I decide to have this baby, I need to find a new job before it happens. Before I start showing, actually."

"Wow. That is a lot to handle."

"It feels like too much. What is Vincent going to say when I drop all these problems on his lap?"

She shook her head. "Talk to him and find out. He's the CEO of an enormous company, I'm sure he's used to dealing with complicated situations. If you don't talk to him about it, I think you'll regret it later."

"And if we break up because we can't work it out?"

"If you guys can't work through an issue like this together, is the relationship still worth it?"

I took a deep breath. "I guess not. Still though. This is so much."

"You don't have to make a decision yet. Like I said, I think you should talk to him. That's what I would do."

That night, I lay in bed thinking about how chaotic my life had become. I was pregnant. It explained how strange I had been feeling lately, but it still left me with more questions than answers. My life had been on the straight and narrow for so long, traveling steadily along a single path. The past two months had been the sharpest detour I could imagine.

Vincent was part of that detour, though, and the more I thought about it, the more I agreed with Riley. I needed to talk to him about my pregnancy. It was unplanned, yes, but maybe it would end up being a pleasant accident. I couldn't rule that out. What I did know was if I made the decision without keeping him in the loop, I would have to hide that from him for the rest of my life. As long as we were together, anyway. I didn't want that hanging over our relationship.

I had a meeting scheduled with him on Thursday. So far, the topic of the meeting would be going over the investment strategy options I had developed for his personal wealth, but it looked like there would be another item added to the agenda, official or not.

Chapter Twenty-two

Tuesday and Wednesday passed by in a blur of anxiety. Most of that time had been spent on thinking about the pregnancy than on actual work. I'd wavered back and forth between wanting to tell Vincent and not wanting to tell him, wanting to keep the baby and not wanting to keep the baby.

By the time Thursday came, I'd made up my mind that I was going to tell Vincent, but I was still unsure about my personal stance on keeping the baby or not. I would need to know how Vincent felt before making a decision on how I felt.

Work before the meeting with Vincent was a morass of emails and memos. I kept having to reread messages to make sure I hadn't missed anything. It was impossible to focus; I couldn't tell if it was hormones or nervousness, but my mind felt dull and fuzzy. Even though I would have usually completed the work in thirty minutes, it took a full four hours before it was done.

Finally, the moment came for me to leave for my meeting. I packed up my stuff and took a cab over to his office. The ride went by in a numb haze. How would I start the conversation? How would he react, regardless of how I started it? The course of my life could depend on this meeting. Funny how it's always the people you least expect that end up changing your life in the biggest ways. A few months ago, I would have never thought I'd have Vincent Sorenson's unborn child nestled in my womb, but here I was.

I took a deep breath and exited the cab. The walk from the curb into his building and up the elevator felt like a sprint. I was going to do this. Striding through the Red Fusion office, I waved to his secretary before reaching his office. His door was half open and I knocked on it.

"Come in," Vincent called.

I eased the door open and walked through. Vincent wasn't sitting at his desk. Rather, he was looking out the window, lost in thought. He wore a slim cut pair of navy pants and a white and light blue checkered shirt separated by a tan leather belt. Casual but neat. I still wasn't used to how sexy he looked in whatever he wore.

He turned over his shoulder and looked at me. "Hello, Kristen. You're a few minutes early."

"Am I?" I asked. I looked at my watch. "Sorry about that. Traffic was lighter than expected."

He waved his hand as if pushing aside my words and smiled. "Don't worry, it's a good surprise. I like good surprises. "

He took a couple steps toward where I was standing just inside his door. "Close that," he said.

I knew that tone. He was seconds away from kissing me, and if that started, there was no way I was going to end up talking to him about the pregnancy. I held up the file I had prepared for presenting the strategy I had in mind for his assets. "We should get through this," I said. "It is important, after all. I also have something else to tell you afterwards, something unrelated to business."

"It must be about pleasure then. I'm looking forward to it, Kitten."

I smiled but inwardly resisted letting his usual effect on me take hold. Vincent didn't need any extra encouragement to keep teasing me and I didn't need him trying to derail my carefully laid plan.

"Not quite, let's just take it one thing at a time."

He sighed. "You're right. Where do you want me?"

In context it sounded sexual and my sex instinctively tightened at his tone. With how busy he'd been the past few weeks and the crazy events that happened, it seemed like forever since we had sex. I needed to focus. One thing at a time. First get through your presentation and then you can tell him about the baby.

He cocked an eyebrow. "Are you okay?"

I shook my head. "Yes, sorry. I was just thinking about my presentation."

He laughed. "I hope you're not as nervous as you were the first time we were in this office. Though I rather enjoyed that conversation . . . "

Even though he got a smile out of me, I knew I had to get this discussion back on track. "Sorry Vincent, don't think that's happening today."

"Okay, well once you're done presenting these materials maybe we can move on to phase two of the meeting."

Vincent clearly had a different idea of how phase two of the meeting was going to go.

"We can just sit on the couch," I said.

How would he react when he found out about the baby? It was clear from our weekend visit with Giselle that Vincent loved Brady, but that was his nephew. He didn't have to take care of Brady every day. Would he feel the same way if the child was his? Would he be willing to sacrifice his lifestyle for that?

He took a seat. "I hope I can have your undivided attention here," he said. "Otherwise I'll have to make sure."

Lewd images of the different ways he'd "make sure" flashed in my mind before I took a deep breath and smiled up at him. "Sorry, I'm just preoccupied with some things at work."

Hopefully a discussion of the facts and figures of his wealth would deflate things. I handed him the binder I had put together for this presentation.

He smiled at me. I waited for him to speak, but he continued to watch me, saying nothing.

I blinked and plowed ahead, opening the binder and turning past the cover page to the executive summary. I launched into an explanation of the different strategies we had prepared for him.

He nodded, attentive, though there was also still a knowing smirk on his face.

"Any questions so far?" I asked.

He shook his head, pursing his lips as if to avoid smiling.

"What's so funny?"

He looked at me a few beats. Still fighting back a smile, he finally spoke. "Are you listening to yourself?"

I scrunched my face. What was he talking about? "Did I say something wrong?"

"No, you've been doing fine. It's just . . ." He trailed off.

"What?"

Then I heard it. I had the tiny rasp I sometimes got in my voice when I was turned on.

I cleared my throat then pursed my lips, trying to think of what to say. This was not going to plan. Not my plan anyway, though Vincent seemed to be enjoying himself. Damn these pregnancy hormones.

"Vincent, this is important."

"Do you know how you look right now?" Vincent's eyes flickered up and down my body, I could almost feel his invisible fingers caressing my curves slowly. His tongue darted out and wet his lips slightly.

"You should see yourself in a mirror, you look too fuckable. I could just tear your clothes off right now. It's been too long. We both know we're far overdue for sex."

The desire in his voice sent a spike of heat to my core. I squirmed, rubbing my legs together. For some reason, I thought about the first time I was here in his office. We were right here on his couch. Except we were lying down, not sitting, and his hands had been sliding up my thigh. I looked at him and blushed, hoping that he couldn't read my mind. I needed to get this back on track.

"Don't you care about managing your assets?"

He moved closer to me, his leg pressing right up against mine. It was good that we were sitting down, because looking into his deep brown eyes, I felt ready to melt. He lifted his right hand, gliding the back of his fingers down the side of my face.

"You're my most valuable asset right now," he whispered.

A shiver ran down the back of my spine. He was being so sweet and it was getting more difficult by the minute to resist him.

"I'm serious, Vincent."

He closed the binder and set it down on the glass coffee table. "Listen, I trust the strategy you've put together for me, and I'm sure I can read through this on my own when I'm less distracted. We don't need to decide on a strategy right this minute."

Vincent turned back to me, a fire burning in his eyes. He caressed my hair with one hand, moving down my tender exposed neck, and with his other gripped my bare leg possessively. I closed my eyes, delighting in the sensations for a moment.

"What if someone hears us?" I whispered.

"These glass walls could stop bullets. No one will hear us."

"Vincent."

"Kitten, I've wanted to take you in this office since the first time you were here."

"There's something I need to tell you . . ."

"Shhh . . . it can wait. I can't."

Who knew what would happen between us after he learned about the pregnancy. I decided I could wait a little longer to tell him so that we could enjoy each other's bodies, in this moment. It might be the last time.

His mouth covered mine, claiming a kiss. My body betrayed me, responding to his touch like it belonged to him. I leaned back until I was lying down on the couch, Vincent's chest pressed against mine.

His fingers eased down toward my pussy, which was on fire. I arched my hips up to give him better access, desperate for him to touch me. He obliged and pressed against my soaked underwear.

"You're so wet for me, Kristen. Tell me where you want me now." He slid a finger around my panties and into my pussy, hitting the perfect spot. He massaged my tender spot slowly, drawing out my pleasure, as if he was demonstrating his control over my body.

It sent me over the edge. I came hard, biting the fabric of his shirt to stop from crying out. Bucking wildly, my muscles contracted in spasms that would have been painful if they didn't feel so earth shatteringly good. Vincent kept hold of me, his lone finger pulsing against my g-spot.

When I had finally finished, I eased up and saw I had left mascara on his shirt to go along with the color on my lips. Turning to his face, I saw a mixture of surprise and arousal in his expression.

He took his finger out of me and grabbed my hips. Looking up at me, he smiled wickedly. "You were ready, weren't you?"

I nodded. "Sorry about your shirt."

He looked over dismissively. "I have another. Do you?"

I looked at my blouse, but it was fine.

He squeezed my hips. In response, I kissed him desperately on the mouth. I loved it when he challenged me. He knew just which buttons to press and when. In this case, he had lit a new fire to go along with my already aching need.

I fumbled with the buttons on his shirt, my mouth still pressed against his. Finding the prize I had been looking for, I relished the sensations of his smooth chest, taut and hard. His nipple rings were polished and surprisingly warm under my hand.

"Kitten," he groaned. "I need to be inside you."

I nodded.

Vincent picked me up, flipping me over. I kneeled on the couch, turning my back to him. He slid his hand up my thigh, groping me possessively. God, I needed him inside me. I spread my legs wider for him, giving him better access, thrusting my needy sex closer towards him. The air felt cool against my skin, making me hyper aware of how exposed I was to him. I heard his belt unbuckle.

My body shuddered as he entered me. I clenched involuntarily around him as he dragged the turgid tip of his cock against my slick inner walls. I didn't know how much more I could take, the pleasure was too intense.

"Vincent, please . . . "

He continued to thrust into me, repeatedly hitting my pleasure center, until we shattered together. I felt him come inside me, his warm seed mixing with my fluids and I followed soon after, arching myself into the air, offering Vincent my body. Afterwards he collapsed on me and we laid there on the couch.

His weight on top of me was comforting. We breathed in sync, recovering slowly from our ecstasy. After he wiped the evidence of our encounter from my leg, we curled up together on the couch. We were both sweaty, but it felt good to have his warmth next to me.

It had to be now or it wasn't going to happen today. I needed to tell him I was pregnant. Now it was time to see how he was going to react. At least I knew he would be in the best possible mood.

I took a deep breath as my heart started beating faster in anticipation of the fallout. "Vincent—"

The intercom buzzed, sending my insides into freefall.

"Mr. Sorenson, security just called up. Mr. Rodriguez and Mr. Bennet are here for you. Shall I let them know you and Ms. Daley aren't finished?"

Vincent untangled himself from me and strode over to his desk. He tilted his head questioningly at me as if asking me if we were done. A loose strand of hair on his face, coupled with his dimpled smile gave him a boyish look.

I couldn't tell him. He—no—we were so happy in the moment, that I couldn't spoil it and drop this bomb on him just before leaving. The important part wasn't so much me telling him as his reaction, and leaving right after I told him wouldn't allow me to see that. With that in mind, I nodded quietly and straightened myself out.

"No Lucy, we're just wrapping up. I'll be down in a minute."

"I'll let them know."

"Thank you, Lucy."

288 | Priscilla West

He turned to me and the anxiety I had before the meeting returned. We needed to have a discussion about how to handle this, but it won't be right now. There will be other opportunities. I had at least a few more weeks before I had to make a final decision about the baby.

"Sorry about that, they're a little early. That's Kurt and Bernie, they're keeping tabs on Marty, just as a precaution. You can stay if you want to sit in."

I shook my head. "No, it's okay. I have to get back to work anyway."

Vincent watched me for a moment then shrugged. "I promise, I'll read through those materials tonight and we can talk about them."

"Thank you. Sorry we couldn't get through everything we needed to."

He smiled. "I think we found a better substitute for our time, don't you."

I returned the smile and continued to straighten out my hair.

He laughed quietly as he went to his closet and found a new dress shirt. "You're good to go, right?"

I was sure I looked a mess, but I could deal with it on my own time. "I'll stop in the ladies room before I head out."

He finished buttoning up. "Good as new," he said.

He opened the door to let me out first. He left, and I headed to the ladies room. Just as I entered, my phone buzzed. It was Riley:

How did the pregnancy convo with V go?

I texted back.

Interrupted. Will do it soon.

I leaned against the bathroom counter and let out a long sigh. It was just a little more time, that was all. I had weeks before I would be showing; surely I could find a good time before then. Missing this chance wasn't the end of the world.

***

That evening, when my head was clearer, I realized my mistake. While it was true that I didn't need to tell Vincent right away, I hadn't counted on the storm cloud hanging over my head every minute I didn't tell him.

After an hour of trying to distract myself with TV and cleaning, I decided that the sooner I told him the better. Vincent was too distracting in his office, dressed in his business attire, but maybe we'd both be more focused if we had the conversation at my place.

I called Vincent at his office and asked him to come over, telling him that I absolutely had to see him to talk to him about something. He sounded concerned and told me he would swing by in a couple hours. That done, I talked to Riley about having the apartment to myself for the evening. Good friend that she was, she called her friend Jen and was out for the night.

As I waited for Vincent to come by, I was determined that there would definitely not be a replay of what happened earlier that day in his office.

Chapter Twenty-three

On my way now. Be there in 10 mins.

After reading Vincent's text, I took a deep breath and set my phone down on the glass coffee table.

I started heating up water on the stove to make tea. It would help calm my nerves along with Vincent's during the delicate conversation. I sat on the couch rehearsing the lines I'd prepared to say to him as I smoothed out my t-shirt and jeans.

A few minutes later, a knock at the door startled me. Three raps followed by the faint sound of a man clearing his throat.

I got up from my seat and walked to the door. Looking through the peephole, I saw Vincent standing on my doormat. He was wearing a forest-green polo with sleeves that stretched against his arms and khaki shorts which showcased the taut muscles in his legs. He must've changed after work. He was shifting his feet, which betrayed his apprehension. Did he suspect what I was about to tell him?

I opened the door. "Hey," I said, pasting on the smile I'd prepared beforehand. It was easier once I saw his breathtaking face.

His expression brightened. "Hey," he said, smiling back at me.

"Come on in." I stepped back, pulling the door wider and gesturing him inside.

"Should I take off my shoes?"

He was wearing a clean pair of sneakers that matched his polo. I half-suspected he was probing me with the question. Telling him to leave his shoes on could be interpreted as a sign that I was breaking up with him. This was going to be a long conversation and he deserved to be comfortable.

"You can take them off."

He removed his shoes and set them carefully next to the pile of flats and heels in the corner near the coat rack.

"Would you like something to drink? I'm in the middle of making some tea." I studied his body language. He was slightly tense, his movements lacking the usual primal confidence.

"I'm fine, thank you."

The formality of his response made the situation even more awkward. "Okay." Once he was clear of the entrance, I leaned forward to close the door. The closing of the door would mark the beginning of a very difficult conversation.

Here goes.

The door made an unexpected thud as I tried to jam it shut. I glanced down and saw a dark brown boot wedged into the door frame.

Huh?

A dull, metallic chrome object slid through the narrow opening in the door. The shape was small and ended in a point—aimed at Vincent's back.

"Stay away from her!" the voice behind the door screamed.

A force pushed me. I staggered backward, my shoulder blades crashing against the half-wall separating the living room from the kitchen. The door flew open and a tall man with white bandages across his nose and cheeks entered my apartment. He was wearing a plain white t-shirt with black athletic pants and looked very pissed off.

Vincent spun around, startled. "How the hell—"

"I said stay away from her," the man shouted, hands shaking the end of the pistol. Sharp, blue eyes blazed behind thick spectacles with a crack on the right lens. Strands of dark brown hair parted down the middle hung haphazardly around his forehead.

"Marty!" I cried. "Oh my god!" My eyes widened when I realized he had a gun in his hand.

Vincent raised his hands in the air and began slowly backstepping further into the living room toward the window. "Calm down. Don't do anything rash."

"Step away from her now." Bandages stretched against his grimace. "I'm not going to let you hurt me or Kristen."

"What are you talking about?" Vincent said, eyes narrowed, his hands still in the air. "You're the one with the gun."

Marty hurried over to me. He wrapped his fingers around my wrist and tugged me to him, while keeping the gun trained on Vincent.

"Where are your goons? Are they in the building?"

Vincent paused. He looked at Marty's hand around me then back at Marty. "They're right across the hall. You fire that gun, they'll hear it and come out armed."

Marty closed the door behind him with his foot. "I know you're lying—like always—but just in case." He released my hand, turning the deadbolt and hooking the chain, locking us in with him. He reached into his back pocket and threw a silver chain at Vincent's feet. "Cuff yourself to the radiator."

"Marty, put down the gun! This is crazy," I cried. My pulse was racing against my chest. Blood roared in my ears, drowning out the thoughts screaming in my mind to escape. I wanted to run but had nowhere to go. No, no, no. This couldn't be happening. I was just supposed to talk to Vincent about my pregnancy.

He turned to me, expression softening. "I'm sorry Kristen, I didn't want to have to do this. But he gave me no choice. Please don't be afraid, I'm not going to hurt you. I'm here to protect you."

"Protect me?" I blurted in disbelief, my breaths coming fast and shallow.

Marty tightened his grip on the gun aimed at Vincent's chest then cocked it. The audible click sent a deathly shiver through me. "I'm not going to ask again. Cuff yourself to the radiator, asshole. Do it."

Vincent twisted his head, spotting the cast iron array of pipes behind him situated below the window. "Okay. Okay." He managed to keep his voice even but his movements lacked their usual ease. He slowly bent down keeping both palms open and in front of him. "I'm doing what you asked. Don't shoot." He brought one hand down and picked up the handcuffs, keeping his eyes trained on Marty—and more importantly, the gun in his hand.

I stared. Stunned. Terrified. I was too scared to move as I watched the events unfolding before my eyes.

There was a click. Vincent had cuffed one of his hands to the radiator.

"This is crazy!" I cried.

"Please, Kristen," Marty said calmly. "Give me a chance to explain. I promise we'll get through this."

294 | Priscilla West

Chapter Twenty-four

Marty directed me to take a seat on the couch. Tears beginning to blur my vision and my legs unsteady, I nearly stumbled into the coffee table as I silently complied.

"Stay there." His words were calm but they felt like a threat.

Seated, I watched Vincent carefully as Marty approached him, gun in hand. Vincent remained standing on firm legs. He wasn't shaking like I was but his dark eyes were wide and focused. A visibly beating vein along his forehead hinted at the adrenaline pumping through his system. It wasn't supposed to happen like this, I was just supposed to have a conversation with Vincent.

Vincent's free hand twitched. Marty took a step forward, aiming the weapon at Vincent's chest. Marty was close enough for Vincent to sock him across the face or reach for the gun in Marty's outstretched hand. Images of heroic scenarios raced through my mind like scenes from an action movie. My fingers clenched against the cushion of the couch. I was gripped by dread that Vincent would actually try something risky—and fail.

Both men stood facing one another, exchanging fierce stares, neither of them blinking. The moment wouldn't last forever. Someone was going to make a move.

Vincent's body tensed. He swallowed hard. His hand curled into a fist by his side. He glanced at me.

No, don't Vincent! I pleaded with my eyes, unable to find my voice.

Vincent returned his gaze to Marty.

Marty raised the gun and pressed the nozzle into Vincent's forehead. "Get on your knees."

"Don't hurt him! Please!" I pleaded desperately, cupping my hands against my face. I was going to watch Marty shoot Vincent in the head and I was powerless to do anything. My eyes pricked. Tears streamed down my cheeks.

"Please, keep quiet Kristen," Marty said, his tone barely concealing his anger. He kept his eyes trained on Vincent.

Marty reached behind his back and produced another set of handcuffs. He snapped one end around Vincent's free hand and the other end around a different pipe on the radiator, ensuring Vincent wouldn't be able to reach for something to throw or a cell phone to call.

"If you try to get out or if your team comes barging in, I'm going to put a bullet through your head. Understand?"

Vincent eyed him sternly.

Marty grabbed his hair and yanked his head back hard. "I asked you a question, you piece of shit. Do you understand?"

"Yes," Vincent groaned through clenched teeth.

"Good." Marty jerked Vincent's head down, making him wince in pain, then released his hair.

Marty returned to the couch, taking a seat beside me. I shifted away, pressing myself against the armrest and curling my legs into my chest.

"Don't hurt her," Vincent said, lifting his head back up. "This is between you and me. I'm the one who punched you, not her."

"Shut the fuck up. Sit still and be quiet. This is all about me and Kristen. There's no way I'd hurt her. If you want to keep talking, I'm not against hurting you though. God knows you deserve it."

Marty turned to me. "Kristen, I'm so sorry it's come to this." He placed his hand on my shoulder.

The sensation made me hug myself tighter. "Please put the gun down," I said, tears wetting the denim covering my knees. "You're scaring me."

He carefully put the gun down on the coffee table. It was out of his hand but not out of his reach.

"Calm down, babe. Breathe. Tell me you're okay. Please."

I tried my best to calm my nerves, taking deep breaths and hugging myself tightly. "What do you want?"

"Kristen, you have to understand. I wouldn't be doing this if there was any other way."

"Marty, you have a gun. You can't have a good reason for this."

"It wouldn't have come to this if that asshole hadn't beaten the hell out of me." He pointed at Vincent. "I have to protect myself. And you. I need to talk to you."

"Okay," I muttered, lips quivering. I kept my eyes on Vincent, trying to find hope in him. Vincent was returning my gaze, nodding slightly, silently instructing me to stay calm. "I'm listening."

"Please, look at me. Don't be scared," Marty said.

I reluctantly turned my gaze toward him. The bandages covering what used to be a handsome face made him look menacing.

"That's better. Are you okay?"

"Yes," I lied, a tear running down my cheek.

"I need you to hear me out. I'm not going to hurt you." He studied me for a moment, ensuring I gave him my full attention. "This isn't easy for me to say, Kristen." He sighed deeply. "My life's been complete shit since you left me."

Not knowing how to respond, I nodded silently.

"It was so sudden. Why did you leave like that? I know what I did was wrong but you didn't even break up with me properly. After two years together, it was just poof. Gone. How could you do that to me?"

I swallowed hard, hoping my answer wouldn't make him angrier. "Marty, you hurt me. I was afraid."

"We've been off and on before. I thought this was just another hurdle for us to overcome. I didn't know you'd react that way. You'd always been so patient and understanding. Do you know what it's like to have the love of your life just disappear from your world? I was heartbroken. When I went to your apartment in Boston, you were gone. But most of your things were still there. I thought you'd come back for them. I waited for you. Days. Weeks. I slept on your couch, didn't go to work. I called you, sent you messages. You didn't answer any of them."

He studied me for my reaction. I remained silent, sniffling.

"You ran. It took me a while to come to terms with it but when I realized what had happened, I felt horrible. Like I was abandoned. Do you understand how that feels?"

"I'm sorry you've gone through a rough patch."

"I fell apart, Kristen. You know my job as an investment banker? I got fired because I stopped showing up. Then I couldn't get another job. Nobody would hire me. I was too depressed to even care. It wasn't long before I stopped trying. Know what I do now? Or at least what I did until a month ago."

"What?"

"I worked at a McDonalds. That's what it came to after nearly two years of taking odd jobs since you left me. I kept getting fired. My coworkers would always make fun of me. They'd laugh at me. 'Look at the Harvard boy. He's no better than us.' It made me so angry. I was just trying to do my job like everyone else but they thought I believed I was better than them. Which wasn't true! It made me lose my temper."

"That sounds terrible." As much as I hated Marty for hurting me, it didn't make me feel good to hear about how rough his life had been the past two years.

"Yeah, I don't understand why people have to be such shitheads. I try so hard to be a good person but people don't see that. They look at me like I'm rotten when it's them. They're the bad ones. Judging me. Accusing me of things that aren't true. I know I make mistakes but really I'm a good person. You know that, right? Can you ever forgive me for what I did to you?"

"I don't know, Marty. You hurt me very badly."

"I feel awful about it all. There's not a day that goes by that I don't regret what I did to you."

"Okay," I said. "Is that what this is all about? You just want my forgiveness?"

"That's part of it. You mean so much to me. The other part is that I love you, Kristen. I've said it to you before and I meant it. I'll never stop loving you. I need to know how you feel. Do you still have feelings for me?"

"How can you ask me that when you just broke into my apartment with a gun?"

"I told you, I had no choice. It's that fucker's fault. Vincent." He turned to Vincent. "I know who you are. Billionaire, playboy, CEO of Sandworks—Vincent Sorenson." Marty returned his attention to me. "Can't you see he's just using you? He's going to break your heart. He doesn't love you like I do."

"You don't know anything about me," Vincent growled. "I'd never hurt Kristen like you did. You're a monster."

"Look at my face," Marty said to me. He unwrapped his bandages, revealing black and blue swollen skin. "You know who did this? Tell me who's the real monster."

I shook my head. "You're upset, Marty. Even so, you've never gone this far before. Have you been taking your meds or seeing the psychiatrist?"

"I want to but I can't afford those things. They're too expensive."

"Can't your family help you?"

"Not really. You already know I dropped out of law school. That pissed my dad off. When I refused to return to law school, he disowned me. My mom tried to talk some sense into him, but she ended up killing herself last month by taking too many sleeping pills."

My stomach dropped. His mom had been a person with serious issues, but any suicide was a sad situation. "Oh my god."

"Yeah." He paused, his eyes beginning to water. He turned his head, blinked away tears then returned his gaze to me. "It made me realize I need you, Kristen. My life's a mess without you. You're my rock. I can't keep going on without knowing if my only chance at happiness is still out there for me. Can't you see how much I care about you?"

I began to play with my necklace as if I'd just discovered I was wearing it. "This isn't right, Marty."

"Let me see your hand."

The image of Marty twisting my finger flashed through my mind. "W-What are you going to do?" I dropped my hand back down and began to hug my knees again instinctively.

He shifted his seat closer to me, backing me against the armrest of the couch. Leaning over, he reached for my hand and gently pulled my arm away my knees. He brought my pinky up to his lips and kissed it tenderly. I felt like I was going to throw up.

Vincent struggled against his cuffs. "Good lord man, what are you doing? Kristen, he's manipulating you. You have nothing to feel guilty about. He's the one who should feel guilty."

"Stay out of this," Marty spat.

"You make me sick," Vincent said. "Look at yourself, using a sob story to keep Kristen attached to you."

Marty picked up the gun and aimed it at Vincent. "I said stay out of this."

"Marty don't! Put the gun down!"

Marty huffed a few times then relaxed. "He's trying to brainwash you, Kristen. Can't you see that? I don't blame you for what happened, and I'm not trying to guilt trip you. It's not your fault. You're just like me."

"What are you talking about?" I asked, frustrated and scared.

"Think about it, Kris. You ran away from me. From us. You have to admit that's not normal. You should've talked to me. We could've worked things out like we always do. That's what couples do. They work things out together." He kissed my hand again. "I have a theory. And please bear with me on this. Remember how we found out I had borderline personality disorder? Well, I did a lot of research and even talked to Dr. Perkins about this. We think you might have an anxiety disorder."

My head swirled. "What?"

"You're afraid of the unknown, of taking risks, of failing. Remember the anxiety you would get before tests?" Marty chuckled brightly. "I would massage your shoulders for half an hour before the exam then hold you after you finished because you thought you bombed it."

"I don't have an anxiety disorder."

Marty rubbed the back of my shoulder. His eyes were warm and his voice was light-hearted. "Come on, Kris. Don't be so stubborn. It's better if you admit it because then we can do something about it."

I remembered how I had suffered from test anxiety numerous times back in college. Marty had been there to comfort me. Maybe I did have a problem. I ran away from Marty. I ran away from Vincent at the restaurant. I basically ran away from my parents. I was thinking about running away from having my baby. I was afraid of taking risks, afraid of the consequences, afraid of getting hurt, of failing. Riley had said so. Vincent had made me aware of it as well. Now Marty was saying the same thing.

Even with all that, he had no right to try and diagnose me. "No, Marty. Don't tell me I have a problem."

"Shh, shh. I know it's hard to admit. I had trouble admitting I had a problem myself. But it's okay, Kris. I get it now. I understand why you ran away. I just want to help you."

"You seem to be forgetting you invaded your her apartment with a gun," Vincent said, struggling against his restraints.

"You don't understand!" Marty cried. He turned to me. "How can you be falling for this guy, Kristen?"

"You don't know anything about him," I said.

Marty threw his hands up in frustration. "I know he's a smooth-talking player who thinks you're the flavor of the month."

His words hurt me. Although Vincent and I had resolved the miscommunication over Ariel Diamond, the issue had still been lingering on my mind. "Why do you keep saying that?"

"'I have some ideas for some new positions we could take at our next meeting'; 'If you're touching yourself right now, it's only a fraction of the pleasure I'd give you'. Give me a break. He's a douchebag. Just like those frat guys we used to make fun of in college—the ones with baseball caps turned backward and popped-collars. I know how smart you are Kristen. That's why I'm surprised you've been falling for this guy's bullshit."

Hearing Marty recite bits of private conversation between me and Vincent made the blood drain from my face. "How did you know about those things? How did you see the text messages he sent me?"

Marty sighed. "Your phone. Remember I have access to it? I can see your texts and hear your conversations."

"What the hell are you talking about? I never remember agreeing to that."

"Yes, you did. We said we would share passwords. You use the same password for your email as you do for your phone." Seeing my phone resting on the coffee table, he picked it up, tapped at it a few times, then showed me he'd passed the security input to reach the home screen. He smiled. "The word of the day is: waddles. You changed your password on your email and Facebook accounts but I guess you forgot to do it for your phone. You have an app that lets me access your phone through the internet. It's how I've known where you've been all this time."

"What the fuck," I said, shocked at the invasion of my privacy. The signs had been there. Repeated warnings from my service provider about going over my data limit. My phone sometimes randomly turning on at night. He'd been watching me all this time.

"This is so twisted," Vincent said. "You've been stalking her. That's how you knew I was coming over here."

"And you don't think it's twisted putting a tracker on my car? Hiring goons to live in the apartment next door. You're the monster here. What's sick is how you're brainwashing Kristen with your charm!"

"Wait," I said, still reeling. "If you knew where I was, why did you wait two years before showing up at my doorstep?"

Marty's eyes became tender. "I was afraid. I didn't feel like I deserved to see you after what I did to you. I thought you'd come back to me on your own when you were ready. I thought I could be a better man by then and we would be a stronger couple. But things didn't go the way I planned."

I tossed my hands up in the air. "You're not making any sense."

"You were going through a phase. You needed to date other guys and then eventually you'd realize we were meant to be together. That's fine. I'm patient. You dated a few guys but it never got far. It was just a matter of time before you came back. But you went further with Vincent. I was afraid for you. Can't you see why I had to step in? Vincent is bad news."

"You know nothing about me," Vincent said.

"I know you're a charmer. You're a CEO who doesn't have time for personal relationships, never mind giving Kristen the kind of love she deserves. You're just like my dad—wealthy, selfish, egotistical; only thinks about his business. He made my mom so miserable she killed herself. I'll be damned if I let Kristen end up like that."

"I'm not your dad. I'm nothing like your dad. Or you. What the hell's the matter with you?"

"Ask yourself. Who beats someone up like this?" Marty pointed at his face.

"Someone who hates men who abuse women," Vincent growled.

"Don't call me an abuser. It was one time. I have a disorder for god's sake, what's your excuse for what you did?"

"I know guys like you. My sister dated one. You're a piece of shit abuser who doesn't deserve sympathy."

"You know nothing about me! Calling me an abuser is bullshit. I hurt Kristen a little bit one time, and I feel awful about it. You have no right to beat me to a fucking pulp when I try to apologize to her."

"Marty," I said softly. "Vincent and I talked about that. But it doesn't justify you coming into my apartment with a gun."

"Kristen, I told you, I didn't want to do this! What else can I do?"

"Take some fucking responsibility for your actions!" Vincent yelled.

"That's what I'm doing now. I'm protecting her from you."

"You're ruining Kristen's life! If you really care about her, you'd leave her the fuck alone."

"You think I like doing this? This is all because of you."

"You're pathetic," Vincent spat.

"You want to see who's pathetic? I'll show you." Gun in hand, Marty stood up and stomped toward Vincent.

"Marty, no!" I screamed.

Chapter Twenty-five

Marty stood in front of Vincent menacingly. Vincent looked up at him with defiance.

"Let's see how you like it," Marty said. "Kris, turn away. I don't want you to see this."

Marty balled up his fist and punched Vincent across the face.

"Stop Marty!" I screamed.

"Not so easy to beat me up when you don't have your goon squad to hold me down, huh?" he sneered.

Vincent tried to shake off the blow but it was clear he was in pain.

"You don't really care about her. You don't love her like I do," Marty said.

Marty landed another punch to Vincent's face and I shrieked. Vincent didn't protest but his nose began to bleed.

"Admit you don't really care about Kristen." Marty punched Vincent in the gut, knocking the wind from his lungs. "Show her I'm right."

I leaped from the couch, my hand around my necklace. "Stop it Marty! You proved your point. You got your revenge. You don't need to hurt him anymore."

Marty wrinkled his brows. "What's that around your neck, Kristen?"

Oh no. I'd planned on macing him but hesitated because he still had the pistol in his hand.

"Don't touch her!" Vincent shouted hoarsely, straining against his cuffs. He was still trying to catch his breath.

Marty hurried over to me and ripped the necklace off. "He gave you this, didn't he? To buy your affection." Marty examined the heart-shaped pendant. He squeezed it between his thumb and forefinger and liquid squirted out from the bottom onto the carpet. "What the hell? What is this thing?"

I could feel my heart beating through my chest. The one chance I had of getting out of this mess was gone.

He brought his finger up to his nose to sniff then he touched the pad to the tip of his tongue and grimaced. "Is this like pepper spray or something?"

I shook my head, horrified.

"You meant to use this on me didn't you? He made you wear this." Marty went back to Vincent. "Trying to turn her against me? Making me out to be some kind of monster? Let's see how you like being treated like that."

Marty squeezed the pendant and squirted fluid into Vincent's face. Vincent closed his eyes and tried to turn away but it got all over his face.

"Oh god!" I cried.

Vincent didn't cry out in pain. He kept his eyes closed but his jaw was clenched tightly. I could only imagine how bad his eyes were burning right now.

"Say that you don't really care about Kristen. Say it and I'll stop."

"Please, Vincent," I pleaded. "Just do what he wants. I don't want you getting hurt anymore."

Vincent hung his head, panting. He tried wiping off the mace with his sleeve and managed to get enough off to crack open his eyes. "I don't care about Kristen," he murmured, blood dripping from his lip.

Even though I asked him to say it, and the circumstances were extreme, the words hurt more than I anticipated.

Marty grinned wickedly. "That's what I thought." He turned to me. "See, Kris? If I hadn't done this, you would've never known what a liar he really is. See how I'm protecting you?"

"You think you've proven something?" Vincent growled, commanding Marty's attention once again. Still on his knees, he threw his shoulders back and brought his head up, his posture like a soldier's. "My feelings for her go beyond caring. I love her."

Marty became furious. He socked Vincent across the face again. The force of the blow made Vincent turn his head and I could see his eyes were red from the mace.

"No you don't. Say it again. I dare you."

Vincent gazed at me. Both his eyes were bloodshot and one was already swelling from Marty's blows. He looked miserable—a man on the verge of dying. "Look at me Kristen. This might be my last chance to say this."

My breath stopped. My heart pounded in my ears.

"I've felt this way for a while. I knew it was just attraction at first. But after taking you to my island, I realized it was more. So much more. I love you, Kristen. I mean truly love you. Not obsession. Not lust. Not selfish possession. Not some kind of blind idealism. Not some sick, twisted version of love—but the real thing. One with eyes open. One with respect. One that never underestimates the hardships to its existence, never takes the other person for granted. The only kind of love there really is."

"Vincent, no!" Tears streamed down my face.

Marty punched Vincent in the face harder than before. Then Marty kicked him in the stomach. "I warned you!"

"I love you, Kristen," Vincent choked.

"Stop saying that. You're a liar!" Marty kicked Vincent again.

"Please, don't say it again," I sobbed.

"I lo—"

Marty pistol-whipped Vincent on the side of the head. "Don't try to act like you're the hero and I'm the villain. Don't forget you're the one who started this."

"No," Vincent panted, his voice barely above a whisper. "You started it when you hurt her." Every word was strained and seemed to require all his energy just to pronounce.

"How can you even say you love her?" Marty said, flabbergasted. "You barely even spend time with her. You're a fucking hypocrite."

"That'll change . . ." Vincent was visibly struggling to hold his head up. Most of his face was swelling and bleeding now but his eyes were burning with intensity. "It'll work."

"You've only been with her for two months. I was with her for two years!"

"You took her for granted . . . You didn't appreciate her. She's unlike anybody . . . I cherish every moment."

"No you don't. You won't settle down. All you care about is money and excitement. How can you even pretend to be serious about what you're saying?"

". . . We'll settle down when the time is right. For both of us."

Marty threw up his hands, frustrated. "You're going to be a terrible father to Kristen's baby. You're too busy. You wouldn't be there like I would."

No. Marty didn't just say that. He didn't just tell Vincent about the baby. How did he even know about that? Was it from my text messages with Riley about the pregnancy?

"Baby . . .?" Vincent struggled.

"You didn't even know Kristen was pregnant? What a piece of work you are."

Vincent summoned the strength to turn his head in my direction. "Is it true?"

Tears streamed down my face. "It wasn't supposed to come out like this. I wanted to tell you. That's why I called you over."

Vincent's eyes locked with mine. Tears ran down his cheeks.

The sadness in his gaze hurt more than anything I could've imagined. The image of his dark eyes filled with tears ripped through my heart like a bullet.

Chapter Twenty-six

Vincent

One week prior

"So, Vincent . . ."

I knew that tone.

"Tell me more about Kristen," Giselle said as she did some preliminary tidying in the kitchen before Brady's birthday party officially ended.

"She's a very capable analyst recently promoted to wealth manager." I fingered a trace of blue frosting in a nearby bowl, tasted it, then chased it down with a gulp of orange soda. It was delicious. I made a mental note to caution Brady about drinking too much of this stuff. But damn did it taste good to have some every once in a while.

"And . . .?"

". . . And she's funny and caring." She's also one hell of a minx in the sack, I thought. Just the thought of her lips wrapping around my cock made me instantly hard even in the most awkward of situations: during business meetings, presentations, even if this conversation. I decided it was better to keep that to myself.

"This is the first time you've let me meet one of your girlfriends and that's the best you can give me? I'm disappointed. Here I thought she was something special."

You don't know how special she is. My mind slipped back to the first time Kristen and I met. Pinching my nipple in that business meeting? I remember thinking in that moment—as her chest was pressed against mine—that she was either the stupidest girl ever or the smartest. Special, for sure. She had quite the set of balls on her. I smiled, suppressing a laugh at the thought.

It wasn't until we started dating that I realized how brave and strong she is—especially with what she'd been through, being in an abusive relationship like Giselle had. It made my blood boil to imagine the silent suffering Kristen endured because of her ex.

"I never said she wasn't."

Giselle shot me a knowing look. "All right, fine. Don't want to tell your sis too much about your love life. I know, I get it. I'm not a gossiping housewife you know. At least not yet anyway."

"You started picking up knitting. I'm not willing to take that risk."

She smiled. "Brady needs sweaters made from love. A boy can't live on trains alone."

"We can agree to disagree on that point," I teased.

Giselle sighed. "You're so fond of Brady. When are you going to have your own kid to spoil?"

I sputtered on my drink.

Kids were something I wanted badly, but it was too early in the relationship to discuss it. It was something I'd hoped for ever since Brady had been born. What I saw in him was what I'd been missing: something worth making money for. Something that made me think beyond the present. Long after I was done risking my life stupidly and working day and night on my company, he would be there, growing and living as I had. I wanted that.

Recovering, I responded, "When I'm with the right person. When the time is right for both of us."

"Mmhmm. I'm not dumb, Vincent. I know you brought her over here for a reason. Maybe to evaluate her reaction around kids?"

Damn, Giselle was clever. I looked around the kitchen, making sure Kristen wasn't within earshot. I could hear her playing with Brady and the other kids in the den. The sound of her laughing and making loud choo choo noises along with the kids made me feel warm and fuzzy.

I lowered my voice. "It's too soon to talk about. Kristen and I have only been dating for two months."

"I know. And yet you've brought her to meet me when you haven't let me meet your other girlfriends. I know you've been in longer relationships than that."

"Those weren't serious."

"Okay. And this one is? Despite being shorter?"

"Quality over quantity. As far as seriousness, it is on my end but we've had some rough patches recently."

"I think she's very serious about you."

"Why do you say that? You guys only talked for a few minutes."

"She seemed very interested in hearing about what I had to say about you."

"Uh . . . what did you tell her?"

"Nothing scandalous." Giselle smiled. "I told her about Mom and Dad and how you changed after that happened."

"How did she react?"

"She seemed very interested in your story."

"Makes sense considering we're dating."

"It's more than that. I think she's really into you, Vincent. I can't put my finger on it but call it woman's intuition. She's probably already thinking about taking things further."

"Let's hope so."

Chapter Twenty-seven

Kristen

Seeing the tears from Vincent's eyes made me want to die. He wasn't happy about hearing I was pregnant with his child; he was torn. The tears from his eyes and the pained expression on his face said as much. I thought about rushing Marty. I could try to tackle him out the window. Or wrestling the gun out of his hand. He'd probably end up shooting me but fine, let him shoot me.

Vincent broke his gaze from mine. He drooped his head and his body went limp in his restraints.

Was he dead? Oh god no.

"Stop this Marty! He needs to go to the hospital!"

Marty turned away from Vincent to face me. He started walking toward me with fists clenched. "Why didn't you say that when he was beating me up?"

"I tried! I stopped Vincent from hitting you. Don't you remember?" Seeing Marty approach me, broke me out of a spell. I suddenly feared for my life again. "Please don't hurt me, Marty."

His face softened. "Hurt you? Why do you think I'd hurt you? I told you. I love you. Do you still love me? You must since you protected me."

"Please, don't. We broke up. Protecting someone doesn't mean you love them."

"Did you love me before?"

"I don't know."

"How could you not know?" he shouted. "All those times together. Everything we shared. I loved you. I still do."

"Marty, our relationship was very rocky. We were breaking up and getting back together constantly at the end. I'm still trying to figure out what my emotions were like at that time."

He shook his head. "Do you love him?" he asked frantically. "Do you love Vincent?"

"I don't know."

"Yes or no, Kristen."

I recalled the sad look in Vincent's eyes. It didn't matter anymore. Nothing mattered. I thought I'd escaped Marty but he had known where I was the whole time. I lost Vincent. I was going to lose my job. I was going to lose my life. I was going to lose my baby.

"Yes! I do love Vincent."

His features hardened into a scowl. "You don't mean that."

"I do," I said, mustering up my remaining strength. "I truly love Vincent. I don't care what you say, Marty. Threaten me all you want. I don't love you."

Marty ran a hand through his hair, staining it with the blood on his fist. Vincent's blood. "You're so frustrating, Kristen. You know me. You know how I feel about you."

"No I don't. I don't understand you at all," I cried.

"Stop crying. Stop being afraid of me. I can't take it when you do that."

"I don't care."

"It's because you're carrying his child. That's the reason, isn't it?" Marty approached me, backing me into the couch. His eyes were on my stomach.

"No, don't come near me." I stuck out my hands and feet, trying to shove him away.

"You can't keep me away." His eyes were still on my stomach.

"Don't hurt my baby!"

"You're making me angry, Kristen. You already know you don't want to make me angry."

A loud crack sounded. Where did it come from? It sounded like a wooden plank snapping. Was the couch about to break?

"Marty, no!"

Marty balled his fist.

"Somebody help!" I screamed as loudly as I could.

"Shut your mouth, Kristen. You're out of your mind."

Another loud crack.

Marty raised his fist. I crossed my arms to shield my body, hoping that the flesh and bones in my limbs would prove sturdier than an apartment wall. He was going to punch my stomach. He was going to punch the baby.

"Forgive me, Kristen. I wouldn't do it if I didn't have to."

In a blur, Marty vanished behind the couch. I sat up, realizing someone had tackled him.

"Vincent!" I screamed.

How had he gotten out of the handcuffs?

I leaped from the couch to see Marty and Vincent rolling into the kitchen and crashing into the oven. The force from the impact shook the stovetop and the hot water I'd been boiling in a saucepan for tea tipped and poured over Marty's head.

Marty screamed and frantically swiped at his face with his hands. His face was steaming.

Vincent was groaning and rubbing his head with the heel of his palm. His hands were mangled, his thumbs twisted inward. That's when I realized what happened.

The two loud cracking sounds I heard were from Vincent breaking his own thumbs to escape his handcuffs.

I rushed over to Vincent to try to help him up. He was dazed and couldn't stand up on his own. I hooked my arms beneath his shoulders and tried to drag him to the apartment door but it was difficult to move him. He's so damn heavy. I thought about escaping just by myself but I knew I couldn't leave Vincent alone with Marty. Not like this. By the time I came back with the police, Vincent would probably be dead.

Marty blindly reached in front of him, knocking over a jar of sugar and a spice rack on the kitchen counter. White dust and parsley spilled across the counter and the kitchen tile. I'd dragged Vincent a foot when Marty found a towel hanging from the oven. He wiped his face vigorously and opened his eyes.

Before I could react, Marty lunged at us, landing on top of Vincent. I fell backward and smashed into a kitchen table chair.

"You bastard!" Marty cried as he began wailing on Vincent.

Vincent snapped out of his daze and raised his arms to shield his face, shifting his head from side to side to avoid a direct blow.

Frantic, I stumbled to my feet and picked up the kitchen chair with both hands, raising it over my head. Marty leaped from Vincent and rushed me. He swatted the chair out of my hands, making it crash across the kitchen table into the corner. "Don't fight me, Kristen!" he shouted. "I don't want to hurt you." Then he shoved me away. I toppled over the coat rack and into the pile of shoes.

Sprawled over a bed of flats and heels, I spotted the a silver object lying beside the couch. The pistol. It must've flown out of Marty's hand when Vincent tackled him. Crawling on my hands and knees across the sea of footwear, I neared the couch and reached for the gun.

The sound of a punch landing on flesh and the sound of a male voice groaning in pain made me realize Marty had mounted Vincent again and was attacking him.

I picked up the gun with shaky hands.

"Stop it or I'll shoot!" I screamed.

Marty continued pounding and shouting at Vincent. He wasn't listening.

"I said stop!" I shook the gun in their direction, but neither of them seemed to hear me. I'd never fired a gun before but I knew how to pull a trigger.

Fearing Marty was going to kill Vincent, I fired a round at the kitchen wall. The sound was almost deafening. The force from the recoil was stronger than I'd expected and I staggered backward, tripping over the coffee table and landing on top of it. The glass shattered under my weight. The back of my head hit something hard.

Was it the ground? The broken frame of the table? I laid on a bed of broken shards, the air knocked from my lungs.

The last thing I remembered before blacking out was that the unexpected weight of the gun combined with the shakiness of my hands made the barrel shift downward the moment I pulled the trigger.

The gun had been aimed at Vincent and Marty.

Chapter Twenty-eight

Vincent

Six years prior

My fist was throbbing. I successfully fought the urge to look at it, but I knew it was fucked up from how bad Jim's face had been. Once he was awake, he was going to have some decisions to make about how to fix his features. That nose would never be the same.

I held Giselle as she cried in the same living room our parents had once held us. Even though they were gone, it was still our home.

"You're going to be okay," I said. "I'm going to take care of us."

"Vincent, look at your hand! I'm so sorry," Giselle cried.

It killed me to hear her feel guilty about what had happened to her. As much as my fist hurt, I put the pain to the side. "Stop it, Giselle. You don't have to be sorry about anything. What that bastard did to you wasn't your fault."

She shook her head. "I should have handled it myself. I should have gotten out as soon as it started. I don't know how I let it keep happening."

"It's not your fault, and it's over now." I squeezed her tighter as she sobbed into my shoulder. It was over. That was the only thing that mattered at that moment.

"What if he does come back?" she choked out.

My jaw clenched. She didn't want to know the honest answer to that question. "He won't. If he does, I promise you he'll regret it for every second of the rest of his life."

She stopped crying for a moment and pulled back to look at me. "Vincent, you can't always be around. You have your company to worry about."

"I'll find a way. The only purpose of that company is to provide for you and any other family we ever have. If it doesn't make the lives of the people I love better, I might as well sell the damn thing."

She nodded and sobbed again. Her eyes were puffy and red, and her makeup had been smudged everywhere. Seeing her so disheveled and upset made my stomach feel like a bottomless pit.

Finally, she calmed down enough to speak. "Vincent," she said, her voice small. "I have something to show you."

My eyes widened. I wasn't sure how much more I could take. "What's that?"

She rolled up the sleeves of her green sweater. At first I didn't know what I was looking for, but then I saw them: several raised pieces of scar tissue in a neat row, each in various shades of pink.

My vision blurred as tears welled up in my eyes. "What are these?" I asked quietly.

"Cigarettes."

"You don't smoke."

"He did. Does. Whatever." Tears rolled down both her cheeks.

My heart sank as I put together the implication. "He put them out on you?"

She nodded. "In a neat row. Once for every time I pissed him off. So I wouldn't forget."

My mouth fell open at the audacity of what I was hearing. "He's sick. I'm so sorry, Giselle. If I had any idea . . ."

"You didn't," she said. "I guess I'm pretty good at covering up, but I just have to show you now so I feel like I've come totally clean. I've been hiding it for so long.

I blinked and felt a hot tear roll down my cheek. "I'm so sorry."

She looked down. "He said he would kill me if I told anyone."

I snapped my jaw shut and flexed my still aching fist. "He said he would kill you?"

She nodded.

My heart was pounding in my chest as I breathed heavily in and out. Could I kill someone who had threatened to kill my sister? How would I get away with it?

"Don't even think about killing him first," she said, as if reading my mind.

I snapped out of my plotting. She was staring at me with a very serious expression etched into her features.

"I'm not letting my brother become a murderer."

"But if it's him or you—" I started.

"It won't be. It can't be," she said.

I sighed and took her by the shoulders.

"Fine. But know this: you're the only family I have, and I'm going to protect you no matter what. Even if it costs me my life."

Chapter Twenty-nine

Kristen

The world was fuzzy. Hues of brown and white swirled like cream being stirred into coffee. I couldn't make out any details in the forms that swirled in front of me. What had happened to my vision?

My ears were ringing. My body felt like it was being poked by a thousand needles. It hurt to move. I remembered a gun in my hands going off. How long had I been out?

A shadow shifted into view. It grew larger and more defined. The outline was a figure. Someone was approaching me.

I blinked. The picture became sharper. I blinked again then a few more times. I was staring at the ceiling, the fan spinning.

There was a face in the picture. It was still. Eerily still. Staring at me from above. Who was it?

Blue eyes. Brown hair. Thick spectacles.

Marty.

My hearing slowly returned, but Marty vanished from my vision almost as soon as he appeared. I sat up and saw that Vincent was still fighting with him. Vincent barreled into Marty with his shoulder, pushing him back until Marty was cornered against the wall.

Vincent pummeled Marty with his mangled hands but it was clear that Vincent was at a disadvantage. I looked around for the gun but it was nowhere to be found, it must have gotten tossed somewhere around the room in the confusion.

I saw a small hole on the kitchen wall inches from where they had been. I didn't hit anyone.

When I looked over at them again, Marty was kneeling on top of Vincent, straddling him and repeatedly punching him in the face. "Take that you piece of shit!"

"No, Marty! Stop . . . please stop Marty . . ." I pleaded, tears streaming uncontrollably down my face. He was going to kill Vincent, the man who loved me, the man that I loved.

Marty ignored me, continuing to hit Vincent. Vincent had his broken hands up, trying to defend his face. He seemed so helpless in that position that it sent another knife of sorrow into me.

"Stop Marty! Please stop!" I sobbed.

Marty looked up at me, chest heaving, fists covered in Vincent's blood. "Stop? Stop?! It's too late to stop Kristen. You made me do this! This is your fault! Look at what you've done!"

This was my fault. My fault. None of this would have happened if Vincent had never met me. I felt sorrow so intense I wanted to vomit. It was because of me that this monster was hurting Vincent. Killing him.

Marty finally got up from Vincent and walked over to the kitchen counter.

I crawled towards Vincent, the room blurry in my vision. When I got to him, I sat down and cradled his head in my lap. He was still breathing. His breath was heavy and ragged but he was still alive.

"Kristen . . ." Vincent groaned.

"It's okay Vincent. I'm so sorry. I'm so sorry. I'm so sorry. I love you Vincent. I love you so much." I chanted, rocking back and forth. Wet droplets fell from my eyes and splashed onto Vincent, leaving streaks in the dried blood caking his face.

When I looked up again, Marty had found the gun. He had it pointed at us.

We were going to die here tonight.

"You brought this on yourself Kristen . . . you didn't even give me a chance . . ."

Vincent was drifting in and out of consciousness. He stirred, pushing himself up until he was sitting upright, putting his body between me and the gun. Even in this state, with his eyes swollen shut, his hands battered and his face bleeding from cuts and swollen from fractures, he wanted to protect me. Vincent wanted to protect me with his last breath even after I had brought this monster into his life.

"I'm sorry Vincent, I'm sorry about the baby, I'm sorry I didn't tell you early. I'm sorry for Marty. I'm sorry for everything."

I wrapped my arms around Vincent, crying onto the back of his shoulder.

"No, Kristen." Vincent coughed. His voice was low and raspy, barely audible. His eyes were half-lidded. His lips were trembling. He was using every ounce of strength left to talk to me.

I leaned my ear to his mouth to hear the faint words riding his shallow breaths. "No. Don't say that Kristen . . . Don't ever apologize to me for those things . . . You didn't do anything wrong . . . I love you Kristen . . . Let's keep the baby . . . I've always wanted a child . . . We'll raise the child together . . . I love you . . . I want to start a family with you."

My heart was shattering. Vincent was confessing to me that he wanted a family together, moments before we were going to die.

He continued, "I'm the one that should be sorry . . . I promised I'd protect you . . . but I failed . . . I'm sorry Kristen . . . Forgive me . . . I . . . " He was losing consciousness again.

Marty stared at us, his eerie blue eyes filled with anger.

I blinked back my tears and took a deep breath.

Goodbye Riley.

Goodbye Mom.

Goodbye Dad.

Goodbye Vincent.

I'll always love you.

The apartment door exploded. A mist of splinters shot through the air, covering my living room.

"POLICE! DROP THE GUN MOTHERFUCKER!"

I blinked and half a dozen officers were fanned out on my right kneeling behind the kitchen wall and the couch, their guns drawn and aimed at Marty.

Before I could feel any relief, I saw the look in Marty's eyes. They were wide and panicked like the eyes of a cornered animal and he still had the gun pointed at us. He hadn't made any motion to surrender.

The cops were shifting around. They were getting antsy. Marty looked back and forth between us and the cops as if he was deciding what to do. I could see the desperation growing in those blue irises.

No. No. We were so close! This wasn't right. Marty was going to shoot Vincent anyway. We were so close. It wasn't fair. It wasn't right. We were so close to being safe, to being happy.

"DROP IT ASSHOLE! THIS IS YOUR LAST WARNING!"

Marty didn't care about getting shot himself. He was going to empty the clip into Vincent and at this distance, he wouldn't miss. I could see the events playing in his mind: he would shoot Vincent then me while the cops shot him down.

I had to try; I had to try one last time to get through to Marty.

I wiped the wetness from my eyes and looked into Marty's face. "No Marty, please . . . Marty you need help . . . Vincent and I . . . we love each other. You and I had something, but that was long ago. You need to get help Marty. Don't take Vincent away from me. Don't take my life away from me. If you ever loved me, if what you said was true about still caring about me, do the right thing. Please Marty, think about what you're doing. You're going to ruin all of our lives."

His brows narrowed. A strange expression crossed his face. Maybe it was a rare moment of lucidity for him or maybe I just imagined it, but it seemed like he suddenly realized what he had become. For a split second, I thought I saw a glimpse of the Marty that I knew years ago. Blue eyes, brown hair, boyish smile.

His arm wavered, then went limp. The gun clattered on the floor.

And then it was over.

Chapter Thirty

When the ambulances arrived, Vincent had regained a bit of his strength. He insisted on riding to the hospital up front in the same ambulance as me, even though he was in a much worse state than me. The paramedics argued with him for a while, before letting him have his way. They must've figured that this way they would at least get him to the hospital, even if he refused to get there on a stretcher.

I lay in the stretcher as the paramedics fussed over him, wrapping up his hands and flushing his eyes with water.

"Kristen, I meant everything I said before. I love you. If you want to have the baby, I'll be right there with you. It's up to you Kristen, but I love you. I'll be here for you, no matter what you decide."

"Is that what you want Vincent?"

He nodded. His eyes were glistening, I'm not sure if it was from the water the paramedics were rinsing his eyes with or from tears.

"When we were back there and Marty told you about the baby, for a moment, I thought you didn't want the baby," I said.

"I've wanted a child for a while now, Kristen. When you told me, I was so happy. . . but I thought I was about to lose it all. I love you Kristen. If you're ready, I want to start a family with you. Do you want that?"

I struggled to find the words."I—I love you too Vincent, and I think I do want a family, but I don't know yet. Things have just been so crazy, we should take some time and think about it in case either of us changes our minds."

He gave me his hand, wrapped in medical bandages and I latched onto it. "I won't change my mind Kristen, but you're right. We'll talk about it later. All I care about right now is that you're okay."

I pursed my lips. He was going to make me cry again. "I'm glad you're okay too, Vincent. I thought I was going to lose you."

Vincent let out a deep breath and chuckled. "You can't get rid of me that easily."

His expression turned serious again. "I'm sorry about all of this Kristen. This was all my fault. Earlier today, when we were interrupted in the office, it was Kurt and Bernie. They had come to tell me that they lost track of Marty. I should have realized that he was more dangerous than he seemed."

"No Vincent, you didn't know. How could you have known that Marty would react that way? I didn't even know. I thought he had changed and got the help he needed and was recovering. I was wrong about him too."

Vincent growled, "Guys like that don't learn their lesson until you bury them under six feet of concrete."

"I wouldn't have wanted you to do that Vincent. That wouldn't have been right. Marty is sick."

He let out a long sigh, "It doesn't matter anymore. Now you're safe and you won't ever have to be afraid of him ever again."

"If you hadn't met me, if I hadn't dragged you into my problems, none of this would've happened. Your hands . . ."

"Don't you dare say that Kristen. If I hadn't met you, my life wouldn't have been whole. I don't regret a single moment I've spent with you. I'd gladly trade my thumbs, my hands or any parts of my body for you Kristen. You're everything to me."

"Did you really mean it when you said you wanted to start a family?"

"I know we haven't been dating for that long Kristen, and I don't know what the future holds, but I know how I feel about you."

"What about your company?"

"They don't need me there all the time. I'll take more time off to be with you. You're more important to me."

"What if . . . what if it doesn't work out?"

"We can't live life based on 'what ifs' Kristen. We'll make it work."

Vincent looked around the ambulance and then raised an eyebrow at me, it looked almost comical on his swollen face. "So . . . 'waddles' was your phone password huh?"

I half-laughed half-sobbed in relief and held on more tightly to his hand. No matter what happened next, we would work through our issues together.

Epilogue

"Ouch."

"Oh, I'm so sorry," I said.

"It's fine. Just try not to put too much pressure there," Vincent said.

He moved his arm out from under me and I stroked it lightly. The cast had come off a month ago, but sometimes it was still sore for him. In addition to breaking his thumbs, Vincent had also fractured his forearm in the fight with Marty.

Marty was prosecuted and locked up. Even though he needed serious help, it was because of his ill-guided actions that Vincent and I were closer together. I wasn't happy about what happened to Marty, but I knew that he would finally be able to get the help he needed in prison.

Sunlight drifted in through the translucent blinds, illuminating small specks of dust floating in the air. Vincent beamed at me, his eyes still squinty from sleep. We were in his New York penthouse. Though I would have preferred the tranquility of his island, Vincent insisted on being in Manhattan so that we could be close to the New York Presbyterian Hospital. He told me that it had the best neonatal care unit in the world.

I snapped back to the present and Vincent was looking at me with a suggestive look on his face. His cock was out and he was nudging at my entrance.

"Wait, aren't you missing something?" I teased him.

He nuzzled his chin against the side of my face. "Like what?"

The light fuzz on his chin rubbing against me made it difficult not to giggle. "Like a condom. That's how we got here in the first place."

Vincent had proposed to me as soon as we had gotten out of the hospital. We had many serious talks while we were both recovering. Somehow, despite it being against hospital policy, Vincent had gotten us placed in the same recovery room. After the events we had been through, it was pretty clear that we both wanted to raise a child together.

Giselle had visited us a few times with Brady and Rob. She gave me a few tips on making the pregnancy go more smoothly and I appreciated the time I spent with her. She wanted to know the sex of the baby, but we didn't even know—we wanted it to be a surprise. I was looking forward to calling Giselle my sister-in-law.

Vincent lifted his head up and smiled down at me.

"But I like where we are now."

"You're not worried about how our lives will change with a baby in the picture?"

He propped his head up with his other arm, his expression turning serious. "I'm excited. In fact, I'm going to come inside you and we're going to make twins."

I laughed. "I hate to burst your bubble but that's not how it works."

"It might be improbable but we've beaten the odds before." Vincent kissed my round belly before laying the side of his head against my chest.

"So you're going to break the rules of biology now?"

I pushed myself up until I was propped against the headboard. Vincent shifted and grimaced as he put his weight on his injured arm.

"Maybe when I get my full strength back, we'll give it a shot."

After we had talked in the hospital, we decided that it would be best if I left my job at Waterbridge-Howser and helped Vincent manage his wealth until I gave birth. With the way things had been going at Waterbridge-Howser, I would've been forced out sooner or later, and I would always have to sleep with one eye open, knowing that Richard had it out for me.

Our plan was that Vincent would help me establish my own wealth management firm afterward. I wasn't sure about it at first, but he'd convinced me that I had all the skills I needed and he had the connections to get me up on my feet. Vincent started delegating a lot of his work in order to spend more time with me, and in preparation for taking care of the baby. He also cut out the riskier aspects of his love of extreme sports, though he still enjoyed surfing occasionally.

I'd moved out of my place with Riley and in with Vincent. Riley had a few blush-worthy comments about sex during a pregnancy, but she was overjoyed for us and insisted on being involved in planning the wedding.

I'd finally called my parents and invited them to the wedding that was happening six months from now. It was still awkward, but they'd seemed happy for me. I don't know if I will ever be close with them, but at least they could still be a small part of my life.

"Not feeling so invincible anymore huh Mr. Risk-Taker?" It felt good to be like this, just lounging around and teasing each other.

"I feel great. How do you feel?"

"I don't know, maybe you can make me feel even better," I said smiling.

"Insatiable." Vincent kissed me and rolled me onto my back. "That's the woman I love."

"The heart wants what the heart wants."

It turned out Vincent had been right all along. Nothing worth pursuing comes without risk. I took a risk in a bar in South Africa with deadly spiders. I took a risk dating Vincent when it could have cost me my job. And I took a risk trusting Vincent, Mr. Trouble-At-First-Glance, when I was afraid nothing good would come of it.

Vincent held me tightly and I relaxed into his arms as two—no— three hearts beat together. Everything my heart ever wanted was right here with me.

Thank you for reading!

If you could spare a moment to leave a review it would be much appreciated.

Reviews help new readers find my books! They also provide valuable feedback for my writing!

:)

Made in the USA
Lexington, KY
17 December 2014